D0912584

The Soil

LIBRARY OF KOREAN LITERATURE
8

The Soil

Yi Kwang-su

Translated by
Hwang Sun-Ae *and*
Horace Jeffery Hodges

DALKEY ARCHIVE PRESS
CHAMPAIGN / LONDON / DUBLIN

Originally serialized in Korean as *Hŭk* in the *Dong-A Ilbo* (East Asia Times), Seoul, April 1932–July 1933

Translation © 2013 by Hwang Sun-Ae and Horace Jeffery Hodges

First edition, 2013
All rights reserved

Library of Congress Cataloging-in-Publication Data

Yi, Kwang-su, 1892-1950
[Huk. English]
The soil / Kwang-su Yi ; translated by Hwang Sun-ae and Horace Jeffery Hodges. --
First edition.
pages cm
"Originally serialized in Korean as *Hŭk* in the *Dong-A Ilbo* (East Asia Times),
Seoul, April 1932–July 1933."
ISBN 978-1-56478-911-2 (alk. paper)
1. Community activists--Fiction. 2. Farmers--Fiction. 3. Korea--Rural conditions--
Fiction. I. Hwang, Son-ae, translator. II. Hodges, Horace Jeffery, translator. III. Title.
PL990.9.K9H813 2013
895.7'33--dc23
2013027138

Partially funded by a grant from the Illinois Arts Council, a state agency

Library of Korean Literature
Published in collaboration with the Literature Translation Institute of Korea

www.dalkeyarchive.com

Cover: design and composition by Mikhail Iliatov

Printed on permanent/durable acid-free paper

1-1

After returning from the night school where he taught, Heo Sung lay down, resting his neck upon his schoolbag and lacing his fingers behind his head to form a pillow. Lying still, he could hear mosquitoes buzzing to and fro as they tried to get around the mosquito-repellent smoke. Now that the seventh month of the lunar calendar was half past, the wind felt a bit cool after nightfall.

For a couple of years, Heo Sung had lived in Seoul with little possibility of hearing the mosquitoes' buzz. In his hometown, even listening to them again pleased him.

"How tall and beautiful Yu Sun has become," Heo Sung murmured to himself. Her image appeared before him, healthy and strong with gently rounded features. Though her face was tanned dark from the mountain region's strong sunlight, her eyes, nose, and mouth stood out sharply without losing the softness of a young woman's features. Reflecting moonlight, her face had been beautiful, almost like moonlight itself. Only her roughened hands did not fit. Used for weeding fields and working in water, they were not the porcelain hands of a city woman. She wore a stiff skirt and a traditional summer jacket of hemp cloth, along with black rubber shoes. She went without socks, which left the tops of her feet darkly tanned. Equally dark were her hands, wrists, and neck, as well as her calves below the short bloomers and shorter skirt, as if the summer sunlight had wished to kiss her body whenever offered a chance, desiring her beautiful and healthy skin.

Heo Sung tried to compare Yu Sun with Jeong-seon. The latter was daughter to Mr. Yun, the aristocratic official in whose Seoul residence Sung was the house tutor. Jeong-seon was a fragile woman with fair skin, almost transparent, and hands so small and soft that they seemed likely to shatter at a touch. She had been one of the loveliest beauties in Sookmyung Girls' High School.

In Sung's eyes, Jeong-seon was the celestial maiden of the moon, so unreachable. He had roomed in the servants' quarters of the Yun family while tutoring their young son in primary school studies, and for such a poor man from the countryside without parents or property, a beautiful woman like Jeong-seon, the only daughter of a noble and wealthy family, was one in whose presence he felt unworthy even to lift up his eyes.

But he might be able to secure at least a woman like Yu Sun for himself. In his current situation, Yu Sun's parents might be reluctant to offer him their daughter's hand, but they would perhaps consider him as a future son-in-law after he had graduated from college.

With those thoughts, Sung sighed over his circumstances.

Sung's family had been among the well-off families in the village. His father Gyeom, a graduate of Daesung School in Pyongyang, had been arrested several times under the Japanese Military Police Government as a suspect in the Sinminhoe, Bukgando, and Seogando affairs, as well as in the independence movement. His various sentences added up to about eight years, but he spent over ten altogether behind bars, including detentions at the police station after his arrest and his time confined during the investigations.

The family fortune had been used up in supporting him those long prison years, and sustaining the household itself was difficult, let alone providing for Sung's school fees. Once out of prison, Gyeom had used the family's rice paddies and other lands as collateral for funds from a financial cooperative to start a business. But having no experience with that kind of work, he failed, losing all the collateral land, and so turned to alcohol out of anger, only to die of typhoid fever. His wife and daughter, Sung's younger sister, also became infected and died, leaving Sung with nothing but the clothes on his back.

Sung thus had no place of his own, and the house where he was now staying belonged to his cousin Seong.

Yu Sun's family lived over a hill from where he was staying. Her parents were simple farmers. Sun's father Jin-hi was still young, and her grandfather had succeeded in the first-level national exam, attaining the title *chosi*. The Heo clan had lived in Sung's village for several hundred years. The Yu clan had lived equally as long in the village over the hill. Both had produced family members who had succeeded in the national exams, or who had lived in the tile-roofed houses of the rich. But according to Grandfather Yu, "There's been no use for scholarship or in being *yangban* nobility since the Reformation of 1894."

As the two villages slowly declined, the courageous gave up their government offices, tied headbands to their brows, and threw away their books and brush pens to wield hoes in rice paddies instead. Some, however, buckled down, sticking to their offices and hoping for the glory of old times. But a few like Sung's father stood "at the forefront of reform," keeping their hair cut short and wearing Western-style clothes. Some of these ended up in prison. Members of Yu Sun's family were among the quiet, sly ones who looked out for their own interests. Heo Sung's family was among those active in affairs, working to improve the world or going to modern schools.

1-2

On the evening before leaving for Seoul, during his last lesson in a week of night school, Heo Sung taught the rest of the textbook with special devotion and even gave an informal, wide-ranging lecture to encourage people.

The night school had been divided into one class for men and another for women. In the latter were some women as old as his aunt or grandmother, but others the age of his younger sister. They listened with open curiosity as Sung explained about personal hygiene, about the spherical Earth and how it rotated daily while the Sun remained unmoving, about electrical light and airplanes, and about how clouds became rain or snow.

"Is it really true?" many wondered. Some women couldn't believe any of it, but none spoke up in opposition. The men's class was different. Some asked questions, or even opposed him.

"What on earth is this?" someone asked. "Why's life getting so hard?"

"These days, I heard even university graduates can't get a job," said another, more knowledgeable of the world.

"You've studied so much. Now's time to get married and start a family. What's the use of studying any more?" With such words, men the age of his uncle or his grandfather would suddenly interrupt the lecture with unexpected advice.

Most were of the Heo clan, but a few members of the Yu clan had come from over the hill. Yu Sun was one of those in the women's class.

Unlike many others, Yu Sun had gotten an elementary school education, but she still came to attend his night school. She was one of the most attentive students.

Thinking of his upcoming departure, Heo Sung felt sad. During class, he had looked at Sun as often as possible. Sun's eyes sometimes met his. He wished that he could continue teaching.

After the course was over, dozens of men gathered under the old zelkova tree to hold a farewell party for Sung. They brought yellow melons, alcoholic drinks, and steamed cobs of corn and sat together in a circle chatting.

"When are you coming back again?"

"I'm not sure. Probably next year."

"When's your graduation?"

"Two years from now."

"You're studying law, right?"

"Right."

"You'll become a police chief after graduation?"

"Well . . ."

"He could also become a county clerk. But to be a county commissioner takes time."

"A lawyer makes good money, I've heard, but there's another test for that, right?"

"Right."

"He's talented, he can become a lawyer."

"A lawyer earns well, I've heard."

"For making good money, a doctor's the best job."

"For the big money, you need to find a gold mine."

"There's no money to be made in Korea. It's dried up like a drought."

"For farmers like us, it's nearly impossible to get your hands on a ten-won note."

"Have some more melon."

"Oh, it's quite late now."

Thus went the conversation. While Heo Sung was listening, his face sometimes flushed, and he occasionally sighed. But he felt a closeness with these uneducated people, an affection for them. Their words seemed to entail boundless goodwill. He liked their humane side, different from polite, careful, calculating city folk.

That evening, Sung suggested that a cooperative be formed. His recommendation received a positive response from nearly everybody, but he would have to leave without being able to implement it.

With his bag and blanket in hand, Sung left his cousin's place before dawn to catch the early train. Listening to the sound of insects in the grass along the road, he walked toward the train station. He had just reached the fork leading off in the direction of Muneomi when he was suddenly startled.

"It's me." It was Yu Sun. Sung was so surprised at this unexpected encounter that he immediately and unselfconsciously took her hands. "When are you coming back?" she asked.

"Next summer." Sung stroked her hair as she stood and leaned her forehead against his chest.

Sun gave him four steamed cobs of corn wrapped in a handkerchief before he continued on his way. She waited until his train rushed through the dark bluish dawn, curving toward Muneomi, and waved with tears in her eyes.

1-3

Sung emerged from a passenger car to stand at the top step, wishing to catch a glimpse of Sun as the train turned, but dawn light left the young woman's form hidden in mountain shadow a kilometer away. Sung waved in the direction he assumed she stood and murmured, "See you next summer, Sun."

The train was running on the steel bridge near Salyeoul Village. "Salyeoul! How lovely is that name!" Sung looked down at the water flowing under the bridge. The water's dark depths were still clothed in summer night. As his eyes followed the watercourse upstream, the milky-white fog of the valley, more typical of early autumn, grew visible. Over the moisture-soaked ground and over the softly murmuring water, the white fog was spreading, one of the most evocative beauties of nature.

On both sides of Salyeoul were rice paddies irrigated by the stream's water. These paddies yielded rice to the bounty of 150 bushels per acre. Originally, there may have been miles of grassland, or of forests that shut out the sky. Into such a wild forest, inhabited by deer and fox, the clear water of Salyeoul might have flowed. There was a hill still called "a hill of bright sky." As a child, Sung had learned from his father that one used to see the bright sky only upon reaching the crest of the hill.

Sung's ancestors had cultivated the forest, very likely in tandem with Sun's ancestors. They must have cut trees, dug out the roots, made water pools for rice paddies, and plowed the paddies in sweat and blood. Eating the rice grown there, these ancestors had dwelt in this place and enjoyed their lives over generations, and Sung's and Sun's own bodies, their bones, flesh, and blood, were like flowers that had budded, grown, and blossomed in this soil, a soil mixed with their ancestors' sweat!

But most of these paddies no longer belonged to their clans. They were all nowadays the property of a company, a bank, a cooperative, or a farm. Those who lived in Sung's hometown Salyeoul were now like uprooted grass. One heard the idle and peaceful sounds of roosters and dogs or horses and oxen less often this year. Not only had their numbers decreased, but the sounds themselves seemed less idle and less peaceful. Life had become anxious, tough, and full of resentment.

As the train rolled along, Sung watched mountains, fields, and villages come and go. He saw the fully ripened rice, yellow millet bowing, barnyard grass, and sorghum, which recalled a bleeding warrior with loosened hair. He saw women bearing jars atop their heads after drawing early water. The morning sun was shining onto the damp water jars, and these flashed golden. A woman brushed away the water overflowing from the jar with one hand and with the other covered her breasts, which would have showed under her short *jeoksam*, a woman's traditional summer jacket. At the loud rumbling of the rushing train, a number of tanned, naked children ran after, excited and shouting. Thatched-roof houses, having survived the long rainy season, looked as saggy and tired as farmers after long summer labor. Like the worried folk who lived in those houses, the black thatch of the roofs appeared weather-beaten. In homes thick with fleas and bedbugs, the people—poverty-stricken, sick with worry over debts and illnesses, and deprived of hope—lived out their lives with a frown.

The train stopped at a station, and Sung could see the stationmaster, a conductor mingling with the station staff, the red-brimmed hat of a Japanese policeman, a gentleman, apparently head of a township, wearing a Panama hat, a young female student with a basket, and an older couple, probably the student's parents, leaving for Seoul.

With a tweet from the stationmaster and a whistle from the locomotive's steam engine, the train soon started to chug along again. After leaving this bigger town with its small station behind, Sung felt hungry. He took out the corn that Sun had given to him. After eating two cobs, he felt a little embarrassed, rewrapped the rest, and put them back.

When he got off at Gyeonseong Station, he was confronted with a swarm of busy taxis, crazy buses, rickshaws like toys, and people with hearts cold as wind-driven sleet. He felt as if he had awakened from a dream.

Sung boarded a tram and returned to Mr. Yun's house in Samcheongdong. After setting his baggage down, he went to the main reception room to find only a few men sitting there wearing Korean traditional hats, but Mr. Yun was not among them. Sung then went to the small reception room, but Yun's first son, In-seon, was not there either. On his way back, he met one of the house servants, an older woman, carrying an earthen pot of stew.

"Oh, tutor, you're back." After greeting him heartily, she added, "The master's son is very ill. Mr. Yun is with him in his room."

1-4

As a house tutor and a student from the countryside, Sung's arrival would be of no more significance than a neighborhood cat's intrusion. Moreover, in circumstances like these, when the eldest son's health was critical and recovery uncertain, the whole house was in a stir, so nobody took notice of Sung except the older woman, who served him food and told him about In-seon's condition.

In-seon was born weak. His mother died a few months later from tuberculosis, a disease she had already been afflicted with. In-seon inherited his mother's constitution. His skin was thus bright, thin, and soft as a woman's, and he had a narrow chest and lanky frame. Though very weak, he was certainly a handsome man and talented, as his excellent school performance proved.

By contrast, In-seon's wife was a woman of health and sensuality. Sung had seen her several times, noting her smiling eyes and coquettish manner. In-seon's friends joked about his weakness, attributing it to his wife.

This summer, In-seon had gone to Seokwangsa Temple on vacation to avoid the heat but had been afflicted there with diarrhea. Since returning home, he had suffered fever as well as indigestion and insomnia. Mr. Yun had grown worried and called in doctors, modern as well as traditional, but In-seon failed to improve. Mr. Yun then invited a famous traditional doctor who was said to have studied twenty years at Jiri Mountain. This doctor prescribed deer antlers and certain roots, such as mulberry, that had to be decocted and imbibed. In-seon took the medicine, but became red and hot over his entire body. He grew delirious, spoke senselessly, and laughed spasmodically. After he had suffered a week in that state, another doctor came to give an injection and other medicine, which made him sleep, but he had been unable to speak or eat properly since then.

In the reception room were still some men sitting together attired in Korean hat and topcoat, doctors of traditional medicine with official governmental titles like *jinsa*, or *sagwa*. They were debating the five natural elements in the Chinese art of divination and the sixty combinations of Heavenly Stems and Earthly Branches to decide on how to change the direction of the sick person's head every day, from which direction the water for the concoction had to be drawn, or at what time the concoction had to be performed and so on.

These men took care of their concoction personally, sitting beside the fire and ordering a housemaid standing nearby to assist. She was forever being ordered to light the pipe tobacco and bring it over.

Mr. Yun had set his heart especially on In-seon not only because he was the first son but also because In-seon had lost his mother very young and was such a fragile child. Moreover, after turning 60, Mr. Yun had given over to In-seon's charge all paperwork regarding his property and the house budget, leaving entailed to himself only the right of veto as the highest authority. In-seon, unlike the other sons of wealthy families, did not squander wealth but knew how to practice economy, and Mr. Yun thus took great delight in such a trustworthy son.

Watching his son now suffering helplessly, he became so upset that he wouldn't take meals properly, but only smoked and drank.

On the morning after arriving, Heo Sung went to the main reception room to offer greetings to Mr. Yun.

"You are back," said Mr. Yun.

Uttering only that one sentence, he turned again to the traditional doctors in their Korean hats and reprimanded them, saying, "Of what use is that medicine?"

The doctors again started to debate the cause of the disease, but without knowing what they were talking about and just mouthing traditional medical terminology.

From outside, the boiling of the medicine pot grew audible, and the vapor with its peculiar odor came seeping through the pot's paper cover.

It was a clear, hot day.

1-5

The ginseng and deer antlers having provided no beneficial effect, In-seon died on an early morning five days after Heo Sung's arrival. The evening before his death, relatives came to gather in the house at news of his critical condition. Among them were Mr. Han-eun, a distant cousin of Mr. Yun and well-reputed in society; some cousins of In-seon; some young men who had studied overseas in either Japan or America; and some other men unknown to Heo Sung, along with their wives. Also came Kim Gap-jin, an older alumnus of Sung's high school and now a law student at Gyeonseong Imperial University. He was the son of Kim Nam-gyu, who had been involved in the Japan-Korea Annexation Treaty of 1907 and received the title of baron. Kim Gap-jin had been well-known as a brilliant student since his early school years, and this had also made him arrogant. His father, however, who had wasted all his money on alcohol, women, and unwise investments, died after going bankrupt and being accused of swindling. His fall had led to loss of his baronetcy even though he was not indicted, leaving Gap-jin to descend into poverty without inheriting the title. His father and Mr. Yun had been good friends, so the latter was supporting his study. For that reason, Gap-jin not only visited Mr. Yun's place to offer the ritual New Year's bow, but even on occasions dealing with house affairs, as if he were a family member.

After In-seon died, people's envious attention was directed toward Mr. Yun's daughter Jeong-seon, whose mourning for the loss of her elder brother only added more beauty to her features. She had been born to Mr. Yun's second wife, daughter of Kim Seung-ji in Namwon, the richest man in the Jeolla Province, where Mr. Yun had been dispatched to serve as a government official. Jeong-seon's mother was famous for her beauty and for having brought to the marriage a large dowry. At the time, some people in Seoul sneered at Mr. Yun for having married the daughter of a rural commoner for money, and there was some truth to this.

Rumor had it that Miss Kim brought land producing 25,000 or 50,000 bushels of rice as dowry, but whatever the case, no one could deny that Mr. Yun's wealth had increased by about 50,000 bushels during his two years of service in the Jeolla Province. A part of that might have come from bribes or extorting people, but at least two-thirds came from his bride.

Through his marriage and position in the Jeolla Province, Mr. Yun became a well-known man of wealth in Seoul, and the changing times that brought the new railroad line connecting the capital to the Jeolla Province raised land and rice values several times higher, increasing Mr. Yun's wealth even more.

But his wife died before she turned forty, having given birth to a daughter and a son. The son had died not very long after birth, and only Jeong-seon had been left as her own flesh and blood. People said that Jeong-seon looked exactly like her mother. She was tall and slender, and her skin was bright and soft. In contrast to her late brother In-seon, she was not weak, but healthy despite being soft. Her only fault, if one needed to be found, was that her high nose and moist eyes made her seem almost too seductively charming for a lady of a well-bred household.

Jeong-seon was the top student at Sookmyung Girls' High School a couple of times, and after entering the music department at the women-only Ewha College, she gained a high reputation for her beauty and brilliance. She was a wealthy noble family's daughter, a beautiful woman, and an excellent student. Rumor had it that she would inherit at least some part of her mother's dowry, so the attention she received from talented young men and various families with sons was understandable. This was especially the case now that Mr. Yun's first son In-seon had died, for his son-in-law would become head of the household until his third wife's son, Ye-seon, came of age, or so people assumed.

Who would draw that lot for the fortune of becoming Jeong-seon's husband? The question aroused great interest.

1-6

After watching his eldest son die, Mr. Yun charged into the reception room and drove out the doctors with Korean hats, the daoist masters. "Fools, what do you know? You killed my son!"

At this furious outburst, they took fright, withdrawing from the house and out the gate. But one of them soon returned to the yard with a plea. "Please give us some travel money."

At this, Mr. Yun shouted, "These fools are sneaking in again! Drive them out! Call the police to come arrest them all."

At this threat, they uttered no further word and ran away.

Mr. Yun then grabbed the boiling pot of medicine and dashed it to the ground. It rolled along, spitting hot black fluid.

Heo Sung, who had been standing behind the door, waited until Mr. Yun calmed down and then came out to offer a word of comfort. "I am wordless for sorrow."

"Yes, In-seon died." With that response, Mr. Yun looked at Heo Sung. Heo Sung remained silent, not knowing what more to say.

"You did right, expelling those ghost-haunted fools." With these words, Kim Gap-jin also came from the room, apparently having stayed overnight. Even in these circumstances, he was wearing his serge university uniform with its initial "J" from the "jo" in "Keijo Imperial University," the Japanese name for Gyeong Seong Imperial University. In his hands, he held the square hat with a badge that read "University."

"In-seon died." Mr. Yun repeated to Gap-jin.

"Yes, what a tragedy. It's because those superstitious fools made him take that poisonous medicine. If you had put him in a hospital at the beginning, as I advised, this wouldn't have happened. What do those quacks know except how to kill a person?" Gap-jin's conclusive and admonitory tone revealed his arrogant character.

"Do you think that I didn't try with doctors?" Mr. Yun retorted. "What more do they know? They just wanted to take my money."

"It was a mistake from the beginning to call Korean doctors. Such idiots, the Koreans, what do they know? The ignorant bastards don't know a damn thing! You should have called Japanese doctors, like Doctor Hujimura or Doctor Ito. In-seon could have survived." Gap-jin continued with such condescension.

Mr. Yun gave Gap-jin a cross look and went back inside, calling for someone.

Heo Sung, unable to endure Gap-jin's manner, reprimanded him. "You shouldn't talk like that."

"What are you yapping about? You're just a private college student. Students of those colleges think they're such patriots. Listen, what do professors at Bosung College know? They don't know as much as freshmen at a real university. As for you, if you're only good enough to get into a school like that, you'd be better off going back home to farm the soil of your forefathers instead of feeding yourself on cold rice and staying in a servant's room of some house, just living off somebody, which is so disgusting." Sneering and shaking his head, Gap-jin left, probably for a nap after his sleepless night.

Sung didn't become upset because he was used to such words, having often experienced Gap-jin that way. Reflecting upon the distinction that yet existed between city people and country people, between noble and commoner, he sighed.

But Sung felt uneasy. He reflected on Gap-jin's words: "feeding yourself on cold rice and staying in a servant's room of some house," "living off somebody, which is so disgusting," and "better off going back home to farm the soil of your forefathers."

The words troubled his heart, almost stabbing it, although not in the way Gap-jin had intended by his insult.

1-7

It was true. Young male and female students from the countryside thronged to Seoul because they didn't want to work the soil of their forefathers but preferred to freeload, which was indeed disgusting. That was true. The rice paddies, fields, and mountains where ancestors had toiled in blood and sweat—which would yield rice, vegetables, clothes, or all necessities of life if one worked them hard enough—had either been hocked at high interest or sold to support sons and daughters studying in Seoul. The only aim now of parents and their children was to lead a life without tilling the soil. With dark-tanned faces, large rough hands, big feet, meek eyes, and rugged bodies, these offspring of farmers who had lived for generations by their muscles working land and struggling against nature now wore ill-fitting city clothes and roamed the city streets. What a pitiful sight it was to watch them, these young men and women, regarded as "rustics" or "hicks" in the eyes of city people even when they dressed in high-priced, fashionable clothes, which only made them look more ridiculous. Their parents sold land and struggled to survive, while they wasted precious money in the department stores and drinking establishments of Seoul's expensive Jongno area.

Even if they finished college or university someday, what could they do to earn their daily bread? Their desire to enjoy life without hard work, or to work in government posts, or as white-collar workers or bank clerks, wouldn't be fulfilled. All that they would get in Seoul were a piece of paper from some college, extravagant spending habits and desires, tuberculosis and sexual diseases, and health problems brought on by a city lifestyle ill-suited to a constitution meant for nature and the countryside.

Nothing more. They didn't want to work the ancestral soil, but would prove unable to get a job that they did want, so their hope of enjoying life without hard work would bring them hunger and unemployment.

"I'm also one of those people." So thought Sung, dispirited. Gap-jin's silly manner of putting on airs seemed rather advantageous.

From inside the room, three women's lamenting voices were audible. One came from Jeong-seon, another from Jo Jeong-ok, the late In-seon's wife, and the last appeared to belong to In-seon's stepmother.

Jo Jeong-ok was the granddaughter of the well-known nobleman Jo of Jaedong, who had high government ranking, and the daughter of Baron Jo Nam-ik. She had graduated from Jaedong Girls' Middle School and then Public Girls' High School, mainly attended by Japanese. There she also wore kimono and *hakama*, a pleated, ankle-length Japanese skirt. After graduating, she went to Tokyo for one year through connections to the office responsible for descendents of the Korean royal family. Mr. Yun was said to have hard luck with sons but to be always surrounded by beautiful women, and Jeong-ok was a beauty. She had, however, smiling eyes and behaved in a coquettish manner, too much for a daughter of a well-bred family. The education that she had received—not only in her family but also in primary school, middle school, and the girls' high school—provided not motivation or training but individualism and selfishness.

She had learned nothing of patriotism, which was in fact not taught in Korean schools, nor of Christian love for humanity, nor of the Buddhist philosophy of sacrificial service, treating everyone as likewise benevolent and interconnected, nor of sacrificing oneself to help other Koreans out of their misery and provide them happiness, nor any practical training whatsoever. The only things taught were filial loyalty, service to husbands, fiscal responsibility, and loving kindness to children, none of which extended beyond an education based on individualism or familialism. Moreover, her father Jo was well known for his disorderly life, and the family of her father-in-law, Mr. Yun, had nothing to offer her but wealth, no philosophy of life. Those with whom Jeong-ok interacted were all more or less her kind of individualists and selfish hedonists.

For a woman like Jeong-ok, to lose her husband around thirty meant losing everything in life.

1-8

Jeong-ok couldn't control herself. The more time passed after her husband's death, the greater her sadness. She wailed. Striking the ground, and even trying to hang herself by her long, untied hair, she cried continuously.

"Jeong-ok, Jeong-ok," Jeong-seon would say, trying to quell her tears, but she would then cry along with her. Older relatives scolded them: "You should stop crying like that in his father's presence!" But Jeong-ok didn't care.

"The young women these days behave so badly—no respect for parents and no shame!" remarked the older women, speaking ill of Jeong-ok. These old ladies were dismayed to see that the strict morals of their youth had been disrupted and felt displeasure at such unrestrained behavior.

Money saved Mr. Yun from his sadness. It was the most important item of his personal holy trinity. First was money, second was women, and third was his son. Although In-seon was now dead, he had yet another son Ye-seon, though very young, and he had money. Managing wealth amounting to one million won was no easy job. Mr. Yun had many men under his command, but nobody was equal to the task. In-seon had been the only one trusted with bank books and official seals, and the loss of In-seon in his capacity as a most faithful clerk was a blow as great as In-seon's death itself. Mr. Yun nevertheless continued his life and business just like before as soon as the funeral was over, despite his sadness as a father who had lost a son.

But what was left for Jeong-ok, the late In-seon's wife? Her family and education had left her narrow-minded. Absent any dispensation from heaven, nothing could be expected of her beyond a desire to enjoy married life and be adorned with new dresses. Even a new dress had meaning only to the extent that it might please her husband, so nothing remained for her now but sadness, darkness, and hopelessness. Moreover, her mother-in-law, a slightly older alumna of the same school, whom she had despised as the wife of an old man, would now despise her in return as an ill-fated young widow. Reflecting on this, she felt miserable. A child would have comforted her, but Jeong-ok's son and daughter had both died before they could speak, and her only other pregnancy had resulted in a miscarriage.

Her crying, overheard constantly from her room, was too heartbreaking to listen to. The only person who could comfort her was Jeong-seon, but with the new semester that had started in September, she went off daily to school until late afternoon, leaving Jeong-ok alone to cry by herself almost incessantly. She could have gone to her family if they had lived close, but they lived in South Chungcheong Province, in Yesan. Besides, her father and mother had both passed away, and only her womanizing older brother still lived there with his wife.

Heo Sung gradually became necessary to the household. Mr. Yun started to trust him after assigning him a few jobs, and Sung began to work as his secretary, taking care of bank business, doing paperwork, and contacting others, even performing the most sensitive jobs. He did the same work as In-seon had done except that he was not Mr. Yun's son. Mr. Yun even let him move from the servants' quarters to In-seon's place, a small reception room, so the servants started to call him "sir" in a highly respectful tone, in contrast to their previous manner, when they had referred to him simply as "the man from the countryside" or "the student." The complex work that Sung was now in charge of interfered significantly with his studies, but he was not displeased that Mr. Yun placed absolute trust in him. Moreover, he was delighted that visitors who had previously not even properly responded to him now took the initiative in greeting him.

1-9

One day while Sung was in the main reception room doing some bookkeeping under Mr. Yun's supervision, Gap-jin came in. He greeted Yun after the Japanese manner, then turned with a sarcastic remark toward Sung, who was making entries in a ledger. "You are elevated in status now."

Without pausing, Sung chuckled.

"Is this guy your manager?" asked Gap-jin, turning to Yun.

Yun smiled. "He is my secretary."

"Should I hire you as court stenographer next year when I become a judge?" Gap-jin asked, laughing loudly before continuing his sarcasm. "If a country fellow becomes butler to a lord, won't his name and title be put on the funeral banner and a memorial tablet?"

After finishing his work, Sung took Gap-jin into the small reception room. Gap-jin was very surprised to discover a desk within and Sung's hat and coat hanging on the wall. Only then did he realize that Sung had moved in. "Is this now your room?" Gap-jin asked, great surprise visible on his face. He was truly astonished.

"No, it's Ye-seon's room. But it's not being used by him yet, so Yun told me to use it," responded Sung. Then noticing Gap-jin still standing, he said, "Have a seat."

Gap-jin sat down where Sung had pointed. But he was so surprised by the fact that Sung had moved from the servant's quarters to this room that he couldn't easily calm down. So it was true that Sung was not just a manager or butler but was being treated as a real "secretary," exactly as Mr. Yun had stated.

"But surely not . . ." Gap-jin thought, gazing at Sung. He had large hands and feet, and his face looked a little rough, features of a country man, but even in the eyes of Gap-jin, who liked to look down upon country people, Sung was a man of bearing.

Sung had been well known already in high school not only for his physique but also for his intelligence, for which Gap-jin had great respect. Sung was also a soccer player, for which Gap-jin had no envy, and was quite proficient in Japanese, for which Gap-jin did have high respect. If Sung had attended the same university as Gap-jin, there would have been no reason to look down upon him except for his status as a commoner from the countryside. But Gap-jin disdained anything done by Koreans other than himself and regarded it worthless. As the student of a private college, Sung was thus held much lower in Gap-jin's opinion.

Staring again at Sung, he reflected, "Surely Mr. Yun would not want Sung to marry Jeong-seon and become his son-in-law. Who should be Jeong-seon's husband except me?"

He had been confident of himself. Upon graduating from university, he would marry Jeong-seon, he thought, and she would come with a dowry of land producing five thousand bushels of rice annually, and so on and so on . . . Thus had he imagined and calculated. Even when some family made an offer of marriage, he had boasted, saying "Oh, no, I haven't thought of marriage. I'm still just a student. Shouldn't I focus on my studies?" He could say this because he had been so confident of himself. For him, the son of a noble if poor family, marriage meant wealth. Women were easy to get. In bars, he could find them in abundance, and seducing female students was easy for him. He had more than he needed. But a wife with money—that would be a most valuable acquisition, one that he still needed.

1-10

Gap-jin saw his bright dreams fading, however, upon his encounters with Sung, who now occupied Mr. Yun's small reception room entirely. "You should celebrate," he said, smirking to cheer himself up as he looked directly into Sung's face.

"Celebrate?" Sung responded, smiling. "For moving from the servant's quarters to this room?"

"Exactly. Your ancestors' status was so low, they would've been allowed to greet Mr. Yun only from the yard. You should go visit their graves and report your achievement next time you go home." Gap-jin's remark was too venomous for a joke.

"The same goes for you," Sung replied in a light tone.

"What's the same?"

"Commoners like my ancestors had to greet nobility like your family from the yard, but nobility like you had to do the same with the Chinese. And now the same with the Japanese, right?"

Gap-jin's face lost its smirk and turned purple with fury.

"Gap-jin, you often talk about nobility, but Koreans are all just country people, commoners in the world's eyes. What's so important about distinguishing between nobility and commoner in this tiny, underpopulated country? Why does it matter so much to distinguish between people from Seoul and people from the country? Or between state schools and private schools? Whether Kim Gap-jin or Heo Sung, we have one thing common—we're 'Koreans'."

"Commoners are commoners. You're an exception, but country people are ignorant by nature. They're sly, though. And they're so proud of their provinces that they hate and exclude people from Seoul. It's true, isn't it? I know a school principal who's from the countryside, and most of the teachers there are, too. The same goes for the banks and newspapers, and you know it. Country people are the ones making distinctions, not city people like me. You've entirely misunderstood things. It's all your own misunderstanding." Gap-jin spoke as if delivering a speech.

"That doesn't make any sense. You say that school has a lot of teachers from the countryside, but what about other schools? There are only Seoul people. And what about other banks? Is there any one from the countryside? And what about other newspapers? Most of the employees are from Seoul. Wouldn't you have to say, then, that these institutions are made up of people proud of their own place, Seoul? You notice only people from the countryside. In your eyes, Seoul people belong here, but if a few from the countryside mix among them, you look at them with suspicion. That comes from the old aristocratic prejudice against any country man who reached a high position usually occupied only by someone in an upper-class family. The nobility regarded it as strange and sinister. They preferred someone whose family lineage was well known. But someone like you, a highly educated man, shouldn't stick to old views. As my friend, you can discuss anything with me, but talking that way about country folk and commoners doesn't help the unity of our country. Someone like you, a man of a noble family, should be at the forefront of breaking down such divisions between nobility and commoner, between Seoul people and country people. You should try to help people love each other for the fact of being Korean, don't you agree?"

Sung spoke with passionate enthusiasm.

Gap-jin was listening intently, looking at Sung with eyes open wide. Sung felt pleased that Gap-jin was not displaying his usual sarcasm. When Sung was finished, however, Gap-jin said, "Have you finished your recitation? You, a private college fool, are you giving a lecture or sermon to me, a university student?"

1-11

Mr. Han of Ikseon-dong was known not only to students of Baejae School and Boseong College but also to many of the middle and high school students in Seoul. Now in his 50s, he had earlier taught English at Baejae High School before moving to Boseong College, but he still taught English composition at Baejae and Ewha High School. He had not received a formal education and so could become neither a professor at a private college nor a full-time teacher in high school. His salary was thus low.

Mr. Han's given name was Min-gyo. In accordance with his name's meaning, "educating people," he took as his life's work the education of young Koreans. He had finished middle school in Tokyo, and while learning English at a prep school for college, he read books on history, politics, and philosophy. Like other Koreans with a similar course of education, he afterwards returned to Korea. He had since been imprisoned for his politics, spent time in Manchuria, and become a Christian and a teacher, but only for the last ten years had he been teaching.

His little thatched-roof house was obscurely located among the winding backstreets of Ikseon-dong. It had a gate of about two square meters, a reception room of two square meters, a main room of three square meters, and an opposite room of two square meters, but the wooden-floored, middle room of six square meters was bigger than usual, and the storage and the outhouse together were four square meters. Naturally, the house also had a tiny yard, a terrace for jars, and a kitchen. This little thatched-roof dwelling was well known as Mr. Han's house.

Because the other rooms were too small for a large gathering of visitors, a sliding-glass door had been placed at the open side of the wooden-floored room, a very unusual addition. The students who frequently visited called it "Mr. Han's Western room" because it had a different style than a Korean traditional room. Four or five chairs donated by individual students were placed there. Some brought their old chairs, unused after graduation, some purchased theirs from a second-hand store and brought them in. The chairs were thus all different in color and shape. Some were of wood, some covered with patterned cloth, some of leather, and one was even covered in red velvet.

Mr. Han's wife had grey hair that made her look almost like an old woman four or five years his senior. They had only one daughter still living at home, and she had just entered high school that year. Their son had been a medical student but had fled overseas during the 1919 independence protests and wrote them only occasionally.

Heo Sung was one of the students who regularly visited this house. Kim Gap-jin sometimes also came to visit because of his acquaintance with Han from Baejae. Students of Ewha College also sometimes came.

One day, Mr. Han was giving a dinner party, and about ten students were invited. It was snowing outside, but in Han's "Western room," a small coal stove furiously radiated heat, bringing the teakettle placed on the heater's lid to a boil that spewed forth white clouds of whistling steam.

In the kitchen, Han's wife was cooking, assisted by a neighbor's woman servant called in for the occasion, and their daughter Jeong-ran was busy running in and out on errands. At some point, Mr. Han arrived and called out, "Open the gate."

"Oh, Father, you're here," cried Jeong-ran. She hurried to the gate, drying her hands on her apron. "Oh my, the snow on your coat!" She tried to brush the snow from his chest and shoulders with her small pale hands.

"Has nobody come yet?" he asked, stamping the snow from his feet.

"So much snow in such a short time," she said, taking his hat and trying to undo his shoelaces.

"I'll do that," he said.

"No," she insisted. "I'll do it."

1-12

After entering the "Western room," Han took off his coat and gave it to Jeong-ran. He looked around smiling, satisfied with the room she had worked to set up for guests.

She took as her responsibility the task of keeping his desk and the room arranged to his satisfaction. The decorations on the curtains for the glass door had been embroidered by her, and though her skill was not perfect, she had put a lot of work into it to please her father. Mr. Han was a man who could appreciate his daughter's heart.

She had also put embroidered cushions on the wooden chairs and spread an embroidered tablecloth across the table. On Han's rather large, Western-style desk, unusual for a traditional Korean home, lay even more, variously sized embroiderings to cushion his arms or support his inkstand, inkstone, and pencil case, almost too many. She probably would have liked to embroider something for the top of the stove, except that the uncouth heater would then have eaten up her carefully crafted artwork.

Han sat down on the wooden armchair she'd placed in front of the stove for him. For such a thin person like him, the weather outside had been very cold. "It isn't too warm?" he asked, opening the stove's door and looking inside.

His daughter was off in the main room putting his traditional Korean clothes on the heated floor. "No, it's not," she said. "It was eighteen degrees just a little ago." She came out quickly to the Western room and checked the thermometer on his desk. "It's twenty-one now," she said, smiling. "Should I keep the door of the opposite room open for a while?"

Han looked very gaunt. He had high cheekbones and sunken

cheeks. He was slightly balding, and more than half of his remaining hair was grey, but his eyes glittered with life. Sturdily built by nature, his body was nevertheless skeletal. From lifelong hardship—suffering through poverty, wandering, imprisonment, worries, teaching, and long talks with young people—his body had grown gaunt, and his face looked tired.

But nobody, not even his wife, who had lived with him so long, had ever seen him discouraged or angry. He was always calm and collected, hardly showing his emotions. This didn't mean, however, that he was cold-hearted. He loved his wife and daughter, his friends and his juniors. Moreover, he wholeheartedly loved Korea. On the wall above his desk was a map of Korea, and on his desk were always some history books about Korea, such as *Memorabilia of the Three Kingdoms* or *History of the Three Kingdoms*, or some literary works by Koreans. He made a habit of reading at least one page about Korea every day.

Guests started to arrive, and they were all students. The first was Kim Sang-cheol, a humanities student at Gyeongseong University. He was a short man with a darkish face.

Following him were students wearing the hats and uniforms of Gyeongseong Medical College, Severance Medical College, Boseong College, Gyeongseong Business College, and Gyeonseong Technical College, then two students of Ewha College. One was quite a beauty, though the other was stocky like a gymnastics teacher. Their names were Shim Sun-rye and Jeong Seo-bun.

Around the time the clock pointed to six and the light was turned on, two young men in suits arrived. One was tall and slender, a Western-style gentleman with healthy complexion and round eyes, while the other was short and slightly built but with glittering eyes. These two were Dr. Lee Geon-yeong and Yun Myeong-seop, an inventor.

1-13

The family had prepared thick beef soup, grilled beef ribs and heart, and pan-fried ice fish coated with flour and egg. Jeong-ran wore an embroidered apron and played hostess.

Saying, "Now, have some food," Han led them in eating.

"It's really a long time since I had a Korean dinner," said Lee Geon-yeong with appreciation. He had recently returned from America after a nearly ten-year stay and was touched by the meal.

"Did you have a chance to eat any Korean food in America?" asked Jeong Seo-bun, the stocky girl.

"From time to time," he replied in perfect English, then continued in Korean, "I had the opportunity with some Korean families when I lived in California, on the west coast of America. I had some kimchi, too. But it didn't taste like this. Mr. Han, your wife's kimchi tastes very good." He scooped up some kimchi sauce with a spoon and savored it on his tongue.

"Beyond any other Korean food, the flavor of kimchi is the quintessence of our Korean spirit," joked Kim Sang-cheol with dramatic flair, for he was a student of Korean theater.

"*Bravo!*" cried Lee in English and added, "You say kimchi is the very food of our national spirit!" He gave Sang-cheol a wink of praise for his clever quip. Sang-cheol returned a wry smile and began gnawing on some *galbi* ribs.

"*Galbi* ribs are very Korean," remarked one of the students. "It's said that the energy to gnaw on grilled *galbi* is the only energy Koreans still have."

"I've heard that, too" said Han, smiling. "They say Englishmen get their energy from eating bloody beefsteak."

"Food would seem to represent each nation's characteristics," said another student. "Sushi is Japan's, the dumpling is China's, and roast chicken is surely the West's."

"Ha ha!" laughed Lee Geon-yeong, picking up a piece of heart to eat. "And here is 'toasted heart,'" he added in English while looking at the two female students, Sun-rye and Seo-bun.

Sun-rye returned a brief, almost imperceptible smile.

"Mr. Kim, what's wrong with you, why so quiet today?" asked Han, turning toward Kim Gap-jin.

"I'm always quiet, am I not?" responded Kim, crunching a piece of kimchi between his teeth.

"He is a man of inscrutable temper," said a fellow Gyeongseong student, laughing.

Others joined in the laughter. Everyone, especially the two new guests, turned toward Gap-jin.

"I have to ask," said Gap-jin, after swallowing some rice with kimchi sauce, "but why are those who have studied in America all such fools? It's hard to find one who speaks English fluently. What's wrong with them?" Playing innocent, he looked over toward Dr. Lee, who was greatly surprised at this unexpected question. Sun-rye looked down as if embarrassed. Other students giggled.

Heo Sung poked Gap-jin in the side. "What are you talking about?" he demanded.

"Mr. Han, did I say something wrong?" asked Gap-jin, pretending even more innocence. "Why are they giggling?"

"Actually, not everyone who studied in America is a good student. Some are good and some are not," responded Han, smiling.

1-14

"Well, I've hardly found anyone who studied or received a doctoral degree in America to be particularly knowledgeable or up to anything significant. Has anybody? All are fools," said Gap-jin, looking at Dr. Lee and laughing, "But Dr. Lee is probably an exception."

All the others laughed.

"Universities like Harvard or Yale must be good, though, I've heard," said Gap-jin, his tone still condescending. "Princeton, too," he added remembering that Dr. Lee had studied there.

No one knew how to react to Gap-jin's remarks. Dr. Lee, struck wordless and apparently stunned, sat in abstract silence.

"Mr. Han, what do you say? Is it not true?" Alone in triumph, he continued, "I thought that their dissertations were little better than our writing exercises from elementary school. If one can receive a doctoral degree for such things, my friends here can all become doctors, don't you agree?" He pointed to his school friends.

"There are surely some frauds with doctoral degrees here, too," suggested Kim Sang-cheol, the drama student.

The mood had been wrecked by Gap-jin, however, and wouldn't be easily restored. It was as if a train had derailed and tumbled from a bridge, making the recovery impossible. In the meantime, dinner was almost over.

At length, Mr. Han placed his spoon in its rice bowl and tried to continue the disrupted conversation, starting with a couple of introductions. "The reason I invited you today is, as you all know, to introduce two respectable men. One is Dr. Lee Geon-yeong, and the other is Yun Myeong-seop. Dr. Lee went to America after graduating from Baejae High School and studied at Stanford for his BA. He then received his MA and PhD from Princeton. He studied Ethics and Education there and also received a bachelor's in theology from Yale University. He pursued his education on his own and supported himself for about ten years. Gaining such a fine scholar and hard worker is a great addition for Korea, and we are pleased to have him.

At these remarks, Lee nodded individually to Mr. Han and each of the others. Gap-jin bowed deeply in response, his nose almost touching the table.

"And Mr. Yun Myeong-seop," Han continued, his eyes grown bright. "He has never gone to school, not even to elementary school. Instead, he has studied religion and real life. As a servant in a farmer's house or a clerk in a shop, whether engraving seals, pulling a rickshaw, or working as a driver, he has always tried to contribute to Korea in his hopes and beliefs. But the overriding aim of his life is to find the rod of Moses. As you know, this was the rod that saved the Israelites, splitting the sea and striking rocks to make spring water burst forth. With equally firm belief and endeavor, he has developed more than thirty inventions and received the patent rights for them. He is now working on another, more important and amazing invention. This one is being kept a secret for now, but it's almost at the stage of completion. In about a year, it will be finished, and it will not only astonish the international scientific community, it will revolutionize human life throughout the whole world. We cannot help but take pride and pleasure in being Korean, a nation that has produced such a great inventor."

Everybody's attention was drawn to the small, shabby figure of Yun Myeong-seop.

1-15

Taking out a piece of paper with writing on it, Han said, "I would like to read aloud Mr. Yun's precepts for daily life. I am greatly impressed by them and want to share them with you all:

> In everyday life, I pledge to God:
> 1. A three-minute prayer every morning (for planning the day while still in bed)
> 2. A three-minute prayer at night, reflecting on the day. Reciting the Bible, too.
> 3. A three-minute meditation, reflecting on the

suffering of the past (remembering the past of great people). Resolving to make more strenuous efforts. Appreciation of people who helped me.

4. My vocation? (To work and think hard all my life in order to practice my ideals and hopes).
5. My devotion to my research and everything I do in life.
6. No hesitation if a chance is given.
7. Three minutes of thought before purchasing anything.
8. Attention to my health.

My Time Schedule:
1. 7 hours at school
2. 3 hours for commuting, meals, writing letters
3. 3 hours for reviewing schoolwork
4. 3 hours for earning money
5. 4 hours for research on inventions
6. 4 hours for sleep
Total: 24 hours
On Sundays: church, entertainment, reading, visits, that's it.

When Han stopped reading and was finished introducing Dr. Lee and Yun, there was utter silence. Everyone seemed to be thinking, "I should also do something important for Korea. I could if I lived with perseverance, devotion, and strenuous effort, like Lee or Yun, or like Mr. Han." Everyone was lost in such reflections, strongly moved by these apparently simple but actually profound things.

"That's it. It's not so difficult!" Heo Sung told himself, reflecting further. "I should go live with farmers. I don't have money, but I can just go and make myself useful. Eat what the poorest of them eat, wear what they wear, live where they live. I can help by doing errands. Like writing letters for them, or going to the police station or district office for them. I can also teach them how to read and write. I can help them set up a cooperative, and clean their toilets and kitchens. I can dedicate my life to doing these things."

He felt confirmed in a decision that he had always kept in mind. He decided to throw away his dreams of earning a lot of money, directing a lot of people, and posting announcements in newspapers of brilliant work to be accomplished for Korea. He now felt that he understood, anew and in greater depth, Mr. Han's motto "From myself, I should start!"

From the drama student Kim Sang-cheol to the Ewha music student Shim Sun-rye, all of those present silently reaffirmed their decisions to devote their lives to helping Korean people. To make Korean art for the people, to write novels and plays and to compose music for the pleasure of the poorest Koreans, these were also important and even necessary contributions according to Mr. Han, contributions that would lay the foundation stones and establish the pillars for building a new Korea.

Kim Gap-jin wanted first to obtain a position as high judge and gain a name for himself, then pursue a career as a top lawyer and become an important person in Korea, earning a lot of money as well as fighting for people's rights. That was what he considered his vocation. Mr. Han also regarded it as necessary work for Korea and indeed thought any work fine if done through individual sacrifice for Korea and the Korean people and if joined with the work of others in organized, ideological commitment. He extended this belief to individuals working together for Korea and was even pleased to know a high-spirited, ambitious young man like Gap-jin from the otherwise corrupt and paralyzed noble class.

1-16

Although Jeong Seo-bun's heart was strongly drawn to Dr. Lee Geon-yeong, Shim Sun-rye's preferred Yun Myeong-seop, if her heart were to be spoken of at all. There were several reasons Sun-rye was interested in Yun. Her own father was born after his father had died, and his mother also died early. He was raised by relatives and worked downtown in the Jongno District at a paper shop as errand boy and clerk until about thirty. He then borrowed money at monthly interest to open his own paper shop and had been working for nearly twenty years since then. Through thrift and careful saving as well as by earning a reputation for reliability, he was now quite well-off, earning money equivalent to about five hundred bushels of rice a year. However, he had only just enough education as was needed for using a ledger.

He didn't drink or seek out entertainment much and didn't take a mistress after growing wealthy (unlike nine out of ten wealthy middle-aged businessmen in Jongno). His life consisted solely of work, from morning to evening, and he moved only within an arc circumscribing only his home and store.

Sun-rye's mother was much the same. Her friends decorated themselves with hairpins of gold or jade and clothed themselves in white silk. Or they regularly did expensive things for their health, like having a shaman perform an exorcism or having themselves treated with medicinal water for bathing or drinking. But she lived without extravagance and would only go for the free medicinal water at a local spring in nearby Akbakgol when her chronic indigestion grew acute. In such cases, she would go early in the morning to avoid other people. Out of frugality, she wouldn't even visit her parents in Siheung unless some important event required it. Raising the late-born Sun-rye had been the source of their joy and happiness.

They therefore sent Sun-rye to school, not only from elementary to high school, but even—against other people's advice to marry her then—on to Ewha College to study music, in which she seemed talented.

"I don't know much about music or college education, but without much property to leave her, I thought she should earn a certificate for a profession she can use to make a living if her life turns out hard." Sun-rye's father would offer these words as explanation for her college education.

Growing up in a family practicing self-reliance, thrift, and restraint, Sun-rye was like a country girl, innocent and well protected from the world, though born with artistic talent. She didn't dress up and was quiet, natural, and virtuous. One might have a first impression of her as too quiet or not yet mature, but inside, she was a sensitive artist. Sun-rye was thus drawn more to Myeong-seop, a thrifty and humble person like herself, although not quite handsome, than to the stylish Dr. Lee.

She had never made the acquaintance of any men other than teachers—and then only in the classroom. Perhaps the only men she had ever met were tram conductors. Occasionally, male students would show interest and follow her, but she just ignored them. They might try for a while to talk to her, but then give up and go away disappointed.

After entering Ewha College, she had met Mr. Han, her first Korean male teacher. She had earlier had no opportunity to have a Korean man as homeroom teacher, not in all her years from elementary to high school, where her male teachers had all been Japanese. She told her parents about Mr. Han. "He's very well-mannered, strict but nice, and a good teacher. He's also well respected in society."

Sun-rye's parents knew nothing about the people recognized in educated circles and higher society, but they accepted her report because they trusted their daughter. Her father therefore went to see Mr. Han for advice about her future.

1-17

"I am an ignorant man, just making money from business. I sent her to college because she liked studying and she is our only child," said Sun-rye's father at their first meeting. Mr. Shim had eyes somewhat larger than usual for a Korean, but his face and chin were round, and he had a typical Korean mustache and beard. Of large frame and chubby, he looked like a typical Korean gentleman.

Mr. Han had a good impression of him as an unaffected man who displayed a number of traditional Korean virtues: humility, dignity, broadmindedness, self-respect, and gravity. Such characteristics were rarely found among the current crop of young Koreans who had been overseas, thought Han. He was quite annoyed by the young men and women who imitated Japanese and Western culture. Such youth were superficial, impatient, volatile as a hot teapot, selfish, nitpicking, and undignified.

With his brief remarks, Sun-rye's father hinted at his hope that Mr. Han might guide his daughter carefully through her college years to teach her good discipline and even assist in finding a suitable man for her to marry, the most important issue for traditional Korean parents. Mr. Han accepted the request willingly.

Some days later, Sun-rye's father sent him a jar of honey from Gangwondo Province. Knowing that Han touched neither tobacco nor alcohol, he decided on honey after long consideration. In return, Han settled upon a dinner party with Dr. Lee and Yun Myeong-seop as an opportunity for finding Sun-rye a proper husband.

Of the potential candidates, he had Dr. Lee most in mind. Han wished Sun-rye, whom he already loved like a father and trusted wholeheartedly, to marry a man whom he loved and trusted just as much. Geon-yeong had been Baejae High School's best student, a well-behaved boy whom he had grown to love while teaching there. After going overseas to study, Geon-yeong continued as a good student at the several universities he attended and had never given cause for rumors about relationships with women or about any other disreputable affairs. As for his knowledge and his ability to express himself, he had been praised for articles published in highbrow newspapers and magazines there. Han had been thinking of recommending Dr. Lee for a professor position at Boseong College, Yeonhi College, or Ewha College, and also of encouraging him to marry Sun-rye.

Some days after the dinner party, Mr. Han met Geon-yeong alone and asked his impression of Sun-rye. He acknowledged having received an entirely positive impression and requested a meeting. They actually met about ten times to talk. Two or three of those times, they ate at a hotel restaurant and watched a movie at the cinema.

Sun-rye was not especially beautiful, but she took after her father with her nice round face, and her Korean eyes were benign and gentle, her skin bright and glowing, her arms and legs well-balanced. Her hands and nose were remarkably lovely. Geon-yeong thought her voice and manner of laughing especially nice, but considered her heart the most beautiful feature of all.

Sun-rye had never argued with anyone nor so much as raised her voice; neither had she laughed too much nor revealed her tears. Like her father and their Korean ancestors, she rarely betrayed her emotions in her face, keeping instead a gentle smile like that of the Buddha. Speaking mostly just "Yes" or "No," she was a true daughter of the old Korea.

"Not many can see Sun-rye's value and beauty," Han observed.

Geon-yeong agreed. "Yes, that's right. I alone can see them."

1-18

Spring arrived just as Heo Sung finished his graduation exam and returned home—to Mr. Yun's house. Unexpectedly, Yun was waiting alone in the main reception room. Sung greeted him from outside. "I'm back, sir."

Yun responded warmly, "Come inside."

Heo Sung went in and stood with bowed head before Mr. Yun, who was sitting in an armchair near the table in the Western-style room. A heater had been turned on.

"Have a seat," he said, indicating with his chin a chair across the table.

Heo Sung sat down.

"Are you now completely finished with the exam?"

"Yes, I've just had the last test today."

"I want to talk to you about something today," he said, touching his beard briefly with his hand. The beard was white.

Heo Sung looked at him, waiting.

"I don't know how you will take this, but I've been thinking about it for a long time. Now that you're finished with your studies, I think you should seriously consider getting married. What do you say?" asked Mr. Yun carefully.

"I'm not yet interested in marriage," replied Sung clearly.

"You say you're not interested in marriage yet? Why not?" asked Yun, quite surprised.

"I would like to study further," Sung responded, giving a common reason. He preferred not to say that he couldn't marry without job or property.

"What do you want to study more?" asked Yun.

"I've studied law and now want to get a certificate to become a lawyer."

"Oh, yes, you should," agreed Yun. He liked the idea. "You have to take the National Exam for Government Offices to become a lawyer, don't you?"

"That's right," said Sung.

"Gap-jin is going to take the exam this year, so you can do it with him. I've heard the exam will take place in July. Is that right?"

"Right."

"Then, you should go to Tokyo in June," said Yun.

Heo Sung couldn't respond because he didn't want to admit that he had no money. To take the exam in Tokyo, he needed at least 200 won all together, including the cost for the round trip. But he had no right to ask Mr. Yun for money.

Yun understood Sung's silence. To ease the uncomfortable situation, he said, "You can go to Tokyo. That's no problem." After a brief pause, he continued, "Actually, that wasn't what I wanted to talk to you about. There's something else important I needed to say. It's about my daughter, Jeong-seon. I'm not sure if she would satisfy you, but might it be possible for you to marry her? Not just for her sake. I have nobody to turn to since In-seon died, and you seem different from most young people these days. I see that from my experience with you. I've been thinking about this for some time now. It's a little awkward for me to talk about my daughter, but she's not so bad. It's also not entirely proper to talk to you directly about this, but there's nobody I can turn to. I hope you don't feel offended."

Yun's words were a bolt from the blue for Heo Sung. He had never dreamed of this possibility. Not knowing what to say, and without much reflection, he simply said, "I wouldn't want to think about marriage until I have the certificate to practice law."

With these words, he bowed his head and left the room.

1-19

The same day, Mr. Yun went to see his cousin Mr. Yun Han-eun, whose opinion he generally respected. He spoke of his marriage plans for Jeong-seon and inquired about Heo Sung as a prospective son-in-law. Han-eun was very surprised and asked, "How did you come to decide upon him?"

"As I have seen, he is a sincere person, and noble even though his family isn't old *yangban*," replied Mr. Yun, revealing an ability to size people up.

"A good decision!" Han-eun immediately agreed. "Marry her to him!" He had in fact been thinking of marrying his own granddaughter En-gyeong to Sung. She was in Tokyo studying English literature at Seongsim Women's College.

Having obtained Han-eun's approval, Mr. Yun returned home and immediately called Jeong-seon in to ask for her opinion about Sung. She didn't answer. Jeong-seon had actually never seriously considered Sung, and wondered why her father wanted her to marry a man from the countryside. Mr. Yun, however, interpreted her silence as acquiescence, not that he considered his daughter in the position to offer her own opinion anyway. He concluded that everything was settled, and assumed that Sung wouldn't reject his request.

But for Sung, the issue was not so simple. Two things already demanded his loyalty. One was his decision to become a lawyer after graduation and return to the countryside and dedicate his life there to the farmers. The other was the promise made to Yu Sun as he had held her shoulders and stroked her head. He had told her, "I'll come back."

The promise, of course, was nothing like engagement. But as he spoke those words, he had also thought, "I will live my life with this woman." For Yu Sun, an innocent with the heart of a traditional Korean woman, to lean her head onto Sung's chest was as much as to say, "I give myself to you. For my life until my death, I am your woman. This is the sign of my pledge, and it will never change." In her traditional way of thinking, Yu Sun probably thought that she had become Sung's wife. Remembering that evening, Heo Sung felt responsible for her, as if they were already married.

What really made marriage to Jeong-seon impossible, however, was Sung's decision to go back to the countryside. For a woman who had lived only in Seoul and had never touched the soil, going to the country and living there was unimaginable. Sung resolved to turn down Mr. Yun's offer of his daughter's hand. If Mr. Yun mentioned it again, he felt sure that he would firmly refuse.

Mr. Yun, for his part, already considered Sung as his son-in-law. For that reason, he didn't raise the issue again.

On a day in June, Heo Sung and Kim Gap-jin departed Gyeongseong Station headed for Japan. Although Mr. Yun had wanted to provide a new suit for Sung, he had refused and set off wearing his old clothes from school time, but he was wearing a new straw hat and carrying a bag given to him by Mr. Yun. Kim Gap-jin cut a stylish figure as a gentleman in suit and spring coat. Their school friends were also gathered at the station to see them off joyfully with heartfelt wishes for success.

1-20

The day was clear and hot, but cool air blew in through the window. As the train moved southward, people in the fields seemed busier planting rice. The rain of the last two days was not a lot but sufficient for planting the fields. Every year, around the time for rice planting, the weather was dry, and people would complain that they wouldn't survive. But just when they were desperately saying that they couldn't survive any longer if the drought continued three more days, the rain would come. This year was the same. It was as if God were saying, "I do my job, so just do what you're supposed to do. Don't think I don't exist. I'm here. I only wanted to show myself since you're inclined to deny my existence."

As Sung watched rice plants gently waving in the wind and farmers bent over planting rice, he felt that the sunlight filling the sky and the life-giving power of the earth were there especially for the farmers. Among human works, farming seemed the only right, holy, and true one. And those riding the train, despite living off the farmers' sweat, seemed not merely unappreciative of their good work but even unaware.

"What are you looking at so intently?" asked Gap-jin, tapping Sung's knee as he settled again in his seat after having wandered off somewhere. He followed Sung's gaze out the window. There was nothing to catch Gap-jin's eye.

"I was watching farmers plant rice," replied Sung and turned toward Gap-jin.

"Why?" said Gap-jin and tried to look out again, but the train had already passed through the fields and was moving between mountains. "You must be missing the work your ancestors did over many generations. That's why people say 'You can't make a silk purse out of a sow's ear.'" Gap-jin was starting to be sarcastic again.

"Does farming look so humble to your eyes?" asked Sung, his tone reflective.

"Sure, in a time of commerce and industry like today, farming is a job fit only for the lowest people, right? Not knowing how to do anything else, they grub about in the soil like earthworms. In your case, we would say that a dragon from the sewer ascended to the sky. Though it's perhaps more appropriate to say a dragon from an earthworm, ha, ha." Gap-jin's voice had risen above the clacking of the train. People sitting nearby smiled. His naïve remarks expressed no malice.

"Are you serious?" said Sung, his voice grown solemn. "Is it so hard for you to see the value of farmers and farming? Do farmers look like worms in your eyes? If they do, then you have a mistaken perception of things."

"Oh, so you're going to lecture me again? You want to preach to me about how 'Farmers are the Roots of Heaven and Earth'? Just drop it, okay? At our place, we have some tenant farmers, and they are all treacherous, greedy like pigs, hardly even human. As farmers who live from working with the soil, they're expected to be genuine and truthful, but no, they'd bellyache for three years if they couldn't swindle city folk. One has to come down hard on such trash. If you release the pressure just a little, they grow ill-mannered. Don't you agree? You've now graduated from college and should slough off that country attitude, instead of dreaming up justifications for it . . ."Gap-jin paused. "Now, what was it you said? You want to go to the country and live with the farmers? What's the use of all your study? But maybe you're right. That might just happen. You'll have no other choice if you fail the National Exam for Government Offices." He laughed at his own joke.

1-21

The train was rushing along mountainsides, turning with their curves, and passing villages crowded with small, shabby farmhouses among fields where men and women were busy planting rice.

Gap-jin, prompted by Sung's words, turned his attention to the visibly poor farmhouses and manifestly hard labor of planting. To Gap-jin, born and raised in Seoul, this rural scene was entirely foreign, having no connection to him. Turning to face Sung, Gap-jin sighed. "How could anybody live in such a place even for one day?"

Curious about Gap-jin's interest in the farms, Sung said, "It's worse inside a farmhouse. The walls are full of bedbugs, the floor is covered with fleas, and lice infest the clothes and blankets.

During the summer, flies and mosquitoes swarm there, too. What's worse, the families don't have much to eat. They have to live on grass roots or tree bark because they don't have even the least grain like millet to make porridge ..."

Interrupting Sung, Gap-jin slapped his shoulder hard and exclaimed, "Yeah, I've heard of eating roots and bark in old times, but who on earth would eat them today? What an exaggeration! Ha ha."

Sung was astonished, not at the slap, but that Gap-jin knew so little about the reality of Korea. After gazing at him in blank surprise, Sung asked, "Don't you read any newspapers or magazines?"

"Don't I read newspapers? *Osaka Asahi Daily, Gyeongseong Daily*, magazines of national institutes, and other magazines like *Chūōkōron* and *Kaizō*, I read all of them. Without reading newspapers and magazines, one would be antiquated, wouldn't one?" bragged Gap-jin.

"Reading only such things, one wouldn't learn about Koreans eating roots and bark these days. Don't you read any Korean papers or magazines at all?" Sung asked, his tone expressing shock.

"Korean papers and magazines?" said Gap-jin, his turn to be surprised. "What's the use of reading those? They're worthless. What would Korean journalists know? I'd rather have a nap than read such stuff."

Sung, stumped with disbelief, was at a loss for words.

More triumphantly, Gap-jin continued. "Also, it's hard to read the Korean papers and magazines today. Koreans now write everything in Hangeul, that vulgar Korean writing system. It's like Greek, so who would read such articles? In the library, there are newspapers, magazines, and books written in Japanese, English, and German. Why spend time reading things in Korean? Only someone like you who's weak in other languages. Or, of course, those farmers out there planting rice, they can read such things."

Gap-jin laughed loudly and looked around.

"There's also a Department of Korean Literature at your university, isn't there?" said Sung, who had not yet given up on leading Gap-jin in a certain direction.

"Yes. There's the Department of Korean Literature. I really don't know what students learn there. I think literature is useless anyway. And to study Korean literature? Even worse. I don't understand the motives of anybody admitted to a prestigious university who studies Korean literature. Then, there's that guy Sang-cheol, who talks about the old *Chunhyangjeon* story or *Shijo* poetry, or about mask-dance groups. That stuff is mere nonsense. Anyone interested in all that is just crazy," concluded Gap-jin, infuriated.

1-22

"Crazy?" said Sung, bursting into laughter but feeling pity. "You're the one who's crazy."

"You're calling me crazy?" said Gap-jin, glaring angrily at Sung, as if prepared to attack.

"Yes, you are."

"Me? Crazy?"

"Yes, you Kim Gap-jin, law school graduate, are truly crazy."

"Why?"

"Looking at everything upside down is nothing but crazy, and you look at everything upside down."

"How?" Gap-jin demanded.

"Isn't it true," Sung explained, "that you've turned all the standards of evaluation upside down? You treat what's important as unimportant. Don't farmers make up eighty percent of Korea's population? Isn't food the most important thing for life, followed by clothing? That makes farmers the roots and trunk of the Korean people, doesn't it? Other classes, such as intellectuals or people in business and industry, are just branches and leaves. Of course, branches and leaves are necessary, too. A tree can't live without any of these parts. But if we're going to rank them, roots and trunk are more important than branches and leaves. Korea's problem is that its leading class, for a very long time—and it doesn't matter since exactly when—has placed high value on the branches and leaves, neglecting the roots and trunk. Frankly speaking, the *yangban* nobility, that leading class of the Joseon Dynasty, was concerned solely with its own wealth and status despite being a minority of just about one percent. That may be true of the powerful class in every country, but isn't it true that the Korean *yangban* class was extreme? They didn't use the state budget for educating the common people, for developing industry, or for long-term projects to benefit the nation and the Korean people. Instead, they spent it on themselves, on their living expenses and entertainment—we call this "expropriation of surplus value" in current terminology. What was the result? As you know, Korea declined economically and ethically, as well as in knowledge, technology, and arts, in every regard. The country is now bankrupt, and the result has been the fall of an entire people, aside from a few *yangban* who still cling to shreds of power. I remember reading certain critical observations made by a Westerner following an inspection of Korea. He said that the bare mountains without trees, the dried-out streams, the poor roads, the people's houses looking almost like sheep folds, the ignorant and sickly people, everything noticeable in Korea was evidence of *maladministration*. Do you have courage enough to oppose his opinion? That the decline of Korea is evidence of bad governance? All that comes from *yangban* selfishness and their misjudgment of values, doesn't it? Now, listen carefully. It's really sad that educated people like you still hold to such distorted values. People like us who've received the new education, shouldn't we appreciate the values of farmers and workers, classes that have been forgotten, even oppressed. Shouldn't we go to them and support their way of life?"

Gap-jin sat in silence.

1-23

By the time Sung and Gap-jin arrived at the Busan port, the long summer day had drawn to a close, but the night was just as pleasant. Fresh wind from the sea revived them after the daylong ride, and the full, summer moon over the Oryuk Islands was refreshment itself.

They walked toward the ferry. On the road from the train station to the port, workers preparing to leave for Japan were strolling to and fro in groups. Some men had their hair cut short, some had a traditional style with their hair rolled up and tied, and others were wearing traditional hats. Women were also to be seen here and there. Among them were young women visible in groups apparently headed for work in textile factories.

All kinds of people were there. Some wore rubber shoes, some Japanese shoes, others sports shoes, and a number wore ill-fitting Japanese *yukata* with stripes. People mostly spoke the local Gyeongsang dialect, but the dialects of other provinces were also to be heard. The Jeolla province with its feeble accent. The dialects of Hamgyeong and Pyeongan, too. Sometimes even the countryside dialect of Gyeonggi with its accent rising on the first syllable of words and the last syllable of a sentence. People seemed to throng from all over.

Men in suits like a school uniform with a high collar and short pants, sporting a red patch on their left arms, were directing people in coercive tones. They were probably the *paejang*, the so-called noble class laborers.

At the line for boarding, ordinary passengers and workers were treated differently than others. The plainclothes police standing near the boarding ladders recognized Koreans immediately and would demand to check their travel licenses. Sung and Gap-jin had to produce theirs.

"Are you checking my ticket?" asked Gap-jin, annoyed.

"Not the ticket!" retorted the policeman, his voice fierce. "The license, the identity license!" He looked suspiciously at Gap-jin from the corner of his eye.

"Let's go." Sung pulled Gap-jin by the sleeve to prevent his causing problems.

Gap-jin gave a disapproving look at the policeman, but followed Sung. Gap-jin had wanted to ride in the ferry's second-class quarters at least, but Sung had insisted on third class, so they descended to the third-class quarters under the rear deck.

The quarters were steaming, the odor disgusting. The majority of those in third class were Korean workers, and passengers who had arrived first had managed to find best spots, spreading out pieces of blankets and lying on them. People arriving later were forced to sit on the floor wedged into the small spaces between those who had come earlier.

Sung found a spot on the side in a corner, but Gap-jin frowned as if he didn't want to stay. Sung snatched Gap-jin's bag, placed it next his own, and pulled Gap-jin along by the arm, pressing down on his shoulder to make him sit. Gap-jin offered no resistance.

There were many people, but they made little noise. Probably reflecting on an unknown future, or recalling scenes from home and even of neighbors—not always especially pleasant to remember—they sat absent-mindedly.

"Hey, Gap-jin," said Sung, taking off Gap-jin's hat and putting it on the bag. "Today is your first day among Koreans. Try to find out how poor they are, how malnourished, how ignorant, how dirty, and what they're thinking, why they left their home and family, what their future is," said Sung laughing.

Gap-jin nodded.

1-24

The steaming third-class quarters grew hotter still. The room was sweltering even before departure, and everyone had already started to sweat.

The workers, especially the women among them, who seemed to be aboard ship for the first time, were trying to catch some sleep. They lay with their heads pressed tightly against cushions to prevent nausea, but the more they tried, the less successful they seemed. To be tossed about, sleepless and insecure, seemed their lot in life. An infant fretting at its mother's breast worsened the gloomy mood. Gap-jin felt particularly burdened to see an old man sitting and gazing blankly into the air.

The ship vibrated as it set off to the audible clank of metal chains. By sitting quietly, one could sense the ship changing direction. Most people were silent, aside from a few young, apparently enlightened men talking to each other in poor Japanese. They were seated like Japanese, their legs crossed and their hands pushing down on their knees. Most passengers seemed to lack time to relax or energy to go on deck for the fresh sea wind or a view of their receding homeland. Perhaps they were asking for a better life somewhere, or any life at all. Maybe they were just being fatalistic, accepting the life to come even though it might be worse.

"Let's go out," said Gap-jin, abruptly standing up, unable to endure the heat or the pressure in his heart.

Sung followed to the deck, where many people lingered.

"Ah, what fresh air," said Gap-jin, spreading his arms wide like a gymnast. The cool sea breeze made his silk shirt flutter nicely.

Dark blue sea, bright moon, cool wind, stars glittering in the sky, occasional white-capped waves, and the ship in the midst of the sea.

"Ah, so fresh," repeated Gap-jin, leaning on the railing below

The Soil

a lifeboat, a quiet spot, and gazing at the sea.

The lights of the Busan port seemed like a mirage. The tiny Oryuk Islands looked like doves nestled between the waves. To the east was nothing but open sea with water and waves stretching out into the unknown.

Sung also felt lighter, as though something bottled up in his heart had poured forth.

"Really, the sea is nice. The night sea is even better," said Gap-jin, his long hair whipping in the wind as though dancing for joy.

"In the midst of the sea, one starts to sense how big the universe is," remarked Sung just to respond. They stood there for a while without speaking further, as if to let fly with the wind all burdensome thoughts borne from the passenger quarters and to become silent Taoist hermits.

"Hello!" intruded an abrupt female voice from behind them.

Sung and Gap-jin turned in surprise. A very young woman of about fifteen or sixteen with long braided hair stood there. Her face in the moon's reflected light was pale as a corpse, and she was wearing a dark skirt of artificial silk that flapped in the wind.

Sung and Gap-jin stood in silence, not knowing how to reply.

"Please save me," she whispered, looking at one, then the other. She seemed to wonder which to turn to. As though trying to avoid other people, she pressed herself rashly between the two of them. Sung moved a few steps aside to make room.

1-25

Quickly recovering from his surprise and standing now beside her, Gap-jin asked in his characteristic deft, cheerful manner, "What's the matter?"

The woman glanced about, her expression worried. To make

53

her feel safe, Sung shifted himself to shield her from sight of the main deck. She finally appeared to feel secure and said, "I'm from Milyang." She continued in her Gyeongsang dialect, "My father fell into debt and sold me to repay it. My father lied about sending me to marry someone in Japan. I've found out that I was actually sold to a brothel." She spoke clearly and coherently.

"How much was the debt?" asked Gap-jin.

"There is hardly a farmer without debt, is there? My father's debt was 150 won. He borrowed 50 won to buy an ox, but the interest grew over time because of poor harvests, and even after his ox had been taken away, he still had a 150-won debt. How could one pay back 150 won? Impossible! That's why he sold me, and got 50 won extra . . ." Saying this, she bowed her head in shame.

She was quite pretty, so much so that Gap-jin could easily think her pretty enough to be bought by a brothel.

"Have you attended school?" asked Sung.

"Yes, I went to the elementary school in my village."

Gap-jin and Sung nodded, her articulate tone explained.

"What on earth do you want us to do?" asked Gap-jin, impatient to know what she wanted.

She gave him an innocent and pleading look, but remained silent.

"You want me to pay the 200-won debt?" asked Gap-jin.

"Yes," she replied, bowing her head lower, "I'll do any work in your house, so please buy me back. I know how to cook and how to clean the house. I don't want to work in a brothel!" She started crying.

"Eh, this is a big problem," said Gap-jin, smiling helplessly and turning toward Sung.

At that moment, visible in the bright moonlight, a man in short pants could be seen hurrying in their direction. He seemed to be looking for something of value.

"That's him! That's the man, the man!" she cried with quiet

urgency, and stepped closer to Gap-jin, cowering with her fists pressed against her chest, like a child who saw something terrifying and was trying to hide.

The man finally saw her skirt fluttering in the wind. Like a bull enraged by a red cloth, he charged toward her, pushing Sung away, and grabbed her arm tightly.

"You bitch, what are you doing here?" Glaring suspiciously at Sung and Gap-jin, he switched to Japanese, "Who do these bastards think they are, luring my girl away!" He pulled on her arm to take her with him.

Grabbing the ship's railing tightly, she resisted. The sleeve of her light, Korean-style summer jacket of ramie cloth tore in the man's grip, revealing her rounded arm.

Looking at Gap-jin and Sung pleadingly, she sobbed, "Save me, please save me."

1-26

"Who is this guy?" said Gap-jin, making a fist as if to strike him.

The man, already angry and believing the girl to have been lured away, slapped Gap-jin's cheek with little provocation. The young woman meanwhile, her sleeve now entirely torn away, stepped close behind Sung and wept, leaning her face against his back.

"Hey!" cried Sung, snatching the man by the collar and pulling roughly. Off balance from the tight grip on his collar, the man staggered away from Gap-jin. "Why lash out before asking a few questions?" Sung demanded. "You expect a man not to strike back if you punch him? You say we lured this woman. Well, that's nonsense. She was telling her story. We were just listening."

As Sung was explaining to the man, Gap-jin spoke up in anger, "This fool, what a clever thief he is! Stealing someone's daughter and trying to sell her to a brothel! What a man! You never imagined you might end up in prison, did you?"

Attempting no defense, the man just stood there blinking.

"Listen," said Sung, releasing him, "This woman doesn't want to go with you, and the law says you can't force her to do that sort of work if she doesn't want to. Let her go home. Now that we know what's going on, we won't just sit and do nothing when we arrive in Shimonoseki or Tokyo. Let her go."

"I paid for her. What law can make me give back what I paid for?" he retorted and grabbed the young woman by her wrist, pulling her away from Sung. "Let's go inside!" he ordered.

"Hey," said Sung, grabbing his arm, "you say you paid 200 won for her, right? Here, I'll give you 200 won." Sung took 200 won from his wallet, all he had. "Now, let her go," he said.

The man was surprised, but a sly smile spread across his face. "Ha," he laughed, "you must really like this girl. But no business-man would sell goods at the same price he paid. Give me one more," said the man, holding up his index finger.

"Three hundred won?" asked Sung.

"Three hundred won is still cheap for this girl," responded the man in the tone of a merchant who knows how to bargain. "A 16 year-old girl is already grown up."

But Sung had no more money. He looked at Gap-jin, who chuckled and took out several 10-won banknotes to count. "All right, you thief," he said, "here's your 100 won." But he hesitated, pulling back his hand, cautioning, "Wait a moment, there must be some documentation. We should get that, too."

The man drew back his own hand to unbutton his jacket and took out a purse on a chain from the inner pocket. He rummaged for the document among various papers, obscure in the moon-light, and after pulling out one of lined office paper with a fiscal stamp and looking at it carefully, he said, "I see you know your business. Here it is." He gave a simpering laugh, looked at Gap-jin and Sung in turn, then gave the document to Gap-jin, who was holding the money in his hand.

1-27

When they got off the ship, Shimonoseki was filled with morning sunlight. Plainclothes police were again checking documents. This time, the procedure was more complicated because of the girl now accompanying Sung and Gap-jin. In a playful tone, the latter boasted to the policeman that they had bought her aboard the ferry the previous night for 300 won. He showed the document as proof. The policeman smiled and looked at the two men as if he were very impressed by their action. Forgetting his profession, he lowered his voice and asked, "So, what are you going to do with her?"

"Well, I don't know myself," admitted Gap-jin, looking to Sung, "This man paid 200 won. I paid only 100. How do you think we should share her? We've studied law and are here to take the national exam, but we haven't yet had experience in legal practice. Perhaps you can give us some idea?" The policeman chuckled at Gap-jin's humorous remark and went away with his colleague.

"What're you blabbing about?" Sung said, pulling on his arm. The two policemen occasionally glanced at them from a distance. They appeared to find the party of the two men and a girl somehow funny.

"Listen," said Gap-jin setting his bag on a bench. "We've spent all our money. How'll we survive in Tokyo? We can't eat this girl, can we?" He tilted his head, as though really worried.

"You still have a hundred won, don't you?" asked Sung, also worried.

"Yes I do, but with just 100 won, how can we both eat? Actually, how can we three, because this girl has to eat, too. My friend, we're in trouble," said Gap-jin scratching his head. "Still, it was heroic, what we did." Patting Sung's shoulder, he added in a playful tone, "Now what prompted a man like you from the countryside to do that? Honestly, my hand was shaking when I paid that extra hundred won, though I did it in pride. But 300 won for our pride was rather steep, ha, ha, ha."

"Well, we can't take this lady with us to Tokyo, can we?" said Sung and turned to her, "You can go back home. We'll buy you a ticket."

"No, I don't want to go back. My father will try to sell me again," she said, sighing.

"Is he your stepfather?" asked Gap-jin.

"No, he's my real father," she replied, blushing.

"How could a father sell his own daughter?" said Gap-jin, his face darkening with anger.

"My father is not the only one. In our village, there are only a few who haven't sold their daughters. The ones in debt all do the same thing. They lack seed money for business, they need food, or they're forced to by their creditors . . ."

"They should sell their own bodies. How could they do that to their own children!" said Gap-jin, becoming more upset. "That's why I say country people are so ignorant! You agree now?" Gap-jip stomped off to strike a match and smoke.

"How do you think the fathers themselves feel, forced to sell their own children? Think about what makes them do that." said Sung, his tone melancholy. The dreary countryside scene, so familiar to him, grew vivid in his mind.

1-28

Finding no solution, Sung and Gap-jin had to take Ok-sun, as the girl was named, along with them on their trip to Tokyo. They made an awkward party.

Purchasing lunch or fruit for three was now necessary. Ok-sun was a quiet girl. She tried to eat as little as possible, slept less, and wore an apologetic face. To protect her feelings, the two men kept their concerns to themselves and didn't speak of money in her presence. But for the entire time in Japan, they privately remained quite worried about surviving their penury, for they couldn't easily make some excuse and ask Mr. Yun for more money. He had actually given them more than enough, so how could they explain about their unexpected expenses?

After their return, on a morning in September when Sung had been sent to Yesan for errands and was not expected back until evening, Mr. Yun received a telegram while standing in the yard speaking with some visitors. "Where's it from?" Mr. Yun asked the visitors.

Looking carefully, they pronounced, "Kio-seuu," Heo Sung's name written in Japanese *gatagana*.

"Ah, that's for Sung," said Mr. Yun and opened the telegram. It read: National Exam for Government Offices, Result: Passed. "Oh, Sung has passed the National Exam for Government Offices!" exclaimed Yun, as excited as if Sung were his own son.

"Who's Heo Sung?" asked one of the visitors.

"He is my future son-in-law," answered Yun and went inside. He called for his daughter in the direction of the inner quarters, "Is Jeong-seon there?"

"The lady is in the backyard," said a young maid and ran to the backyard.

Yun settled into an armchair on the wooden floor between the main room and the room opposite to wait for his daughter.

Jeong-seon came with two school friends from the backyard. She was no longer wearing mourning garments, but a sky-blue skirt of Japanese silk *habutae* and an elegant summer jacket of Chinese silk. The weather was still warm, despite being September.

Her friends politely greeted Mr. Yun and went into the opposite room. Jeong-seon was about to follow her friends when Yun called her back. "A telegram came," he explained. "Sung passed the exam. Here it is. You can have a look."

Reluctantly, she took it and started to read. Her friends from the opposite room made eyes at Jeong-seon.

"That's nice," she said and put the telegram on the tea table.

Smiling and expecting some expression of pleasure, her father watched her, but her face betrayed no emotion, and she went to join her friends.

"Who is Sung?" whispered one of the friends, leaning close to Jeong-seon's ear.

"Who else could he be? He must be her future *husband*," answered the other friend, sniggering.

"What're you saying?" Jeong-seon retorted, tweaking her friend's nose.

"Is it true? Is he your future husband?" asked the friend who had whispered.

"No, he's our house tutor, a hardscrabble college student," responded Jeong-seon indifferently.

"Ah, you mean the man in the servant quarters, that student at Boseong College?" said the other friend, astonished.

"What? You're going to marry him?" asked the first girl, also astounded.

"What are you two talking about?" Jeong-seon retorted, avoiding the issue.

1-29

That same evening, Sung returned and had not even finished his greetings before Mr. Yun informed him, "You received a telegram." He opened his desk drawer to take it out and hand it to Sung.

Sung read it and was very pleased. He had to take a few deep breaths in his excitement despite trying to act as though the results were not so important. He was especially happy at being one of those few who had passed the exam out of nearly 800 of the smartest people from all around Japan and Korea.

"What about Gap-jin?" asked Sung, trying to hide his joy.

"I've heard nothing yet," responded Yun, retrieving the telegram from Sung's hand. "Have a seat," he added, and as soon as Sung sat down, he continued, "You've now passed the exam, so it's time for you to think about marriage."

"I appreciate your support for my study, and that you paid for the trip to Japan. And the offer of your daughter's hand is such a great favor that I cannot properly express my gratitude. But I have no money or position, so it's impossible for me to think of marriage now. I passed the exam, but finding a job will take time . . ." explained Sung, trying to express his refusal.

"That's no problem. I know your situation very well, so you need not worry about that. If you don't like my daughter, that's a different issue . . . but as I told you last year when we first talked, I trust you like a son. You know I'm now old and need somebody who can take care of the house. Naturally, I know of other people, but finding someone trustworthy isn't easy. Also, Jeong-seon is now 20 years old and should get married as soon as possible. I worry about her. Quite a few girls are over 20 and unmarried these days, but parents worry about them. For me, a prospective son-in-law doesn't need to be from a noble family or have property. I see the man as he is," explained Yun. He then sat there waiting, a man of the world and of wealth, a father concerned for his daughter and seeking Sung's approval.

Sung should have responded firmly, saying, "I appreciate your proposal, but I can't marry your daughter. I've already promised to marry another woman. Yu Sun is her name, and I've already made up my mind to live in the countryside with her and educate farmers as my life's work. I can't marry your daughter. If I did, I'd have to break my promise to Yu Sun, and also to the farmers. I should go back to them and to her because they've trusted me and are waiting for me."

Sung should have given a response like that, a statement directed by his character and his conscience. If he had responded that way, how admirable he would have been . . . but he lacked the fortitude. In that moment, he vividly recalled Jeong-seon, a young woman famous in Seoul for her beauty. She had not been unattractive to him. Although they were not equals, for their connection had been one of master and servant, he had had enough opportunity to see her at a distance and more closely over the last two or three years while staying in Yun's house. He had recently even had occasion to speak with her since he had become more involved in house affairs, especially from being put in charge of the house budget after In-seon's death. Jeong-seon's skin, like polished white jade, her small, lovely hands, her contemplative eyes, her graceful skill on the piano, so appropriate for the daughter of a noble family, all that had touched Sung's heart deep inside. Jeong-seon also had property. People said that she would receive more than 15,000 bushels of rice annually, or surely at least half of the property that her mother had brought as dowry from her maiden home in Jeon-ju.

There was no practical reason in any respect to refuse the marriage offer. Sung accepted it in his heart with enthusiasm. But he needed to express himself with a form of refusal worded in such a way as not to sound like a real refusal.

1-30

Sung remained silent for a while. He was thinking of Yu Sun in his home village, how she had waited for him near the station at dawn, hiding the wrapped steamed corn in the folds of her skirt, how she leaned against his chest without saying a word, how he held his arm around her and touched her hair, how he promised to return to her, "Next summer," and how the innocent Yu Sun would have since been waiting for him, cherishing him in her heart. He hadn't been able to return to his home village so far, and the month was now September, because he had gone to Tokyo to take the National Exam for Government Offices and had since been waiting in Seoul for the results. How ardently had Yu Sun been waiting for him? How often had she watched the train from Seoul, expecting every time to see him? How sad would she be if Sung married Jeong-seon? How disappointed and resentful would her tears be? Wouldn't she, as a faithful Korean woman, throw herself into a deep well to die? Worst of all, wouldn't it mean that he himself broke his promise?

What about his decision to go back to the farmers? The decision to educate the poor farmers—the roots and trunk of the Korean people—to make them strong and to lead them to a better life, through sacrificing himself and giving up his own welfare for his whole life? What about Mr. Han and his colleagues, who had all heard of his decision? "No, no, I have to refuse Mr. Yun's proposal. I should marry Yu Sun and go back to the country"! exclaimed Sung, but only to himself, for when he lifted his head and saw Mr. Yun, he couldn't utter those words.

"It's ridiculous," thought Sung, changing his mind, "I'm not engaged to Yu Sun. I haven't touched her, so why this loyalty? Who else knows of my love for her? Who else knows of her love for me? God? Does he even exist? Even if he does, what sin have I committed?" Sung's thoughts wandered further. "Yu Sun is a good woman. She is physically strong and lovely of heart. But Jeong-seon is more beautiful. Yu Sun is a country woman, with only an elementary school education, whereas Jeong-seon is a daughter of a noble family, highly educated in both old ways and new . . ."

His own thoughts caught him by surprise. He had never liked Gap-jin's distinction between the countryside and Seoul or between commoner and nobility. He had so often criticized Gap-jin, but now realized that he himself preferred Seoul to the countryside and nobility to the commoner, divisions rooted deeply within his heart. "Someone like me with higher education and pursuing an intellectual life," he continued, accepting his thoughts, "how could I lead a life with an uneducated country woman? Wouldn't I be unhappy? Yes, of course I would! My thought of marrying Yu Sun was just an impulse, and following through would be a mistake. I'd make both myself and the innocent Yu Sun unhappy. Yes, that's true. I might have the right to make myself unhappy, but I have no right to make her unhappy. That's clear!" Sung suddenly felt so relieved and enlightened, as if he had awakened from a nightmare. How had he been unable to see such a clear truth? He felt a path open wide before his eyes.

"What about my work for the farmers?" The cry came from another corner of his heart. But he now managed to detach his conscience by cutting the entangled threads as with a knife. He felt as if clouds had broken up and fog cleared away. "I can work for the country with Jeong-seon. Actually, she can be a good co-worker, a real partner. Ah," Sung exhaled in relief, "the problems are solved now." He felt as if a weight had fallen away from his heart. His future, like a path adorned with lilies, promised to lead him through a garden of delights. His conscience, his loyalty, and his sense of truth all vanished in the vision.

"You should give me an answer."

Urged on by Mr. Yun, Sung expressed his approval clearly. "If it's your wish to have me, I'll do what you ask."

1-31

The marriage of Sung and Jeong-seon was announced. Though she did not love Sung and even felt insulted at her father's suggestion that she marry a man from the countryside who had been doing errands for the house, she knew that her father's decision was like her own. Because she had been raised in a tradition that mandated daughters to obey their fathers in the affair of marriage, disobedience was unthinkable, so she tried to love Sung. She considered all his merits. Sung was a strong and healthy man, almost like a savage, rare among the Seoul nobility. His manner was masculine and serious. He might not be a fine man, with his rough hands, broad shoulders, and large chest, but his intellect, his honest facial expression, his voice that made no attempt to curry favor, his indifference toward other women, his tanned skin, his thick eyebrows and lips, and his near bulky physique and attitude, all these were regarded by her as characteristics of a manly, even heroic husband. Especially his thoughtful eyes and his firm and straight nose impressed her. She noted with discomfort only that he was of the country, one of those low-class people who had been looked down upon for a long time and were almost like foreigners for her. She could imagine only water-sellers, oil-sellers, managers for landowners, or custodians of tombs if she even thought of the country people. With such individuals, she had always used only the least polite form of address in the Korean language. If that were not enough, she had another reason for discomfort. She had endured too much whispering about her own mother having been merely a commoner's daughter from the countryside.

Her only comfort was that Han-eun, the most respected man in her father's clan, had married all his daughters to men from the countryside. One son-in-law was from Hamgyeong Province, another from Pyeongan Province, and the third from Hwanghae Province. Han-eun always said that he would also see his favorite granddaughter Eun-gyeong married off to a man from the countryside. He did that strategically in order to do away with discrimination based on class and locality, but he also wanted to have a strong, healthy family bloodline.

All these circumstances pressed Jeong-seon to obey her father's decision. Gap-jin was the one truly shocked by the marriage arrangement. He had believed that Jeong-seon would become his wife and that half of Mr. Yun's property would fall to his hands. In the meantime, however, he learned that he had failed the exam. He made excuses. His exam for the administrative section was harder than Sung's for the juridical section. He had originally wanted to become a scholar, so he hadn't taken the exam as seriously as he should have. Much as he hated to have failed, however, he was even more upset to think that he had perhaps lost a chance to marry Jeong-seon and gain half of Mr. Yun's property through that failure. In fact, if Sung had not become his competitor, Gap-jin might have won Jeong-seon as his wife. Probably even without him passing the exam, this would have happened.

He had turned up his nose at Sung in the train to Tokyo, saying, "Hey friend, why not stay home? What's your point in taking the exam?" But he had now been taken down a notch or two. He had other problems as well. While they were staying in Tokyo, the girl freed for 300 won had turned to Gap-jin more than to Sung, becoming his lover. She was now back in Milyang, her home village, and would soon give birth to Gap-jin's child. He had insisted she return there, despite her many tears, rather than accompany him to Seoul because he feared for Mr. Yun to learn of her.

After the engagement of Sung and Jeong-seon was announced, Gap-jin no longer dropped by Mr. Yun's house.

1-32

The wedding day was scheduled for the 15th of October. Coincidently, that was the day of the ninth's full moon according to the lunar calendar. At 3 o'clock on the 15th, Sung and Jeong-seon were to be married at Jeongdong Church, in the presence of many envious guests. The wedding invitation had already been sent out early in October, and also printed on the invitation was the name of Sung's groomsman, Han Min-gyo.

In his heart, Mr. Han was against Sung's marriage but decided to wish the couple a happy life together because nothing could be altered now that everything had been arranged.

When Mr. Han heard the news from Sung, he advised him in terms that recalled an earlier, different intention. "Sung, you should now consider working as a lawyer in Seoul."

Sung felt Han's simple statement pierce his heart, as though Han had seen into his sordid thoughts and scorned them for what they were. Feeling uncomfortable, he responded, "I'm going to the country."

"No, you can't. How could a woman who has grown up and lived only in Seoul endure life in the country? Anyway, working to help farmers in the countryside is not the only work you can do for the Korean people. Practicing as a lawyer is also one. Being a lawyer not for money but to help the disadvantaged would be good for Koreans. A lawyer encounters many individuals, so you might happen to find some good people. Lincoln was a lawyer, wasn't he?" said Mr. Han, trying to make Sung feel better.

Sung felt as if he had found a door leading from a smoky room where he could hardly breathe to a place outside with light, fresh air. He realized that Mr. Han's statement was intended to help him feel better, and that made him so appreciate the man that he could have knelt at his feet and bathed them with his tears.

"Whatever you do, don't do it for selfish reasons. Your own benefit or welfare shouldn't be the criterion. Let what benefits the Korean people lead your actions. Keep this in mind, and it won't matter what kind of work you do or where you work, whether in Seoul or in the country," said Mr. Han.

At this remark, Sung felt burdened again. "Will my marriage help me sacrifice for the Korean people?" he wondered. But he avoided an answer.

When Sung arrived home—to Mr. Yun's house, now his future father-in-law—a tailor was waiting.

"Where have you been so long?" complained Jeong-seon, giving him a look of disapproval. That showed that she already felt close to him.

"Why do you inquire?" asked Sung, speaking very politely. "Were you worried about me?"

"Why are you being so courteous? You shouldn't talk to me like that. You've still not overcome your rural deference," she said, shaking her finger at him like a Westerner. Sung was still using the most polite form of Korean despite their betrothal. He couldn't change his habit so abruptly. Whenever he began speaking in too deferential a manner, she decisively prevented him. To help him relax, she would sometimes approach and throw herself into his arms if nobody else was present, or she would place her small hand within his large hand.

"Well, let's see if your suit fits. I've chosen the cloth," she said, and tried to unbutton his traditional Korean jacket. The young tailor, a pencil squeezed behind his ear, watched the lovely couple, smiling.

"What's the suit for?" asked Sung, also smiling and taking off his jacket.

"Oh goodness, what are you saying? Come on!" she admonished, smiling.

1-33

A tail coat, a morning coat, suits for spring and winter seasons, and a spring coat and a winter coat with extra pairs of pants were ordered for Sung, and Jeong-seon had her wedding dress and various suits tailor-made for each season. Several temporary seamstresses were hired to assist the house seamstress in preparing these clothes, along with bedding for the bride and bridegroom.

Some Western furniture and a bed along with traditional Korean furniture were purchased. Mr. Yun, thinking that Sung would open a law practice, bought a house of about seventy square meters built on good dry soil in Jeongdong and furnished the place with appliances after renovating part of it and repapering some of the walls. He also had some servants ready for them.

"It will be your place, to decorate as you like," said Mr. Yun, giving Sung and Jeong-seon full permission to redo the house.

Sung waited for Jeong-seon each day at the corner of the American consulate around the time that she got out of school and walked with her to their new house to direct the workers and servants on what to do. They discussed what they would do for the house, but their plans changed every day.

Jeong-seon was not quite happy about the place because it was not so big as her father's house. She particularly complained that it had no western room and lacked a bigger yard. "It's so small! How can we live here?" she would complain.

At each complaint, Sung found himself surprised and distraught, wondering how he could satisfy Jeong-seon in the future if she were already unhappy with such a large house. "Wait until I earn money as a lawyer. I'll get you a house like a palace built of shining white stone," Sung would promise, smiling. But in uttering these words, he was surprised at himself. "What's happened to me that I think only of a bigger house?" he wondered. "Am I just being self-centered and selfish? Aren't I forgetting the Korean people?"

Another of Jeong-seon's complaints was that the front gate was not imposing enough. It rose no higher than the servant's quarters. Moreover, cars could not pull up to it. Sung comforted her on these points as well, promising to change things later when he earned money as a lawyer.

Sung's engagement to Jeong-seon caused great sensation among the young people of Seoul. The marriage of a penniless student from the countryside to the daughter of a wealthy, noble family, a brilliant student wedded to a gifted woman of beauty, all that and more was surely cause for sensation. The October issue of a certain magazine printed photos of the happy couple, describing them in words as lovely as a poem.

Another wedding ceremony was scheduled for the same place on that same day, the marriage of Han-eun's granddaughter Eun-gyeong to the young inventor Yun Myeong-seop. Han Min-gyo was also involved with this marriage. He had introduced Yun Myeong-seop to Han-eun to request financial support for the inventor's research. Han-eun had been so impressed by the Yun's personality and background that he decided to offer him the hand of his granddaughter.

There was, however, a complication that had arisen in these nuptial matters, and it had to do with Dr. Lee Geon-yeong. He and Shim Sun-rye had been dating and had professed their love for each other. Lee had even told Mr. Han, "Miss Shim is the very woman I've been looking for." But he had suddenly shown a change of attitude within the past month and had since been try-ing to avoid Sun-rye. She informed her father of the change, and he went to see Mr. Han on the matter. "No, that cannot be true," said Han in reassurance before seeing him off.

Han then invited Lee to his home to find out what was going on. Lee explained, "I've given serious thought to this and come to realize Sun-rye would be unhappy married to me. I decided I'd better stop seeing her before our relationship gets more serious."

1-34

Mr. Han was shocked at this reply that he had never expected to hear. Lee seemed a different man than the one he had trusted. His reason for breaking up with Shim as easily as tossing away an old shoe meant he had either lost his sense of loyalty or just been toying with her all along. Either possibility was unthinkable, given Mr. Han's image of Dr. Lee.

"Is this true, what you've just said?" asked Han, dumfounded.

"Yes, and I believe I've done the right thing," Lee replied with confidence.

"You mean you don't love Shim?" asked Han.

"No, I love her."

"But?"

"But I never promised to marry her," said Lee.

"Isn't profession of love a promise of marriage?" Han countered.

"Love might be a condition for marriage. But love and marriage aren't the same, I think."

"You mean you can't marry her even though you love her?"

"That's right."

"What's the reason?"

"I think the marriage would make us both unhappy."

"Why do you think that?"

Lee remained silent.

"You mean you started a relationship with her without intending to marry?" asked Han.

"No, I don't mean that."

"You were thinking of marriage?"

"Yes," responded Lee.

"Why did your love change?"

"My love hasn't changed."

"Then what has?"

Lee again remained silent.

"Has something happened to prevent you from marrying Shim?"

"No, nothing really."

"Then why did you suddenly break off all contact after courting her for nearly six months? Shim and her family expected marriage, understandably so, and were preparing for a wedding."

"To be frank, my parents are against the marriage," admitted Lee, lowering his head.

"Your parents?"

"Yes."

"Why are they against it?"

"They think the marriage would be improper."

"Why do they think so?"

"I can't tell the reasons."

"You mean to say you didn't anticipate your parents' disapproval while you were courting Shim with the intention of marrying her. And now that your parents have come out against a wedding, you say you can't marry her. Have I got that right?"

"Yes, that's right. As a son, I cannot marry a woman against the wishes of my parents. I owe them this consideration because I've been unable to care for them these past ten years." Lee spoke these words solemnly.

Mr. Han looked carefully at Lee, reflecting seriously and trying to read the truth in his face and eyes. Finally, in a tone pained and sorrowful, he said, "I trust you as a patriot and love you as a friend, so I will say honestly what I think. Your decision on this issue is a big mistake. You're trying to cover your own lack of resolve with filial loyalty to your parents, which sounds quite noble. That's what you're doing, I believe, and nothing else."

1-35

"Sir, you make me out to be a very low person by that remark," said Lee, upset.

"I said it because I'm very disappointed after putting so much trust in you," said Mr. Han, looking straight into Lee's face with reproach in his eyes.

"Why can't you understand my filial obligations?" protested

Lee, his voice growing harder.

"Do you yourself agree with your parents' opinion that Miss Shim is not a proper partner?" asked Han in a soft voice.

"No, I don't agree. It's certainly not because I think she's not good enough for me. It's just that my parents are against her. I can't let myself love a woman I happen to like if I have to go against my father and mother. Why am I wrong about that? I don't like it when young people these days ignore their parents' wishes and pursue their love freely. I believe that a good son takes his parents' opinion seriously in important affairs like marriage," Lee stated, his voice grown proud.

"What you say is right," responded Mr. Han, changing his posture and leaning back against the chair. "But you are wrong in two things. First, if you have such a high respect for your parents' opinions, you should have listened to them before falling in love with her. Second, you're misjudging the impact of the blow to your parents and Miss Shim. If you marry against your parents' wishes, they would naturally feel very offended, but that's all. If you don't marry Shim, she'll suffer a bigger blow than she's ever experienced in her life. She might try to kill herself. If not that, she might decide never to marry, and just lead an unhappy life. Your parents might be temporarily felled by the blow, but she would fall and never get up again. It would be such a terrible blow." Mr. Han paused and softened his tone, "As for the loyalty, it weighs more in a distant relationship than in a close one. For example, one's debt to strangers weighs heavier than to family or friends. The latter can understand circumstances better and forgive better. Strangers cannot do that. Ethics teaches us not to harm others to benefit ourselves or our families. You, who have studied ethics, should know that better than I." Han again raised his voice, and with more strength added, "Your parents don't know Shim and have no reason to be against her personally, but just because of their opposition, you're going to drop her after leading her in word and deed to expect marriage. That's doesn't sound praiseworthy. However, I'll try to understand you. What's your view?"

"I don't agree with you. I believe it's right to call off a relationship if you know the marriage won't bring happiness," responded Lee in a defensive tone.

"Dr. Lee, if you want to become a leader of the Korean people, you should give up your ethical theory based on the happiness of an individual," said Mr. Han, rising to walk a few paces away.

1-36

Standing at the edge of the wooden floor and looking far away toward Namsan's modest heights, Han occasionally turned his head to glance at Lee. He half expected to hear him admit, "I have been wrong." But he had already heard a rumor from someone that Han-eun was thinking of Lee as a prospective husband for his granddaughter, Eun-gyeong. He had already invited Lee to dinner at his place and introduced his wife and other family members to him. Eun-gyeong had been there as well.

She was, in Lee's eyes, quite noble in appearance. A fragile woman, her fragility added to her nobility from Lee's perspective. Her face and bearing were so elegant that she seemed not to belong to this world. Lee didn't see that quality in Shim and ruefully reflected, "Oh, why did I let myself get so close to Shim? Why did I think of her as my future wife? A woman much nicer than Shim is waiting for me. I was too hasty!" But with great relief, he found a way out. "I'm not engaged to Shim. I haven't announced any engagement yet."

Lee was in fact not actually engaged. When Mr. Han had asked him about getting engaged at Mr. Shim's place, Lee had said, "Sir, that's just a formality. We don't need an engagement ceremony."

Mr. Han had accepted his opinion, as had Mr. Shim along with his wife and daughter. They all expected the wedding as soon as Lee found a job. In fact, Mr. Shim's family was already preparing the wedding. From the letters sent by Lee every other day while he was staying in Gongju, nobody could have had any doubt about their marriage. Any of the letters picked at random would offer such lines as "Last night, I couldn't fall asleep. Do you know why? Because of you. I longed to hold you in my arms forever." Or he'd write, "Ah, my Sun-rye, my one and only, you make my pulse race. With your gentle eyes and soft skin, you make passion I thought I'd outgrown flare up again. Oh, the feeling of your skin, its warmth!" Such were his words.

But he stopped writing her letters like those after leaving Gongju. From his time in Gwangju and Mokpo, and even upon his return to Seoul, he neither wrote nor spoke a word to Sun-rye.

The long silence came after he had learned of Eun-gyeong. He first heard of her while he was in Gonju. Through a distant nephew there, Han-eun sent Lee word to pay him a visit upon returning to Seoul. The nephew, who knew Lee from their college days in America, told Lee about the possibility of a marriage arrangement.

Mr. Han did not know all the details but had heard something similar. He trusted Lee, however, and tried to ignore the rumor. Even when Mr. Shim caught wind of it and came to see him, he firmly denied the possibility. "Dr. Lee isn't that sort of man. He wouldn't do that even if he and Sun-rye couldn't see each other for ten years."

"Sir," said Lee, standing up, "I'm going."

"You have nothing more to say?" asked Han in a stern tone.

"No," was Lee's brusque reply. He left.

Mr. Han followed him through the front gate, only to find Sun-rye unexpectedly walking their way. Upon glimpsing Lee, she cried out in shock and seemed unsteady on her feet. Han quickly rushed to catch and support her in his arms.

1-37

Seeing Sun-rye faint into Han's arms, Lee was startled, and dropped his walking stick. But quickly retrieving it, he strode off with rapid steps down the alley.

Han took Sun-rye to a room and laid her comfortably on the floor. Both his wife and daughter Jeong-ran stood nearby, aghast. "Bring cold water!" Han ordered. He sprinkled it onto Sun-rye's pale face and began to massage her hands and feet.

At that moment, Sung entered wearing a smart tweed suit and carrying his coat draped over one arm. He looked the fine gentleman in his suit, far different than in his student uniform. Nobody would imagine that he had recently been a working student running errands in someone else's place. His face, moreover, showed more complacency and less fighting spirit.

Sung had come to consult with Han about his own wedding, but looking anxiously at Sun-rye, he asked, "What happened?" At that moment, she came to herself and opened her eyes.

Han responded to Sung's question only with his own eyes, and in them were tears. Sung had just encountered Lee at a cross street in Andong and quickly grasped the tragic circumstances. He too had learned of Lee's marriage arrangement with Eungyeong and didn't need to hear any words from Han because he understood clearly what had happened.

Leaving Han's place at the impropriety of remaining any longer, he felt his own stab of guilt. "Yu Sun!" Her memory had pierced his heart. Once she discovered his marriage with Jeongseon, she would collapse in the same way as Sun-rye. Or something worse might happen. At these dark thoughts, Sung shuddered, and he walked on wherever his feet might lead.

In the meantime, Sun-rye had come to herself and started to cry, bowing her head to the floor in front of Mr. Han.

"Sun-rye!" cried Han, holding her shoulders with his hands.

She raised her head slightly and asked, "Sir, what should I do?"

"You should become a bigger person," responded Han. "So far, you've believed that marrying Lee would give meaning to your life, but you should now think of finding purpose through becoming the wife and mother of Korea. I feel very sorry, and truly saddened, for misjudging Lee's character and introducing him to you. We can only trust that it was God's purpose to make you a bigger person. We must try to find a new, more important purpose for your life." He stopped, falling into awkward silence.

"But I cannot endure the pain," said Sun-rye, and continued crying. Seeing her vehement tears and trembling shoulders, Han closed his eyes, and some tear drops flowed down his own cheeks. In a corner of the room, Jeong-ran stood and also cried.

Sun-rye had wondered at Lee's long silence, and had also heard rumors, but like Mr. Han, she had trusted him. Only that morning had she finally learned from her fellow students that Lee and Eun-gyeong would undergo an engagement ceremony that very same evening at Eun-gyeong's home.

1-38

Mr. Han finally asked her, "Shouldn't you meet and talk to Dr. Lee?"

"What's the use of seeing him now?"

"Then, what do you think you should do?" said Han.

"What should I do?" she replied. Mr. Han could get no response after that except Sun-rye's tears because words could not express her pain, the trampled heart of a spurned woman. She eventually left his place after being unable to do anything but cry.

As soon as she arrived home from Mr. Han's, she took out all the letters and photos from Lee and burnt them. "Why are you doing that?" asked her mother. "You should keep them and use as proof later when you give him a big scolding."

"What difference does it make?" she replied. She could only cry to herself.

Her mother later tried to comfort her. "You should forget such a rake."

"How?"

"Well, you should at least see him and give him that big scolding."

"What's the point?" she said. Sun-rye tried to keep her pain and hurt private and mourn without burdening others. But she didn't sleep at night and could be heard repeatedly getting up and lying down, which made her parents feel terrible.

After Sun-rye had left his place, Mr. Han had sat for a time in silent anguish. Eventually, he put on his hat and readied himself to go out.

"Father, are you coming home for dinner?" asked Jeong-ran.

"Yes," he promised, heading out the door, "I'll be back." When he reached Yun Han-eun's home, he found him sitting in the reception room.

"Ah, Cheong-oh, you've come to visit!" exclaimed Han-eun in welcome. "Cheong-oh" was what people called Mr. Han's house and by extension Mr. Han himself. "Good that you came," he added in obvious delight, stroking his grey beard. "I was about to send someone to bring you here."

Han-eun was in a cheerful mood. "Today, we're going to have the engagement ceremony of Dr. Lee Geon-yeong to my grand-daughter Eun-gyeong. A small dinner party with family members has been prepared. I heard then from Lee that he studied under you and learned a lot, so I was going to invite you, too. I'm happy you're already here," said Han-eun. He interrupted the nearby play of his seven- or eight-year-old grandson and ordered him, "Go and tell Dr. Lee to come here." The child immediately rushed off to the inner room.

"How are you doing?" Han-eun finally asked Mr. Han.

"Oh, I'm all right," said Han, trying to control himself, "The reason I came is I wanted to talk to you before the engagement. But if it's already taken place, I'd better not say anything, I think. Are they engaged?"

Han-eun was very surprised and could only ask, "You mean Lee and Eun-gyeong?"

"Yes," said Mr. Han, and what Han-eun was told next shocked him even more.

Late in the evening of that very same day, a young gentleman was sitting on a bench in Tapgol Park, his head dropped down in despair. The man was Lee Geon-yeong.

1-39

Slumped on the bench, Lee felt like one fallen from the seventh heaven to the bottomless pit. He no longer had Eun-gyeong, daughter of a wealthy, noble, and respected family. He would most likely also lose out on the job at Yeonhui College, previously a good bet for him because Han-eun was one of the trustees and had been strongly recommending him. As bad as his future prospects might be, the events at Han-eun's place that evening had so embarrassed Lee that he would as soon hide himself under the bench or even disappear into the ground.

Upon encountering Mr. Han seated with Han-eun, Lee's heart had sunk, but he tried to think positive thoughts as he waited for them to speak with him. Guests started to arrive, and Lee's father was the last, traveling from his country home. The dinner table was ready.

Han-eun talked about this or that, things going on in the

world, as if nothing had happened. He seemed almost to have forgotten the engagement. Lee grew nervous waiting for Han-eun's announcement, sole purpose for the day's gathering, but Han-eun breathed nothing of the engagement until the dinner was almost finished. Lee's worried expectation of a terrible judgment grew so great that he could not even glance toward Han-eun. He chewed on pieces of food but did not even recognize what he was putting into his mouth.

When the dinner was finished, Han-eun remained silent for a while, seemingly deep in private thoughts. The guests sat in quiet bafflement. As Han-eun finally opened his mouth and began to speak, Lee's breath caught in his throat, and he felt as though a shower of sparks were pouring upon him from a blazing bonfire.

"Today, we were going to have the engagement ceremony of Dr. Lee and my granddaughter, but it has to be canceled for a reason that I prefer to keep private. I can say one thing. This is partly my fault because I was mistaken." Han-eun had spoken emotionlessly but solemnly. He looked at Lee's father. "I'm so sorry for this. I know you came a long way today."

Oily sweat rolled down Lee's back. His father's face turned pale though he understood what was meant. Mr. Lee had known of his son's relationship with Sun-rye and had been pleased. After hearing from his son about the marriage arrangements with Han-eun's granddaughter, however, he had also changed his mind, moving his heart from Sun-rye to Eun-gyeong.

Mr. Lee had to protest to save face. "You should tell us why your granddaughter cannot marry my son." He tried to keep his voice calm but failed to hide his nervousness.

"It's better that you not hear the reason from me. If you really want to know, ask your son," replied Han-eun, refusing to say more.

At that point, Lee quietly stood up and left the room. He walked where his feet led him and eventually found himself at

Tapgol Park. He didn't know what had happened in the room after his exit, but he felt certain that his life was destroyed.

1-40

That's how Lee and Eun-gyeong's engagement fell through, with the consequence that Eun-gyeong and the inventor Yun Myeong-seop would be fated to marry instead. As fate might also have it, that wedding would be scheduled for the same day and place as Sung's wedding, October 15th in Jeongdong Church.

Sitting on the bench in Tapgol Park, Lee knew only that he had lost both Eun-gyeong and Sun-rye, no longer able to reach high enough or low enough, so to speak. He blamed Mr. Han and felt like hunting him down and breaking his legs if possible. But he lacked courage, even enough to confront him and protest, let alone break his legs. Everything was his own fault anyway, and he had no energy left to undertake anything.

Lee felt empty and wondered what to do next. There were many women in Korea, he mused. He could find women other than Sun-rye or Eun-gyeong to love. Such thoughts flitted through his mind. But the more he tried to keep one of those thoughts, the more he realized that finding another woman like them was not so easy.

"Should I go back to Sun-rye?" he asked himself. "She's a good woman and might forgive and accept me even now. Yes. She's a good-hearted, generous woman, loyal to her values and to whatever she has set her mind. She is truly so. Should I return to her?" Reflecting on that possibility, Lee felt his heart glow, as if a faint light glimmered there and were increasing to brighten the way out of darkness.

A nearby drunken voice abruptly interrupted his thoughts. "Hey, who's this? Isn't it Dr. Lee?" Someone clapped his shoulder. It turned out to be Gap-jin with two other, unfamiliar young men.

Lee jumped up in surprise, flushing as if caught out in his thoughts.

"What are you doing here?" said Gap-jin, putting his arm around Lee's neck and pulling him closer. "I heard that you're engaged to Yun Eun-gyeong. You should buy us a drink to celebrate."

Pulling his friends over with his other arm, Gap-jin continued, "Here, I should introduce the three of you. This is a man who went to America and earned a doctorate. Ha, ha, Dr. Lee, these are a couple of former students from my university. They graduated but haven't even gotten a job at an elementary school and can't feed themselves. Actually, I'm not much different." He laughed.

"You should talk," retorted one of the two, poking Gap-jin's cheek with his finger. "You've lost your girl, haven't you? We haven't fallen that far even if we do have no jobs and spend all our time in bars. But you, you're just an all-around loser."

"Hey," complained Gap-jin, bowing his head and scratching it, "stop it! Let's not talk about that." He laughed again. "Hey, Dr. Lee, don't believe anything these two say. You wouldn't think of me like that, would you? Anyway, let's go to a bar and have a drink. Someone like you, whose ship is sailing so smoothly with a fair wind should buy tramps like us a drink. Ah, life's a curse. Let's go," said Gap-jin and pulled the three men along with his arms hooked about their necks. Lee was annoyed at the younger Gap-jin taking liberties like that, but he had no energy to push the arm away.

1-41

Gap-jin led Lee and his friends from the park to a bar in Nakwon-dong. In a dusky room only obscurely illuminated by colored lights were few if any customers other than one who seemed to be a student talking with a waitress at a corner table.

"Welcome," greeted several women, variously in Japanese or Korean. Their faces were powdered white, as if with chalk, their lips painted red as a cat's mouth after a recent kill, their eyebrows lined long, and eyes darkened at the edges to look big. They were as familiar with the male customers as with brothers, or rather husbands, tilting their heads boldly and swaying their hips.

"Oh, darling, why is it so hard to see you these days?" said a woman dressed in a Western suit. She took Gap-jin's hand in her own and lifted it to stroke her cheek.

"When have you ever been close enough to me to dare this?" he retorted, slapping her hip sharply enough to make a smacking sound.

"Ow! Oh, help me!" she cried and ran off as though in anger, but not before giving him a sharp pinch on his cheek.

The four men took a table and sat down in soft, warm chairs. They found the table covered with an oilcloth unpleasant to the touch. "Whisky, whisky," ordered Gap-jin in a loud voice. He took one of the girls, a pretty one, onto his lap and hugged her tightly. Girls sitting beside the other three men seemed to be waiting for similar embraces.

Four glasses of whisky were set on the table. "Hey, you girls aren't drinking?" demanded Gap-jin. Then in Japanese added, "This won't do!" He motioned toward where the alcohol was kept and ordered, "Bring a whole bottle, the White Horse brand!"

"All right," agreed one of the women and went to the bar. Seated behind the bar and putting on airs were a male bartender and a woman with a cash register.

After another four glasses were filled with the golden whisky, Gap-jin held his glass high and offered a toast, "Ladies and gentlemen, I congratulate honorable Lee, a doctor of philosophy from America, for his engagement with Yun Eun-gyeong and wish them good health."

Gap-jin's two friends held their glasses high, but Lee didn't. "Hold your glass high!" urged one of the men. Gap-jin, his own glass still raised high, gazed at Lee with blank eyes, but his expression verged on annoyance.

"I . . . I'm," Lee began, his lips trembling. "I'm not engaged. I don't expect to be engaged any time soon, either, and . . ."

"What are you talking about?" Gap-jin demanded, abruptly setting his glass on the table again. "What the hell! It's like a light's gone off during a toast for your engagement. What's wrong?" The others also put down their glasses.

"Oh, you're engaged?" asked the woman beside Lee, slipping an arm around his neck. "I gave you my heart without knowing!"

"No, I'm not engaged," responded Lee weakly.

1-42

"What on earth happened?" asked Gap-jin, his voice now gentle, even genuinely sympathetic. "You say you're not engaged, right?"

"That's right, I'm not," replied Lee, his voice sad. The others looked at him, wondering.

"Your woman left you for another man?" Gap-jin suggested, his eyes sparkling. Dr. Lee chuckled. The others relaxed and chuckled, too.

"Okay," decided Gap-jin, "let's drink with this man who's lost his woman. Everyone help cheer Dr. Lee." Gap-jin laughed and downed his whisky in one shot. The others followed his lead, except for Lee.

"What's this?" said Gap-jin, taking the glass and holding it up to Lee's mouth. "A man shouldn't be so downcast at losing a woman. It's not like losing your parents. Drink it down. She's not the only girl for you. Don't worry, the world's full of them. Hey, you girl, Shizuko! Why are you just sitting there? Open the man's mouth and pour in some alcohol!" Gap-jin gave a sidelong scowl at the girl beside Lee. Shizuko was Korean, but like other women in bars, she was called by a Japanese name. Her eyes were a bit small, but she looked quite pretty with her soft, clear skin and rounded curves. She also seemed less vulgar than the other girls. Lee thought that her hands looked like Sun-rye's.

"Here, have a drink!" she said, slipping one arm around Lee's neck and pouring the whisky into his mouth with the other. Alcohol flowed down his throat.

Glass after glass, the powerful shots of whisky killed the conscience, so vulnerable to alcohol. The men openly displayed brutish instincts, pawing at the girls, speaking obscenely, fondling private parts, lustfully kissing . . .

"Honestly, marriage is an anachronism, and getting engaged just means binding oneself to that anachronism. Don't you agree, friends?" announced Gap-jin, opening a new theme.

"Of course, you're right," chimed in one of his friends, a literature student who had remained quiet until then. He had tiny eyes and a small slanted mouth, giving him a sly expression. "What use is marriage? We can have all the women in the world as wives. Take Shizuko today, Yasuko tomorrow. What do you girls think?" He grabbed Shizuko by the waist, apparently favoring her.

"What are you doing?" Shizuko objected, shaking off his arm. "I'll get engaged to this man instead. Dr. Lee. Or was it Dr. Kim? No, I'm sorry. Doctor Lee, right? Please get engaged to me. Not for marriage, just engagement, okay?"

"Hey, Zuko, how many times you been engaged?" asked Gap-jin's other friend, who had studied medicine.

"Me? First time with this man," replied Shizuko, looking askance at the swarthy man, bulky but small.

"This girl also lost her man, right?" said the former student of literature, poking Shizuko's cheek with his finger.

"A woman lose a man? Never! She just makes the man lose her," Shizuko retorted.

"What'd you say, bitch?"

"Who you calling bitch? I like Dr. Lee." Turning to Lee, she said, "Let's get engaged. Here, have a drink. Drink half, and give me the other half." She held the glass close to his mouth.

1-43

Mr. Yun's house was buzzing with guests milling about and presents arriving on the day before the wedding. Sung returned late in the evening that day after making some final wedding arrangements with his best man and other guests. To his surprise upon entering, he came face to face with a furious, glaring Jeong-seon.

Anger can of course make a face look vicious, but hers was truly scary. With eyebrows raised in contempt and mouth turned down in grim anger, she actually made him shudder. This was not the usual face of gentle Jeong-seon, but of a fury with a wrathful heart, for her eyes shot poisonous darts into his soul.

Sung stood dumbfounded, immobilized by her rage. "What's wrong?" Sung finally asked, concluding that he should perhaps speak first to find out the problem.

"You despicable man!" she cried. "Just despicable!"

At these words, Sung shuddered again, but he also felt the insult, and grew very angry. "You shouldn't speak like that," he said, reproving Jeong-seon in an effort at maintaining his dignity.

"Shouldn't speak like that?" She sneered at him. Her face changed expression from anger to ridicule and sarcasm.

"What on earth is wrong?" asked Sung, dropping down into a chair. He then glimpsed some slips of paper in Jeong-seon's hand. Immediately, he thought of Yu Sun.

"What's that in your hand?" he asked, stretching out his own to take it.

"Yes, have a good look." A tremor of emotion passed across her face, and she started to cry, collapsing in tears upon the table beside his chair.

Sung unfolded the slips of paper Jeong-seon had gripped so tightly, and he glanced first at its several pages. The handwriting was awkward and written in pencil on pages torn from a small notebook. It was, however, written clearly enough in small letters, like a homework assignment being turned in and bearing some traces of erased letters. Altogether three sheets filled on both sides, it ended with the signature "Yu Sun" written more freely. Sung began to read.

This will be your first and last letter from me.

In the past, I had a strong desire to write you, but couldn't because I thought it was not proper for a woman to write to a man. After your visit here during that summer two years ago, I expected you to return the following summer, and I waited the whole summer last year watching the train from Seoul, but you didn't come. This summer also I waited for you the whole time, but you didn't come, and I heard nothing from you. I was worried and wondered why I had heard nothing until I saw a magazine the other day at a friend's place and learned that you are going to get married to the daughter of a well-known, wealthy family.

When we read in the newspaper of your success on the exam, I was so happy, together with the whole village. The later news that you are engaged to marry a woman of a wealthy family has pleased the whole village, except for me and my parents. We are very sad.

1-44

Yu Sun's letter continued:

> Please forgive my foolishness. I had believed I would become your wife because you showed affection toward me that summer two years ago. Since last year, my father urged me to marry, and I foolishly told him I had already given my heart to you. My parents were pleased. They intended to have an engagement ceremony last year if you had come during the summer, but we waited to no avail. They advised me to marry somebody else, assuming that you must have forgotten me, but I refused in tears.

> As you know, no woman in our village has ever married another man once she has given her heart to a man. My great aunt was engaged to a man who died before they could marry, but she spent her whole life living in his family's house as his wife. I have heard that a woman from your family hanged herself from the chestnut tree that grows on the hillside near our village after a year mourning over her husband's death. Some of our villagers think such loyalty is old-fashioned, but I must be a foolish woman because I feel bound to that tradition. Women are loyal to their husbands even without knowing them beforehand because the marriages were arranged by their parents. How could I then forget you and marry someone else just because you forgot me, a woman who loves you with body and heart and was once in your arms even if for only a brief moment?

> But as you are going to get married with a beautiful woman of a wealthy family, I wish you both happiness.

I have no skill in writing and hesitated long before writing this. I've written and rewritten it several times, even tearing it up again and again. I'm sending it now because I wanted to pour out my heart before you get married. To write a married man would not be right.

The letter was dated the 5ᵗʰ of October and signed by Yu Sun, but it had a postscript.

I wrote this letter a week ago but delayed sending it because I feared such an action might be inappropriate. Finally today, though, I have taken courage and intend to give it to the postman. Yu Sun.

When he finished reading the letter, Sung let its pages drop from his hands to the floor. He could not sleep the whole night for anguish.

"Should I run away to see Yu Sun?" he wondered. "Or should I be a man, directly and honestly talk to Jeong-seon and Mr. Yun, and then return to Yu Sun?" Considering this latter alternative, he felt liberated. But his thoughts soon strayed. "Tomorrow is the wedding, and after three in the afternoon, everything will be resolved—but resolved toward happiness?" he asked himself.

These three thoughts were like apexes of an ineluctable triangle, and Sung ran from one corner to another the entire night, through the next morning, and even up to the moment of the wedding.

Putting on his tuxedo, he was torn from thought to thought, and also during the ride to the church. He was still distracted while standing next Jeong-seon before the pastor, and in trying to slip the ring onto her finger, he fumbled to find the right one and almost dropped the ring, which alarmed him.

He failed to hear the wedding march, nor could he clearly see the people gathered around him. In leaving the church to the strains of a march that he didn't hear, he was so distracted that he nearly stepped on his bride's foot.

2-1

The reservoir in Salyeoul filled up with the long-awaited water. Rain had poured continuously for several days, making the river flow with vehemence, but farmers were finally able to begin the rice planting, so long delayed by drought.

In every field, people were bent over their work, and the wailing melody of a folk song was to be heard rising from their lips. Though hungry, the young people had energy.

It had still been raining that morning, and women had labored in traditional bamboo hats. But the rain had now stopped, and a blue sky strewn with torn fragments of clouds was reflected in the rice fields that gleamed like small lakes. Women's hats became toys for children playing along the paddy dikes.

Boys and girls, naked or wearing only light summer jackets or loose underpants, gamboled in the water or played house upon the dikes. Their bodies were tanned and dark. But they looked less well-nourished than city children. How could they be? They ate only millet from Manchuria and soybean paste swarming with maggots. As for the infants, suckling at the breast of a mother who had eaten no more than once a day provided them not milk but something more like the rinse from a milky bowl. Only the water for drinking and the sunlight for tanning were still free, neither privatized, on loan from government, nor on sale through cooperatives. Children could thus tan as freely as they could drink the water filling their stomachs. Formerly dry wells now overflowed from the rain.

Women's legs, revealed by clothes rolled up to the knees, were strong but never so beautiful as those of Seoul ladies in translucent, white-silk stockings and white high heels. The legs of the young farming women, married or unmarried, were swollen. From standing too long in the water, and also from not eating enough, they had been stricken with some kind of swelling disease. When they straightened up to ease the pain from long bending and resembled anchors as they held both hands apart from their body to keep their clothes from trailing in the water (as if that could harm their shabby clothes), their faces, which had only once been dusted with powder, and then solely for the married ones, also appeared distorted and swollen from sunlight, hunger, weariness, and long bending. The sour body odor from their clothes mixed with the sweat, rain, dirt, and heat. Would it smell the same to the hard-working country men in the field as the sweet scent emanating from the bodies of soft-skinned Seoul women with their healthy complexions, visible through cloth as light as mosquito netting?

Old and young, married and unmarried, the women held rice plants in one hand and divided them into small portions to stick into the soft soil beneath water that reflected the sky with its scattered clouds. The freshly planted rice shoots swayed green in the wind. Soon their roots would reveal the pain of transplantation, turning sickly and yellowish before putting down new roots of life and growing vigorously. They will then bloom with small flowers, produce their grains, and ripen yellow-brown, bending over to finish their lives' work. Afterward, they would be harvested by the same hands that had planted them, and then separated from stem and husk. Of this grain planted and harvested by the people, half would go to the storehouses of the landlord. The other half would pass through storehouses of several debtors for transport by car and ship providing dealers their profits before ending up as food or alcohol in the mouths of people who had never worked in fields or seen their reflection in the water. But those who had worked so hard in the fields, using their bodies as fertilizer, would remain forever poor, forever servants in debt, and forever hungry.

A whistle blew. The train from Seoul to Bongcheon was passing.

At the whistle, people in the fields raised their heads. Among them was Yu Sun.

2-2

Yu Sun had become a fuller woman now than in the late summer two years earlier when she was held in Sung's arms. After trying to push her long hair braid aside to keep it out of the way, she finally took and fixed it above her breast with the strings of her high hanbok skirt. That coarse hemp skirt, now no longer stiff with starch, was tied lightly, and the summer jacket, made from similar hemp, stuck to her sweating back and revealed the gently rounded features of a young woman. Her clothes were shabby and her face darkly tanned, but her round, clear-featured face with large, dark, if somewhat worried eyes, a straight but gentle nose, and a firm mouth revealing a certain character made her an attractive woman even if merely glimpsed as she stood there holding the young green rice plants with their white roots in her left hand, apparently stretching her back.

Despite its tan, her face seemed lacking in the blush of youth. Was this from the summer heat, from weariness, from malnourishment, or from worries hidden in her heart? Probably all of these.

Yu Sun's heart had in fact broken at the news of Sung's marriage. She had not expected a man whom she trusted wholeheartedly to change so easily. Sung had been for her an icon of fidelity. Her honest, innocent heart had brimmed with devotion, respect, and love for him. He was like heaven and earth, sun and moon, even life itself. Sung was still the only man, the only husband for her, a woman unlike the modern urban women who taste and savor various men before spitting them back out. Yu Sun had no other man before Sung, and wanted none after him.

When Sung changed his mind and married another woman, she lost her heaven and earth, her sun and moon, her life itself. Had she not been a traditional Korean woman but a modern city one instead, she would have headed for Seoul to make a big scene by disrupting the wedding or disturbing Sung's new family home. But she endured the pain that cut her heart and tried to remain calm, as if nothing had happened. Even to her parents and siblings, she revealed nothing of the pain in her heart. Busy all day working, she had no chance to sit somewhere hidden and lament her sadness as feely as she wished. She could sigh deeply only as trains whistled past the field, and she would then gaze at the dark rush of its cars rumbling loudly by.

Couldn't she rid herself of this habit of waiting for Sung every summer, forever watching the trains pass by and wondering if he were on one? Was she still waiting in hopes that he might one day come to see her?

After briefly watching the rollicking train, she sighed deeply, reflecting, "I have no one to wait for," and then returned to planting rice, realizing the impropriety of a woman standing too long in evident contemplation as others looked on and whispered to each other, seemingly pleased by this distraction from their boring work.

"Why the hell aren't you working?" came a loud voice from behind. It was from Mr. Shin, the landlord. The people were planting rice in his field for day wages of only thirty jeon per man and twenty per woman, one-third and one-fifth of a single won. "Humph, if I don't keep an eye on things, you just stop working." Mr. Shin was rushing toward them, infuriated and swirling a wooden stick, his traditional ramie overcoat stretching out behind him like dragonfly wings. A short man in a suit following him was the agricultural agent, a government official supervising the right technique for planting rice.

2-3

"These idlers never change." Shin spoke now in Japanese, his voice thick with contempt and his short, fat neck twisting pig-like as he turned his head to glance back at the official.

People had been planting rice without a break in the heat of the day and had even forgotten that they were working in Shin's field. They had been so accustomed to farming for their own needs since Dangun's time that they had yet to grow used to re-calling that they now worked somebody else's fields. Most of the people laboring here had planted rice in their own fields until five or six years earlier. Those without their own land at that time could still work another's land and take half the crop for them-selves after handing over the first half to the landowner. But for five or six years, landlords had been having their lands farmed by hiring people just for labor instead of by sharecropping the fields. Workers offering their labor were abundant. At twenty or thirty jeon per day, more than enough people thronged for work. Since the modern money had come into use twenty years be-fore, cars and other new products had come onto the market, and things had gradually, imperceptibly altered for the farmers. As small, independent plots slowly ended up in the hands of a few wealthy people, previous landowners became tenant farmers, but even that form of sharecropping had become difficult to main-tain. Some therefore turned to double tenant farming, contract-ing with a landowner as a tenant farmer but lending the plot to another farmer for the actual labor and making a profit that way. The most common form of this was called *mareum*, but variant forms were possible. Others turned themselves purely into work-ers hired for farming without the choice of sharecropping. There was a reason for this. Landowners had moved to better places for living, such as Pyeongyang or Seoul, and quickly found that dealing with individual tenant farmers was no longer convenient. They entrusted others to oversee their land and took no further interest so long as they received a satisfactory amount of crops every year.

Mr. Shin was not yet a man of great wealth and so lived in the district town nearby, enabling him to deal with his own lands in hiring farmers for the labor and avoiding problems inherent in lending plots for tenant farming or similar sharecropping ventures. But his approach to avoiding problems resulted in some twenty families losing the source of their livelihood.

"Hey!" cried Mr. Shin, turning his attention again toward those planting rice. "That's why you'll never have even a mouthful of rice your whole life." He came closer to the people working in the rice paddies and tapped the edge of the dike with his stick. "Why are you standing around watching trains pass instead of planting rice? If you try to cheat me like that, I won't give you any more work. If I don't give you work, how'll you survive? Will you live on dirt? You can't even have that! The mountains belong to the government, and the fields are private property. If you slack off work that way, you'll all starve. Humph, what idlers! And idling's about all you've done today. You women and girls are useless except for getting men hot and bothered. And you young men, trying to look up their skirts at their crotches! No wonder you're not doing any work! Starting tomorrow, I should either fire the women and girls or make them work separately. Hey, Mun-bo!" he called, singling out the overseer. "Why are you letting them slack off like that? You think I like to pay you three times as much because I've got so much money? Humph, what ingratitude!"

Mr. Shin's insults made people more and more resentful. Farmers who had worked countless generations out of love for the soil and the plants, unconcerned about land ownership and habituated to the labor, now began to feel bitter anger in recognizing their servitude.

2-4

Having abruptly lost any desire to work, the farmers felt the full weight of their overwhelming burden. Steam rising from muddy water, odorous smell of rice plants, mucky soil about hands and feet, salty sweat dripping from foreheads and flowing into eyes and mouth, one's own sweaty body odor inhaled by nostrils with every breath, stale sweat smell of others, sun burning skin through coarse hemp cloth, hunger pangs in the pit of one's stomach, backache from bending too long, all of that had formerly been experienced as pleasure but now became unbearable under Mr. Shin's insults, and the people seethed within.

"What a jerk! Made his own money just by luck! How disgusting!"

"Bastard! How foul-mouthed he is! Has he no wife or daughter at home?"

"If I could just take out my anger on that swine, I'd throw him into a rice paddy and trample his fat belly."

"Just to feed my stomach, I have to endure all this . . ."

The farmers, seething with these thoughts but remaining as silent as dumb animals, continued to draw individual shoots of rice from the clumps grasped in their left hands and stick each one into the muddy earth.

"That's no good, not aligned right," muttered the agricultural agent, walking here and there on the dikes between paddies. "The rice seedlings should be planted in straight lines at equal distances, but look how these have been done!"

The agent approached a spot where people were working bunched together and told Mr. Shin, "That's no good! Look there. Everything's planted so crooked, it's useless! That furrow there looks especially bad."

He pointed his stick toward the furrow where Yu Sun had been working. Those who had been planting the rice seedlings stopped at the agent's critique and stretched their backs. "What the hell can we expect? These are pigs, not people," said Mr. Shin. He rapped the ground with his stick for attention. "Listen up! What do you think you're working for? How could you do shoddy work like that for my good money? You hear what this gentleman said? How do those furrows look? Crooked! Are you really using your hands to do this?" He turned again to the agent. "It's like talking to the deaf. No matter how many times I tell them, they don't listen. I must've told them a thousand times how to plant straight." He then spoke again to the people. "You're no better than animals! You deserve to starve. Even thin gruel's too good for you, let alone millet from Manchuria." He turned back to the agent and pleaded, "What can I do? Farming with those idlers makes my blood boil. They're not really even a human breed, but maybe you can reason with them and teach them to do it right from now on. Could we just leave the ones already done as they are? Redoing those furrows would cost me several dozen won. Please have some understanding."

The agent remembered being well treated for lunch and hoped to be well treated for dinner. In fact, what had been done so far was not so bad as to call for redoing. He simply needed to say something in his capacity as field manager to maintain his authority and also thereby to prove himself in front of Mr. Shin. Besides, he had noticed Yu Sun, a woman of beauty not often found in the countryside, and desired a plausible reason to approach her.

The agent called out to the people. "Hey, come here everybody!"

Men walked over to him, but the women held back, their

faces averted from him because such was how a woman ought to behave.

"Everybody come here! No exceptions!" shouted Mr. Shin. "Do as the government official says!"

2-5

Reluctantly but with no choice at Mr. Shin's command, the women trudged over to the agent. They knew that resisting Mr. Shin would result in immediate loss of their livelihood. Children who had been playing in the distance with the bamboo hats came running to see what was going on. They looked back and forth from their parents to the scary people and grew worried.

The women took their places behind husbands or older brothers, maintaining female propriety. Yu Sun stood behind a widowed woman. As everybody gathered around, the agent started to explain the planting technique, but in a hectoring tone and using an impolite form of address, pronouncing words as if he were foreign. The man had a sunburnt face with a flat, misshapen nose, and the back of his head was like a brick. He looked vulgar and was said to be the son of a farmer despite putting on airs.

"There is a special way of planting rice seedlings," he explained, beginning a long lecture using difficult terms that even he didn't quite understand and even grasping at Japanese words. Scarcely had he finished when he pointed to Yu Sun and ordered, "You, come here!"

Yu Sun didn't budge.

"What are you doing? You're embarrassing her," said the widow, speaking out for Yu Sun.

"Mind your own business. I'm not talking to you!" snapped the agent, annoyed.

The widow sighed, but didn't open her mouth again.

"You, come here. Do what he says!" This time, Mr. Shin was

ordering her. Yu Sun, however, stood silently behind the widow.

"What a bitch!" exclaimed the agent, growing very angry. "You won't come when I tell you to? I need to explain something, you arrogant, rude little bitch. Don't you know who I am? You still not coming?"

The agent shoved the widow aside to snatch Yu Sun by the wrist. As he jerked on her arm, muddy water from the seedlings that she held splattered stains on the agent's white suit and Mr. Shin's ramie overcoat, annoying them both. "You bitch," cried the agent, angered because of the muddy stains. He slapped her face, hard, and demanded, "Pull out all the seedlings you've planted and redo them."

A young man stepped forward. "Listen, Mister!" he demanded, snatching the agent's arm and twisting it to free Yu Sun's wrist. The young man's grip was so tight as almost to crush in its power. "What sort of official doesn't know how men should behave with women? Who taught you to grab the wrist of a full-grown woman and slap her in the face? Don't you have a mother or a sister?" The young man who protested was a tall, robust, stouthearted man with a high-bridged nose and firm voice.

"Who the hell are you? You dare touch a government official?" The agent struck the young man in the face. Hit hard, his nose started bleeding.

Ignoring the blood, the agent struck him in the face several more times. The young man at first endured without resistance, letting himself be repeatedly struck. But as the agent was about to kick him in the side with his hard dress shoe, the man moved quickly and was already pressing the agent's neck down with his hand. Blood from his nose dripped onto the upper, back part of the agent's suit.

2-6

"You brute!" The young man's voice was trembling. "How dare you grab a young woman's wrist and slap her face? Don't you fear heaven?" He easily pulled the agent off his feet with one hand and tossed him down onto his back in the dirt.

"Kill him!" cried some people, coming after the agent. But the young man pushed them back with outspread arms and said, "Stay away. I can deal with this myself. I may as well die with this son of a bitch." He then kicked the agent in the side, the buttocks, the head, everywhere.

"Ohh, ohhhh," he screamed, as if being killed.

"What the hell are you doing?" cried Mr. Shin, grabbing the young man's arm. As the kicking stopped for a moment, the agent escaped and fled in such a rush that he forgot his hat on the ground.

"Catch the bastard!" people shouted. The agent fell into the paddy in his hurry to get away but quickly scrambled to his feet again and ran off.

The young man made no attempt at pursuit, but returned to the field and resumed planting rice seedlings as though nothing had happened.

The women, infuriated but worried at the same time, had watched the scene trembling but now also went back to the field to start working again because they knew they would lose their wages if they took too long a break. In their hearts, however, both men and women were shadowed by knowledge of the terrible revenge in store. Yu Sun herself also grieved over what had happened because of her.

Mr. Shin felt relief that at least the young man hadn't beaten the agent any further and that he himself had not been attacked. He left without a word, running off breathlessly to catch up with the agent.

As the people dragged on listlessly with the unwanted work, the blazing sun of summer, seemingly fixed in the sky, had finally lowered enough to brush the ridge of Mt. Dokjang. The day's labor was finished. After washing hands, faces, and feet, they set off for home on heavy legs that seemed no longer their own. Bent from hunger and backache, they looked to the ground with eyes strained listless from the day's hard work. Even saliva was too scarce to wet their dry lips.

Wondering when the police might come, they glanced back and forth between the path leading to the district town and the sturdy young man on their own path. But police were yet to be seen.

Approaching the entrance to Salyeoul, they met those who had worked in other fields also returning, children riding oxen that they had fed during the day, and dogs trailing their owners. All walked in silence, tired and hungry, their heads hung low as though following a funeral bier. Even the children were too hungry to act like children. The dogs themselves looked boney, as if fed too little. The silent mass formed a hungry, cheerless crowd.

From the houses, however, smoke rose as with promise of sustenance.

Old women bent from age and small girls of about ten with dirty naked feet and lacking skirts and upper clothing were cooking in the kitchen. Millet porridge would be the most to expect, a dish made by boiling several spoons of Manchurian millet with a handful of herbs in a big pot of water heated over a fire fed by a few damp little branches rather than coals. That was what awaited them as a meal.

2-7

Not every home had even the soybean paste swarming with maggots. Not every home enjoyed even the gritty Chinese salt. But no matter how bad the dinner, even worse was to come. As darkness fell, people had to endure swarms of mosquitoes, and when they lay down to bed, fleas and bedbugs would attack. Closing doors against mosquitoes was too hot, but leaving doors open let the pests in to buzz and bite. How hellish night in the country is! Burning mugwort to smoke out mosquitoes made eyes water, but no sooner had the burning gone out than the pests swarmed again for attack. How hellish nighttime is!

"But in the past . . ." the old would lament. "In the past, we had our own house and land, and life was enjoyable," they mourned, recalling how they had lost both house and land and taken on hard, burdensome lives.

"In the past, the elderly and the young women received enough to eat without working in the fields," lamented old people or men like Yu Sun's father, forced into sending his daughter to work for field-hand wages among men laboring for their livelihood.

"If we just had full stomachs, we wouldn't mind the mosquitoes."

"If the paddies and fields were still ours, we wouldn't complain about having back pain—just watching the rice plants grow would please us like seeing our own children growing up. I wish I could again see the day that I might eat from my own field."

Old farmers, sleepless in the night from mosquitoes, bedbugs, and worries over debts, would think on days gone by and lament again and again in a single night. "How did it happen that we lost house and land and fell into such misery?"

Old farmers sometimes wondered what had brought on their current state of poverty. But they could not explain with their own reasoning. "We didn't do anything bad, and didn't change much—didn't drink more, smoke more, or spend more on things. And we didn't get robbed, either. We worked hard and lived frugal as always, and we actually reaped more due to the new fertilizer and new seeds."

The old farmers would grieve and try to understand the riddle, without success. "Higher taxes to pay, and the higher cost of clothing, education, alcohol, and cigarettes!"

They would remember how they had once harvested enough tobacco for the whole year through planting a few shoots in a corner of the vegetable garden, and from about two liters of rice fermented with around twenty liters of leavened barley, how they had made enough alcohol to celebrate holidays with neighbors and perform memorial rites for ancestors. But tobacco and alcohol now had to be purchased, and even silkworms could no longer be raised for their cocoons and the silk sold for extra income.

They saw riches everywhere, however, and wondered. Wide new roads with cars, trains on tracks, electricity, banks, companies, big governmental office buildings, wealthy people in Western suits earning big salaries. "What do these all have to do with me?" they wondered. But they found no answer to the question. "It's just fate" they concluded. "The world has changed."

With these thoughts, they would give up. They lacked the wherewithal to explain their own circumstances or plan their future. They would just continue to plant rice seedlings, weed the fields, and reap the crops. They would go on with their debt-ridden lives, bitten by mosquitoes and bedbugs. This life of theirs, burdened with worries, would leave them no energy for thoughts on planning or doing other things. They vaguely believed that they would somehow survive, much as parents expect care from their children someday. They didn't resent, but just endured. That's the way Koreans thought.

2-8

After hearing Yu Sun tell of what had happened that day, her father was sleepless with anxiety for her. "Starting tomorrow, you shouldn't go work in the fields any more. What did I always tell you? Even if we starve, my daughter shouldn't have to go into the rice paddies. Don't go work there again. It's all my fault." He felt so embittered.

Yu Sun was also troubled. Han-gap, the young man who hit the agent, might now suffer greatly because of her, and she sorrowed to think on it. The son of a widow, he loved Yu Sun, and she had noticed. He had been three grades higher, and they had often walked to school together. Sometimes in crossing a stream, he had borne her on his back. He was quiet, sincere, and never tried to shirk responsibility by complaining and making excuses over hardship or disfavor. Though still young, he was respected by the older people and was in fact the most trusted individual in the village despite his family background not being comparable to Yu Sun's. His father had settled in the village some time ago but died when Yu Sun was so young that she hardly remembered his face. Han-gap's mother had raised him herself by doing odd jobs for other households, along with spinning yarn and weaving cloth during wintertime, and she was welcome everywhere for her work. Han-gap took after his mother more than his father, for she was also quiet, hardworking, and trustworthy.

Such was Han-gap. He had affection in his heart for Yu Sun but dared not express it to her father because he was poor and from a family of commoners. Yu Sun's older brother had some education and considered himself too good for manual labor but spent his time drinking, so Yu Sun's father turned to Han-gap for help with hard chores about the house. He was the one who had always gone to market for them.

Yu Sun felt so sorry to think that she might have gotten him into serious trouble.

She got up early as usual the following morning and went out with a bowl and jar to fetch water. Because the well was located at the west end of the village near a shortcut to the station, and also because the train from Seoul came early in the summer mornings as she walked to the well, Yu Sun had always looked down the fork toward Muneomi as she drew water, wondering if Sung might come. Although he was now already a married man, wedded to the daughter of a wealthy family in Seoul, she still did the same out of habit.

Over the well hung a spiderweb laden with dewdrops like tears. They glittered, brilliant as pearls in the early sunlight, and appeared almost uncanny, as if some charm were protecting a sacred well, preventing her from drawing water. She gazed at the dewdrops for a while and then drew some water with the bowl, taking care not to tear the web. She washed and dried her face, using her skirt as a towel. After the sleepless night, cold water from the well refreshed her tired eyes.

She filled her jar with water and capped it with the bowl turned upside down, then put a coiled, protective pad on her head. Before placing the jar there, but holding the string from the pad gripped between her teeth, she looked again toward Muneomi. The grass still bathed in dew was dark indigo, but above cloud-capped Mt. Dokjang, the red sun glowed radiant. Waiting every morning for one who would never come, her heart weighed heavy as a stone.

Sighing deeply, she bent over to lift the jar. A verdant grasshopper was poised on the upturned bowl, but sprang quickly away into the wet grass when her hands drew near. As she lifted the jar and prepared to set it on her head, a man wearing a suit and carrying a large suitcase appeared before her. She was so surprised that she almost dropped the jar.

2-9

Just managing to hold onto the jar, Yu Sun stood dumbstruck. It was Sung. Outfitted in a suit with white pants and a vest instead of a student uniform, it was clearly Sung. Carefully, she placed the jar onto her head and walked homeward without even a backward glance although she obviously recognized him. That was the code of etiquette for a Korean woman upon encountering a married man.

Sung dropped his suitcase onto the wet grass and quickly followed her. "Don't you recognize me?" he said. "It's me, Sung."

"Yes, I know," Yu Sun replied, walking further.

"How is your father doing?" he asked, not knowing what else to say, but feeling the need to say something.

"Fine," she answered, as briefly as possible.

Discouraged, Sung stopped following. He stood there stiff, like a *jangseung*, the traditional totem pole at a village entrance.

Sun walked on, never turning back to look. Her only gesture was to wipe away with one hand the water drops that trickled ceaselessly from the brim of the jar. The sun had risen higher, and the drops traced countless golden lines in the reflected sunlight on one side.

Her rubber shoes trod the moist soil of the path, sometimes touching the low-bending blades of grass on either side as she moved further away, growing smaller with each more distant step. Sung gazed after her, his eyes on her old hair ribbon, its tint imperceptible between red and black from discoloration through long use, as it hung down to brush against her coarse hemp skirt, no longer stiff from starch, which swayed as she moved, and when she was lost to sight, he dropped wearily down onto a rock at the side of the path.

Cradling his head with one hand, he closed his eyes, but the tears still flowed. He felt that he lost his home, his way, and all hope.

His thoughts turned to the night before, when he had left his house and Seoul. He remembered how his wife Jeong-seon had cursed him, shouting, "You stupid bumpkin, you worthless piece of dung!" She had then banged his head with a washbowl. Her rage came from his refusal to take on the case of Baron Yi's family lawsuit. This suit resulted from a distasteful and complicated affair concerning adultery, divorce, a legal filing concerning cohabitation, and strife over property in which Baron Yi, his wife and son, and other relatives were involved. The retainer's fee was 2,000 won, and the case was every lawyer's dream. It had fallen into Sung's hands through an acquaintance of Mr. Yun, but also because Sung had become well known in Seoul through winning a lawsuit brought by Viscount Kim over property. Rumor had it that if Sung should win this new case, he would earn almost 100,000 won as remuneration. Sung, however, had come away from the Kim lawsuit with a guilty conscience and had sworn never again to take such an ugly case. When he rejected the suit, it eventually went to a couple of other lawyers, a Japanese and a Korean. That infuriated Jeong-seon.

"Yes, that's you!" Jeong-seon declared. "Just a commoner from the countryside, living in servants' quarters all your life, how could you act any different?" She felt scornfully certain that Sung had rejected the fortune merely because he was nothing but a common farmboy.

This particular conflict, however, was not the only reason that he left. The closer they had grown and the longer they had lived together, the more they had come to realize how opposite their ideas and attitudes were. Their views of life were completely incompatible, and that became ever clearer over time.

2-10

"Money is the most important thing in the world."

That was primary among Jeong-seon's basic axioms. Of secondary significance was an axiom inferred by Sung, for Jeong-seon didn't directly express it herself. This was her belief in the importance of living her life based on the sensual pleasure of sexual stimulation. He sometimes thought that her slender, lovely form was the embodiment of nothing but sexual desire, and that possibility displeased him. He believed that even those without higher education could strive for human dignity, or at least shun lust, and that married couples should control their sexual desire and avoid expressing it explicitly. He acknowledged that his view might be too strongly influenced by the traditional ethic for married couples expressed in the proverb, "Treat each other as guests," so he tried to respond to his wife's desire as best he could. But he felt uneasy, for it seemed to diminish him. With regret, he felt his faith in human dignity slipping away.

He tried to hold on to that sense of dignity, but Jeong-seon nagged at him for his sexual reserve, accusing him of not loving her or of being unable to forget the girl Yu Sun.

A woman's face marred by resentment and jealousy appeared ugly in Sung's eyes. When his wife shot words like poison darts, or her eyes flamed with jealousy, he would shudder in dismay, saddened to find such ugliness hidden within his lovely wife. As the incidents recurred, her beauty started to diminish in his eyes. The outer beauty of a woman desired by an innocent young man, along with his trust in the inner beauty of her heart, gradually vanished, and she seemed little more than a bundle of flesh uniting carnal desire, unreasonable jealousy, bitter resentment, and explosive anger. Whenever Jeong-seon, to all appearances a lovely, well-behaved, and virtuous woman, revealed such base ugliness, Sung was painfully forced to see the falsity and pretense of women. He despaired over his wife being neither well-behaved nor virtuous. Trying to think better of her, he wondered whether he might have misogynistic tendencies. But Jeong-seon's character gradually came to seem lower than the average woman's.

As a last resort, Sung made a fervent decision to inculcate higher thoughts, principles, and viewpoints within her, but she merely ridiculed his ethical advice. Jeong-seon's preconception that her husband was her inferior appeared deeply rooted. She spurned with derision whatever Sung suggested and seemed to derive deep satisfaction from nagging him and ridiculing his remarks.

Coming home from his work at court, Sung never felt any peace or joy. He abhorred entering his house. Even when Jeong-Seon might smile to greet him, he had to work hard at maintaining her mood for an entire evening until bedtime. But if something went wrong, the armed truce immediately broke, and home became a chaotic winter battlefield whipped by a cold wind.

"Ah, I can't stand it anymore," Sung finally lamented. "If this continues, my life will be wasted quarreling with my wife." After several more incidents, the big fight had broken out the night before, prompting him to leave home.

As he now sat lost in such reflections, three Japanese policemen approached with fierce expressions on their faces.

2-11

Sung stood up in surprise.

One of the three policemen, a shrewd-looking one, drew too close to Sung's face and bluntly asked, "What are you?"

Annoyed by the man's rudeness, Sung retorted, "I'm a human being."

One of the policemen standing nearby turned on him and snapped, "What kind of answer is that?"

"What kind of question was that?" Sung snapped back. "Asking what I am?"

"And who taught you to speak like that?" demanded the third policeman, slapping Sung in the face twice, with such force that his hat was knocked to the ground.

The policeman who had spoken first took out a notebook and began an interrogation. "What's your name?"

"I've done nothing wrong," Sung protested. "Why are you treating me this way?"

"Maybe this bastard incited the farmers here to attack the agricultural agent," said one of the policeman, speaking Japanese. "Let's arrest this guy first."

Sung at first stood dumbstruck, uncertain what was going on. He surmised that the policemen were not after him but had come to arrest some farmers for fighting with an agricultural agent. Reflecting as a lawyer, he decided to avoid any additional problem for himself now, but he also realized that a serious legal issue confronted the farmers in Salyeoul, a village that he intended to dedicate his life to.

Sung switched to Japanese and spoke calmly. "I've just arrived from Seoul with the morning train. I'm on the way to my home village Salyeoul."

At his fluent, polite Japanese and calm manner of speaking, the policeman holding the notebook changed his attitude slightly. "Have you just gotten off the train?" he asked, his Japanese tone softer than his Korean.

"Yes."

The policeman with the notebook then turned and spoke to the other two policemen. "In that case, you must have seen him, right?"

The two gazed at Sung, and one of them finally hazarded, "Yes, I think so."

Thus was the potential storm averted. And as they soon learned that Sung was a lawyer, their demeanor altered even more. The one who had slapped him looked somewhat embarrassed. Sung himself was still quite annoyed by what had happened to him, but he hid his feelings and endured the foregoing insults, reasoning that such things commonly occurred in the countryside. In fact, he had no other choice.

Carrying his bag, Sung followed the policemen. Village dogs started barking in furious uproar. Within half an hour, eight people were arrested on suspicion of involvement in the previous day's altercation. Neither resisting nor offering alibis, they calmly lined up like people preparing to head off together in a group. Only their wives and children stood crying at the gates of their homes. As the primary suspect in the attack, Maeng Han-gap had been struck and kicked while being placed under arrest.

Sung stood blankly watching the entire scene.

After the arrests, the policemen first paused for a cigarette break, then led the eight suspects to the district town.

2-12

Refusing invitations from relatives, Sung went directly to Han-gap's house. Relatives who had earlier treated him like a bitter melon now made a big fuss over him as he walked along, greeting him as a lawyer and the son-in-law of a wealthy man.

"You came back a man of worth," remarked older women, welcoming him.

Women like older sisters beckoned, offering to put him up for his stay, calling out, "We heard your wife is a woman of beauty." Sung, however, turned down all their offers and went on to Han-gap's place, the smallest, poorest house in the village.

"Oh, goodness, an important man like you staying in our shabby place?" worried Han-gap's mother. "There's no rice or proper side dishes." She expressed her concerns openly.

"I'm satisfied with what your son eats." Sung replied, soothing her unease.

Worrying about her son and wondering if he would return safely, she asked for Sung's opinion each time she came from the kitchen as she bustled to and fro preparing a meal.

"He must have hit the agent because that man grabbed Sun's wrist and slapped her face. You know how Han-gap is. Just like in school, when he meddled in other people's business. But how could he dare strike a government official? How childish! Oh, why does he cause me such heartache?"

She spoke coming from the kitchen and going back, sometimes just protruding her head, sometimes stepping out with a wooden spoon in her hand, sometimes just letting her voice be heard.

"What did Han-gap do wrong?" Sung said, deeply moved by the young man's action, "Should a man just stand and watch a woman get grabbed and slapped? He was right to strike back."

"You're probably right," agreed Han-gap's mother. Gladdened by Sung's praise, she emerged from the kitchen and stretched her stiff back. "But these days, people who plow the soil aren't treated as humans. Some officials still wet behind the ears but with titles like *seogi* or whatnot go around treating elders like dogs. Even their own fathers and grandfathers! They use coarse language and slap elders in the face if they feel like it. Just a few days ago, someone from the government tobacco company got angry at the old noble man who lives in that house made of pagoda wood"— she lowered her voice as if to divulge a secret—"and he kicked that old man with his hard dress shoes! The old man passed out right there and woke up later with problems passing water. Isn't he well over seventy now? That's not all. Shameful health checks, grillings about tobacco and alcohol, taxes on farming, and other things! Whenever people come from the district office, there's tension. The young officials don't balk at stepping into a house and poking around in the main bedroom or kitchen. They'll even argue with young married women! Is that how things are done these days? Does this happen in Seoul, too? How can the government allow it? How can people endure such officials? Also, why does the government need to have so many new roads paved? We're forced to do that without pay, along with picking up rocks or plowing and weeding fields. We can't refuse unless we want trouble. Just because the government thinks my son and me are a household, we've got to do everything they demand without exception. I don't know how to survive. Is Seoul the same? Or is our district governor just bad? How can the higher-ups let things be run this way?"

She sighed deeply and continued, "But I just hope my son comes home safely. Why did he go and hit a government official? What a foolish boy!" She shed a few tears.

2-13

Han-gap's mother felt profoundly sad and anxious but showed these emotions only indirectly in her words and physical expressions, unlike city women. She possessed self-control, a virtue of traditional Korean mothers.

She looked so haggard, however, as she brought out the little portable table to serve Sung his meal. Not yet sixty, she had few teeth, leaving her with drawn cheeks and puckered lips. Her eyes were deeply sunken, and the skin of her bony chest, where it showed above the traditional jacket that she wore, looked like wrinkled oil paper. Her hands were also bony and callused, signs of ceaseless labor, worry, and malnutrition her entire life.

Sitting at the small table, Sung remembered the well-nourished, well-adorned ladies of wealthy families in Seoul. Their only job was nagging at servants, and they nourished themselves on food that was not only nutritious but delicious too, much more than enough and really too much to digest. Suffering predictable stomach problems, they tried all kinds of medicines for their health.

That little portable table! It was the one with eight angles that had been passed down through several generations in Han-gap's family. Half a century had likely passed before its paint peeled off entirely, and another half until it had become completely recoated with dirt and dust. Only three of its eight decorative figures on the edges still remained. Despite its state of disrepair, this little table was an artifact attesting well that Han-gap was descended from a relatively noble family. His mother used it with pride in serving the head of the family. Although not of silver and no longer serving meat, it was not a common square form but octagonal. When Han-gap's grandmother had married into the family, her grandfather-in-law had been served with it. No one recalled how many generations it had seen use, but it afterwards served Han-gap's grandfather, then his father, and finally Han-gap himself. The table was a family treasure ordinarily reserved for serving only the head of the family. Sung felt greatly honored in having his meal served on it.

Not only the table but also the soup bowl and rice bowl placed upon it were both old. The brass soup bowl had found use for so many generations that its thick bottom was worn through with a hole that had to be plugged fifteen kilometers away in a shop specialized for selling brass bowls.

"These days, you can't find such good metal," remarked the shopkeeper without a hint of irony at the sight of the antique bowl. The brass bowl from the Joseon Dynasty was in fact of better quality, both thick and well-shaped, not like the small and fragile-looking modern ones. Sung compared this generous and aesthetically shaped soup bowl with the straitened circumstances into which Han-gap's mother had fallen. He reflected on the considerable spirit of the Joseon people in contrast to the meager spirit of his own time.

The brass rice bowl now contained only steamed Manchurian millet so light when dry that it would have floated off at the slightest puff. There were a couple of humble side dishes. The repaired bowl held chopped green onions in cold water. Another bowl contained squash stems that had been peeled, cut, and mixed with soybean paste prior to being wrapped in a squash leaf and broiled over an open fire. The squash dish was cooked in a leaf not simply because Han-gap's mother had no pan but also because as the dish grew hot, the maggots in the soybean paste would crawl out and be easily picked off.

A bowl of firmly pressed millet, a full bowl of cold, green-onion soup, and a bowl of squash stems mixed with soybean paste broiled in a squash leaf, this was Sung's first meal upon returning to his country village.

2-14

"Aren't you eating?" asked Sung, looking at Han-gap's mother.

"You go on. I've got some left for me in the kitchen later," she replied. Instead of eating anything, she took the dried squash leaves, rubbed them between her palms, and stuffed the wad into a short pipe, probably used by both her and her son. She then stuck the pipe's bowl into the brazier nearby and inhaled to light the so-called squash-leaf tobacco. Until autumn, when bean-leaf tobacco was available, people lived on such squash-leaf tobacco. Who in the village could afford even a cigarette? The authorities controlled tobacco so strictly that punishment was meted out just for receiving only a few free tobacco leaves or for giving a bowl of the leaves free to a friend. When Han-gap sometimes bought a pack of cigarettes called Long Life Tobacco for his mother with money earned selling straw shoes that he had made, his mother would protest, "Why did you buy this? You don't have enough money, do you?" She would worry but still smoke with enjoyment.

Sung could not easily swallow his food. Not because of the steamed Chinese millet. Nor because of the cold soup's bitter taste. Nor because he imagined maggots crawling from the soybean paste. Neither did his difficulty stem from the miserable state of the people described by Han-gap's mother. Rather, her tragic existence, which confronted him point blank, and the mere thought that somebody like her existed made a lump rise in his throat.

But thinking that by eating well, he would at least comfort her, Sung finished more than half the bowl of millet, having mixed it with the cold soup but tasting nothing as he ate.

"Thank you. I'm done," Sung announced, putting his spoon down.

She set her pipe away and turned to him. "It's hard to eat without proper side dishes, but you should try to finish it all. Here, have some more." Taking his spoon herself, she was about to spoon the steamed millet into some water.

"No, no," Sung insisted, holding her arm. "I can't take any more."

"What a pity it is! Serving only Manchurian millet and bitter soybean paste to a guest from Seoul who lives in luxury there! What a life we have!" She then poured the water into the millet and started eating it along with the squash dish.

Sung was initially surprised, but realized that the old woman had cooked enough only for him and was intending to eat the leftovers, or nothing at all if he had finished everything. In fact, she always cooked only enough for her son and either ate the leftovers or just drank tea brewed from the millet that had scorched on the bottom of the kettle during steaming. If her son happened to ask her, "Mother, don't you have any food for yourself?" she would respond, "Yes, there's some for me in the kitchen. I just don't have much appetite now, I'll eat later." She lived this way on a single meal a day, or just half of one, between spring planting and the new harvest. She worried only that her hardworking son might eat enough, not that she provide any for herself. In this way, the old woman had used up all the fat under her skin, probably also the fat around her intestines and bones, and was now held together almost literally by skin and bones. Her eyes were cloudy, and her dark-blue lips lacked blood. Sung noticed this and surmised that she ate far too little to regenerate enough blood for her body.

Finishing the leftover food and carrying away the portable table, she said, "I heard that you became a lawyer. What brought an important man like you here in this hot weather? You must've missed your home, right? How long are you going to stay? You won't go back on tonight's train, will you?" As if suddenly remembering her son, she implored, "Please help my son return safely. I'm old and can't survive without him. God must be helping us since a lawyer like you has come."

2-15

"I'm not going back to Seoul. I came here to live." Sung spoke in a loud, vigorous voice, as if she were deaf. She was not, but her emaciated features gave that impression.

"Here to live?" she echoed in surprise. "Why would a lawyer want to live here? We stay because we don't have any choice. We can't eat rice or smoke freely these days. We sometimes used to make rice cakes and liquor, and we'd slaughter pigs and share them with other villagers, but people became selfish when food grew scarce. Where there's food, there's generosity. No food, no sharing. I don't know why, but our village has gotten so poor these days. Most of the families here are dirt poor now. Only the *chosi* family and the village head's family probably still do any business these days and manage to have some food left after spring planting. But even Sun from the Yu *chosi* family is working in the field for wages these days, so what more can I say? She grew up as such a precious daughter in that family! We've all gotten so poor, how could a lawyer live here?" Han-gap's mother caught herself and offered a little, embarrassed smile, as if thinking she might have taken Sung's statement too seriously. But the smile, ephemeral as smoke, faded away.

"I mean it," Sung insisted. "I came back here to live. I'll find a little place and do some farming. I won't go back to Seoul."

"Your wife will come, too? Did you lose your job?" she asked, still unbelieving but worried.

"My wife can come if she wants to follow, but probably won't." Sung said little, preferring to drop that topic.

"Well, I heard your wife's the daughter of a wealthy noble family. Sun told me she's also very pretty. People say your father-in-law bought you a house in Seoul and gave you some of his farmland worth several thousand bushels or more. Oh, I see, you came here to buy some land. You want to buy some land here in Salyeoul. If you do, please lend some to my son for tenant farming. It's easy to buy rice paddies now. They'd been controlled by some government company or financial cooperative, but they can now be put up for sale. People are ready to sell even for just a little extra money. They're sometimes asking for only fifty or sixty won a quarter acre. People just make ten won at that price, but they're still willing to sell. By the end of the year, hardly anyone in the village will own land. Tenant farmers will lose their land, too. The new owners won't keep the old tenant farmers, they'll give land to people they like. Living here is a bad idea. Everyone's become so poor. In other villages, people left for West Gando, in Manchuria, but the people of Salyeoul have never left home for other places. They all had their own homes and land. Even just a few years ago, people still felt safe here because they had land to plant. Your family was well-off, a wealthy family. You became better off because your family's place was well located. For other folks, selling land to survive was like pouring water onto sand. They can't get it back. Our family, though not so well-off as yours, was not poor like now . . ."

That evening after dinner, Sung visited the old pagoda tree. It had originally belonged to Sung's family, but both it and the house now belonged to someone with the title *chosi*. People had always gathered beneath the tree's branches day and night during summer months for meetings or to chat and relax. Also that evening, people were sitting around under the tree, keeping a low fire smoldering to repel mosquitoes. The old, the young, and the children sat in their separate groups. Sung joined the gathering and immediately became the center of attention.

2-16

Nobody knew how old the pagoda tree was. People said that in the days when boats still traveled up the Salyeoul River, the tree had been used for mooring, but nobody knew when that had been. One now had to go about sixty kilometers downstream to reach the place where boats still came up and docked. Long ago, when the forest was thick with trees, the river was called Dalnae, meaning "moon stream," and it was deep. Perhaps boats had come right up to the edge of Salyeoul Village. The first villagers themselves might have reached the spot by boat. At that time, the forest must have been thick and teeming with roe deer, musk deer, and tigers. Those ancestors must have first cut trees, built houses, cleared land for fields, made roads, dug wells, and given names to the village, the mountain, and other things. The river was probably called Salyeoul because it moved fast as the arrow indicated in "sal," but also Dalnae because it reflected the moon, and because the river flowed close by the village, the settlement was called *Dalnaebeol*, meaning "land of moon stream," like a place of milk and honey. In those days, the valley, the mountains surrounding it, the Dalnae River, the grass and trees, the meat and crops produced there, even the croaking of frogs and the fragrance of flowers, all belonged to the people. Things were not labeled with signs identifying owners, nor was this even necessary.

The pagoda tree and the ground where it stood had legally belonged to various people in recent years, but it belonged to the village by custom and tradition. Any villager could enjoy its cool shade. Not only people but also cows, horses, dogs, and hens with chicks were allowed to dawdle or nap under the tree, and even a traveler could stop to rest weary legs in the shade of this old, respectable tree without hearing an objection.

If all this sounds unbelievable, ask the pagoda tree itself. It has a lot of experience, having witnessed the history of Salyeoul Village at least for four or five hundred years. The tree has gone through the same joyous and sad times as the village. It knew exactly how the old greybeards coped with legislation, administration, and jurisdiction, discussing village affairs, judging offenders, and disciplining people. They may have lacked written law with its many complicated articles, but they had a revered oral law passed down from ancient times and the law of conscience written clearly in their hearts. They had never imagined harming one person for another person's profit or impairing the gain or honor of the village. The pagoda tree knew all this very well. The people of the village pursued the ideal of harmonious coexistence between individual and community, a perfect harmony of "I" and "we."

The tree also remembered the countless feasts that had taken place under its branches. With simple but healthy food like corn, melons, mixed-vegetable rice cakes, or dog meat soup, and drinks like the Korean rice wine *makgeolli*, people happily gathered as if for feasts even when working to weave twisted-straw ropes, woven-straw baskets, and straw shoes, both ordinary and square, all the while soothing babies and keeping cats around.

When unavoidable death paid a visit, people gathered under the tree to join in crying over the dead for the farewell ceremony, and on the first full moon of the lunar year, young girls were seen dressed up beautifully and holding hands in a circle around the tree like an enormous wheel. They would chant back and forth:

"Which herald?"
"From Jeolla."

"Which gate?"
"Through East Gate."

Laughing in the cold weather, they would play like that.

Voices of cursing and even fighting were also sometimes heard, but the conflict was immediately resolved at the decent voice of an old man saying, "Stop it."

Sung was imagining all that.

2-17

"You little brats shouldn't play with fire," warned an elderly man known locally as "Old Man of Hillside House." He was weaving straw shoes and admonishing the shirtless children who whirled mugwort stems lit at a fire kept smoldering to repel mosquitoes.

"Brats, do that, and you'll pee your pants tonight," a young man threatened, shaking his fist. The children scattered, giggling and making red circles in the darkness with the glowing mugwort stems. But they stealthily approached the fire again when the stems went out.

"What'll happen?" wondered Old Man of the Hillside House, as he pulled the straw shoe that he was weaving tight against his heel. "They won't easily get out of trouble, will they?" He didn't address anybody in particular, but he was clearly asking Sung.

"We can't expect them to be safe after hitting a government official," came a hasty response from a man who was shaping a pine tree root to plug a hole in a wooden bowl.

"But even a government official shouldn't grab a young woman's wrist and slap her face," said Old Man of Hillside House, his anger growing. "In the old days, they'd have broken his leg for that." He measured the shoe against his palm.

"That was then, this is now. Even a low-ranking government

official won't hesitate to enter the main bedroom of a house, a room meant for intimacy, so what's the big deal about grabbing a young woman's wrist and slapping her in the face?" argued the man mending the wooden bowl. He was around forty with hair cut short, and he seemed to have experienced the world, or at least to have suffered a lot, given his way of speaking.

"It was wrong to hit," observed a grave voice heard by all. It was the village head who spoke as he sat leaning against the lower trunk of the pagoda tree, smoking a pipe. The aroma was of genuine tobacco. "One shouldn't hit. Even if the other did something wrong, hitting is battery. Although Mr. Hwang the agricultural agent did wrong, one should have talked to him instead of using violence. Han-gap made a mistake." The village head spoke in a tone of judgment.

"Who struck first?" a young man protested. "Hwang hit Han-gap first and bloodied his nose, so Han-gap pushed him down by the neck and kicked him several times. Boy was I glad! I'd been grinding my teeth in rage." He looked clever but sickly, as if wasting away.

"Whatever, it's wrong to use violence," retorted the village head, offended. "I should know better than you. Han-gap will be locked away for several years. I stopped by the police station earlier, and the police chief told me Han-gap's in big trouble for obstructing official duty and committing assault. Why did he even think to use violence? And why against that agent? People can't get out of trouble if they use violence against government officials. So take care. It shouldn't happen again." With these words, the village head stood up, loudly spat some phlegm, and walked off into the darkness.

"What a bastard!"

"Is 'village head' such a high office?"

"Putting on airs!"

The younger men spoke ill of him, but only as the footsteps of the village head were no longer to be heard.

"What do you think, Sung?" asked Old Man of Hillside House. "You're a lawyer and should know better. How serious are the crimes of Han-gap and the others?"

"Well, it looks like it'll be hard to get them out of trouble." Sad at being unable to give a better answer, he offered some comforting words. "But it isn't such a big crime."

2-18

"How terrible!" said Old Man of Hillside House, stuffing squash leaves into his pipe as he rested from weaving straw shoes. "They live just hand to mouth and are now to be locked away for so long. How terrible!" He was a traditional old man, still wearing his hair in a topknot, and his body was like a tough old pine tree.

"What's the problem? Being imprisoned means you're better off. You don't need to worry about food or clothes in prison. They won't kill you anyway. Even getting a meal as a prisoner is better than starving," observed a young man of sallow complexion, smiling. He was watching over a sickly baby, ensuring that it did not crawl away.

"What about the rest of the family?" countered the man mending the wooden bowl, half rising to reach for a knife.

"Does staying home do any good? It only keeps you debt-ridden. They shouldn't arrest just one person but the whole family," insisted the young man with sickly face.

"Home is still better," suggested a swarthy-faced man of about twenty. "Even a beggar would be happy to have a home." The young man spoke cautiously, as if bashful about meddling in the affairs of his elders.

"Humph, you haven't suffered enough," said the older, sickly-faced man. "A home's only home if it provides food. If your stomach's empty, a home's worthless."

"What would you need to live without worries?" Sung asked, hoping to change the topic.

Everybody perked up when they heard the phrase "to live without worries."

"Depends on how many family members," replied the man mending the bowl, wanting to sound intelligent.

"For five people," proposed Sung.

"Still depends on who they are," said the man with the bowl, "but if two of them can work, well, about an acre of rice paddy and enough field for two days of plowing would be more than enough to live on. Also a piece of mountain land for firewood to cook with."

"With about an acre of rice paddy, you could be satisfied with only enough field for one day of plowing," corrected the old man. He was again weaving straw shoes.

"That's right," agreed a middle-aged man who had been silently weaving straw baskets. "With about an acre of rice paddy, I wouldn't envy any wealthy man."

"But the landowner's share of rice should be less. These days, the amount is too much. At the current amount, we'll have to live in debt our whole lives," complained the man with sickly complexion.

"Still," insisted the man with the wooden bowl, "if you have about an acre of rice paddy and field for two days of plowing in addition to a little piece of mountain land for firewood, you can easily survive."

"That's true, yes, that's right." Most of the people agreed.

"Of course it's right," said the man with the bowl, satisfied that his opinion was finally accepted.

Sung tried to calculate the cost of the land if it were to be bought rather than sharecropped. About an acre of rice paddy would make four hundred won, the field for two days of plowing six hundred, the piece of mountain land for firewood one hundred, and the total would be one thousand and one hundred won. About a thousand won's worth of land would be enough to support an entire family of five not only for one generation but over generations. "About an acre of rice paddy and enough field for two days of plowing." Repeating these words, Sung returned to Han-gap's home.

"You're back now," said Han-gap's mother, her voice audible in darkness. Only the burning squash leaves in her pipe gleamed as she smoked.

2-19

For Sung's bed, Han-gap's mother had prepared another room by driving out mosquitoes and shutting it up well to keep them out. Entering the room and groping to find the mattress and pillow, Sung lay down. He was worn out.

Sung first noticed how hot the room was. The tiny space was so tightly closed that it was even hotter than the worst summer heat. Sweat was oozing from his skin's every pore. Sung vividly saw his house in Seoul's Jeongdong area with its front and back doors ajar and a fan turned on.

He tried to endure the heat, closing his eyes to sleep. But the change of environment didn't let him relax.

"Leaving home and wife . . ."

Thinking this, he felt unhappy. Even though his wife didn't understand him and was often immature, he had not done right in leaving her. Moreover, although he hated her like an enemy during their fights, his affection was as deep as the hatred. Wasn't a fight so fierce because love is so deep?

"Why can't you just accept my flaws? Why can't you love even my flaws?" she had asked. "I grew up without my mother. Is it too much to want to be spoiled by my husband?"

Remembering what his wife said, crying after the fight, he shuddered, feeling so sorry for her.

"I'm not a bad woman. I don't hate you, either. You are a precious husband for me, but I'm so immature that I nag at you. Can't you just understand and forgive me? Can't you just accept me as I am and still love me?" Jeong-seon would sometimes implore at the end of a quarrel, leaning her head against his chest.

The nape of his neck burned where a bedbug had bitten, and he could feel fleas moving in his armpits. The mosquitoes that had been dizzy from the mugwort smoke came back out and buzzed around the room, looking for someone to bite. The top of his foot started itching.

"Damned mosquitoes!" Sung slapped the top of his foot.

In his house in Seoul, Sung used a silk mosquito net in the main bedroom and a white Western one in the reception room. Mosquito nets were actually not even necessary in the Jeongdong area.

As he lay attacked by fleas and bedbugs in the heat, Sung wondered how anxious Jeong-seon would now be after having unexpectedly lost her husband.

The night before, as Sung was leaving the house with bag in hand and swearing that he would never return, Jeong-seon shouted back in anger that he never should return. But when the clock struck midnight, she started to wait for him, wondering where he was. Several times, she ordered the servant, "Go see if the master is in the reception room."

Lying in bed with the lights on, she closed her eyes. When she opened them again, she turned to see if Sung were there despite knowing that she had lain awake the whole time. Finding only his pillow, she burst into tears. The whole time since their marriage, almost a year, they had never been apart. Jeong-seon fell asleep at some point. When she woke up, the electric lights were turned off, and the light of dawn shone through the window toward the east.

"Is the master not yet back?" Jeong-seon shouted, so loud that she herself was startled. But around that time, Sung was already at the well of his home village Salyeoul. Jeong-seon lay face down on her husband's pillow and cried.

2-20

That day, Jeong-seon called the courthouse several times, asking, "Has Mr. Heo arrived?"

"No, he's not yet here."

Whenever she heard the clerk's answer, she almost wanted to hurl the receiver.

Sung may have been unable to fall asleep in his home village Salyeoul, plagued as he had been by mosquitoes, bedbugs, and fleas, but Jeong-seon also had her concerns and waited for him with impatient anxiety.

"He might be gone to Seokwang Temple," she thought, trying to reassure herself. She felt embarrassed even in the presence of her maid and servants. If her husband had left her forever, how could she go out and see other people?

Sung had also been thinking of his wife as he lay in his borrowed room, unable to sleep. Except for the parts of her that he hated, she was a beautiful woman. Not only her face and body but also her heart and voice were beautiful. The only problem was that she didn't understand him. Sung sometimes thought that she might have been a good wife for Gap-jin. In her head, thoughts on the Korean people or mankind were scarce. She was interested only in herself, her husband, and her home. She would never imagine suffering or giving up her own wealth for others or some larger purpose. Sung felt sad about that. He had often tried to influence her in this matter, but that never worked out. Whenever Sung's ideas or behavior went beyond what Jeong-seon understood or had sympathy for, she would turn on him in anger as though insulted. She seemed intent on limiting him to her own way of thinking. In fact, if he had been willing to limit himself in that way, they could have become an ideal couple and lived happily together.

Sung, however, was an utterly bullheaded farm boy, according to her, and she didn't have him in the palm of her hand. Her view of life was determined primarily by generations of upper-class prejudice, or so Sung thought.

He listened to Han-gap's mother snore and envied her ability to relax despite what must have been great sorrow of heart to know that her son was in police custody. Or had she grown indifferent from experiencing so much sorrow in her life? Perhaps she believed in fate and accepted whatever happened? Or was it that characteristic Korean trait of hiding emotion, whether joy or sadness?

Stifled in his room and craving fresh air, Sung opened the door. A cloud of mosquitoes swarmed in, crowding him out as though he were alien to the village.

Sung left the house.

The sky was a dark indigo blue, and clear with glittering stars, a sign of imminent autumn. The top of Mt. Siru, the mountain passes Meok and White Sky, the Dokjang mountain range, all of these traced dark curves against the indigo sky. Sung started to walk as his legs took him, toward fields without houses. All was quiet. The season was still too early for the sound of crickets. So quiet was the night that Salyeoul River could almost be heard.

Sung approached and presently stood at the river's bank. When he was a child, ancient red pine trees had grown there, but they were all gone now. Only a willow tree of some three or four meters remained. In the dark night among fields, the water looked pale, and its flowing current was now audible. From further upstream, somewhere, came the gentle sound of other water rolling into the river.

His mind wandering in endless thoughts, from the river's

continual flow to his childhood dreams, the perplexities of life, the unfortunate village of Salyeoul lying deep in sleep, the wife whom he had left abandoned in Seoul . . . Sung walked up and down along the riverside.

2-21

A rooster crowed. What did it have to eat? The rooster would probably be as thin as Han-gap's mother, thought Sung.

The eastern sky's indigo blue was something that one couldn't see in Seoul. He watched it turn lighter, changing to purple. The line of the mountains was getting more distinct but still appeared dark against the sky. As the world slowly awoke, even the flowing water seemed to grow louder.

Though usually seen only in late summer, early morning fog rose from the valley. The season was still early for that, but the mist was probably because of the river's course through high mountains. Here and there, the murky fog rose, but rather than dissipating, it stopped to quietly hang in the air.

The water of the river reflected the indigo above as a deep, liquid blue. From somewhere came the distant ringing of a bell.

Sung thought of the road leading from Muneomi past Salyeoul and around Bangameori and Gutmoru before finally reaching the market at Geomeunori. That road was just a short way outside the village. The bell probably hung about the neck of a donkey bearing the load of some peddler who had stayed overnight in Muneomi and was now on the way to the Geomeunori market. On the donkey's back were probably artificial silk, cotton cloth, rubber shoes, hair ribbons, traditional combs, both wide- and fine-tooth, and fans, among other things, all wrapped in worn-out cloth. Behind the donkey . . . but at that, Sung drew a blank.

In the old days, the donkey would have been followed by a man in straw shoes with long braid and a rain hat over his traditional hat during the rainy season. But today, no one wore that outfit. Sung couldn't quite imagine how the man trailing the donkey appeared.

The bell clanged on into the distance, muffled by the valley fog as the donkey moved further along. Sung's thoughts followed the sound. He reflected that with the new roads now built in Korea, traveled by cars and trucks, the clanging bell of horse or donkey had become rare. This was the natural result of a developing civilization, but Sung felt that something had been lost. He wondered how all those people who had followed donkeys were now living. He also recalled how people in Salyeoul had once used hemp to make shoes called *mituri* to earn extra money, but rubber shoes were now used and the frame for *mituri* no longer seen.

The east sky was getting brighter and redder, promising the sun in its round hot glory. "I should see the sun rise before going back," Sung decided. He walked up to a spot protruding from the skirt of the mountain near the river. A grove of very old pine trees had grown there earlier, before he left for Seoul, and the old had brought children there to play, but only a single bent pine stood there now. It was probably saved because it was bent.

Sung seated himself on a narrow spot where the old tree's roots protruded, and he softly exclaimed, "Anything of worth is all used up!" His body was still sticky from sweating all night, but the early morning breeze cooled him. Two sleepless nights had also left his head heavy and his eyes sore. Worse than his physical discomfort was the indescribable fear and pain roiling within his heart.

"What should I do from now on?"

Sung gazed at the wheel of the sun rising over White Sky Pass, moving with casual self-assurance as it radiated its marvelous light. To sit in nature and watch the morning sun climb into the sky had been denied to him for several years! He felt its light shine into his heart as he watched.

"The light, the power!" Not quite a poet, he marveled at the morning sun with a few simple words of exaltation.

Mount Dokjang, the fields about Salyeoul, the water of the Dalnae River—all were awakened by the light and the power. The world around was so bright. Water of the river and rice paddies, dew drops on edges of grass, everything glittered golden. The village, after its harassment by heat and insects all during the night, awoke in the sunlight like a person recovering from malaria.

"I should go back to the village now," decided Sung, and he stood up.

2-22

Since arriving in Salyeoul, Sung had stayed up for two nights. Plagued by insect bites at night, he could also find no rest by day from the bother of flies. But in those two days, he had learned some things about the village.

There were three villagers sick of typhoid fever, four of dysentery, five of malaria, two without clear diagnosis, and one pregnant woman coming due. How many would be healthy if seen by a doctor? Many others seemed in fragile health, though not seriously ill, as their sickly faces bore evidence of infection by parasites or weakness from malnutrition. After spending only two nights in the village, Sung felt his own head and body disturbed, as if he had suffered a serious illness. But he had the good fortune of remaining strong in spite of eating poorly, suffering sleepless nights, growing exhausted, and anxiously worrying. He lamented to realize how harsh their village life was. Flies that had crawled across excrement from villagers sick with dysentery or typhoid fever would fly around everywhere and alight with tainted feet upon food or dishes in the kitchen or a baby's mouth and hands.

At night, mosquitoes teeming with malarial parasites would be biting into people's blood vessels, and fleas and bedbugs disgorging the typhus bacteria would go from room to room, house to house, and village to village, making the rounds.

Is there no doctor in the countryside? The diseases of poor country people hold no interest for modern doctors beyond serving as objects of study in a thesis. Healing those diseases brings no money. To call a doctor to the countryside would require a villager to sell an entire shack just to pay for the cost. To cover the doctor's travel expenses, the house-call fee, the medical bill, and the prescription charge would require so much money that dying and being reborn would be much less expensive and far more convenient. Besides, no doctor would go to the trouble anyway. Students today turn to careers in healing just as a way to earn money, and even if a villager were to sell a shack, the funds would cover only the bare minimum of care. The countryside in these times receives healthcare assistance only after cities are first equipped with hygienic facilities run by public health officials. If the cost for the water supply of one city were invested to improve rural wells, how many villages might enjoy hygienic water?

People of the countryside are afflicted with all kinds of disease and die early. The death rate is high, and the rate for children even higher. These people help produce food for all and lay the foundation for culture, but they have little to eat and enjoy no cultural benefits.

Sung felt his sorrow and resentment rise at these thoughts. "But isn't that why I've returned?" He clenched his fist in determination. "All right," he decided. "Let me try to improve conditions in Salyeoul as much as I can. Regardless whether Marx was right or wrong about class warfare, I'll see how much can be improved without changing the social structure. Can't I do at least that with the villagers' help? Instead of promising a future paradise, I can try to help revive the farmers now. Maybe not completely, but at least reduce their suffering and increase their profit. Don't I have that freedom?" Sung began to feel renewed confidence, self-respect, and satisfaction. "Salyeoul has about a hundred households, nearly five hundred people all told," he reckoned. "I can dedicate my life to helping the farmers here!" With this decision, Sung started to reflect on projects to bring work for the villagers.

What should be done first? What severe hardship most needed easing? And how could about an acre for rice and enough land for two days of plowing be provided? Finally, what kind of life should Sung himself lead?

2-23

The first thing needed was to bring a doctor from town. Second was to find food for those without. Third was to rid homes of flies, mosquitoes, and bedbugs. Fourth was to obtain release of the eight arrested, including Han-gap. These four had to be done as quickly as possible within the next few days.

Sung left for town early that morning.

In town were the scattered remains of an old fortress. The gates were all demolished, and the only parts of the fortress left were rocks too heavy to carry off. Even these still showed holes made by firearms. The fortress had seen many battles over time. During the ancient Goguryeo Dynasty, there were several battles against Chinese armies of the Sui and Tang Dynasties. Afterwards, it had been always an important battle site in various wars against Khitans, Mongols, Qing Chinese, and Russians. It had even witnessed domestic conflict, such as the revolt of Hong Gyeongrae in the early 19th century. Famous men had left traces on this fortress. General Eulji-mundeok, who fought a Chinese army of the Sui Dynasty. General Yang Man-chun, against a Chinese army of the Tang Dynasty. Or King Seonjo of Joseon, against a Japanese invasion. Not even the Sino-Japanese War or the Russo-Japanese War had left the fortress in peace. Knots full of gunshot were still to be found on trees thirty to forty years old. The remains of the fortress provided a stubborn reminder of how much the Korean people had suffered from invaders.

Some two hundred of the five hundred households in town were Japanese, and the mayor himself was Japanese. The first big house encountered upon entering town sported a tin roof and stood on the highest ground. This was the local house of *gisaeng*, the Korean geisha, and it bore the Japanese name "Asahi," which meant "morning sun." Sung could recall it being there even during his childhood days. The next big houses were the district office, the police station, the post office, the local bank, and a few restaurants. As for the common Korean houses, most were thatched-roof, but a water-supply system was under construction, and some already had electric lights and telephone service. Among the town's seventy telephones, seventeen were owned by Koreans.

Sung first went to the police station. The small building was originally used as a district office in the old government system but had since been renovated and used by the police.

A policeman at the gate blocked Sung's entrance. "What's your business?"

Sung stopped. "I want to see the police chief," he replied.

"The police chief?" The policeman scrutinized Sung closely, as if to demand, "Who the hell are you to ask about seeing the police chief?" However, he stepped aside for lack of a reason to hinder, but then followed, asking for some identification.

Sung handed over his business card. It stated, "Heo Sung, Lawyer."

That must have quite impressed the policeman. Knowing that a lawyer first had to pass the National Exam for Government Offices or work as prosecutor or judge, the policeman showed a little more respect.

"Wait just a moment," he said and rushed into the police chief's office. A few seconds later, he returned to say, "Come in this way." He even bowed his head a little saying it.

The Japanese police chief remained sitting and greeted Sung by just bowing his head, then invited him to sit down. "When did you arrive?" he asked.

Sung noticed that the man was well-fed and plump. "A couple of days ago," he replied. Then added as a lead toward conversation, "I'm from around here."

"Oh, you are? You're a successful man." The police chief showed surprise to hear that a man from the countryside had become a lawyer. "Which school?" he asked, his tone friendlier. "Did you graduate in Japan? Tokyo? Or Kyoto?"

"I graduated from Boseong College," responded Sung, observing the man's face.

"Boseong College?" The police chief again seemed surprised, but then disappointed.

2-24

"You're so young . . . Anyway, that's great." The police chief praised him in the indulgent manner of an official expressing pride over a local who had made good. The chief's surname was Abe, and he had a middle rank called *Gyeongbu*.

He ordered the clerk to bring some tea and then asked as he fanned himself in the morning heat, "Now, what did you want to talk about?"

"Well," Sung began, "I came to see you for a favor with regard to the incident in Sitan-li," He used the official name for Salyeoul.

The chief stared at him over his glasses, saying nothing.

"Sitan-li is my home village. The incident happened the day before I arrived, and I'm well acquainted with those arrested. They're usually as meek as lambs."

At this, the police chief sneered and retorted, partly in Japanese, "Lambs? Hardly a flock, then. More like a gang of them!" He lit a cigarette and started smoking.

"Please listen to me. As for the truth about what happened, here's what I learned. The agricultural agent, Mr. Hwang, first grabbed a nineteen-year-old woman named Yu Sun by the wrist, and when she resisted, he slapped her face. That was the start of the incident. As you are aware, to insult or touch a woman you don't know is unpardonable in Korean tradition. That's why Maeng Han-gap grabbed Hwang's arm, to restrain him, but Hwang struck Maeng in the face three times. Maeng was trying to talk to him and avoid any violence, but when Hwang bloodied Maeng's nose, he pushed Hwang down. That was a legitimate self-defense to protect himself from being hurt. And the other seven men were only trying to pull the two fighting men apart. The blood stain on Hwang's suit is from Maeng's nose. Clear evidence for this is that the stain is on the back of the suit. It supports witnesses who can tell you that Maeng pushed Hwang down by the nape of his neck to keep from getting hit. Besides, if those seven people had really ganged up on Hwang, that man wouldn't have managed to run away as he did. All this evidence goes to show that these eight people, including Maeng Han-gap, are guiltless."

"Moreover," Sung added, "these people live hand to mouth. If they can't work, their families will starve. Now if they were guilty, they should certainly be punished, but Hwang is clearly the one responsible for what happened. I hope that I've managed to help you understand the circumstances clearly. I ask you please to quickly free these poor, unfortunate people, simple farmers unable to defend their own innocence. This is what I want to ask you, as a favor."

"Mr. Hwang's statement is quite different from what I've just heard from you," said the police chief. He pressed the call bell on his desk.

A policeman came in and looked surprised to encounter Sung. He was the man who had slapped Sung's face at the well. Sung was also taken aback.

2-25

"What's the standing with that case of assault on Mr. Hwang and the criminal charge of obstructing official duty?" asked the chief.

"Haven't they already confessed?"

"Ah, they've all confessed except for one guy named Maeng Han-gap. He's a hardened individual. He still insists he was first hit and didn't disobey the order about the right technique for planting rice. But I'll finish the case today." The police officer sounded confident.

"Is there any agitator behind all this?"

At this question, the officer answered, "Maeng Han-gap must have acted as agitator but hasn't confessed who put him up to it. He's got only an elementary school education and wouldn't know much about the proletariat or imperialism. But according to Mr. Hwang's testimony, Maeng used expressions like 'class warfare' and agitated people to attack the government officer as a servant of imperialism, so we suspect an intellectual agitator behind him." The officer gave Sung a sidelong, baleful glance and said, "These days, Koreans who studied at colleges in Seoul are all arrogant and have rebellious ideas."

"What did Mr. Shin say?" asked the police chief.

"He agreed with the accusation and testimony of Mr. Hwang."

"Okay. You may go."

After sending the officer out, the police chief gave Sung a smile of triumph and said, "Who can believe the statements of farmers? And you didn't witness the incident yourself." He then turned to the documents on his desk as if he were finished with Sung.

"I don't doubt the police authorities know what to do, but I'd just like to say something for the record," explained Sung, drawing the attention of the chief before he continued. "If Mr. Hwang made a false testimony to cover his own guilt, what would happen?"

The police chief stared at Sung with annoyance and said, "There's certainly evidence, a medical certificate issued by a doctor, a state doctor, that Mr. Hwang has been bruised on one side and will need treatment for two weeks."

"Aren't the bloodstains on Mr. Hwang's suit and on Maeng Han-gap's clothes also evidence? I believe there is a difference in defining the criminal charges depending upon motive. There is a big difference between stepping in to stop the assault on Yu Sun by Mr. Hwang and stepping out of line to obstruct an agricultural agent teaching the right technique for planting rice. And is there even any evidence for the latter?" Sung asked.

At this, the police chief became infuriated and retorted, "You're a lawyer and should present your theories later in court. Defense is not allowed in a police station or a prosecutor's office." With these words, he again turned away.

"Calm down. I'm not here as their lawyer. I'm here only because the accused are all from my village. I know them very well and how they usually are, and I believe their story. I came to see you with the hope of getting this incident resolved smoothly. I truly apologize if I offended you."

But Sung's effort to placate the police chief had no effect.

"Much as you may know those farmers, I know Mr. Hwang and Mr. Shin even better," snapped the police chief.

2-26

Sung realized that there was no use in further discussion, but he didn't consider his visit a total waste of time. His words about the actual event would remain in the police chief's head. Moreover, he had obtained important information useful later in court for defending the farmers. From the conversation between the police chief and the officer, he could piece together Mr. Hwang's accusation and Shin's testimony. Hwang must have maintained that he was doing his job as agricultural agent by encouraging people in the right method for rice planting when a gang of eight farmers led by Maeng Han-gap and incited by communism rebelled against him, shouting insults, and beat him up. Mr. Shin had given testimony in favor of Mr. Hwang, and the state doctor had prescribed at least two week's treatment for the bruise. As for the police, thought Sung, they always accused the farmers of being communists revolting against authorities and trusted government officials instead. That was the formula.

Sung left the police station and went to see the state doctor. His office was located at one corner of the marketplace set up on the extensive grounds of an elementary school that had earlier served as a government guest house. Sung found the place, located just before the arrow-shaped stone bridge leading to the town's south gate. Originally a building in Korean style, it was now renovated and vaguely Japanese or Western in a mix as confused as the rice and vegetable dish called *bibimbap*. At the gate hung a sign indicating the doctor's practice and a doorplate providing the doctor's name along with his position as a member of the Japanese Red Cross.

Sung went in and saw rubber shoes and dress shoes lying on the stepping stone at the entrance to an open space with a sign that announced a waiting room. Seated there were a woman with an eye disease, a man with a boil on his head, and a farmer with a festering leg. Just emerging from a room was a woman holding a smoldering cigarette between the index and the middle finger of her left hand, chortling and moving her hips sensually as she walked. She looked like a *gisaeng*, or even a common whore, in her thin dark-blue skirt of voile and her oiled hair put up in a chignon. She didn't seem to be an ordinary patient.

Sung approached an aperture in the wall with a sign indicating reception and pharmacy. A middle-aged man, miserably haggard, was eating cold noodles with cucumber slices.

"Is the doctor in?"

At Sung's question, the man looked up with a mouthful of noodles and said, "You need to see him?"

"Yes, somebody's sick and needs to see the doctor."

"Is the patient with you?" asked the man setting his bowl down and sticking his head out the hole to see the patient.

"I came to request a house call," explained Sung. He took out a handkerchief and wiped sweat from his forehead. The small reception room that doubled as a pharmacy looked less than four square meters and had only a few medicine bottles and a rusty scale. It was evidently hot inside.

"What's wrong with the patient?" asked the man.

"Are you a doctor?" retorted Sung, annoyed.

"Where are you from?" the man asked.

"Let me see the doctor first," Sung replied, his voice more imperative.

The man seemed unembarrassed but went to inform the doctor.

Sung glanced into the room with the sign that announced "Doctor's Office," but he saw only an empty chair and a table.

"Is the doctor in there?" asked the farmer with the festering leg.

"How long have you been waiting?" Sung said.

"We've been waiting long enough for a pot of barley rice to

cook," he replied, shoeing the flies from his pus-filled leg, "but the man at the reception won't tell us whether the doctor's in or not."

2-27

"He just ignores our question," said the farmer in anger. "People like us from the countryside aren't so important, are we?"

"Some who came later than us have already gotten treated," said the woman with the eye disease, trying to open her eyes, but failing.

"They think we don't have money, but I brought some with me," said the farmer and showed a crumpled one-won note held tightly in his hand. He spread it out for Sung to see.

The doctor came in from a nearby room wearing slippers. Surprised at Sung's appearance, his clothes and his bearing, he asked in respectable manner, "Oh, where did you come from?" His swarthy face sported a mustache, and he peered at Sung over gold-framed glasses set on the middle of his nose. He seemed to have just had some alcohol and food because his face was red and he was trying to suck out some meat stuck between two long, gold teeth.

"Are you the doctor?" Sung asked, bowing.

"Yes, I'm Dr. Lee," he replied, still polite.

The woman who had been laughing and slowly heading away when Sung entered turned back at the doctor's voice, looking at him and Sung in turn as she walked toward them. "Mr. Hwang is still here, right?" she asked, making eyes at the doctor.

The doctor shot her a look of rebuke.

"Oh, that Mr. Hwang!" she exclaimed. "Supposed to be in treatment for two weeks, but just watch him drink!" She laughed, nearly in hysterics.

"Alcohol can have medicinal effect," the doctor joked, having failed to quiet the woman.

"Out of my way! I'll go make fun of him." She pinched the doctor's arm, pushed him aside, and entered the nearby room, just next to his office.

From the room, a man's voice was overheard. "You bitch! Where'd you go? To service a husband?"

"Hey, how could I service a husband just for a minute?" She laughed loudly.

"Oh, you little bitch!" replied the male voice. "So you need a whole night to service a husband?"

"What did you call me? A bitch? Ouch! Don't pinch! That hurts. Mr. Hwang, you're such a womanizer. Messing around with a sweaty girl planting rice and getting into a tussle with those hicks! Ah, how dirty! Back off! Ahhh, why'd you pinch my groin? How awful!" A slap was heard.

"Ah, this wench hit me," cried the man's voice.

"Why not? You deserved it," she retorted, laughing again.

"What a saucy bitch!"

"What's wrong with me being saucy? Get another medical certificate, this time for a three-year treatment, then sue me," chattered the woman.

"That's all? Come on, give me a kiss," the male voice demanded.

"No. I don't want to. The mouth that kissed that country girl planting rice smells like dung," retorted the woman.

"Hey, I was attacked before I had a chance to kiss her! I just had time to grab her wrist! But she was a pretty one. A woman like you can't hold a candle to her. I'll have to get that bird in my hand sometime," the man said.

"Humph, you think that's so easy? Now that you've filed suit, be careful you don't get your throat cut by one of those villagers," she warned.

The whole time that the two could be overheard, Dr. Lee paced the room nervously, repeating, "Why are they talking so loudly?" Sung detained the doctor as long as possible, gaining valuable information.

2-28

"Who is the patient?" asked the doctor, looking at Sung.

"There are about seven or eight patients, and they are all poor. I couldn't just sit and watch without doing anything. That's why I came to ask for a house call. You might be busy, but please come with me to see them." Sung watched for the doctor's reaction.

At the word "poor," the doctor's look of respect changed to one of derision. "House calls have to be paid in advance. You know that?" The doctor's tone had become stiff.

"Paid in advance?" asked Sung, scarcely controlling his fury. "Fine. I can pay in advance if that's the case. How much do you charge for a house call?"

"Five won every four kilometers. Taxi costs also have to be paid by the patient, and if the car can't reach the place, the cost doubles."

As they discussed costs, Hwang and the *gisaeng* could be heard flirting and chasing each other in the room next to the doctor's office.

"Can anybody afford such an expensive house call?" asked Sung in an aggressive tone.

"Who would make a house call without being paid?" the doctor protested.

"What can poor farmers expect when they get sick? In an emergency, what do you do? Don't you at least go if someone comes to ask you?" Sung looked into the doctor's eyes.

"I can't do much about that. I don't have my practice for charity. In fact, I don't even like to treat country people. They think they don't have to pay, and they lack any gratitude. Let them have their traditional medicine if they want. Why do they ask a doctor for a house call if they have no money? How dare they!" The doctor sounded almost belligerent.

"But you can't refuse to see patients if they ask you. That's the law, even if you want to refuse. I'm therefore asking you to visit them without being paid in advance. There's more than one patient, probably seven or eight, maybe even ten. Some are seriously ill, so you should go to see them. I'll call a taxi for you," Sung spoke with an imperative tone.

Dr. Lee looked at Sung anew. He felt anger surge, overcoming his tipsiness. "What are you saying? Are you here to judge me? It's my decision to go or not, so who are you to order me around? What impertinence! Tell me, what'll you do if I say no?"

The doctor was about to turn away. Sung took him by the arm and said, "I came here to ask you to see patients in an emergency. If you refuse, I'll be forced to call the police." Then pointing to the woman with an eye disease, the farmer with a festering leg, and a man with a boil on his head, Sung softened his tone and spoke to persuade. "They came from a village far away and have been waiting long to see you. Attend to them first, then prepare for the house call. In the meantime, I'll get a car ready."

As Sung and the doctor were loudly arguing, the nurse, Mr. Hwang, the *gisaeng,* and the haggard man at the reception had all come out to watch, their eyes glancing from the doctor to Sung in suspicion and worry.

2-29

Sung stared at Mr. Hwang. The man's features were somehow unbalanced and his face dark, giving an impression of ill-mannered cunning. From the drooping, thin-lined tails of his eyes, he seemed a man of lascivious desire and immorality.

Intimidated by Sung's words, which were reasonable—or rather legally correct, more than reasonable—and recognizing

Sung's bearing as different from a country hick's, the doctor called to his nurse and said, "Ask the patients what their problems are, and let them come in one after another." He then turned away from Sung without saying a word and went into his office.

Mr. Hwang and the *gisaeng*, realizing that something unusual was afoot, returned quietly to their room, glancing again and again back at Sung.

The nurse addressed the patients in a brusque tone, then asked, "Who's first?"

"This woman can go in first," replied the farmer, conceding to the woman with eye disease.

"Oh, no, I came later. You go first," the older woman insisted.

"Whoever, hurry up," said the nurse, annoyed.

"All right. I'll go in first." The farmer went into the doctor's office, dragging his infected leg.

The nurse helped the doctor into his scrub suit and tied the strings behind his back. "What happened?" asked the doctor looking at the boil oozing pus.

"It was itchy, like a mosquito bite, so I scratched it, and it got red. Now, it looks like this. I tried different ointments, but nothing helped," explained the farmer, an earnest plea in his voice.

"Haven't you heard 'If it ain't broke, don't fix it'?" the doctor asked. "You shouldn't have scratched it, should you?" He pressed several times about the edge of the boil with his finger.

"Ow, ouch!" the farmer cried out.

"Don't scream! You're not a child!" The doctor pressed down hard again.

"Is it possible to cure it without cutting it open?" asked the farmer in a trembling voice.

"You think it's possible to treat without cutting?" The doctor took out his anger toward Sung on the farmer.

"It hurts so much even at the least touch," said the farmer, "I heard a shot would deaden the pain. Can you give me a shot?"

"A shot costs two won," said the doctor, starting to bargain. "How much money do you have?"

"I've only got this, but after harvest, I'll pay the rest," promised the farmer. He showed the crumpled won held tightly in his hand.

The doctor took it and gave it to the nurse, then turned back to the farmer. "Asking for a shot with just one won? That's scarcely enough for consultation. Surgery alone costs three won, and five with a shot."

The farmer opened his eyes in wide astonishment to hear that surgery would cost so much. "As much as five bushels of rice!" was his immediate thought. But until his leg got healed, farming would be impossible, he realized. Finally deciding, he said, "I'll pay one won first for surgery. Later at harvest, I'll pay the rest."

"Surgery can wait till tomorrow, so come up with at least enough money for that." The doctor stood up and went to wash his hands in the sterilizing water of a nearby basin, telling the nurse, "Call in the next patient. Ask if they have money. If not, tell them to come back tomorrow with money in hand." With those words, he went into the room where Mr. Hwang was staying.

2-30

Sung gave six won to the farmer with the festering leg, telling him that he should undergo an operation and stay overnight.

The farmer protested, "I don't know if I should take this." But he accepted the money with appreciation in his eyes and looked at it for a while, as if reflecting that it was a pity to waste such a sum on an operation. He then limped away, favoring his festering leg. Six won in his hand, such a windfall—more than he could usually save in an entire year—and he couldn't spend it. If only he could just buy some cheap ointment and take the remainder home, he seemed to think. Sung watched him with moistened eyes.

Sung went out for insecticide against bedbugs, material to make mosquito netting, some medical ingredients made from petroleum, and other kinds of disinfectant, returning to the doctor's office in a taxi about thirty minutes later.

Dr. Lee hesitated but climbed into the taxi. Sung took the medical bag from the nurse and also got in. The entire way to Salyeoul, they didn't talk to each other at all. Sung was reflecting on what he had experienced at the police station and the doctor's office, while the doctor was thinking about the unpleasant experience with Sung.

In Muneomi, they got out of the taxi. After asking the driver to return for him in about two hours, Dr. Lee stopped by the police station and then followed Sung to the village.

At the well, they encountered Yu Sun. She had come to draw water for the daytime. It was the first time for Sung to see her again after his initial encounter on the morning of his arrival.

When Yu Sun saw Sung and the doctor, she turned away. The doctor seemed to have been drawn to her because he stared as if he had forgotten Sung's presence. Sun stood with the coiled pad on her head, waiting for them to pass by.

"She's the woman," said Sung, turning toward the doctor and smiling.

"Pardon?" responded the doctor. He had been too charmed with Sun to listen carefully.

"She's the woman from the incident with Mr. Hwang," said Sung, looking directly at the doctor's eyes, visible over his glasses.

"Is she?" The doctor didn't know what else to say.

"When Mr. Hwang grabbed her hand, she shook him off, so he slapped her. That's how things started."

"Oh, I see," said the doctor, and gave a forced smile, but then felt cold sweat run down on his back when he remembered that Sung had overheard the conversation between Mr. Hwang and the *gisaeng*. Reflecting on this, he finally offered his business card and received one from Sung. Dr. Lee was taken aback to see Sung identified as a lawyer, and his surprise bordered on real fear. He had read about Sung's legal career and had also heard people talk about him.

"Oh, you are the lawyer Sung?" he observed, trying to calm himself with the remark. He changed in attitude toward Sung completely, his tone more than friendly, even humble.

By the time they were finished tending to the sick in the village, they had grown familiar enough to joke with each other. "I'll pay the medical fees, so make sure they get better," Sung said as they rested under a shade tree by the river after the visits.

"I'll do my best," said the doctor. He looked at the river and added, "This village has nice scenery."

2-31

Sung decided to settle at a site looking down onto the river and to have a thatched house built there. He hired some jobless people from the village and had them begin construction work. The wage was one won per day. This was not decided by Sung alone but also by the people, who had gathered for a meeting to discuss the issue. They decided on eighty jeon a day, and Sung added another twenty to make a full won.

The people of the village started their work with joy. An old man who was the most experienced at building houses offered to be, or became as a matter of course, director of the construction work.

A site under the pagoda shade tree was first considered, but not wanting to appropriate for himself a spot used by every villager for recuperation, and feeling uneasy for even considering it, Sung refused that offer and decided to settle north of the village on a hillside facing southeast. The Dalnae River ran directly in front of the gate. Before one's eyes to the east stretched out the *Dalnaebeol*, and beyond that were White Sky Pass near Dolgoji, the peak of Mt. Siru, and several other mountains. From the property to the river, one followed a downward slope for about twenty meters.

The village elders tried to dissuade Sung from settling there, arguing that the site was good enough for a pavilion though not for a house, but Sung insisted on it.

Sung handed out the insecticide against flies, fleas, and bedbugs and also fly swatters for each household, telling how to use them, and he himself sprayed insecticide on maggots swarming in the manure compost pit.

On the day for tamping the ground to harden it into a proper foundation, the whole village came out in high spirits.

"We shouldn't be paid to build a house for a fellow villager," they would say every time when they got paid, and on this day at least, they refused any pay. Sung instead prepared abundant rice cakes, alcoholic drinks, and yellow melons to feed the people.

"Evening is the right time for tamping," they agreed, deciding to prepare the site during the day and tamp the ground in the evening.

Now that mid-July by the lunar calendar had passed, the heat had subsided, so as the sun went down, a cool breeze was blowing. The moon soared high over White Sky Pass, and with that rising moon, old and young, men and women all gathered on Sung's new property. Reflecting the moon, the Dalnae River looked as if dusted with golden flour.

"*Aha uhu, tam tamp.*"

"*Uhu yeocha, tam tamp.*"

The sound of people chanting as they tamped echoed far and wide.

To the rhythm of the chant, the big tamping stone fastened with twelve ropes draped over a sturdy wooden structure went up into the moonlit air and came down hard upon the ground with a loud boom.

"When this good house is fully built to stay," one person would shout.

"*Aha uhu, tam tamp,*" the others would respond, pulling the ropes down tightly.

Up soared the stone in the air.

"If son is born, he'll be a great, good son."

"*Aha uhu, tam tamp.*"

"If daughter's born, she'll be a good, chaste one."

"*Aha uhu, tam tamp.*"

"If you keep chicks, to phoenix they will grow."

"*Aha uhu, tam tamp.*"

"If you keep cows, fast horses surely show."

"*Aha uhu, tam tamp.*"

"Within, without, piles heaped-up unhulled rice."

"*Aha uhu, tam tamp.*"

"From field and paddy, more than will suffice."

"*Aha uhu, tam tamp.*"

"High piled-up luck from fields of the Dalnae..."

"*Aha uhu, tam tamp.*"

"...to heap up high in this new house this way."

"*Aha uhu, tam tamp.*"

In a short time, the people grew festive. Filled from feasting, gladdened with *makgeolli*, brightened by the high-risen moon, transported through the joy of work, all this raised them to convivial spirits. Seemingly forgotten was all the bitterness of life.

2-32

Sung looked around to see if Yu Sun had come. He secretly wished for her to live in the house together with him, thinking that to establish a family with her in a house offering such a nice view would be perfect.

Sung walked around pretending to look for something. Yu Sun's father was there, sitting and smoking, and some young women of the village were to be seen, but Yu Sun was nowhere to be found. Sung was disappointed. It was as if the moon were missing from the sky, as if the Dalnae River no longer shone in its reflected light.

Sung slipped away from the gathering and headed off for the village. The way was quiet because the most sociable of the villagers had gone to Sung's property for the tamping. Sung walked faster and soon stood before the house where Yu Sun lived.

Mr. Yu's house, with its roof half tiled and half thatched, was fronted by a gate and had a reception room that people said used to stay open as a welcome sign to any visitor. Mr. Yu's grandfather had served in several high government positions during the Joseon Dynasty and was thus well known in the area. Some poems and writings of his had even been collected and published as a book. But that world was now gone, and the Yu family had lost all its property. Only during the grandfather's yearly memorial service were the title and name of that illustrious man mentioned, much to Mr. Yu's proud satisfaction.

Government officials had once bowed in the yard before the guest house when visiting, but neither the police nor the officials from the government's tobacco company offered respect any longer to the Yu family. That had at first upset and hurt Mr. Yu, but he had learned to reconcile himself to what could not be changed.

Sung lingered near the house so brightly lit by the moon. The gate was half ajar, and though he had never hesitated to go in and out during his childhood, he couldn't cross that threshold now.

He had been gazing for some time when Sun emerged from the house. Sung stepped aside into the shadow of the old royal foxglove tree next to the vegetable garden and watched. Sun came through the gate and lightly descended the steps from the yard, which lay on a slope. She gazed at the moon for a while, then walked toward the foxglove tree, and was startled to encounter Sung. Her heart beat faster, and not only from surprise.

"It's me, Sung," he said, stepping from the tree's shadow.

"Oh," she said, greeting him with a slight bow. "But what are you doing here? I heard that today's the tamping day for your house." She spoke more cordially than a few days earlier, when she had met him at the well.

"All the villagers came, but you weren't there, so I left to find you," Sung explained, clasping his hands and speaking in a sincere tone. "Everyone on earth might be gathered together, but without you, the world would be so empty . . ."

As his voice trailed off, Sun bowed once again. "Nice to hear that," she said.

"To live in this village, to live here my whole life, that's why I left Seoul and came here. It's also why I'm building a house for myself. But not because this village is my home. It's only my home village on official documents. I don't really have a home, and this place still holds such bad memories for me, but I've decided to spend the rest of my life here. Do you know why?" His eyes bright with fervor, Sung gazed at Sun's bowed head, her hair so long uncared for.

2-33

Sun remained silent, unresponsive. She understood what Sung was saying, but knowing that he was married to another woman, she wondered what he really meant.

Troubled by her silence, Sung asked her again, "Do you know why I came back?"

"How can I know? For the villagers, I suppose." A sudden sound startled Sun, and she glanced back, but it was only her dog, which had woken up and come out to find her. It barked a couple of times at Sung, a stranger, but stopped at a wave of Sun's hand and rubbed its nose against her skirt. The dog was a special Korean species, the kind with a long, gentle face and large eyes.

"Yes, I also came back for the villagers' sake. But if you weren't here, I might not have come. What's the point of building a house?" asked Sung, revealing his heart.

"Your wife will surely follow you here, but if you offer any work for wages, I'll do it," said Sun. She bowed one more time before retreating to her house with the dog.

Grief-stricken, Sung returned to his house property, where the work was ongoing. People were still in a convivial mood, shouting, "*Aha uhu tam tamp.*" But Sung no longer heard the sound. He felt as if his ears, eyes, and other senses had shut down. His head and heart seemed shut off as well. But he assumed a pretense of cheerfulness to make the people working so hard for him feel comfortable.

Over the following day or two, the cornerstone was laid, the pillars set, crossbeams erected, and rafters raised. Using thin, round trees as lumber made the work easier, and thatching the roof with straw and mud was also easy. Rooms were constructed, and the floor was laid. From the mountain came brick-sized rocks used uncut to make an embankment against the riverward slope, a job completed in a single day. Doors, both regular and sliding, were bought in the market and fitted into the doorframes. An outhouse was arranged simply by setting up a reed fence as a blind and positioning two large stones either side a narrow trench for squatting upon. Paths to the village and river were quickly made and paved with stones. Papering the walls and laying linoleum in the rooms were done in two days. Within two weeks of the tamping festivities, Sung's home was completed. Even the wall surrounding the house had been finished. It was constructed of mats bound together by interlacing long bush clover and oak tree branches. That took three days, done leisurely during smoking times after dinner. Even a well was dug. Two rooms, a floor, a kitchen, a shed, a platform for crockery, a well, the wall, the front yard, and the spacious backyard—all this was accomplished for under two hundred won.

"It looks like the office of a district head," people said, praising the neatness of the house and envying Sung. After disinfecting his belongings of bedbugs, he moved into the new house on the last day of July. The floor smelt of wood, and the rooms of oil. Only past midnight did the people head for home, leaving him alone. Sitting by himself in a room, his mind blank, he began to reflect on times past and times to come. His thoughts were interrupted by the sound of insects, and the insects by his thoughts. He felt proud that he had managed to have his own house built just five years after losing his parents and everything else. At the same time, he detested himself for getting into a marriage that had failed within a year and for desiring a woman that he shouldn't desire. He also felt physically and mentally drained from the work taken on to help the farmers. Though he had barely started, he worried that it was beyond his capacity, and he felt at a loss for how to proceed. The clamor of insects was incessant as rain, and his jumbled thoughts buzzed just as loudly. Unable to sleep at all that night, he remained restless. At times sitting up, at times lying down, sometimes stepping outside, only to come back in, Sung stayed awake that whole night after moving in. Such restlessness seemed a portent for his life.

2-34

Much lay heavy on Sung's mind. Building a house and helping the sick among the villagers was one sort of burden, but there were more. He regretted the decision to leave his wife in Seoul, but also felt anxious for Sun through his resurgent love. Anxiety and relentlessness afflicted him in his unsettled life and work. He felt misunderstood by the villagers, even infuriated by some of them who at times obstructed and hindered his work out of ridicule and malice. For all these worries, Sung had become completely exhausted, physically and mentally. Despite his weariness and constant desire to lie down, he couldn't sleep when he stretched out to rest. He sometimes doubted his decision. But he braced himself by force of will and endured everything by thinking of Mr. Han.

From among the sick, only one person died. The rest recovered, but these now looked pale as ghosts, scarcely skin and bones, whenever they came to visit him. As promised, Dr. Lee returned every third day for two weeks to treat the sick, but he kept his promise mostly from a desire to see Yu Sun. After visiting the sick, he would roam the village, hoping to catch a glimpse of her before leaving.

During this time, Sung had learned how to treat typhoid fever. He knew to avoid medicine for reducing the fever, but he also knew better than to induce excessive sweating. Medicine should only be used for digestion or strengthening the heart and against inordinate thirst. He knew to sterilize urine and feces, to feed patients rice water fortified with vitamins, and to be alert to intestinal bleeding. He knew the necessity of rest, of being alert to various dangers, and of a number of other things. He learned all this from doing, not from study, even how to give enemas and shots. He had about the same level of knowledge as a practical nurse.

Family members of a sick person would rush to Sung in their fear even deep at night. He would in turn hurry to the patient with simple medical instruments and medicine kept ready at home. If the patient was in critical condition, he would sometimes even stay overnight beside the patient. Things like that had worn on his own health severely.

Around the time when the other patients were almost

recovering, Sun's aunt, a widow staying at Mr. Yu's, got sick. Being sickly for a while, she eventually came down with a high fever. In Sung's opinion, she had contracted typhoid.

Mr. Yu himself had diagnosed it and treated her with Korean traditional medicine, to no effect. Meanwhile, Mr. Yu himself had gotten the fever and had taken to bed. Around the same time, Sun's older brother, a man leading a dissipated life, was arrested in the district town for beating up Mr. Hwang to avenge the violence against his sister. This news burdened Mr. Yu with more worries, because his grandfather's annual memorial service was also coming up.

Mr. Yu called for his daughter-in-law, who was staying in her parents' place, to remind her of the service. She didn't come, pleading the excuse of being sick. She had been ill-treated by her husband, and knowing that his family had nothing to eat, she had run away to her better-off parents six months earlier and never come back. The memorial day for Mr. Yu's highly respected grandfather was the most important event in the affairs of his family. Learning that his daughter-in-law would not come for the service, Mr. Yu fell into a fury and loudly cursed her, but he went ahead with the ritual. Mr. Yu had always secretly made a crock of rice wine in his shed to use on the occasion, for he insisted on making his own privately rather than buying an inferior product. Still feverish, he got up, brought out the crock, and prepared the clear rice wine for the service. He then ordered Sun to set up the ritual table arranged with food. His eyes were bloodshot, and his body was weak and unstable.

He hastily and nervously went to the room where his sick sister was lying and looked into her face. "If it's not too bad today, you should get up and help. Sun alone won't know what to do, you know." That was an unreasonable demand, but he considered the ritual important enough for any sacrifice.

2-35

When Sung came to Mr. Yu's place after dinner, Yu was sitting in fresh clothes with hair combed, face washed, and the headband known as a *manggeon* on his head, while Sun was busy popping in and out of the kitchen, also in clean outfit.

"What's the matter? Why are you up?" Sung asked, surprised at the sight of Mr. Yu.

"Today is memorial day for my grandfather," Mr. Yu responded, his shaking hands busy at his calves tying on *haengjeon*, the ritual pads that go between ankle and knee.

Sung took his wrist and felt for the pulse. Although an old man, Yu's pulse was beating too rapidly for Sung to count. Kneeling before Yu, Sung spoke with urgency. "The night air and this activity will further harm your health. You must lie down!"

"Oh no, I can't. In my house, nobody stays in bed on a memorial day. Unless I pass out, I have to conduct the service as long as my mind is alert."

Confronted by Mr. Yu's passionate devotion and powerful will, Sung had no heart to rebuke him.

"Oh, no, you shouldn't come out, too!" Sun cried out. At Sun's voice, Sung looked into the yard. There was Sun's aunt stumbling in the moonlight as Sun rushed to her side. Sung knew that she had a high fever, over 39 degrees. He watched her take a few steps toward the kitchen, then fall holding Sun's shoulder.

Mr. Yu looked out the window and clucked his tongue. "Isn't she younger than me?"

Sung rushed to support the suffering woman, helping her into the house. "I should set the table," she murmured, but without energy, letting herself collapse in his arms before passing out.

Sung carried her and laid her back in her bed. Her body was burning with fever. "Cold water and a towel, please," Sung told Sun.

"Is it serious?" Mr. Yu asked loudly from the other end of the veranda.

"Yes, very bad," Sung replied.

"She should stay in bed, then," said Mr. Yu. "Sun can do the preparation." He coughed up phlegm.

"She's really sick," Sung said to Sun as she returned with water and towel. "Your father is also quite sick. We're in big trouble."

"What should we do?" she asked, bursting into tears.

"You should ask some relative to come."

"Nobody will come," Sun said, controlling her emotions, and went into the kitchen.

Her aunt, delirious from suffering, cried out, "I want to go, too. I don't want!"

Sung sighed deeply. People in the village had become hard-hearted and wanted no contact with any typhoid-ridden house, whether of family or neighbor. Moreover, police orders blocking visits to typhus-ridden homes offered a good excuse for the heartlessness of modern times. Sung left Mr. Yu's place and went to ask Han-gap's mother for help. She had been like a nurse helping the sick suffering from typhoid, visiting them in their homes. She fed them rice soup, washed their clothes, and helped the women relieve themselves. Sung asked her to nurse Sun's aunt.

Mr. Yu remained on his knees conducting the service up to the point where the door is temporarily closed as part of the ritual. During that time, he went out to the yard and looked up at the sky once before fainting. Sung carried him into a room, then finished the rest of the ritual for him.

2-36

Mr. Yu recovered consciousness but was seriously ill. Sitting up for the memorial ritual's entire preparation and procedure had severely weakened him. His sister's condition was even worse, for she had not yet regained consciousness.

As soon as the sun rose, Sung sent someone from the village for Dr. Lee. Around noon, the doctor came. After tending to the sick, he told Sung that both were in serious condition, especially Sun's aunt.

Mr. Yu asked the doctor, "Am I going to die?"

"Don't worry," the doctor assured him, responding with the usual tone adopted by doctors speaking to patients.

"I'm an old man and can die, but what about my sister, is she very ill?" He seemed intent on preserving his dignity even in such dire circumstances.

"She looks quite unwell, but may be all right," replied the doctor, speaking in a friendly manner and trying to comfort the old man.

"Please do something for her, she shouldn't die," implored Mr. Yu, though he scarcely had energy to speak. "If she and I both die, who will take care of my daughter, a young child? My son's now in prison and can't help. We're not wealthy enough to pay you well, but please, doctor, save my sister at least." Mr. Yu then closed his eyes, but the tears seeped out anyway.

"I'll do my best," said the doctor. He often glanced to the yard in expectation, obviously looking for Sun.

After a while, Mr. Yu turned his head toward the window and called Sun. His voice seemed drawn from far down inside, scarcely loud enough to reach Sun's ear in the other room. But she heard and responded, "Yes, Father," before hurrying from her room and approaching his window to bow her head and say, "Father, I'm here." Her face was tired from lack of sleep, but that made her even more beautiful.

"Warm the alcohol left over from the ritual to serve the guests. They wouldn't like to eat at a patient's house, but alcohol should be all right. Fruit should also be fine, nothing else, no cooked food. It's not proper to serve cooked food to guests at a patient's house. Do you understand?"

"Yes, I understand," Sun replied and went away. Dr. Lee's eyes followed her movements from shed to yard, from yard to kitchen. Some five minutes later, when Sun brought in a portable table with alcohol and fruit, he observed her openly, his mouth agape and revealing many gold teeth. Sun placed the table between the doctor and Sung, straightened her father's covers, and went out holding her dress so that it didn't flutter.

Sung lifted the kettle and poured the amber rice wine in a brass cup placed upon an old-fashioned high saucer. As he offered this, the doctor initially demurred, saying, "You drink first," but accepted it at Sung's insistence. He took a sip and smacked his lips. After a couple more sips, he smacked them again before gulping it all down. He seemed to like the drink. "It's very good," he praised, "better than sake."

"It's not sour?" asked Mr. Yu, satisfied.

"It's excellent," the doctor said. "I've never had anything like this. Where did you buy it?"

"Yesterday was my grandfather's memorial day. For a frugal household like ours, the small service isn't worth the permission required for making rice wine, so I make a little secretly once a year for ceremony," Mr. Yu explained and closed his eyes.

2-37

"Your daughter is ready for marriage," observed the doctor, finally broaching the topic after three cups of wine.

"Oh, she's still young," said Mr. Yu. The image of his lovely daughter rose in his mind, but he frowned as if from a headache.

"She's quite good-looking," said the doctor, looking to the yard in search of Sun. She was nowhere to be seen.

"She's had little education," said Mr. Yu, coughing and swallowing phlegm. His throat rose and fell.

"Would you give me your daughter's hand? She wouldn't live in luxury, but she wouldn't have a hard life either, I assure you." The doctor spoke openly. He worried that he might sound too bold, but there was no time to lose because the old man might not live another day.

At the doctor's request, Mr. Yu opened his eyes and gazed at him for a while without expression. He seemed to be evaluating the man's suitability as a son-in-law. With a groan, he tried to sit up and face the man more directly. "Are you not yet married?" he asked.

"Actually, I've been married."

"Oh, you're widowed?"

"Not exactly."

"You mean you're divorced?" Mr. Yu's eyes opened wide.

"Not yet. But if I found a good woman, I wouldn't mind getting divorced. Even if I didn't get a divorce, your daughter would have her own household, so it doesn't really matter, does it?" the doctor ventured, smiling shyly.

"You mean you'd take my daughter as a concubine?" Mr. Yu's voice rose to a high, shaky pitch.

"I'd treat her as a wife, so she wouldn't be a concubine, would she? I'd see that you're also well taken care of, with a lump sum or a monthly arrangement, whichever you like, and . . ."

Interrupting the doctor, Mr. Yu abruptly sat up with unexpected energy and cried out in rage, "You reprobate! You vile creature! Offering to buy my daughter as your concubine? Isn't that what you're saying? Get out, you scoundrel! Leave now! Curse you!" Mr. Yu paused, laboring for breath. "Shameless scoundrel! I'll live till my daughter has you and your wife as servants. You brazen scoundrel!" He grasped at his pillow, intent on throwing it at the man, but his boney fingers were nearly too weak to move.

"What did you call me? A scoundrel?" The doctor sprang up, yelling wildly, "Old man, don't you know what you're risking? If you weren't sick, I could have you thrown in prison."

"How insolent you are!" cried Sung, rising to Mr. Yu's defense. He grabbed the doctor's arm and hustled him to the veranda. "Talking back like that to an elder!" The doctor, off balance, would have fallen had Sung not gripped him more firmly.

Sun and Han-gap's mother rushed out together and stood nearby, trembling with anxiety.

At the force of Sung's grip and dignity, the doctor grew fearful. He snatched his bag without a word, slipped on his shoes without tying them, and hurried from the veranda. Only safely beyond the gate did he venture to mutter, "Just you wait . . ."

After the doctor was gone, Sung returned to the room and helped Mr. Yu lie back down. The old man's body was as stiff as a long-dead corpse. Sun knelt at his pillow and softly cried out, "Father, Father."

2-38

Less than an hour after the doctor had left, two policemen came to search Mr. Yu's house. They confiscated what remained of the rice wine and nailed a wooden sign to the gate warning, "Quarantined: Residents with Typhoid Fever." Confronting Sung, they demanded, "What are you doing here?" and ordered him to leave.

"There's nobody but me to care for the sick," he replied, explaining that he had been inoculated, and he requested permission to stay.

Sometime after midnight, Mr. Yu passed away, but he regained consciousness before dying and told Sung, "When I die, please take my daughter under your wing and find her a husband." He turned to Sun and confirmed his words. "When I die, trust Sung as your elder brother, and marry the man he chooses."

Mr. Yu didn't trust his own son. Even if he were someday

released from prison, he was hardly the man to be entrusted with his sister's welfare. Mr. Yu despaired at foreseeing the Yu family's decline with his death and inwardly mourned that he had failed his ancestors. But he knew that revealing sadness was improper, so he suppressed all his pain and grief. In this abject state, Mr. Yu breathed his last, attended by his daughter and Sung but without son, daughter-in-law, or grandchild. On his burial date four days later, Sun's aunt hanged herself with the strap from her *hanbok*.

The daughter-in-law, her hair let down in mourning, came riding in the special palanquin reserved for close relatives of the dead, but left immediately after the funeral service. She excused herself for having to nurse her baby, whom she had left at her parents' house.

Sung saw to all the funeral procedures by himself and even paid for the service. Creditors afterwards confiscated the house, as the Yu family went down completely.

Mr. Yu's son Jeong-geun was the legal heir, and his agreement was needed for disposing of the household's few goods. The trial concerning Han-gap's assault on Mr. Hwang was near, however, so Sung planned to visit Jeong-geun in prison to resolve the Yu family's legal issue during a break from conducting Han-gap's defense. Placing Sun under the care of Han-gap's mother and allowing both to stay together in a room of his new home, Sung headed for court.

Only a few people were in attendance at the trial. The prosecutor demanded six months imprisonment for Maeng Han-gap as the main culprit, charging him with assault and obstruction of official duty. Three months were demanded for each of the seven remaining individuals. The accused other than Maeng denied assaulting Mr. Hwang.

Sung sat dressed as an attorney and kept a pencil ready in one hand for taking occasional notes as he listened to the prosecutor's summation. He stood when his turn came and began the defense by emphasizing that the accused were usually good people. He explained what had sparked the incident and how it had run its course. Mr. Hwang had grabbed Yu Sun's hand and slapped her face. Maeng had grasped hold of Hwang's arm only to stop the violent abuse. Hwang in turn assaulted Maeng and bloodied his nose. That blood dripped onto the back of Hwang's shirt and stained it as Maeng defended himself by pushing Hwang down face first. Sung then told of his unexpected encounter with Mr. Hwang at Dr. Lee's office. Although Hwang was supposedly undergoing two weeks' treatment for bruises, he was found drinking, gossiping, and carousing with a *gisaeng*. Concerning Yu Sun, Hwang had even been overheard admitting to the *gisaeng*, "Hey, I was attacked before I had a chance to kiss her! I just had time to grab her wrist!" Sung added that the police chief acknowledged placing more trust in government officials than farmers. Sung wrapped up his defense by insisting that the accused were without guilt. He called for the court to summon as witnesses Mr. Hwang, Dr. Lee, the *gisaeng* Choe Gang-wol, and the farmer who had witnessed everything at the doctor's office.

2-39

The judge appeared to listen carefully to Sung's defense, and sometimes made notes. He declined the request to summon witnesses but declared that he would need more time to consider his judgment. He then adjourned the court. The judge had apparently decided to give Sung's defense his generous consideration.

No sooner had the courtroom excitement faded than Sung felt a great aching pain throughout his body. He barely managed a meeting with the imprisoned Jeong-geun for authorization to deal with Mr. Yu's estate before rushing to catch the evening bus back to Salyeoul.

Seeing his return, the villagers, especially those with jailed sons, gathered around for news. Barking dogs soon alerted Sun and Han-gap's mother, who rushed out to find Sung walking home on the hillside between the village and his house. Han-gap's mother took his hand and asked, "How's my son doing?" She hardly noticed that his hand felt hot.

"He's fine," replied Sung, barely audible. He felt dizzy.

"How about Sun's brother?" asked Han-gap's mother, speaking for Sun.

"I met Jeong-geun, and he's fine. They're all fine." Arriving home, Sung sat down at the edge of the veranda to untie his shoes.

About ten or more people who wanted to hear details of their sons or husbands had followed Sung and were now gathered at his house. "Are they coming home soon?" someone asked.

"The judgment hasn't yet been announced."

While the others were talking, Sun went into Sung's room to prepare his bed, lighting a lamp and arranging the mosquito net. Sun instinctively noticed that Sung was not well. She straightened the pillow and returned to the veranda.

"Please get me a cup of cold water," said Sung and went into the room, where he collapsed onto the bed without taking off his suit. He started groaning and began to slip into unconsciousness.

"Are you sick?" Han-gap's mother finally noticed clearly that he was unwell. She touched his brow and was surprised to find it so hot. "You should eat something. Should I make some rice soup?"

Sung didn't answer, having caught typhoid at last. He regained consciousness the next morning, but fell into delirium by evening. Whenever he groaned in delirium about the pain in his arms and legs, Sun and Han-gap's mother massaged him in turn, and whenever he complained of headache, they took turns cooling his fever by applying wet towels to his brow. They cared for him like mother and sister. If he woke in the early morning around three or four, he discovered Han-gap's mother or Sun sitting beside him. They would moisten his dry, darkened lips, trickling water into his mouth with a spoon.

Sun knew that he had fallen ill from overtaxing himself in helping the villagers and caring for her father and aunt without regard to his own health. Moreover, he had further exhausted himself going several days without sleep during the funeral services for her father and aunt, and he had served as defense attorney for a few days at court. She therefore felt a responsibility to save Sung even if she had to sacrifice herself.

2-40

Sung didn't recover for more than ten days. During this time, and indeed ever since he had left Seoul, Jeong-seon spent her days holed up at home wailing and raging over her husband's absence. She was too ashamed to see her father or friends, for she partly admitted her fault, but she also resented Sung for leaving her and not letting her know his whereabouts even after several months.

During this period, Gap-jin sometimes dropped by and asked, "Hasn't Sung come back yet?" Or he would drop a sarcastic line. "A country boy like him must have run back off to the countryside."

Jeong-seon had also considered this possibility, thinking of the country girl Yu Sun. But she pushed the thought aside until she happened to read one day in a newspaper of Sung defending farmers in a district court and realized that things were as Gap-jin had suggested. Sung really had gone off to his home village in the country. She felt her jealousy over Sun and animosity against Sung flare up inside. Buying some wine, she drank a whole bottle and thought in her drunken anger that she would even be willing to lie in Gap-jin's arms if he were there. But he didn't come to visit that night, fortunately.

One morning, a letter was delivered to Jeong-seon. The writing looked somewhat familiar, and she made out Yu Sun's name on the envelope. Exploding from an unstable mixture of jealousy and displeasure, Jeong-seon cast it to the floor and cried, "What's this? Damn her!"

But curious about its contents, she opened the letter. It was written in pen this time, not pencil:

> Mr. Heo is seriously ill, and you should come see him. He did a lot to cure the poor people in the village and did other things for them, too. Even when he was in weak health, he stayed up the whole night taking care of my ill father and aunt. After they died, he had to go straight to court in a state of exhaustion. Since getting back, he's suffered high fever and delirium every day. I considered writing earlier, but didn't for fear the news might shock you. I think the time has now come to inform you.
>
> Mr. Heo calls your name in his delirium. He suddenly opens his eyes to look for you, calling out, "Jeong-seon," before closing them again disappointed. It's hard to watch him in this state. Please come as soon as you get this letter. Bring a good doctor with you.
>
> I'm doing my best to care for him because he did so much for me and my family. But I'm an ignorant person, so I hope you come soon.
>
> Sincerely,
> Yu Sun

As she read the letter, Jeong-seon's jealousy and displeasure vanished, and her pure soul of hidden love and sympathy emerged. "Ah," she thought, "my husband went away to work for the country people he's always talked about. He still loves me. Yu Sun isn't a malicious woman trying to seduce him."

"Everything's my fault," she decided. "I'm the one to blame.

I'll go to you soon, I will. I'll go take care of you." Jeong-seon, filled with love for her husband, began to prepare for leaving on the evening train. "Oh, how much quicker it'd be to fly than take a train," she thought impatiently.

2-41

The first thing Jeong-seon did was call her father.

"Father, it's me, Jeong-seon. Yes. Sung is seriously ill in his home village, and I need to get him a doctor. Yes, right. I'm leaving on the evening train. Could you please find a doctor for me? Yes, I have enough money. No, you don't need to come. Yes, I'll drop by before leaving." Such were her words over the phone.

Mr. Yun was surprised by the news, but also gratified. He had worried that Sung and his daughter might separate, but now learned that affection yet remained. He considered even the possibility of widowhood for his daughter preferable to her being divorced, kicked out of Sung's household.

That evening, Jeong-seon stood on the platform of Namdaemun Train Station, being seen off by her younger siblings. Dr. Gwak was there to accompany her. Mr. Yun had paid him well and even arranged a nurse to go along. Three people thus waited to board the Bongcheon train, scheduled for 10:40.

When they climbed aboard and the train started moving, Jeong-seon stood at the door to her car, waving good-bye to her siblings until they could no longer be seen. She was wearing a traditional jacket of Chinese silk that looked too light for the autumn weather and through which her skin was visible, a voile skirt with blue circular patterns, and lacquered leather shoes. Her hair was so teased up at the whorl of its parting that her chignon scarcely drew attention. She wore glasses with a golden frame and looked like a student, not a married woman. Her skin shone under the electric light like beautiful amber, as though to reveal lovely bones through its near transparency, scarcely obscured by the thin silk jacket. The way the short grey skirt fluttered about her straight legs clad in amber-toned stockings was utterly flattering.

To travel on a train was an adventure for Jeong-seon, who had rarely ever left her home. Even on the Gyeongui line, she had gone only as far as Gaeseong, so she now felt as if she were heading into a foreign country. And she was on the way to her sick husband!

As she headed for her seat, she heard someone call out, "Oh, Mrs. Heo!" She turned and saw with surprise Dr. Lee Geon-yeong holding out his hand to greet her, inquiring, "Where are you off to?"

Jeong-seon smiled unwillingly and stretched out her hand. Shaking it, Dr. Lee said, "Mrs. Heo, this is Miss Choe, Choe Yeong-ja. She graduated from Nara Women's College of Education in Japan and has started her new post at an eminent high school in Seoul." Dr. Lee turned to Choe and looked into her eyes, seemingly with affection.

"I'm Choe Yeong-ja," she said to Jeong-seon, bowing in the Japanese way.

"Oh, I'm Yun Jeong-seon," she replied, and bowed her head lightly in a Western way.

"Mrs. Yun is the wife of lawyer Heo. She was the best and most beautiful student of Ewha College," Lee said, his facial muscles twitching.

Jeong-seon looked at them, wondering how long they had been together. After jilting Shim Sun-rye, Dr. Lee had soon gone after two girls of the same school simultaneously. He had completely lost credibility and honor among Ewha students, as rumors of him went around, and now he was chasing women who had studied in Japan. Miss Choe was one of those women, and Lee was probably seducing her on this trip, Jeong-seon surmised.

2-42

"By the way, are you traveling alone?" asked Lee, offering a seat.

"Oh, I'm traveling with a doctor."

"A doctor!" Dr. Lee imagined Jeong-seon running off with the doctor as a lover after losing her husband.

"My husband is sick in his home village, so I'm taking a doctor to see him," she said, greatly satisfied at being able to state that she was underway to her husband.

"Who? Mr. Heo?" Lee was again surprised.

"Yes. He's given up his job as lawyer to live in the countryside and help farmers." Jeong-seon was happy at being able to use this chance encounter to provide an excuse for her husband's absence from Seoul, helped by what Yu Sun had written in her letter. Unpleasant rumors had been going around concerning Sung's disappearance. She particularly detested one scandalous rumor whispering that Sung left her after discovering her in an intimate relationship with Gap-jin.

"Oh, that's admirable work," Dr. Lee remarked. He thought of his own earlier decision to work for farmers and was overwhelmed with emotion at how everything had turned out differently than expected. The entire year after returning to Korea, he had done nothing but chase skirts, enjoying women's lips and bodies. He had lost his reputation in both church and academy and could nowhere land a university job, but enough women still remained with desire to be loved and kissed by him. Women in the church recognized him for the philanderer that he was, but other women were yet willing to be seduced by a man of good looks, impeccable words, and a doctor title. Moreover, outside the church community, he was a perfectly new man among women, and of these women, Miss Choe was the one with the most wealth and cultivation. Dr. Lee couldn't expect a prosperous life on a salary in Korea, so he intended to marry the daughter of a well-off fam-

ily and lead a comfortable life. His reason for earlier loving Shim
Sun-rye was her status as the daughter of a businessman, and his
reason for leaving her was his discovery that her family was not
well-off. Only a woman of beauty and wealth was qualified to become Dr. Lee's wife. The church community offered too few with
those qualifications. He was even willing to marry a daughter of a
dishonored aristocratic family if the money were enough and the
daughter not too ugly. "Money is the important thing. Dishonor
in the family doesn't matter. Money is more important." That had
become Lee's philosophy of life. Miss Choe was the daughter of
a family that traded in strong drink, and her father had obtained
a government position in one of the provinces. She was not a
woman of beauty whom Lee would find attractive without first
having had a few stiff drinks.

"Why do parents matter? She herself is important." Or so Dr.
Lee would boast among old friends opposed to his dating her. Of
actual importance, though, was not Miss Choe herself but her
father's wealth.

Jeong-seon persuaded a reluctant Dr. Gwak to go to the sleeping car, while she remained alone in her seat. For a young woman
either to sleep alone in the sleeping car or to share that car with
an unrelated man was improper, in her opinion.

She observed Dr. Lee try to persuade Miss Choe to go to the
sleeping car, but the young woman refused, perhaps for the same
reason as Jeong-seon. Apparently embarrassed, Dr. Lee went to
the bathroom to wash and comb his hair, then returned to his
seat.

2-43

Jeong-seon dozed off for a moment, but woke again upon sensing the train stop. She was very tired from having been in an
agitated state the whole day since receiving Sun's letter. She saw

Dr. Lee walk to and fro, his red necktie flapping. The train had reached Gaeseong City. Jeong-seon looked out the window expecting to see acquaintances. Many people were walking about carrying baggage.

"Good bye," came the voice of a Western woman, a familiar voice at that. Jeong-seon turned her attention back inside the train to discover who was speaking English. The voice belonged to Mrs. Hall, a woman who had long taught at Ewha College and was now principal at a school in Pyeongyang. Koreans called her Mrs. Hall, but she had never actually married and so was really a Miss. Standing at the window nearest the door, she was bidding good-bye to the people who had come to see her off.

The train started to roll, and Miss Hall looked around for a seat, a small bag in her hand. Jeong-seon approached to help with the bag.

"Oh, Jeong-seon!" Miss Hall, happily surprised, took Jeong-seon's hand and patted her shoulder.

Dr. Lee, who didn't know Miss Hall, simply watched them from a couple of seats back.

Someone behind Miss Hall touched Jeong-seon's shoulder and exclaimed, "Jeong-seon!"

"Oh, Sun-rye, you're here, too," said Jeong-seon, grasping her hands.

"Where are you going, Jeong-seon?" asked Sun-rye, holding onto her hands and seeming very happy to see her.

At the name "Sun-rye," Dr. Lee turned red. Avoiding her face, he quickly turned his own toward the window beside his seat and pretended to be looking out. Miss Choe noticed Lee's startled reaction.

"Come this way," Jeong-seon said. "There are seats here." To prevent Sun-rye from noticing Lee, Jeong-seon linked an arm in hers and kept her close to block the view as they went to their seats. But Sun-rye noticed Lee from behind, and his back alone was enough for her to recognize him.

She froze, unable to move, and glimpsed Lee's face reflected in the window. It was the man who had left her for being less wealthy than expected, even after holding her so tightly and pressing his lips to hers. It was the man who had left in her heart a painful, burning scar that would never entirely heal in this life or even beyond. It was the man who had left a parched, aching sorrow in her, a woman who had never before known such sadness. It was the man who had left her to think every man a beast and a devil—her, a woman who had only ever thought good of people. Sun-rye had heard the rumors that Lee was chasing women, enjoying their lips and their flesh.

She would never have expected to see him here now.

Sun-rye hadn't gone out much since being forsaken by Lee. She was afraid of encountering him, utterly terrified at the thought of seeing him at all. Although she missed him deep in her heart, she feared seeing him, his face, his eyes, his lips, and his hands that had touched her body. She felt certain that upon encountering him, she would faint as if confronted by a ghost. Or falling into a frenzy, she would rip off his suit and strangle him with that blood-red necktie, bite off the tongue that spoke such seductively lovely lies, crush between her teeth those lips bruised blue from pressing so many women's lips, or slice off with a fine-honed blade those hands that had touched so many women's bodies.

2-44

Jeong-seon pulled Sun-rye to their seats, nearly having to carry her. Looking at her face now so pale, she whispered, "What's the point of looking at him? Just forget him. He seems to have seduced another woman, a Miss Choe. She studied in Japan and doesn't know his reputation. Anyway, she's got a job at some girls' high school. What a dirty skirt chaser he is!"

Sun-rye was not by nature a weak woman, but even the thought of Dr. Lee left her dizzy and close to fainting. She tried to brace herself against today's encounter but felt her head spin. She leaned on Jeong-seon's shoulder and closed her eyes, her only means of controlling the terrible pain.

Miss Hall, sitting across from Sun-rye, seemed to be quietly praying for a while. She had loved Sun-rye almost as a daughter while teaching at Ewha College and had actually called her a daughter. Miss Hall loved Sun-rye because she was innocent, quiet, and serious, but also wise and sensitive, the valued characteristics of a traditional Korean woman. Sun-rye had never spread word of her engagement with Dr. Lee, not even telling Miss Hall. When Miss Hall had otherwise learned of Sun-rye's deception by Dr. Lee, she had sought out Mr. Han to commiserate.

Having noticed Sun-rye's sudden reaction, Miss Hall finally asked, "Jeong-seon, is that man Dr. Lee?"

"Yes, that's right." Jeong-seon nodded.

Leaning slightly, Miss Hall glanced sideways in Lee's direction. She clasped her hands tightly as if to control some strong emotion, then murmured to herself.

For a while, the three remained silent.

"I can't ignore this," Miss Hall remarked. "I have to talk to Dr. Lee." She took off her hat and got up, walking over to Dr. Lee. "Are you Dr. Lee?" she asked.

Dr. Lee sprang from his seat.

"I am Miss Hall." She bowed her head briefly toward Miss Choe and sat down beside her. Dr. Lee had extended his hand, but Miss Hall ignored it. "Dr. Lee," she asked, "have you ever loved Shim Sun-rye?" Her tone was sharp as a knife edge.

"Well, yes, briefly. Somebody had introduced her to me," explained Dr. Lee, a little disconcerted. With Sun-rye sitting so close at hand, he was discouraged from employing his otherwise eloquent speech.

"I know what happened. Mr. Han trusted and loved you, and that's why he introduced Shim Sun-rye to you. You told Mr. Han you liked her and would marry her. That's why you and Sun-rye dated evenings, arm in arm like a married couple though not yet married, and you led her to believe that you would become her husband. But you abandoned Sun-rye for another woman—I know her very well, she was one of my students, though I won't say her name—a woman of wealthy family. You then went through another two or three women, leading them trust you like Sun-rye did. You now have Miss Choe." She turned to Miss Choe. "Excuse me please, Miss Choe. I know who you are, and that's why I'm saying all this in front of you." After this excuse to Miss Choe, she continued, her eyes fixed on Dr. Lee. "He wants your money, Miss Choe. It's not because he loves you. He loves women for their money. I know that. He now loves you, Miss Choe, because of your money. That ought not be so, but it is. God is surely watching you, Dr. Lee. You can deceive people, but not Almighty God. I love Sun-rye like a daughter. She's such a good woman, but she's now pining over you. Because she's so heartsick and unable to study, I'm taking her to Pyeongyang. She was afraid of seeing you in Seoul, so afraid that I'm taking her to my home. Repent, Dr. Lee. Trust God again and remember what Jesus taught." She then got up, intent on leaving without waiting for an answer.

2-45

Having stood up, Miss Hall glanced at Dr. Lee and Miss Choe before turning away. Dr. Lee's face was pale, his trembling lips purple. Miss Choe seemed to be crying, her head bowed, pressed against the window frame.

"It's a misunderstanding . . . a misunderstanding," Lee tried to say in English, but the words scarcely left his mouth.

"A misunderstanding?" said Miss Hall, who had been about to walk away. She turned around and stepped closer to Dr. Lee. Smiling at him, she said again, "A misunderstanding? You say I misunderstood you? That would be nice. I would like to believe you are not such a bad person. Dr. Lee, you are a gentleman, a Christian, and a man who ought to become a leader among Koreans. I don't want to believe you are such an ignoble person, a man who would steal the heart of someone's daughter, only to drop her. If I've misunderstood something, that would be nice. Could you tell Sun-rye and me what I've misunderstood?"

Dr. Lee hardly dared even glance up at Miss Hall. With a feeble voice, he merely repeated, "Madam, it's a misunderstanding."

"Just telling me it's a misunderstanding doesn't help. Now, I'm giving you one last chance to explain what was misunderstood, and if you don't use this opportunity, I'll know that you have nothing to explain." Miss Hall then returned to her seat.

Only a few people were in the second class car. Rumor had it that Manchuria was in tumult, with some disease going around, making for few travelers. Some of those passengers had already left for the sleeping car. Only a couple of people were present, other than Miss Hall, Jeong-seon, Sun-rye, and Dr. Lee with Miss Choe.

While Miss Hall had been talking to Dr. Lee, Jeong-seon tried to comfort Sun-rye. "Listen, just forget that guy," she advised. "He's a dog, not a man."

Sun-rye replied, "It's not so simple. I can't just forget him."

"Didn't you say you're afraid of him?"

"Yes, but what should I do? I can't forget him. I don't like people speaking ill of him," she admitted, hiding her face, though whether from crying or smiling was unclear. She was, in fact, trying to smile through her tears.

"You think of him in that way, expecting him to come back to you?"

"Naturally not, Jeong-seon, but still."

"If he came back to you, would you accept him?"

"If he came back, why not? I can't marry any other man now anyway."

"Why not? People even get divorced all the time these days. What's so wrong with you? You surely didn't let him have his way, did you? You're not deflowered, are you?"

"What's a virgin? I don't feel like one. I feel like his wife."

"What? You don't know the difference between a virgin and a married woman?"

"I don't know. But I don't feel like a virgin. My heart feels bound to his," said Sun-rye, crying.

At that moment, Miss Hall returned to her seat. Ignoring Sun-rye's tears, she looked out the window, but her own eyes were also wet. To change the subject, she asked Jeong-seon, "Where are you headed, Jeong-seon?" She had previously had no chance to ask that question because of Dr. Lee.

"My husband fell ill in the countryside, so I'm going to him with a doctor," Jeong-seon answered, suddenly realizing that her situation was much better than Sun-rye's.

2-46

After hearing about Sung's intentions, Sun-rye was impressed. "I wish I could do that, too," she said, and meant it sincerely.

"What are you saying?" Jeong-seon asked, wiping Sun-rye's tears away with a handkerchief and trying to brush the hair away from her face, like an older sister doting on her younger sister, or a mother on her daughter. "You think you can live in the countryside? Where urine and manure stink, and bedbugs and fleas swarm? Where people live in mud huts without wallpaper and linoleum or electric lights and telephones? Where you meet only ignorant country people all day long? How could you live there, you, a city girl who grew up in Seoul?" Jeong-seon laughed loudly, intending to cheer Sun-rye up.

"Why not?" replied Sun-rye. "I've heard that country people are simpler and nicer than Seoul people. I'd like to live in the countryside if I had some work there." She looked at her hands. Other than her own wash water, those hands had never touched dirty water. They had never held a poker, let alone a scythe or a hoe. Jeong-seon's hands were not much different. Their hands, if ever put to work, were used for nothing more laborious than handling utensils for mealtimes, scribbling with pencils at school, or playing the piano. White as facial powder and soft as the tip of a writing brush, such hands lacked any calluses or hangnails. They would be useful only as toys for men of the city. By contrast, the hands of country women, who produced crops, fruits, and textiles, were dark, rough, big, callused, and so tough that mosquitoes couldn't bite through or leeches suck.

Sun-rye could only compare her hands with those of her house servant, an old woman. A fortunate city woman wouldn't use her hands to earn a living. Such women earned their living with pretty faces, soft skin, and coquetry for men's favor. If a woman had these three things, she would secure for herself a pleasant life, a life so well nurtured and delicate, she would have to take medicine for her health and digestion, and her only duty would consist in being a toy for her husband. Such a life is indeed fortunate if such a fortune is good.

"What about you, Jeong-seon? Your husband's now working for farmers in the country, but you're staying alone in Seoul?" Sun-rye seemed to have recovered some vigor, enough at least to control her pain and sorrow.

"Yes. You think I can't be alone in Seoul?" asked Jeong-seon, unsure herself.

"Well, do you think you can?" Sun-rye laughed, but with a shade of sympathy.

Miss Hall was happy to see her laughing.

"Why not?" Jeong-seon protested, though herself unconvinced.

"We can wait and see," said Sun-rye, and laughed more heartedly.

Jeong-seon joined her in laughter, as did Miss Hall.

Early the next morning, still before sunrise, Jeong-seon arrived at her destination. Miss Hall and Sun-rye had gotten off the train in Pyeongang, and Dr. Lee seemed already to have left the train as well, for only Miss Choe, her eyes red from tears and sleeplessness, greeted Jeong-seon with embarrassed courtesy as the latter made ready to get off at her stop near Salyeoul. As Miss Choe bowed her head in the Japanese way, Jeong-seon asked, "Are you engaged to Dr. Lee?"

"No. My father wanted . . . but not yet." She blushed.

Jeong-seon didn't ask where Dr. Lee had gotten off. Apparently rejected by Miss Choe, he had probably left the train in Pyeongyang to hunt for the daughter of some wealthy family there. Or had he decided to follow Sun-rye, who had gotten off there with Miss Hall?

"I'm sorry to say this, but be careful with Dr. Lee. He's not a trustworthy man," warned Jeong-seon, getting off the train and waving back to her. She saw new tears flow from Miss Choe's eyes.

2-47

On the train station platform, a man from Salyeoul was waiting for her, alerted by the telegram that she had sent early the day before. He was watching passengers get off the second class wagon, and he approached Jeong-seon to ask, "Are you Mrs. Yun Jeong-seon from Seoul?"

Taking the bags from Jeong-seon and Dr. Gwak, he led them

from the station. A few more villagers were waiting outside. These were the men been arrested in the incident concerning Mr. Hwang but released after being found not guilty of assault in the first trial. Only Maeng Han-gap, the main defendant, had been found guilty and had received three months' imprisonment. He now was appealing the verdict. The other seven had not been found guilty of assault, though some were placed on probation. They knew that they owed their freedom to Sung's legal skills, so they were taking care of him and his household after their release.

Asked about Sung's condition by Jeong-seon and Dr. Gwak, they said that his illness was quite serious but not critical.

At Muneomi Pass, dozens of men and women were waiting to meet Jeong-seon. Since people had been released after the trial, the villagers had even more respect for Sung. They also felt strong sympathy for him because he had fallen ill in nursing the sick back to health when even their relatives feared to help. Except for a few proud men with money, the villagers all dropped by Sung's place daily to see him and provide food, firewood, and other necessities.

Jeong-seon was very surprised that so many villagers came to greet her. She wondered if they had come simply out of curiosity, but they seemed as glad at seeing her as if seeing a family member after long absence.

The villagers in fact felt awkward at first, as if encountering a foreigner, and didn't speak much to Jeong-seon, maintaining distance from her, but after noticing that she responded to questions, they felt more comfortable and opened up. An older woman even talked to her as if to a close family member, "Dear, you must be tired from spending a night on the train."

In the meantime, Jeong-seon looked around, trying to glimpse Yu Sun, but saw no young woman who fit her image of the woman.

"You should hurry now, not stand around here," an old man urged, and the people around made way for her to walk toward the village. On their way, a policeman came to stop them and ask Jeong-seon and Dr. Gwak a few questions.

As they approached the well with Dr. Gwak leading, Yu Sun was already coming toward them, but stopped and turned aside to the edge of the path to let Dr. Gwak pass by, as it was the custom for women. She then took a few steps but noticed Jeong-seon and stopped again, making herself unobtrusive.

"Sun, this is Sung's wife," a woman informed her.

Overhearing this, Jeong-seon took the opportunity to stop and turn around. She held out her hand and took Sun's, saying with a smile, "Are you Miss Yu Sun? I'm Yun Jeong-seon. Thank you for sending me the letter."

"Hello. Yes, I am Yu Sun," she responded, bowing her head as before a schoolteacher.

"She's been looking after Sung, showing more care than a family member would," said an old man standing nearby.

"Thank you very much," said Jeong-seon, bowing her head to express gratitude.

Yu Sun blushed.

2-48

As Jeong-seon and others passed the village on their way to Sung's house, a lot of people came out to meet her. Some worried over Sung's health and said, "He could have a good life, but he came to help us." Jeong-seon gradually began to understand what her husband's work and ambition were.

When she arrived, Dr. Gwak was already examining Sung, who had regained consciousness around this time. He had a fever of 39 degrees Celsius and some intestinal bloating that could be treated with an enema. The doctor explained all this to Jeong-seon after she entered the sickroom and saw her husband's suffering. His parched lips, his dark beard, his disheveled hair, hardly a face to look at.

Dr. Gwak moved away from his patient, making room for Jeong-seon. She sat beside her husband, took his hand in hers, and began to cry helplessly, her tears streaming down. Sung looked at her blankly, then tears flowed from his eyes. The two cried together but did not speak.

Two weeks later, Sung could walk in the yard supported by Jeong-seon. She took care of him with all her heart and strength, and even saw a beautiful side of her sick husband's character that she hadn't noticed before. Sung in turn saw the beautiful side of Jeong-seon's character.

"Let's go back to Seoul when you're well," said Jeong-seon one day as they were sitting by the Dalnae River in the late autumn light.

"Instead of going to Seoul, you can stay here with me." Sung hugged her waist with his arm, and she let herself be drawn to him, leaning against his body that had now recovered so much strength.

"Well, I'm not sure," she responded, undecided about staying in the country.

"You think the clear water of Dalnae River isn't as good as that dirty water in Cheonggye Stream?" asked Sung, looking into her face with affection.

"Naturally, Dalnae is better," she replied, smiling.

"And the fields and mountains? Or the air and the light? What Seoul has doesn't compare. A frail woman like you should live in a quiet place with clean air and bright light. Your brother passed away from a respiratory illness, didn't he? Let's stay here. Let's live with the farmers. If we try, this village can become like new, a place where people can live in comfort. The people here have better character than those arrogant city slickers. Eight out of ten

Koreans are farmers. That's sixteen million. The other four million just live off the farmers' labor. We've also lived so far thanks to the farmers' sweat. If we have any conscience, we should repay what we've received. Jeong-seon, don't even think of going back to Seoul, you hear me?"

Sung kissed her for the first time since their reunion, and she blushed as if kissed by a man for the first time. She looked around to see if anyone was nearby. There was nobody but a calf. Still too young for a ring through its nose, it alone was looking in their direction.

"If you want me to stay, I will," she said smiling into his face, which was less thin but still sickly.

2-49

Although Jeong-seon had promised to stay, her heart remained in Seoul. The city was not only where she had grown up but also home to several generations of her family. Yesan may have been her ancestral hometown, but the ancestors holding government office lived in Yesan only after retirement, spending most of their lives in Seoul. Jeong-seon had experienced country life only on summer vacations in Sambang and at Seokwang Temple. The countryside was like a foreign country, an alien land where savages lived, a barbarous country where people from Seoul could not survive, where women walked about barefoot, men visited other people's houses with their swarthy legs exposed, and children often stole things. She couldn't imagine truly living among such crude and ignorant people.

"But why are the people so ignorant? They're not so innocent, either. The children steal, and I'm afraid of them. I wonder how you could be from this village," Jeong-seon said, laughing. "Now, don't get upset. I know you don't like to hear people running down country folks!" She laughed again, carefully, and searched his face, wondering if she had been too harsh for a man recently recovered from a serious illness.

"Well," Sung gently replied, "some traits of country people are better than those of us city folk, some are worse. They're basically good people but have lived long under pressure from the upper class. In recent years, they haven't had enough food, so they've become hardhearted. You know who made them like that?" Sung gazed at Jeong-seon's pretty face and graceful body.

"Let's see now, who?" she said, playing the coquette in pretending to think.

"The *yangban*, the noble class did," replied Sung, his voice sharp. "Seoul *yangban*, country *yangban*. That class has destroyed Korea."

"You're attacking the nobility again," she observed, her tone and face sullen.

"Your family is high nobility. My ancestors were low nobility. But regardless whether high or low, it's all the nobility's fault," said Sung, but in a tone less sharp.

"All right, we can acknowledge that the nobility didn't govern the right way. They didn't lead the people properly, and that's why Korea's in such trouble now. But what about the people? Why didn't they revolt against it? Why didn't they push the nobility out and govern themselves?" Jeong-seon started attacking the commoners.

"That's because they didn't receive any education. They were kept ignorant and indoctrinated with Confucianism, especially the dogmas of Neo-Confucianism, which left them little better than slaves. Distinctions were enforced among upper, middle, and lower classes. Only members of the upper class, the *yangban*, were allowed to retain government positions. Those in the middle class, the *jungin*, were allowed to work only in technical areas, such as yin-yang theory, medical science, and mathematics. Lower class people, the *sangnom*, were allowed to take only the lowest government positions in the provinces or to take up farming, commerce, and manufacturing, and things were to be this way every generation. These three pursuits are not lowly in nature, but the *yangban* class defined them that way. The *yangban* focused on politics, but what they understood by politics was their own self-interest, as we'd now call it. They used their position to get wealth and power. They cared nothing about improving farming skills, nor about developing business and manufacturing. What about the country's defense? They ignored it, having interest only in their own careers and accumulating wealth. Some were concerned about the country, of course, but such people have been hard to find in our modern time. Since the nobility bears responsibility for conditions in the countryside today, they should pay for their mistakes. How about helping farmers as a representative of the nobility since you're from a noble family?" Sung suggested, laughing.

"You mean I'm representative of the high nobility, and you're of the low nobility?" Jeong-seon replied, and also laughed.

3-1

Sung recovered as the days passed by. Jeong-seon could finally share the bed with him the three days before she left for Seoul. They felt affection for each other like newlyweds. She asked him to accompany her to Seoul, but he refused. She took the early morning train, and for the first time since he had recovered, he walked to the station, not a short distance.

"Is it all right for you to walk so long?" Jeong-seon worried, repeating the question several times on their way to the station.

"I'm all right." Sung insisted, trying to sound confident, but cold sweat dripped from his brow, and more rolled down his back.

At the station, Han-gap's mother and Yu Sun, and more than ten villagers, men and women, were waiting to see her off.

"I will ask Father to sell our house and property and come back," Jeong-seon promised her husband, holding his hand, still cold from the lengthy illness. Tears welled up in her eyes and flowed down, and the skin around her nose, eyes, and mouth twitched. For some reason, she felt great sorrow.

As the train started moving, she tried to open the window and look out, but the double-framed window wouldn't open. She sat down on her seat and wept.

The past fifty days were like ten years for her. During that time, Sung's condition had been critical a couple of times, and they had experienced unnumbered conflicts because of their differences, emotionally and in their views. She had, however, managed to learn more about him through that experience. Sung had a firm aim, and his ambition in life involved all of Korea, different from hers, and he was an emotional person who tried not to let his emotions rule over him. Such were the things that she discovered about him. From that, she came to realize that he was not some foolish country bumpkin but someone deserving respect, a man with merits that she would have never imagined on her own. But she also came to see that he was not the sort of husband for whom she had wished. Her ideal husband was an average man of the upper class, selfish and thinking only of his wife. She probably didn't think in exactly these terms, but a deeper analysis of her heart would fit that description. Sung seemed to be a great man for others but not a good husband for her. She remembered their conversation by the Dalnae River.

"Do you think that you alone can save Korea?"

At her question, Sung had responded, "Well, how could I? I only try to save one village, Salyeoul. But I don't know if I'll be successful, either. I just try to do my best. There's nothing else I can do, is there?"

"Well, if you say so, but why waste your life on work even you're not sure of?" she protested. "Isn't that a foolish thing?"

"Probably you're right. It's likely a foolish thing to do. That's why crafty people wouldn't do that."

"Then why not," she tried to dissuade him, "use your talent? You could do good work for Koreans as a lawyer. You don't have to suffer in the countryside. You can earn good money and fame, and still do good work for people, can't you?"

"As a lawyer," Sung insisted, "I can't help starving farmers much. I can at most represent a rich family in a lawsuit concerning some sort of corruption. I'd rather help the poor farmer, writing official documents for them. It'd be very helpful for them if I could deal with the district office or police station in their stead, wouldn't it?"

3-2

Even to Jeong-seon's ear, one might say to her conscience, what Sung said sounded so true and so solemn as almost to be religious doctrine. She had actually learned about things like truth and justice at school. But who today, anywhere in world, would follow such old lessons about truth and justice? If Peter and Paul had been reborn, they would have stood by her side, she thought. Sung was surely a foolish dreamer. He was not a man who would be the sort of husband to whom she could entrust her life.

As the train ran further away from Sung, as it more closely approached Seoul, she felt him fading from her heart.

"The pleasure of life!" she thought. She felt this as almost a categorical imperative putting irresistible pressure upon her. Among family, relatives, and friends, nowhere could she find such a foolish dreamer like Sung as a model. She knew Mr. Han. She had even heard her distant uncle Han-eun often praise him as a great man. But what about the man himself? The face of a needy person, the shabby clothes. What if Sung should become like him? "No, no!" she protested inwardly. "I don't want to be his wife!" Mr. Han, a man over fifty, still lived in a rented place. He earned only about a hundred won a month as his salary. "Ah!" she felt disgusted just to imagine it. "Is that a proper life for a human being?"

After passing Shinchon Station and emerging from the tunnel, Jeong-seon saw spreading out before her eyes the great sea of Seoul's electric lights and felt as relieved as if she had leaped from hell into a bright paradise. Such happiness filled her heart.

The crowded Gyeongseong Station appeared, its taxis lining the street and waiting for customers. Off they would dash, their headlights bright like wide-open eyes, as soon as customers had climbed in.

That was life. Salyeoul, Dalnae, the thatched houses, farmers—they were like things of a distant country for her. The farmers seemed to be from a different world, people with whom she had nothing common. More than insignificant, they were even unpleasant for her.

"Oh, welcome Lady," said the old female servant, the nanny, the seamstress, and the young female servant Yu-wol, all four welcoming her home. "You have stayed so long away. How is our master now?" they asked. "Is he well recovered? Why didn't he return with you?"

Jeong-seon looked around her familiar home. She had wondered how they were keeping the house while she was off taking care of her husband although she had entrusted things to her nanny. She was so happy to see all the furniture in the room again— her standing closet, hanger closet, wardrobe, large looking glass, bedding closet, desk, and telephone. They made her happier than to see her husband. Wondering if everything remained as it was, she opened the closets and wardrobe before changing her clothes. In the wardrobe, she saw her clothes as well as her husband's. Finally, she felt tired and sat down on a chair at the desk in her husband's room used for reception. The room smelt of cigarettes, and in the ashtray on the desk were many cigarette butts.

Suspicious, she asked her servants, who had followed her, "Did somebody come into this room?"

"Mister Kim of Jaetgol sometimes visited," Yu-wol explained.

"Mister Kim of Jaetgol?" said Jeong-seon in surprise. "Why?"

"He'd just drop by. He'd ask if you'd returned and order us to open up the reception room. He'd then come in and stay here for a while before leaving," the old servant explained. She was a woman with a nice face, and good at talking.

"Sometimes, he brought his friends with him," said Yu-wol, sullen, "and wanted to have Chinese food delivered, or to have a table of drinks and snacks prepared. It was so tiresome."

3-3

"What're you talking about!" said the old servant, looking at Yu-wol sideways and delivering a rebuke. "He did that only one time. Not so often as you say!"

"Only one time, was it? Last time, they even stayed past midnight, acting crazy, or don't you remember?" Yu-wol said, glaring back at the old servant with a look of reproval.

Jeong-seon felt displeasure to hear that Gap-jin had come with friends to stay deep into the night when she and her husband were absent, and not just once but several times. She felt insulted.

That night, she lay down alone on the bed where she used to lie together with her husband. She tried to feel desire for this man who had chosen to remain in the country, but the more she tried, the further he seemed to drift away. Instead, the easy-going Gap-jin appeared in her mind, and she even felt an insuppressible urge for him.

Comparing Gap-jin with Sung, she realized that Sung was undoubtedly a man of character, more respectable than Gap-jin. But Sung was not a husband to satisfy her or any young woman who longed to be loved passionately and with sexual pleasure. Jeong-seon respected Sung but felt unfulfilled in her heart. That emptiness of her heart seemed in some way connected to Gap-jin. He might be a fun husband, she thought—at least in a sexual way. Jeong-seon perhaps inherited this strong sexual desire from her father, but she tried to rationalize her feelings, telling herself that any young woman would feel the same as she.

Her weariness from the trip as well as her many thoughts, imaginings, and even agonizings kept her long awake, and she thus fell asleep late and woke up late. She went to her parents' place that evening for dinner, and when she returned around nine in the evening, Yu-wol opened the gate to let her in and said,

"Lady, Mister Kim of Jaetgol has come again. He went into the main room and is reclining in there, waiting."

Hearing Jeong-seon's voice, Gap-jin came from the room to stand on the veranda, where he loudly pronounced, "Ah, finally, you're back. I've been waiting for you so long. I wondered if you'd also gone crazy like Sung and decided to live in the countryside. If that happened, it would be so sad, not only for the people of Seoul but also for all humankind. Worse, it would make me wail in despair." Like some character on the stage, Gap-jin spoke half-jokingly, half-seriously. Perhaps he was quite serious even though he was pretending to joke.

Jeong-seon looked displeased, bowed slightly to greet him, and went into the main room, leaving him behind on the veranda.

Feeling a bit embarrassed, he then asked in a polite tone, "Didn't Sung want to come home?"

"He didn't," responded Jeong-seon halfheartedly.

"Well, is it true that he's in love with a lowborn country girl? Did you find any evidence?" pursued Gap-jin, more encouraged.

"I don't know. Who knows?" she replied, still sullen.

"That fool, why on earth would he stay in the countryside unless he's bound there by the sweat of that country girl ... what's her name? Anyway, the crazy fellow! He's a real fool." Gap-jin then entered the main room, where Jeong-seon was sitting blankly, to pick up his hat and coat. He said, "I'm going. Sorry for bothering you." He then went back out and began putting his shoes on.

3-4

Watching an embarrassed Gap-jin preparing to leave, Jeong-seon felt sorry. She followed him to the veranda and asked in a soft tone, "Why leave so quickly?"

He stood abruptly up in the act of tying his laces and gazed at her blankly with a stunned face. "I'm leaving because you hate me."

"I hate you?" she said, smiling.

"Should I stay instead of leave?" He let his coat down onto the floor. Jeong-seon burst into laugher, as did the old servant and Yu-wol. Gap-jin stayed at the veranda's edge, and Jeong-seon didn't ask him to come up. "Well," he finally said, "what's the reason the fool didn't want to come back?" He spoke as if interested in Sung.

"Oh, he wants to work for farmers and wants me to join him." She sat down herself, leaning against the door.

More encouraged, he asked, "What's he do for farmers? Teach the dunces? What the hell's he thinking? These days, jobless people say 'Help the farmers! Help the farmers!' But what can they do? The world follows the market's rules. Let the bastards try, nothing'll change. It's all useless. Sung should be a lawyer instead. Does he want to be Gandhi? What a load of garbage! Being Gandhi's not easy, anyway. I hear he's fasting again. That'll get him released, but he'll soon be back in. It's ridiculous! And even three meals a day isn't enough for life's demands now. In and out of prison, fasting one day, at a spinning wheel the next. What's the point? Didn't Sung also work a spinning wheel? Like this, *bung, bung, bung*." He mimicked turning a wheel with his right hand and pulling threads with his left.

Jeong-seon burst into heartfelt laughter.

"Where did you see anyone work a spinning wheel, mister?" said the old servant, her plump body shaking with laughter.

Jeong-seon then turned solemn and asked, "What work does Korea now offer other than manual labor for farmers?" She tried to stand on her husband's side.

"You can work for wages," said Gap-jin, making a surprised face, as if it were so obvious.

"Earn wages and then what?" Jeong-seon's tone had changed into a jocular one.

"Visit bars and drink, as I do."

"What else?"

"There are many things to do. A man could seduce women or get opium from dealers if he likes, or buy some *indan* to refresh his mouth. Like this," he added, popping some into his mouth. Chatting in such a manner, he remained at Jeong-seon's place until around ten and then left.

After he had left, she suddenly felt again that inner emptiness. Gap-jin remained in her thoughts, making her suffer, as though she had taken a powerful love potion.

Her plan of selling the house and property to go back to her husband in Salyeoul grew harder to keep. She tried to resist the inner temptation, but hers was a powerless resistance, as if her body and heart, bound to an invisible rope, were being drawn more and more to Gap-jin.

3-5

At Jeong-seon's place, women gathered every evening for fun and chatting. They were mostly either former schoolmates or old friends. Some had jobs, but most had none deserving that label. Most of them were between twenty-three and thirty years old, though a few were in their mid-thirties. Some were married like Jeong-seon, but many were unmarried, and one or two were divorced.

They had no worries about food and were not busy, so Jeong-seon's house was a good place to gather for chatting and having fun. Jeong-seon, for her part, tried to forget her loneliness and agony through these gatherings. What they talked about in their meetings was merely idle chatter. The main topics were gossip and love stories, though occasionally also their views on work surfaced. In short, they were living out a sort of pseudo-religion, that variegated mixture of the erotic, the grotesque, and the nonsensical popularly known as "Ero-Gro-Nonsense" that had originated in Imperial Japan and had come to dominate even Korea's female intelligentsia.

Moral terms like patriotism and idealism, the substance of women's conversation ten years before, had long been tossed forever into the dustbin of history along with long skirts and *daenggi*, the traditional hair ribbon. Even Shim Sun-rye, who sometimes joined the gathering, would occasionally respond to the topic of Ero-Gro-Nonsense. This topic simply seemed more conducive to the modern mind. Or if that nonsense were like bacteria, then not only modern people generally but even the contemporary women of Korea, a place still a hinterland for the modern world, seemed to have lost power to resist.

The people mentioned in their gossip were teachers, doctors, journalists, bachelors, skirt chasers, concubines, and loose women, among others. They never talked about books or anything related to scholarship or the arts. As for the love stories that they related, these were entirely different from the words about "sacred love" of merely ten years earlier. What they discussed was the matter-of-fact love process from holding hands, hugging, kissing, and trysts to the living together of unmarried couples and the living separately of married couples, all of these unburdened of the ceremony and etiquette of Korea's earlier court society. The love relationships of the day were truly scientific and businesslike.

"Marriage?"

The gathered women would pout their mouths. For marriage, they wished only to find a rich, healthy, and humorous bachelor whose parents had died leaving property and whose name had some renown. Such a bridegroom, however, seemed as rare as the virtuous bride. That's why they couldn't marry. Or perhaps they even preferred not to marry so as to pursue various relationships with men, to experience different personalities and body types, and to find sources for the money spent on taxis and dinners. They found diverse if partial satisfaction from each man that way (though the same was true also for men). Getting just a piece here, a piece there, a crumb here, a crumb there from each man for their desire, Korean women of the day never sated the hunger of their hearts though they employed every artifice to advertise for love, like neon lights constantly flickering and moving. Until late in the night, they would wander in search of something, and as they fell into bed around one or two in the morning, they would find no sound sleep, but troubled dreams from bellies as unsettled as their cluttered hearts and minds on account of always eating so irregularly. After much restless tossing in the darkness, they would rise late that morning with bitter tongue, heavy eyes, dry lips, and unfulfilled yearning.

The women gathered at Jeong-seon's house were mostly those who led that kind of lifestyle.

3-6

The nail embedded in Sun-rye's heart seemed to be pressing deeper over time. Although not genuinely interested, she joined her friends as they gathered for fun and chats, and she tried to forget her pain. But whenever she heard them gossip about Dr. Lee, how he had chased such-and-such a woman or had gotten engaged, her heart whirled in agony. She tried to control herself, thinking her emotions inappropriate, but that was not easy. Whenever her heart was thrown into turmoil, she would lament her own bad character.

"If I truly love Doctor Lee, why can't I wish him happiness?" she would ask herself, struggling to overcome her feelings. A sentence that she found in a book only made her suffer even more: "Jealousy is ugly." She strove desperately to rid herself of this ugliness in her heart, yet realized how weak she was.

Whenever she felt forlorn sorrow deepen or spiteful jealousy burn, she would sit down at her piano to play arbitrarily and roughly, striking each key with great force. Such performances grew so habitual, she even composed a piece of music from them.

"I can't stand it anymore!" her mother finally cried. When her mother cried out this way in frustrated anger, Sun-rye laughed like a child. Ever after that, she would play until her mother again erupted, and would miss her reaction if she failed to cry, "I can't stand it anymore!"

One day at school, she heard some friends talking about Dr. Lee, and the topic was particularly unpleasant for her, so she went to the practice room for piano and played the piece of music composed out of her hopeless loving anger for him. Because the piano at the school was of better quality than the one at home, the sound was quite impressive. Knowing that her mother's reaction was not to be expected, she repeatedly played the same piece, totally absorbed in it, even moving her shoulders and body as she pounded the keys with great force.

As she was playing, the music room door suddenly opened. Caught by surprise, Sun-rye stopped and turned around. It was Miss Mary, the music teacher.

"Were you playing that piece, Sun-rye?" Miss Mary asked, looking down at her where she sat.

Embarrassed as if caught doing some wrong thing, Sun-rye blushed and bowed her head, admitting, "Yes."

Miss Mary approached Sun-rye, her heels making a tapping sound, and patted her on the shoulder. "My girl," she asked, "what is this piece of music? From which book have you learned it?" Miss Mary's gentle voice helped Sun-rye relax.

"Not from a book. I made it up myself." Sun-rye lifted up her eyes to look at Miss Mary.

"Don't worry," Miss Mary said, shaking her head. "I'm not criticizing you. The piece you've just played is very powerful and passionate. There are some parts that don't quite fit, that don't follow the rules, but the piece is overall 'very nice.'" She said "very nice" in English, and touched Sun-rye's chin to show affection for her, as though with a cute child. Sun-rye couldn't control the tears welling up. Quickly turning her head aside, she took a handkerchief from her sleeve and wiped away tears, pretending to blow her nose.

Miss Mary, her hand stretched over Sun-rye's shoulder, touched the girl's cheek, now wet with tears. With sorrow for Sun-rye, she bowed her head till her own cheek rested lightly upon the top of Sun-rye's head. "Sun-rye, my girl," she asked, "did I make you sad? I'm sorry. I didn't intend to."

3-7

Sun-rye was clearly not crying over being upset by Miss Mary, a teacher who loved her and whom she admired. Miss Mary was the teacher who best understood the dreams and worries of a young woman at a college teeming with marriageable women. Sun-rye had never talked to her about her inner conflict, nor had she ever done so with anyone else, but Miss Mary might have been able to surmise the reason for her sorrow through Miss Hall, the retired teacher who had earlier taken Sun-rye to Pyeongyang, for the two were good friends who had shared the same house in Seoul.

But what was the proximate cause of Sun-rye's tears, Miss Mary wondered. She had played the piano somewhat at random to forget her heartbreaking sorrow, and the fact that her playing had become a piece of music was already sad enough. To have it praised for its quality and beauty, however, must surely be what had filled her with such abrupt sorrow.

"You didn't make me sad, Miss Mary," said Sun-rye, trying to smile. "It's not because of you. I was thinking of something else . . ." Closing the keyboard cover, she stood up.

"Yes, I see . . . I see." Miss Mary took a pen from her breast pocket and, using a sheet on the piano, wrote down three titles in English: "An Angel's Lamentation," "The Morning Storm," and "Virgin's Sorrow." Showing them to Sun-rye, she asked, "This piece of music you've just played, what's it called?"

"It doesn't have a title. I played it just arbitrarily, it's not serious." Sun-rye smiled.

"I'll provide a title, then. Choose one from these three if you like."

Sun-rye took the sheet from her hand, and after studying the titles for a while, she underlined only the word "Sorrow."

"Sorrow, Sorrow," Miss Mary nodded. She patted Sun-rye's back lightly and left the room with the sheet.

A bit later, Sun-rye also left the room. The poplar leaves scattered across the lawn, along the road, and up onto the stone stairs of the campus were being rolled by the late autumn wind, rustling as they scattered. Students who had played tennis were walking back to their dormitories in the thin light of the setting sun, rackets in hand, hungry and restless.

Sun-rye passed through the gate and walked homeward. Her sorrow was now better dispersed, but her heavy heart still ached. She was intending to go home directly, but knowing that the hour was too early for dinner and wanting to have a chat to distract herself, decided to visit Jeong-seon.

"She's not home," Yu-wol told her.

"Where did she go?" asked Sun-rye.

"She went to watch the baseball game at Gyeongseong Stadium with Mr. Kim of Jaetgol," Yu-wol said. "Please come in," she added, preceding Sun-rye in and glancing at the clock. "She might be here soon." The wall clock in the main room showed six.

3-8

Sun-rye sat down on the edge of the veranda as Yu-wol invited her to wait for Jeong-seon. She let thoughts form and gather in her mind, like a sky giving way to burgeoning clouds. Who among her friends was happy? Even among the married ones? Jeong-seon herself was unhappy, as she told her friends. The married women who gathered at Jeong-seon's place were not all happy, or so their lives often seemed from what they told people of their circumstances. One was unhappy because her husband had no job, another because her husband possessed too little virility to provide a happy sexual relationship, or because a husband with sufficient money and health had too little education, or because a husband had everything but chased other women for the emptiness in his heart, or loved his wife less and less, or became stingy, or because the woman had a bad relationship with her in-laws, and so on. Everyone seemed unhappy for some reason.

"Does happiness belong only to a virgin, just a woman who hasn't known a man?" Sun-rye sighed.

At that moment, the phone rang. Yu-wol rushed to pick it up. "Where are you? Yes, Lady, I'm Yu-wol. Yes, yes, a visitor. Yes, oh, are you returning after dinner? Yes, Dr. Lee came around four, and he said he'll come back in the evening. Miss Shim is here waiting, yes," said Yu-wol, and was about to hand the receiver to Sun-rye, saying, "Here, you should talk to her."

"No, it's okay," Sun-rye said. "I'm fine. She can have dinner there. I'm going." Only then did the thought occur, "Oh, Jeong-seon is having dinner with Gap-jin after the game. Is it right for her, a married woman, to do that?" But she kept her thoughts to herself and headed for the gate, only repeating, "I'm going."

She was fearful of encountering Dr. Lee, who was supposed to come back that evening, but she also found herself wondering, "Why is Dr. Lee visiting Jeong-seon? Does he now want to seduce a married woman?" Sun-rye felt a sudden flash of anger. She had already reached the gate but turned around to go back in. At that instant, Yu-wol, having hung up the phone, was coming to see her off.

"Does Dr. Lee come here sometimes?" asked Sun-rye, blushing with shame and feeling self-conscious at asking such an indecent question.

"Recently, he has sometimes come to visit. But as soon as he sees Mr. Kim of Jaetgol, he leaves," said Yu-wol, proud of her cleverness in seeing through the relationships. She chattered on. "Mr. Kim of Jaetgol always makes fun of Dr. Lee, sometimes so much, it's hard to listen to."

Sun-rye wondered if her own name ever entered into such talk. Imagining that Yu-wol might know that she had been forsaken by that heinous sex maniac, Dr. Lee, she felt suddenly dizzy, as if all the blood had rushed to her head. "Ah," she cried inwardly, "why can't I just forget that devil? Why doesn't his shadow leave me as he himself did? Wasn't it enough for him to kill my soul? Does he also want to kill my body and leave only skin?" Bowed down with emotional pain, Sun-rye left the house. She had gone only a step or two from the gate, her eyes downcast, when she noticed somebody in front of her. She lifted her head, surprised. It was Lee Geon-yeong.

3-9

Doctor Lee looked startled for an instant but then smiled as he removed his hat and greeted her. "Oh, Sun-rye, how nice to see you. Where are you going? Are your parents well?" He spoke calmly, as if nothing had passed between them and she were merely a good friend. He seemed to feel neither pity nor embarrassment.

Sun-rye, though, felt almost as though she were losing her mind, as if she had been dashed headlong against stone and were broken in heart and body. But quickly recovering from the shock, she felt fury flare through every vein. She was no longer the same girl who had fainted in Mr. Han Min-gyo's arms at the sight of Dr. Lee. Suffering and sorrow—an ordeal that she had first undergone as a young woman—had tempered her strength and resilience. Lee Geon-yeong had caused her grief, but also made her strong.

"Shame on you!" she cried. "Even if you can't feel sorrow and repent, you should at least feel embarrassed! After seducing so many young women, is your eye now on a lonely married woman? Is a scholar to behave like that? Is a noble man to behave like that? You learned all that in America? You learned all that shamelessness? What's with that red necktie? What's with that glistening hair? What's with that brazen face that won't blush even at such a shameful deed?"

Revealing neither annoyance nor sarcasm, Dr. Lee listened calmly and cool-heartedly, as if hearing a business report, a reaction intended to show his 'heroic' vigor. He waited for her to finish, and even then held his silence for some time, as if reflecting and trying to understand what he had heard, or as if offering her an opportunity to speak her heart fully. He finally spoke with calm words. "There must be some misunderstanding. I have never seduced any woman, certainly not a married one. What you've just said betrays some misunderstanding. Sun-rye, you're very agitated. You should go home and rest." He turned as if to walk away.

Sun-rye well knew that he was quibbling, his words merely of deceptive, false, and evil intent. But such an inexperienced young woman as she little knew how to argue logically enough to pierce Lee's malicious heart. She felt only the nearly explosive pain of her own heart, and so regretted her insufficiency to properly respond that she would have torn out her heart if she could.

Thoughts even more terrible occurred to her. "Should I stab

him to death with a knife? Then tear off that mouth that speaks so shamelessly and rip out that belly so filled with selfishness and lust?" Shocked at her own thoughts, Sun-rye strode quickly away from Lee before he had taken even a first step.

Lee closed his eyes, reflecting a while with his head bowed, then turned to follow Sun-rye instead of going on into Jeong-seon's place.

Sun-rye was moving at a rapid, rhythmic clip through the gathering darkness, her black skirt obscured, but her white jacket and the line of her neck and shoulders visible under the street-lights that shed their glow from above house roofs.

3-10

At the moment that Sun-rye had turned from him, Lee had be-gun trembling. He felt as if all the blood in his body were rush-ing to his chest to explode there, leaving his extremities empty. His hands and feet grew cold, but his eyes felt hot, as if burnt by flame. Had night not already fallen, his hot, dry lips would have shown pale, and he tried to wet them with his tongue, but his mouth was just as parched.

Falling into a sudden rage, he exclaimed, "How could she say such things, that nasty girl!" He clenched both fists and won-dered how he had managed to control his fury and offer her such a calm, cool façade when she had been so impudent.

In the next moment, however, he realized that he missed Sun-rye. Her soft voice, tender hands, warm breath, all that he remem-bered made him sorrow over losing her. He begrudged the loss of one who had entrusted him with her heart and body, as meekly as a sheep entrusts itself to the shepherd. He reflected upon his interest in Eun-gyeong, daughter of a wealthy family, but Eun-gyeong was now gone. He had since chased several other women of wealthy families but lost them all. He was currently interested in Jeong-seon, the wife of a friend, though with prospects of a divorce, but she was already occupied with Gap-jin. He wondered if he should have just stuck with Sun-rye.

In Lee's heart, money was everything. One way or another, he wanted it, but he could not quickly build up wealth on his own, and he discounted the idea of striving to earn money in the long term over several dozen years. What he had in his favor were being single, having a very respectable doctoral degree, and being handsome enough to attract women's interests. These were his seed capital—no, his bait for simultaneously catching wealth and a beautiful wife. When Lee had crossed the Pacific Ocean upon returning from America, he had possessed but one desire, to marry a wealthy beauty. Unfortunately, his wish had not come true, forcing him to endure several humiliating rejections, and he now bore the stigma of skirt chaser, further reducing his chances with any woman who might otherwise have shown interest. In such circumstances, he had found himself unexpectedly humiliated by Sun-rye. Finding himself at the end of his luck, and despite his fury, he despaired, only to feel anew a desire to have Sun-rye back.

"Sun-rye is a foolish girl," he told himself, for he understood her innocence as foolishness. "If I showed my affection toward her again, she would come back to me." Lee felt better for thinking this way, and even managed a smile through scorched, pale lips.

He began to calculate. "What should I do? Drop by at Sun-rye's house with some gift? Admit my wrongdoing and officially ask her for her hand? If I did that, things would work out immediately, but . . ." He paused to collect his thoughts. "Her family isn't wealthy, so how could I afford to build a modern house and buy a piano after marriage? Without such things, what sort of life is that? It wouldn't match my dream."

That worried him. "Right," he thought. "And if I married Sun-rye, no wealthy family would be able to offer me the hand of its daughter. I'd have to give up my dream of wealth."

He reflected further. "I have no job now. What could I live on? Should I go to Mr. Han to beg forgiveness and seek help? If I did that and married Sun-rye, I might get a job. Perhaps not at a women's college, which would be my ideal, but at least at a school for male students . . . Wouldn't that be the right thing to do? If I continue on my current path, what will become of me?"

Lost in such thoughts, Lee walked aimlessly, his eyes downcast. When he raised his head, Sun-rye was gone.

3-11

"Winning back Sun-rye's heart shouldn't be so difficult," he thought. Feeling better, and even satisfied, he turned to go see Jeong-seon after all, telling himself, "For the moment, I might as well visit Jeong-seon. She must be home since Sun-rye was just there. If Gap-jin isn't there, I can enjoy her beauty as much as I like. That shouldn't be any hindrance to marrying Sun-rye. I can visit her house tomorrow, but I'll have fun at Jeong-seon's place tonight. If Jeong-seon's alone, I can take her out to Town Hall for a dance show."

With high expectations, Lee entered the alley to Jeong-seon's house. Imagining her beside him watching half-naked dancing women, he completely forgot Sun-rye's insults and felt entirely cheerful.

Lee stood at the gate and shouted, "Come open this gate!" In the electric light, the white doorplate that read "Heo Sung" was clearly visible. It as yet bore no stain though the marriage was showing cracks, as if wearing out. Lee reflected that as he was chasing women for their kisses, Heo Sung had left his lovely wealthy wife behind and gone to the countryside to share the joys and sorrows of farmers. He felt his own life of little worth compared to Sung's life of service and high ideals.

Dr. Lee had studied history, sociology, and even ethics and the Bible. He not only possessed great knowledge of noble works, he had also studied logic, rhetoric, oratory, psychology, and literature to prepare himself for teaching young men and women. His selfish, hedonistic character, however, remained unaffected by such studies. He used all that valuable knowledge, training, and ability solely to seduce rich, beautiful women. If only Korea had provided him a wife of beauty and wealth, he might have used his abilities for Korea and Koreans, as he always claimed that he would. If that were the case, truly the case, all those wealthy families with pretty daughters had surely sinned against Korea by preventing him from doing his great work for the people. Han-eun would number among them for not allowing him to marry Eun-gyeong.

"Who's there?" Yu-wol said, opening the gate.

"Has he come back from the country?" inquired Dr. Lee, pretending he were visiting Sung.

"You mean our master? He hasn't come back yet."

She had to restrain herself from bursting into laughter. Dr. Lee always asked the same question. Moreover, no train on the Gyeongui Line to Seoul was scheduled between his afternoon visit at four and now, which meant that Sung could not possibly have arrived. Lee's obvious pretext made her laugh inwardly.

"Well, why doesn't he come back? Is Miss Jeong-seon in?" Lee expected that she would be.

"Miss Jeong-seon!? Don't you mean *Mrs. Yun?*" Yu-wol corrected. She felt only disgust at his presumption in referring to her master's wife as "Miss."

"I'm not yet used to calling your lady 'Mrs.' because she's so young. I'm sorry about that." Inventing such excuses, Lee made as though to touch Yu-wol's cheek, but she turned her head away in irritation.

"What a brazen, shameless cad!" Yu-wol thought, and mentally spat. She hated Gap-jin, Dr. Lee, Dr. Gwak, and the other fools who came to visit Jeong-seon for chatting and laughing. They were no better than dogs, and she disliked dogs.

"Mrs. Yun hasn't returned. She phoned to say she'll be late," Yu-wol informed him, hoping to forestall his return.

3-12

"Listen, Yu-wol," Lee said, taking out his wallet, "you want to make some money?"

"No, why should I?" She moved away, into the shade of the gate, and rather harshly asked, "Why should I take money from a man for no reason?"

Slipping a silver, fifty-*jeon* coin into her hand, Lee asked, "Hey, your Miss—no, excuse me, your Mrs.—did she go out with anybody? Did she mention where she went?" He was whispering, his voice nearly inaudible.

Yu-wol didn't immediately reject Lee's money. She reflected, "The old maidservant got money from Mr. Kim of Jaetgol this way. That's why she was always happy to see him."

"Did you hear me? Did she go out with anybody?" he again asked.

"She went with Mr. Kim of Jaetgol. They were heading for the stadium and then off to dinner. She said she'd be back late."

The effect of the fifty *jeon* had been almost immediate, but it did nothing to bring Jeong-seon back home alone. Disappointed, Lee went away. "Where should I go now?" he wondered. "To Sun-rye's house? Or should I see Jeong Seo-bun?"

Jeong Seo-bun, the physical education teacher from Mr. Han's dinner party, was plump with a light complexion, and her voice was husky. She had taught both Jeong-seon and Sun-rye. Despite her having a crush on Dr. Lee, he didn't fancy her. But he would be generous enough to talk nicely to a woman who loved him and perhaps hug her once. Sensing some openness on his part, Jeong Seo-bun harbored hopes of requited love from him.

Seeing no other choice, Dr. Lee dropped by her place.

She welcomed him, delighted, and in great haste prepared fruits and tea. Anyone else watching would have felt pity to see her doing all that in such a manner. Lacking money, beauty, or youth, she had fallen for Dr. Lee as her first love. Even if he were not to prey upon her affections, she probably would be unable to love any other man. Perhaps her firm, Christian ethical view would not allow her to love any other man once she had fallen for Dr. Lee.

Even a woman like Jeong Seo-bun could appear feminine and attractive in the privacy of an evening under soft electric lights. Lee's keen eyes caught that. He had failed to meet Jeong-seon that day and had even gotten insulted by Sun-rye. Moreover, he had found no opportunity for several days to enjoy the softness of a woman. All of this led him to self-pity, and he thought, "I could at least have Jeong Seo-bun."

After peeling an apple and cutting it, she pierced a slice with a fork and offered it to Lee, saying, "Here, have some." He didn't take it with his hand. Instead, he opened his mouth. A little reluctant at first, she slipped the fruit between his lips and sat on the floor nearby with her head shyly bowed, like a teenage girl.

At that, he reached out and slipped an arm around her neck, and her body fell into his arms without resistance. Her heart raced furiously, and as her panting breaths came ever more rapidly, she grew dizzy from joy and happiness.

Seo-bun lost her virginity that night at the age of thirty-three. She had always considered sex outside marriage a sin, but she excused herself to think that she had given more than her body to the man whom she loved, her husband for life. She felt happy in believing that she alone, among many rumored women, had successfully made Dr. Lee her own.

Disheveled and messy after the act, she called out to Dr. Lee as he was about to leave. "Dr. Lee," she cried, "Dr. Lee! I'm now your wife. Forever. Even after the resurrection, I swear to remain your wife."

Dr. Lee remained silent.

3-13

Around one in the morning, a taxi arrived at Jeong-seon's gate, and out stepped none other than Jeong-seon and Gap-jin. They had visited the Oryujang Hotel for a bath and dinner but had stayed so long that they missed the last train back to Seoul. Taking a taxi that dashed along Gyeonin Road to Seoul, they had finally arrived. Both reeked of liquor, and they stumbled as they stepped out of the taxi. Ignoring the driver, Gap-jin threw his arms about Jeong-seon's neck and kissed her passionately. He then got back into the taxi and ordered the driver, "To Jae-dong!." He collapsed into the seat and closed his eyes. Moving his head with the motion of the car, he gave a crazed cackle. The driver was startled enough to turn his head and look.

"Where are we?" Gap-jin asked.

"The intersection of An-dong," came the curt reply.

"Is it? Then drive to Jongno." Gap-jin looked out the window.

The driver slowed down. "You said Jae-dong, didn't you?"

Gap-jin laughed. "Today's such a great day I can't go home yet. Where should I go? Let's go to a bar."

The driver stopped. "Which bar?"

"Oh, it doesn't matter," Gap-jin replied, his tone boastful. "Just take me where pretty girls like Jeong-seon serve—lovely, obedient girls with soft skin!"

From a small police station at the intersection appeared a policeman stepping out to investigate the halted taxi. The driver grew worried and quickly drove on again, moving along the street in front of Gyeongbok Palace.

Gap-jin opened his eyes. "Where are you going?"

"Tell me where you want to go. If you just order me to take you to any bar, how would I know where to go? There are lots of bars in Seoul. Tell me which one you want." As he spoke, they passed the provincial government building.

Fuddled with drink, his eyes vacant, Gap-jin tried to think. Girls in different bars came to mind. Korean girls, Japanese girls, this or that girl. "Let's go to Arirang," he finally said, and burped loudly. The driver drove as ordered, toward Jangchundan.

Most customers had already left Arirang Bar. Only a couple of drunken men still remained, also a shameless older man crazy over some girl there. Gap-jin staggered up the stairs to the second floor and called out, "Hi, Aigoku . . ."

"Oh, Mr. Kim!" exclaimed several women as they came out to surround him. He was welcome among bar girls as a man of good cheer and even better talk, a generous tipper attractive to women.

"Ah, here you are, Judge!" chirped Aiko in Japanese. A short, voluptuous girl, she pulled Gap-jin by the hand, and he quickly kissed her. "No! I don't like that!" she exclaimed. Shaking his hand away and wiping her mouth with a handkerchief, she ran off to clear a table for him to sit down.

"Hey!" he called. "Some whisky!"

3-14

Gap-jin downed the whisky in one shot.

"Wow!" exclaimed the girls sitting beside him, surprised.

"Hey, you!" Gap-jin ordered one of the girls. "Get a bottle!" He then draped his arms over the shoulders of the girls to either side and started loudly singing a vulgar Japanese drinking song, but off key, "Is the liquor tears or sighs?" The girls joined in. They swayed sideways, holding his hand dangling from their shoulders as he moved his body to the tune. Beyond a partition further away, the shameless older man broke off from pestering a baby-faced girl of about seventeen who was sitting on his lap and turned his head to look over toward Gap-jin's table. He had a square, insipid face with a broad expanse between the eyebrows. Probably not a man of great wealth or high position, just someone who had managed to accumulate a bit of money one way or another.

"Hey, mister!" Gap-jin spoke in Japanese and lifted his glass of whisky high. "Let's drink a toast to more hairs for your head and your grey hair to turn black. Here, girls, let's drink together."

The man, however, grew embarrassed and shrank back, but glanced once more toward Gap-jin, apparently resentful at the younger man's boldness.

"Hey, mister! Mister!" Gap-jin called, spilling his whisky. "Why'd you draw back like a turtle at the sight of a human being? We can drink a toast!"

"Stop now! You'll upset him," whispered one of the girls beside Gap-jin, poking his side with a finger.

"Upset him?" He placed his glass on the table and turned solemn. "Why should my toast upset him? I was just uncomfortable at seeing an old man hold a girl young as his granddaughter on his lap and fondle her for such a long time, so I wanted to drink to his youth. Why should that upset him? All right. Let it be. We can drink a toast to ourselves!" He raised his glass again.

"For what?" asked a girl grabbing a glass and playing the coquette. "To your becoming a judge?"

"Becoming a judge . . ." he mused, staring at the floor and burping loudly.

"What else then?"

"To becoming a prosecutor . . . a prosecutor," he decided, now more drunk. "As prosecutor, I will arrest you all." He laughed and looked around at the girls, seemingly fond of them. "Are you frightened?" he asked, making a scary expression with his eyes.

"There's no reason to be afraid. We didn't do anything wrong," responded a girl, her tone abruptly sullen.

"She's right," the other girls agreed.

"You've done nothing wrong, you say?"

A girl turned on him. "What've we done? Tell us!"

"Should I list your crimes?" He chugged a shot of liquor and said, "You seduce men like us under the pretense of love and drain our wallets. That's not all. Playing the coquette on a shameless old man's lap, uh . . . that's a crime according to Criminal Code 2222 . . ."

Upset at these words, the man got to his feet, looked sideways at Gap-jin, and left.

3-15

Around nine the next morning, Gap-jin left the place of an Italian girl in Shinmachi, an area lined with brothels. Out of fifty won gotten from Jeong-seon the day before, not a single note was left, just some coins, a few silver, jangling in his pockets. He didn't remember how much he had spent at Arirang, nor the amount he had tipped the girls. Upon leaving the Italian girl's flat after drinking a cup of black tea, he found the street outside filled with sunlight but his heart somewhat darkened. Chilled by the morning's late autumn wind, Gap-jin hurried to enter a by-way, concerned lest he encounter some acquaintance, and headed for the trolly terminal in Jangchundan. He bought a ticket to Seodaemun, electing to go to Jeong-seon's, where he would eventually arrive to find her still in bed.

When she had returned home the previous night, she immediately suffered pangs of guilt. Remembering that the old servant and Yu-wol opened the gate and came out scarcely a moment after Gap-jin had kissed her, she still felt so ashamed to think that they must have seen her in his arms. Without the solace of alcohol, she might have killed herself for shame the night before, but she managed to shift all blame onto the alcohol.

"What's wrong with what happened?" Jeong-seon asked, trying to justify herself by shutting the mouth of her protesting conscience. If not for alcohol, she—a married woman—would never have given her body to Gap-jin in the hotel. But glass followed by glass had worked like keys loosening one moral scruple after another. Exhilarated in that liberation, she drank still more, and even as that alcohol removed the protective garb of her conscience, so were her clothes removed until she stood naked before a man other than her husband.

Upon awakening in her own bed, she found herself sober and deeply regretful over what she had done. In such a frame of mind and still lying in bed, she received a letter delivered just that morning from her husband. Seeing "To Yun Jeong-seon" written on the envelope, she let it drop to the blanket and covered her face with both hands, turning to lie on her side and weep into her pillow as she writhed in an agony of conscience.

Quietly observing all this, Yu-wol put Jeong-seon's clothes under the bedding to warm them and left the room. In doing so, she caught the startled old maidservant eavesdropping at the end of the veranda. The old servant stepped back in alarm, then slinked off toward the kitchen, silently beckoning to Yu-wol, who followed. Inside, the breakfast tray was almost ready, only the stew still boiling on the fire, waiting for the lady to rise.

"Hey," the old servant asked, putting her hand on Yu-wol's shoulder, "why is she crying?"

"I don't know. She just looked at the envelope, then hid her face behind her hands and burst into tears." Yu-wol then picked a crust of *nurungji* from atop the wood-burning stove and chewed on the dry, overcooked rice.

"Ah, probably a letter from the country," the old servant re-marked, displaying her understanding. Glancing at the bubbling stew, she exclaimed loudly, "Oh, that's boiling down too much!" She chuckled, then slipped out of the kitchen and crept along quietly toward the main room to eavesdrop.

3-16

After many agonized tears, Jeong-seon sat up and took the letter again in hand. She inspected both sides of the envelope. Written in Chinese characters on the back were the words "From Your Husband." Each stroke of the ideograph for "Husband" seemed to stab her body like a knife.

She opened the letter and read: "My dear wife," began the heading, and the letter was written all in Korean, as Sung was wont to do. She continued reading:

> I haven't heard from you since you left, and I'm be-ginning to wonder. I assume that you've received my two previous letters. I've become healthier than when you left. People now trust me more, and we've set up a coop-erative using this year's harvest. I had eight hundred won left and used it to fund the coop. If this cooperative can provide enough food and clothes, it'll be worth dedicat-ing my life to.

> But it's just a beginning. "Well begun is half done," we say, but you can't start cooking and eating at the same time. There are still a lot of things to start, to do, and also a lot of difficulties to go through.

> But Jeong-seon, my dear wife! Your promise to work with me provides great encouragement and happiness. Although I'm not a perfect husband for you, I believe that you'll be a wife full of love. You might have had

some suspicion about the relationship between Sun and me, but there is none. Earlier, I regarded Sun as a nice girl, but you're the only woman for me. No other woman can love me, and my eyes and heart will never be distracted by other women. I give you my word on that, so you can believe me.

If you were to die before me, I would never love any other woman. I believe that if I died before you, you wouldn't love any other man. At least, I want to believe that.

Jeong-seon ... you might consider this old-fashioned, but I hate any kind of betrayal and disloyalty. I can love and forgive anybody except a disloyal person. If my wife became disloyal to me, what would I do? I really don't know, but I do know that if I, your husband, were to betray you, my wife, if that were actually to happen, you could stab me with a knife. I would deserve it.

What nonsense I'm talking! These days, I miss you a lot. I feel nearly as if we're still dating, and I'm so anxious, longing for you. Why haven't you written? What are you doing these days? I assume you're busy dealing with the house and property before coming back. Don't try too hard. If the house doesn't sell, you can leave it in the charge of your father. Just come. What I'm waiting for is only you, your body and heart.

If you don't come within a week, we can return here together because I'll be in Seoul around mid-November appealing the case concerning our villagers.

The women of the village all miss you.

Take care and be careful in going out with people.

At the end was written, "On the night of October 23rd, from your Sung."

3-17

In reading the letter, Jeong-seon had to stop several times. She hid her face in her hands and collapsed onto the bed each of those times. She felt almost as though her husband had known what had happened the previous night and had written to admonish her.

Once finished with the letter, Jeong-seon fell face-first onto the bed cover, but she now felt far more fear than shame. "If I, your husband, were to betray you my wife, if that were actually to happen, you could stab me with a knife." Obsessing on these words from the letter, she could vividly imagine Sung with a sharp knife in his hand.

At precisely that moment, Yu-wol entered to say, "Ma'am, Mr. Kim of Jaetgol has come."

Still collapsed upon the bed, but angered, Jeong-seon shouted, "Tell him I'm not yet up."

But before Yu-wol could step back out, Gap-jin burst into the room through the side door, addressing Jeong-seon in overly familiar terms, "Aren't you up yet?"

"Don't come in here! Get out!" Jeong-seon screamed, her body shaking as she lay still face down upon her bed.

Ignoring her demands, Gap-jin said, "Oh, what's wrong with you? Actually, you look beautiful in that position, too. A true beauty can never fail to be beautiful no matter what the circumstances. I really should've brought my Kodak camera. Hey, Yu-wol, you're the one who should get out! Why are you just standing there?" He gave her a sidelong glance.

"How dare you speak like this? How can you just burst in here when I'm not even up? Get out now!" demanded an outraged Jeong-seon, turning toward him a face stained with tears and distorted by anger. She glared as if she could bite off his head.

Only then did Gap-jin realize that she had been crying and

really was furious. Surprised because he hadn't expected this, he looked at her in wonder for a while, then burst into laughter, as if witnessing something funny.

"Oh, I see. The so-called conscience those simpletons at church talk about must have thrown a fit. Yes, that's it. A daughter of God repenting in tears. Wow, you could yet wind up in heaven. But I've heard there aren't any love affairs in heaven, only simpletons who call out 'Lord, Lord' and weep tears blander than water, like you're doing now . . ." Gap-jin rattled on, half laughing.

Jeong-seon trembled through her entire body and screamed at him, "What did you say? Where did you learn such a way of speaking? You devil!"

"A devil? Oh, that's nice to hear. I've been always a devil. But the simpletons wouldn't call a married woman cheating on her husband an angel, would they?" He laughed again.

Seeing Jeong-seon's hysterical reaction to Gap-jin's extraordinary rudeness, Yu-wol glared crossways at him and screeched, "How dare you speak that way?" She ground her teeth in hate and rage at him for the shameless liberties that he was taking with Jeong-seon. Her fury was only increased in knowing that the old maidservant, whom she detested, sided with Gap-jin, and she felt such animosity that she could have stabbed him with a knife.

"Bitch! How dare you!" retorted Gap-jin, shaking his fist at Yu-wol before turning again in irony on Jeong-seon, "A devil, eh? A man for one night is as good as a husband, and you call me a devil!"

3-18

"Oh, my God, that devil, that devil is going to devour me," gasped Jeong-seon, speaking with difficulty and almost losing her breath. "That devil tricked me into corrupting my body. . . . You devil . . . oh . . . you devil."

"Tricked you? Now, who do you think tricked whom?" Gap-jin stepped closer to Jeong-seon, protesting, "You were the one hanging onto me, asking for it, and you're now trying to say I raped you?"

Yu-wol stepped behind Gap-jin and pulled at his coat, yelling, "Leave now! Oh God, what're you doing! Please get out!"

"What's this bitch doing!" He grabbed Yu-wol's hair and pulled her off balance. She fell to the floor.

"My God, how brazen!" Jeong-seon screamed in outrage. "You were the one who invited me to the baseball game! I wanted to come home after that, but you made me stay for dinner, or don't you remember? I wanted to come home after dinner, too, and you said you'd escort me home by taxi. But in the taxi, you decided to take a drive along the Han River. I wanted to leave the river and go home because it was late, but you wanted to stay a bit longer. Somehow, you got me to Origol and suggested going to see the Oryusang Hotel, remember? I didn't want to, but you insisted and said I could catch the train coming from Incheon in an hour because a taxi home would be too cold. But when it was time to head for the station, no matter how I begged, you wouldn't listen to me, so we missed that last train. I got upset, so you said you'd call a taxi. As we waited, you convinced me to drink some whisky as protection against the cold taxi. You made me to drink too much . . . got me drunk. You say that you didn't trick me. Oh, I . . ." Out of breath, Jeong-seon groaned, "Aah, aah," and fainted.

Gap-jin, startled and suddenly serious, rushed to take Jeong-seon in his arms and help her sit up. "Bring some cold water," he ordered Yu-wol. "Quickly!"

Alone, he kissed Jeong-seon's wet mouth, rubbed his cheek against hers, and gently squeezed her breasts and feet, caressing her. He stopped only when the old maidservant and Yu-wol with other servants rushed into the room bearing water.

As soon as Jeong-seon recovered consciousness, she struck

Gap-jin in the face with her fist, breaking his glasses and pushing him off as she moved away. His brow, scratched by slivers of
broken glass, began to bleed.

"Get out! Get out!" she demanded. With trembling hands, she
plucked a book from the low desk and threw it at him, screaming,
"Get out!"

Gap-jin quickly ducked to one side. The book flew through an
open window and landed on the veranda.

"Okay," he agreed, "I'll go." Taking his hat, he stood up to
leave, but added, "You might have my seed in your belly. If a child
is born, come see me. Or come see me earlier if you want, and I'll
meet you." He then left.

As the gate slammed behind him, Jeong-seon again blacked
out. Yu-wol cried as she put Jeong-seon back onto the bedding,
placed her head upon the pillow, and covered her with a blanket.
Jeong-seon seemed to notice nothing.

3-19

Only past four in the afternoon did Jeong-seon finally get up,
wash her face, and take some food.

She had, however, enough mental strength to prepare for going out. That was a woman's instinct. She combed her hair and
put on make-up. And she changed her clothes. As she opened the
wardrobe to choose what to wear, she saw the purple, traditional
jacket and brown dress that she had worn in the night before and
felt an urge to rip them apart. She wondered if she should wear
a Western suit, but her frame of mind told against it, and she
settled on a black serge dress and white, traditional jacket, something unnoticeable, and drew over that a black, traditional overcoat made of specially processed cotton yarn. Standing before the
full-length glass, she felt wearied with her pretty face and lovely
clothes, regarding them worthless.

Jeong-seon left home and headed for Dr. Hyeon's practice in Dabanggol, walking by the Anglican Church in Jeong-dong on her way.

The cross atop its steeple recalled for her a pastel picture drawn against the background of a setting sun. She thought of the nuns inside wearing their black robes with the white conical hat. She felt that she now better understood them, these women who spent their lives in such a desolated place, and wondered if they had pasts like her own.

On the gate was a sign with great white letters: "THE ANGLICAN CHURCH." Jeong-seon looked past the name-plate and into the quiet yard and buildings that seemed imbued with the silence of death. She felt a desire, an urge to see those nuns who spent their lives glorifying God, praying fervent prayers, and repenting in tears. She was surprised at herself. She had never previously paid the least attention to things like convents, sneering at such a life, but she now felt an interest.

A phrase heard sometime before came to mind: "Religion is for sinners." The thought pierced her heart, and she walked on in dejection.

At that moment, she suddenly heard a familiar voice. "Hey, isn't that Jeong-seon?" Somebody tapped her on the shoulder.

"Oh!" exclaimed Jeong-seon, turning around to discover two high school friends, Miss Seok and Miss Yeo.

"My goodness," Seok said, surprised and laughing, "Where are you going dressed like that? You look like some woman kicked out of her in-law's place in the middle of the night. Or a seamstress just hired to work for a family. What's wrong with you, a lady of wealth?"

Jeong-seon forced a smile, but Seok's joke had pierced her to her heart.

"Where are you going?" Yeo asked, grasping her hand and glad to see her. Yeo was a shy woman, but smiled easily.

Jeong-seon tried to hide her troubles behind the smile, but she was feeling so down that she could offer only a feeble reply, "Oh, I'm on my way to Dabanggol."

"Are you sick?" Seok asked, showing concern and making to embrace her.

"No, I'm fine," Jeong-seon responded, holding onto the smile.

"When is your husband coming back?" Yeo asked. She and Seok had happened to be speaking of Jeong-seon just before they encountered her. Rumors had been going around among her friends that she was going to get divorced or was already divorced, or that she was carrying on an affair with Gap-jin or living with him, and so on. Encountering Jeong-seon in strange circumstances after such talk made them all the more suspicious and curious.

Maintaining her smile, Jeong-seon simply answered, "I don't know."

"Well, Jeong-seon," replied Seok, beginning to talk more seriously if carefully, and trying to study her face, "you know, we hear a lot of things about you. That you're going to have a divorce or other kinds of rumors. Naturally, we don't believe any of them, but that guy Kim Gap-jin, people talk about you having something with him. It's not good to make people talk like that. It wouldn't be good at all if Mr. Heo hears of the rumors."

3-20

Jeong-seon felt as if her friends Seok and Yeo knew her secret and were willfully tormenting her. She feared their looks and their words. After they departed saying, "See you this evening at your place," she again started out, heading toward the State Hospital. But feeling that her friends were pointing at her behind her back and making fun of her, she turned around to check, only to find them already gone.

Jeong-seon walked on faster, like a criminal who had somehow escaped surveillance. She envied her unmarried friends, their purity and their freedom. Compared to them, she felt like dirty clothes, like a body covered with boils or bound with a filthy rope. Only yesterday, she had prided herself as the happiest, most successful of women.

Turning onto the riverside road in Dabanggol, one could walk down toward Sogwanggyo Bridge to find a traditional Korean house renovated half in the Western style. On the gate hung a signboard with the words "Gynecologist" and "Pediatrician" taking up two lines. Beneath these were the name of the practice in large letters and the name and title of the doctor in smaller letters, off to one side. Just below its middle part, the signboard was stained from a large flood years earlier, indicating that the practice had been there for a good many years.

Inside the gate stood a rickshaw.

Jeong-seon went through the gate into the inner quarter instead of entering the practice, located in the quarter ordinarily used as a reception room. She took quick steps as though to avoid anyone coming in behind her. Standing outside a glass door on the main floor, she called out, "Hyeon, it's me."

The house had a spacious, clean yard and was itself a large structure, but quiet, without many family members.

At Jeong-seon's voice, the door of the room opposite the main room opened, and a girl of about fifteen named Bok looked out, opened the glass door, and welcomed her with a smile. "Oh, please come in. Dr. Hyeon is seeing patients now." Dr. Hyeon didn't allow her servants to call her Mistress or Lady. They were to refer to her as Dr. Hyeon.

As Jeong-seon was removing her shoes, the girl ran through the gate to the quarter with the practice, her tail ribbon fluttering.

Jeong-seon flopped into a rattan chair set on the main floor. "Oh," she wondered, "how can I ask about this?" She had been turning it over in her mind at home for hours already, but how could she raise the issue that she wanted to ask Hyeon?

Soon after the girl had rushed off, Hyeon came in. She had gotten her hair permed and was wearing a dark purple suit. At the first glance, she might look like a young woman of about twenty, but a closer inspection revealed her as past thirty.

"Hey, Jeong-seon, you're here," Hyeon said, her tone like that of a man talking to a man, a habit of hers. She switched briefly to English to ask, "How are you doing?" Grasping Jeong-seon's hand, she shook it, then hugged her and kissed her brow, amost like a lover, before stretching out on a couch covered with a blanket.

"Bok, bring some cigarettes!" Hyeon ordered, but in a more feminine tone.

3-21

"Well, any news?" Hyeon uttered the phrase in English, lighting a cigarette and enjoying it as she exhaled. She continued in Korean, "Isn't your husband back yet? I don't understand what he's doing, leaving such a beautiful wife as you all alone. If I were him, I would take you everywhere, even for a walk." Hyeon spoke gazing at Jeong-seon, like a mother looking at her cute baby. She blinked from the smoke, then added, "My Jeong-seon is so pretty. You always look beautiful, but you look even more beautiful today. Did something good happen to you? Is your husband back? Am I right?" She blew smoke toward Jeong-seon who didn't mind having the soft odor fill her nostrils.

"Should I try one?" thought Jeong-seon, gazing blankly at the cigarettes in their round case with the blue label "Three Castles." But Hyeon's questions pricked her conscience. "Did something good happen to you? Is your husband back?" Jeong-seon grew fearful that Hyeon had seen through her secret, so she smiled and quickly replied, "Yes, he has come and left." But in that moment of her trickery and lies, she was like a sly, deceptive snake.

"He returned and left already?" asked Hyeon in surprise, "Didn't he have any time to see me before going back? Or maybe you wanted him to avoid seeing me, afraid that I might take him away from you. Am I right?" She chuckled, but grew more serious, shaking her head as if disappointed. "I was only joking. I just wanted to ask your husband about something. I don't like to go to other lawyers."

"He said he'll come back soon," offered Jeong-seon, "because of some appeal at the High Court. He'll come back soon. If it's not too late, you can ask him then." Jeong-seon sighed to remember her husband's letter and her own reaction in reading it.

Hyeon seemed to be thinking with her eyes closed, but they were startled open at Jeong-seon's sigh. She glanced with clear eyes at Jeong-seon's bowed head, then blinked slowly several times, thinking. She tried to infer something from Jeong-seon's sighs, expression, posture, and other smaller details, then nodded as if she had understood, inhaled smoke deeply, and tapped with an index finger to loosen ashes from her cigarette. They tumbled into a white enamel ashtray. Hyeon became melancholic, like a summer sky suddenly darkened by rain.

No words passed between the two, and only the smoke of Hyeon's now neglected cigarette hovered between them in bluish wisps before dispersing.

Bok brought in steaming hot tea. Called black tea, it was in fact of reddish tint. On the tray were bowls of sugar cubes and cream, along with silver teaspoons. The entire set was Western.

Hyeon sat abruptly up and stubbed out the cigarette, still one third left. "Jeong-seon," she announced, "have some tea." Putting sugar and cream into her own cup, she drank first.

3-22

"Jeong-seon, are you worried about something?" Hyeon asked, elbow on the table and chin in hand, gazing at Jeong-seon. Her eyes were not clear this time, but seemed moist and sad.

"No!" came Jeong-seon's firm denial, and she even smiled to prove it.

Hyeon didn't believe the denial but made no forceful effort to uncover the truth. She could sense the new shadow of worry and sadness in Jeong-seon's heart.

"Hyeon," said Jeong-seon, drawing her chair close, "Hyeon, I don't want to have a baby, but my husband was with me yesterday. What can I do to avoid getting pregnant?" She blushed deep red. To Jeong-seon's further embarrassment, Hyeon laughed deeply, like a man. Jeong-seon pinched Hyeon's leg. "Hey, why are you laughing?" she protested, like a little girl, but felt as if stabbed in the heart.

"Ouch, ouch," Hyeon cried, still smiling. "I'm not laughing at what you said, but because I thought of a patient I saw today. You suddenly reminded me of her." Hyeon laughed again, in delight, her cloud of melancholy cleared up.

"A patient? What kind of patient? Why the laughing?" Jeong-seon smiled awkwardly.

"Listen," Hyeon said. "Just a little while ago, a young patient came to see me."

"You mean just before I got here?"

"Right. She came in the rickshaw. She looked nice. Soft skin, and such a voluptuous body. Actually, that's the reason men like her and cause problems. And her problem today was exactly like yours. What a coincidence! That's why I laughed."

Jeong-seon tried to ignore Hyeon's jocular tone.

"Anyway, I asked her what'd happened," Hyeon continued. "At first, she tried to explain in a way no one could possibly understand. It was all vague, all *sidoromodoro*. But I wouldn't let her do that with me, and she eventually broke out in a tearful confession." Hyeon swallowed once and continued, "She was the wife of a teacher, and her husband left for the countryside a month ago. Last night, she was seduced by a man. She says he forced himself on her. Either way, she slept with a man who wasn't her husband. She's now worried she might get pregnant and wants me to keep that from happening. How unpleasant! I'd have liked to say, 'Hey, how could a married woman like you not stay chaste for just a month? You had to go off and have an affair with some man, and you now want my help to avoid having a baby?' But I couldn't say that. A doctor has ethical responsibility and ought to help regardless whether the patient is a thief or a married woman having an affair." Hyeon then sighed, picked up her cup, and downed the rest of the tea.

"So . . . what did you say?" Jeong-seon asked, careful but bent on learning the important point.

"What did I say?" Hyeon lighted another cigarette and smiled. "I said, 'I can't stop you from getting pregnant.' I then felt sorry for her, so I added, 'You should go sleep with your husband today.' I guess that advice puts me in the wrong, don't you think?" She laughed again.

3-23

"What happened next?" Jeong-seon asked, anxious to know if Hyeon had treated the woman anyway.

"She then told me," Hyeon responded, "that her husband is suffering from tuberculosis and staying in a sanatorium. She could go to see him but can't sleep with him. Well, it's really a pity, isn't it, Jeong-seon? So ironic. She couldn't do what I advised, so she asked what to do instead. I told her that and more. That the best way is to scrape or remove the uterus. That twenty hours had already passed, and the sperm would be deep-rooted in the womb, dividing and sucking the mother's blood. That the sperm would no longer be someone else's but would now be connected to her as her son or daughter. That removing that is like killing her own child and that according to the law, a doctor is allowed to carry out an abortion only if the mother is in critical condition. I pointed out that she is healthy and not allowed to have an abortion. She then said that it would be terrible for her husband as well as for her if she is pregnant and cried a lot asking me to help her no matter what. Well, Jeong-seon, I don't know what I'll do in her case, but how could she think of removing a life from her body? She shouldn't have had an affair. Is it so hard not to have an affair? As for me, I wouldn't have such an overwhelming desire for a man. Even if she did, she should have been prepared to accept responsibility. What does she want? How horrible she is, just wanting to have the poor baby removed after an affair! Don't you agree, Jeong-seon?" Hyeon seemed to enjoy talking.

Jeong-seon couldn't bear to listen any longer. Every word seemed directed at her. She wanted to leave, but that would raise suspicions, so she changed the subject, smiled and asked, "Hyeon, you really don't like men?"

"Do you?" Hyeon retorted, only half joking. "Living alone means being free. Not one of my married friends is happy. Are you? Men! They only smell of . . ." She frowned, as if she smelled something unpleasant. When she did so, she looked prettier.

"Smell? What smell?" Jeong-seon laughed.

"Bad breath, smelly feet, rancid hair. A lot of smells. Also the stink of behaving so disgustingly. Why? Don't you smell anything on a man?" Hyeon also laughed.

Jeong-seon remembered the smell of Gap-jin's armpit. In her memory, however, it was pleasant, even exciting. She then thought of Sung, but he ate neither green onions nor garlic and thus had no odor, whether on his breath or from his body. "Hyeon, you must suffer from the disease of hating men. Don't you ever think of getting married? I've never heard of you seeing a man. You don't feel lonely?" Jeong-seon asked, feeling sympathy for her. She was reflecting on what she knew of Hyeon, a woman who looked virtuous, was stylish, and of wealthy family, but was never rumored to be in relationships with men.

"Sure, I sometimes feel lonely. I'm also a woman. But knowing this or that man would only lead to a gossip. Besides, there's also no man I'd want to marry. Or if there are any, there's only one I'd really consider marrying." Hyeon smiled meaningfully.

3-24

"Who? Who is he?" Jeong-seon asked, her tone already badgering.

"Well . . ." Hyeon resisted, as if the answer were difficult, testing Jeong-seon's patience. "Do you really want to know?" She tapped on the table with her fingers. "You shouldn't be too surprised, and don't get angry . . ."

"Don't worry. Just stop playing games with me!" Unburdened of her weighty thoughts, Jeong-seon now pretended to be upset.

"Wait a moment. You expect me to reveal my secret so easily? No way!" Hyeon suddenly stood up, went to her room, and returned with a box. She set it down in front of Jeong-seon and opened it. "Here, have a look. Try to find who loves me most, and whom I most like. You figure it out."

Curious, Jeong-seon looked inside. There were a lot of letters. Letters in various envelopes, Western and Korean. Letters written with fountain pens and calligraphic brushes. Letters in various styles of penmanship, well written, badly written, hastily written, and aesthetically written. The differences indicated letters from various people.

"Wow!" Jeong-seon opened her eyes wide, as if alarmed at the sight. "What are these? All the love letters you've received?"

"Exactly. No, actually, just some of them. I'm keeping only one from each writer to make a sample collection. When I first started getting love letters, I used them for toilet paper or for starting fires, but I came to the idea that a sample collection might be interesting for later. Besides, it's fun. Anyway, I started collecting them last year. But however many I might have received, you must have received a lot more. You're prettier and younger, and you're also a more cherished daughter of a wealthier family."

"No, not many. I've gotten some, but no more than twenty. Not as many as you. You're the beauty, not me, right?"

"Oh yeah. Right. You're not a beauty at all . . . By the way, Jeong-seon, you should be careful about meeting some people. There's some talk about Dr. Lee and Baron Kim's son visiting you a lot. I don't believe anything is going on between you and them, but if your husband gets wind of these visits, that wouldn't be good. You're a young, married woman. You shouldn't be meeting any men. It'll just set off rumors. Do you imagine that men want to visit you for your knowledge, your character, or your influence? They might say things to make you feel good, but what they really want is your body and beauty. They're the same way with me. These men! Falling in love, sending letters, gifts, whatever! They really just want to have me once. Some of them might have an eye on my wealth, this house that's mine alone because I don't have parents or siblings. I see through them all, I know what they want! Why should I fall into their traps? I'm not that crazy." Hyeon scoffed.

3-25

"Yes, you're right." Jeong-seon could not but agree.

"These days, Korean men think only of seducing women. Maybe they think it's modern. Here, look at this," Hyeon said.

She spread the letters across the entire table top like *golpae* sticks for ease in selecting. Picking a jade-green Western envelope with writing in English, she showed it to Jeong-seon. "Recognize the handwriting?"

"Well, it looks like Dr. Lee's," Jeong-seon responded in surprise. She had sometimes received the same kind of letters.

"Exactly," Hyeon said, taking the letter out and starting to read:

> Oh, my dear Miss Dr. Hyeon, whom I admire and love!
>
> I have received no response to any of the letters that I've sent, but I don't resent you. I feel no resentment because my heartfelt love for you allows no other emotion than love and because you have yet to understand my character and sincerity.
>
> Various rumors about me are making the rounds, but all are groundless, all invented by envious people who wish to damage my honor. I have had several female friends, but the woman I love—I swear it!—is you alone, Miss Hyeon, not only yesterday and today, but forever . . .

Hyeon stopped reading and looked at Jeong-seon. "Just listen to this guy. The other women were merely friends. His true love is me alone, only me. Hah! Does he imagine I wouldn't know he says that to every woman? He must have made the same profession of love to Sun-rye and Seo-bun. Hasn't he done the same with you? In fact, he's not the only one to write like this. Most of these men call me their first love. If they can lie about love, they'd lie about anything. That's why I don't trust them. So-called men of character, but just liars in disguise. They're all selfish men. They concoct all sorts of stories! Some claim to be virgins, or widowers, or aristocrats—how laughably amateur they are! Some swearing they cannot live without me, others speaking of their chivalrous sympathy for me, a woman living alone, in need of protection and comfort . . . All sorts of stories. Want to see this one?" From a long white envelope, Hyeon drew forth a letter with stylish, ink-brush writing and showed the signature at the end, "Have a look! Know who this is?" It was the signature of an educator and religious man.

"This man wrote you?" Jeong-seon was surprised.

"Well, here's another," Hyeon said. "Look. Know this guy?"

Jeong-seon was dumbfounded. It was a well-known pastor.

"How about this one?" Hyeon asked, picking up a rather large envelope.

Jeong-seon couldn't help but burst into laughter. It was an old man of wealth. Hyeon laughed with her.

3-26

After revealing these highly distinguished letters, Hyeon called out for Bok to switch on the heater and waited for that to be done before turning again to Jeong-seon and asking, "Want to see a very interesting letter?" She then rummaged through the letters with two long outstretched fingers and picked one out from beneath another big letter, a yellowish envelope with writing scrawled in ink across it. The thin, yellowish paper with the scrawled words stood in noticeable contrast to the other letters in their high quality envelopes decorated with careful writing, which made the scrawled writing look quite childish.

"Recognize the writing? You must know it." Hyeon winked, as if to tease Jeong-seon.

Jeong-seon had not yet seen the writing clearly but presumed it to be Gap-jin's, based on Hyeon's manner. Without thinking, however, she replied, "No, I don't."

"Have a look. It's from your lover. Among all the letters I've received, I fancy this one the most. The other writers compose their letters carefully and embellish them with ornamentation, but this fellow doesn't do that. Here, listen, I'll read it."

Hyeon started, half laughing. The top edge of the paper was irregular, as though carelessly torn from its letter pad:

> Doctor Hyeon, I don't understand you. How can such a young, beautiful woman like you remain uninterested in men? What could be more joyful than pleasure between a man and a woman? Fall in love with me. I'll give you a new perspective on life.

Hyeon paused. "What do you think of this guy's spiel?" She read again:

> I'm now the best man in Korea. An immature, uncultured Korean woman wouldn't be proper for me. Only Dr. Hyeon could be my partner.

Hyeon paused again and chuckled. "You hear what this guy's saying?"

Jeong-seon, caught between tears and laughter, sat quietly with clenched jaw.

"Listen," Hyeon said. "The end is magnificent." She continued:

> I've never failed in getting any woman I wanted. But there are three women I haven't yet had. You, Dr. Hyeon, and Yun Jeong-seon your favorite, and another woman whose name you wouldn't recognize. I haven't had you three yet, though I'd like to. Jeong-seon is my friend Sung's wife, but I had my eye on her before she married him. He just managed to steal her from under my nose.

But a real man never leaves a thing unfinished once he's made up his mind to act. Within a week, I'll have Jeong-seon. That's my plan. After that, I'll get my revenge on the other girl. I will then have put my complicated love life behind me to love only you, darling, sincerely.

Pausing, Hyeon observed, "He now calls me darling," then continued:

So far as I hear, you have no contact with men at all. No matter what they try, you don't fall for them. I'm really impressed there is still such a woman as you in Korea!

Hyeon seemed quite satisfied on this point. "Yes," she noted, "he actually now uses the formal form of address for 'being impressed' instead of just the informal one."

3-27

Hyeon continued reading Gap-jin's letter:

If a woman doesn't fall for me, for my seduction, I'll either admire her or kill her. Unfortunately, I've not yet encountered such a woman. Dr. Hyeon, I beg you! Make me either an admirer or a killer.

Hyeon finished, returned the letter to its envelope, and tossed it on the table. "What do you think?" she asked. "This kind of love letter is probably quite rare in the world. Isn't it great?" She seemed to enjoy it.

Jeong-seon, however, her feelings a confusion of rage, shame, and worry, could barely reply, "You think him a nice guy?"

"Nice guy? Gap-jin's certainly no nice guy. He's entirely

obsessed with sex. But among sex maniacs, he's several orders above someone like Lee Geon-yeong. In the first place, he's masculine. He doesn't plead with a woman; he makes demands. He's a totally different sort from those slimy men who'd stoop to lick the sole of a woman's foot. Another thing I like is his honesty. How frank he is! He's a delight compared to those guys who say one thing but think another. You know, Jeong-seon, I'm quite disappointed with Korean men. There's hardly a one who's manly and honest. It's really pathetic to see men with their noses to the ground, trying to sniff out the scent to money, power, and women. This fellow Gap-jin, he's college educated but doesn't have an honest job and just chases women, so he's clearly a man to detest. But he's more delightful and *gawaeyey*, cute, than those guys who do precisely the same thing, but cloak themselves as patriots, moralists, and Christians. Besides, he's right, isn't he? If girls were *sikari*, if they were firm, the guys wouldn't flit from one to another. Girls are easy these days, and guys know it. For example, people don't talk about you and Sun-rye, right? In Sun-rye's case, Lee Geon-yeong is at fault, not her. And as for you, people might talk about you and Gap-jin, but they just don't know you. My Jeong-seon wouldn't fall for him so easily, right? But I'm worried now. Gap-jin said he'd either admire us or kill us, so which will it be? And who's the other girl he was talking about? Maybe Sun-rye? This Gap-jin fellow's already had all the easy girls and now's setting his sights on the harder ones." Hyeon laughed and added, "If the other woman's Sun-rye, he won't find seduction so easy. He'll get a painful lesson about what a Korean woman really is." Hyeon gave a throaty laugh. Jeong-seon laughed along, but without pleasure, as cold sweat trickled down her back.

Jeong-seon abruptly stood up. "Hyeon, I'm going now."

"So early? Why not stay for dinner?" Hyeon tried to dissuade her.

"I should go home." Jeong-seon insisted, smoothing the wrinkles of her clothes.

"Don't think of removing the baby!" Hyeon admonished, "That would be cowardly and very irresponsible. Remember, people say that love for a child is deeper than for a husband. Keep the baby. Father and mother are both nice and talented, so your child would be great to have. I promise to be a good aunt." Hyeon patted Jeong-seon on the back.

3-28

As soon as Jeong-seon reached home, she packed and took an overnight express train for Salyeoul at seven in the evening, intending to act on Hyeon's advice to the other woman: "Go sleep with your husband."

Jeong-seon stayed awake the whole way and got off at the stop after the Salyeoul station because the express didn't halt at small stops. It was still dark. Jeong-seon awakened a still-sleeping taxi driver who initially refused to drive her anywhere. But by pleading and paying ten won, big money for four kilometers, she persuaded him to take her to Salyeoul.

Even when she arrived in Salyeoul, the sun had not yet come up. Some 280 kilometers northwest of Seoul, the place was much colder than the city. Carrying her suitcase, occasionally switching hands, she avoided the main road to the village and walked instead along the Dalnae River toward her husband's house. A few village dogs with acute ears barked once or twice at the faint sound of her steps.

Setting her bag down upon the hillside by the river where she and her husband had sometimes sat together before she left for Seoul, she gazed at the ice that had formed along each bank, remembering that earlier time.

Her husband's house appeared purple, even dark blue in the

faint early morning light. She picked up her bag and trudged on up the hill like a daughter-in-law kicked out of the house for sinning but going back to seek forgiveness. At a newly dug well was to be seen a pottery bowl containing tofu and edible ferns in clear water. For Jeong-seon, that looked like something from a different world. Unconsciously, she stared down into the well. From the well's dark depths flickered a light no bigger than her palm, wavering like the sheen on a pool of mercury. It almost seemed to waver at Jeong-seon's breath in a manner indescribably mysterious and even scary for her. Growing up in Seoul, she had never peered into a well, but her feelings stirred at the sight were not just because of this first encounter. Like those few drops sprinkled onto the head for baptism into Christianity, the well water made a big impact on her, almost spiritual though impossible to explain.

Jeong-seon suddenly had no courage to go further. "If I had come to see my husband without any problem," she thought, "how energetic and proud I would be."

She saw only darkness ahead.

"Why did I come here?" she asked herself. "To hide my sin, to cheat my husband and the world?" Feeling herself on the verge of falling, she clutched a pillar of the well and leaned against it.

The sun rose. In the clear air, pure of dust and smoke, it looked young, like a well-nourished baby awakened and raising its head. The clean yellow sunlight illuminated Jeong-seon leaning upon the pillar in her agony, almost like a picture.

Her husband's house was still several meters away, but up the hill beyond the well and so not visible from where she stood.

Jeong-seon looked again down into the water. The palm-sized pale sheen seemed to grow larger and brighter, reflecting her face. Startled and even frightened at what she saw, Jeong-seon stepped back in alarm.

At a sudden clattering sound, she turned her head to discover

Yu Sun coming down the hill, a water jar balanced on her head.

"Goodness!" exclaimed Yu Sun, abruptly frozen in mid-stride and too surprised to utter another word.

Jeong-seon said nothing, but her breathing grew quicker. Anger? Jealousy?

Neither found the encounter pleasant. Emotions approaching fury and hate shot with almost identical sharpness through the two women as they faced off. Their cold scene perfectly matched the winter morning.

3-29

Jeong-seon first broke the painful silence. "Oh, how much you must have done for my husband." She had spoken only with difficulty, recovering her sense of superiority as an older, educated lady of a noble family, a person of status. "How have you been?" she added, pretending gladness at the sight of Sun.

"When did you arrive?" responded Sun, offering the only possible polite greeting from a country woman. She set the water jar down near her feet.

"Is my husband doing well? Is he still sleeping?" Jeong-seon asked, recalling her purpose in coming, suddenly as alert as a cunning serpent testing the air with its tongue.

"Oh!" exclaimed Sun, again surprised. "You two must have crossed paths."

"What?" Jeong-seon's heart began pounding strongly.

"Yes," replied Sun, looking at Jeong-seon in sympathy. "He went to Seoul with the morning train the day before yesterday."

"What? The morning train the day before yesterday?"

"Right, the day before yesterday."

"Not the morning train yesterday?"

"No, the day before yesterday was market day. He left market day," Sun responded, her face expressing puzzlement.

Jeong-seon collapsed upon her suitcase and began sobbing so hard she nearly writhed in agony.

"Calm down," Yu Sun implored. "He will return quickly when he learns you are here." Almost crying herself, Sun sympathized with Jeong-seon, assuming her tears to be in disappointment after traveling the whole night to see her husband, whom she had awaited so long to no avail. All trace of lingering jealousy vanished entirely from Sun's heart.

"Come on, let's go in, it's so cold." Sun gently tugged at Jeong-seon's arm.

Without resisting, Jeong-seon let herself be raised up and drawn along by Sun, who left her water jar at the well, took Jeong-seon's bag, and started walking up the hill, leading the way. The morning sunlight was like a brush that painted the two women walking among trees with leafy branches that trembled against a background of brown hills and an indigo sky so characteristic of Korea. The dark tears continuing to spill in Jeong-seon's heart, however, blurred her vision.

Han-gap's mother, making breakfast in the kitchen, came out in surprise and hailed her gladly. Jeong-seon returned the greeting and forced a smile through a countenance twisted with anxiety and damp with tears.

Jeong-seon was soon alone in Heo Sung's room. "Ah," she thought, "my husband's room!" A desk and a bookshelf, both unpainted, and a shoe frame for *mituri* were there. Hanging on the walls were ears of corn, grains of millet, healthy-looking sorghum, bountiful rice, and worn clothes made of coarse cotton cloth, a strange contrast to the bedroom they used in Seoul.

Gazing about the room, Jeong-seon glimpsed a photo on the wall above the desk. It was of her. While she had neglected and forgotten her husband, he had looked upon her image everyday, reflecting on her. The thought made her sad.

On his desk lay a notebook that an elementary school child

of the countryside might write in with a pencil. She opened it and read:

___ of October. Still no letter from my wife.

___ of October. We worked on the road of the village today. I was happy to see people working hard but enjoying the labor. We are going to dig a well and construct the water line tomorrow. This way, Salyeoul is changing and getting better every day. Salyeoul can represent Korea. But why hasn't Jeong-seon written yet?

Such were the entries.

3-30

Jeong-seon read further in the journal:

___ of November. It is cold. People are happy that the price of rice is going up. Without the low-interest loans from our cooperative, farmers would have sold their rice at a low price. If only the rich of the village would join the cooperative, we would have less trouble securing funds. But we will succeed in the end.

I don't understand at all why she doesn't write. Is she sick? I miss her a lot.

After some entries, he wrote:

It's not possible. I can't believe what he wrote. It's just an intrigue to make me suspicious of my wife!

The letters were scrawled in a large hand, with no date given. Jeong-seon was surprised. What did it mean? Who was "he"?

What was it that this "he" had told Sung? Something that made him suspicious about her, and he was very upset, so it must have been doubts about her faithfulness. Did that mean somebody had repeated rumors about her closeness to Gap-jin? Who could have done that?

"Oh, of course, Lee Geon-yeong!" she exclaimed to herself, realizing that he might have written out of jealousy toward Gap-jin.

"If that's what happened, I can talk my way out of it—I can say that it's just a groundless rumor." As she decided on this, her heart split in two: half secure, half ashamed.

"There's no way other than lying now." Jeong-seon tried to think through what to tell her husband when they met. "Well, it's not really lying if I just say nothing. If I confessed, that would be terrible. I feel so ashamed. Admitting it would be too shameful! If I remain silent, everything will be all right, so why confess? Country people are said to be fierce, and I don't know how my husband will react. I shouldn't say anything, just keep quiet. I'm bad for cheating on him, but did I do anything so bad? It was only once, and very brief. I didn't plan it, I fell for a trick. All right, I won't confess!" Jeong-seon clapped her hands, as if making a successful bid in an auction. "Just don't spit out the truth," she admonished herself, "and in the future, never do it again."

The one thing unsolved, however, was that a child that might grow in her belly, a thing she feared like an omen. She might try to belittle her fling with Gap-jin as having left little more than a needle mark, describing it as "only once, and very brief," but what if this single, brief moment had left not just a small, if ineradicable emotional mark, but also a new life establishing a larger, enduring relationship of father, mother, child?

"Perhaps I should have my womb scraped," thought Jeong-seon, with regret.

She considered returning to Seoul by night train, but they

might miss each other again. She couldn't, however, simply wait for her husband's return, which might be delayed. She needed to see him as soon as possible. Not because she missed him but to quickly erase all trace of her sin.

"The meal is ready. May I come in?" asked Yu Sun, opening the door slightly. She had prepared breakfast in the meantime.

The rice was from the mill, and it offered life, unlike city rice, which was mixed with stone dust but lacked the cereal germ and other nutritious parts. Also prepared were bean paste stew, radish salad, kimchi, tofu, and some meat.

3-31

While eating, Jeong-seon asked Sun about this or that. Though she sounded heedless, her words held a secret intention, a well-honed skill of women.

"Did he worry that I didn't come?" Jeong-seon asked, seeking Sung's thoughts through Yu Sun.

"Certainly," Sun assured her, wondering what more to say, and carefully studying Jeong-seon's face with eyes sharp, but softened through a smile. "He waited for you every day. Around the time of the train's arrival, he would stand on that hill—you see that hill there?" She opened the door to point. "He'd stand there looking toward the station and say in disappointment, 'She didn't come today.'"

"Did he also wait for letters from me?" It was an unnecessary question.

"Of course. Every time the postman came without a letter from you, he was very disappointed," said Sun. She would have liked to depict in more detail how deeply Sung had sighed and how quietly he had remained in his thoughts, but she stopped short, concerned that Jeong-seon might think her improper in having shown so much deep interest in Sung.

"Did he say anything before leaving for Seoul?" Jeong-seon asked, finally posing the very question of her real interest, but indifferently.

Before answering, Sun blushed to recall Sung's actions early that morning of his departure for Seoul, how he had softly hugged her shoulders, promising, "I'll return." That had happened on the main road in front of the police station as she was carrying his bag, having accompanied him that far. It was the first time since his return to the village. Loyal to his wife Jeong-seon, he had never till then touched Yu Sun, not even to brush against a single finger of hers. Why then had he shown such kindness that day? Was it simply a gesture in departing for the long trip? Or did his disappointment and worries over Jeong-seon loosen his matrimonial bond? Or did he briefly reveal his deepest feelings, in that cold, dark, emotionally overwhelmed moment, a spontaneous response to her true love for him, love she had thought to keep so well hidden?

"He didn't say anything. He never says much," Sun finally replied, unwilling to offer Jeong-seon an opening into her thoughts.

"Did he get any letter the day before?" Jeong-seon asked, casually adding some rice to the scorched-rice water.

Just as casual, Sun said, "I think he got some sort of letter."

Dipping her spoon into the bowl of scorched-rice water, Jeong-seon asked, "What kind of envelope? Western? Japanese?" As if she had found a clue.

"It looked Western."

"Oh? Did he say anything about the letter?"

"I didn't pay much attention. Later, though, I saw it all torn up."

"Really? Where are the pieces?"

"I burnt them all in the kitchen fire. He told me to."

"Not a single piece left? Just a little one? Even with one letter on it?" Jeong-seon sounded anxious despite herself. She wanted to know, somehow, who had sent the letter.

"No, there's nothing left." Sun was firm. "It's all burnt."

"Still, go quickly, see if anything's left," Jeong-seon wheedled, trying to sound friendly.

3-32

Yu Sun went to the kitchen to look. "There is surely nothing left," she thought, and promptly returned to report, "No, there was nothing."

"Look more carefully," insisted Jeong-seon, somewhat annoyed, as if Yu Sun had intentionally neglected to search thoroughly for something that could have been found. Jeong-seon failed to realize how ridiculous she looked fretting over a few scraps of paper immediately upon arriving to visit her husband after long absence.

Such behavior displeased Yu Sun. Her sympathy for Jeong-seon crying at the well had vanished completely. Sun still found inexplicable Jeong-seon's arrival two days after Sung had left for Seoul. And what was this business about that letter? Why did she beg for even a scrap? Had she done something improper? Did the letter inform on her? Come to think of it, Sung's reaction of tearing the letter to pieces immediately after reading it was quite suspicious. Sun began to wonder and now even wanted to see how Jeong-seon might react upon reading a scrap if she should find one.

Yu Sun went back to the kitchen and looked for scraps, lifting pieces of unburnt wood and searching everywhere.

"What are you looking for now?" asked Han-gap's mother, turning to Sun. She had been sitting in front of the fire scraping potatoes.

"Scraps of a letter," replied Sun, trying to hide a smile, and asked "Have you seen any?"

"Not a whole letter? Just scraps of a letter?" Han-gap's mother grew curious.

"Yes, from a letter that can create big problems. Isn't anything left? Did it all end up in the fire? How nice it'd be to find a piece! Oh, here's one!" Sun snatched it up and blew off the ashes.

"You found one?" Han-gap's mother sounded relieved. "Let me see," she added, stretching her neck for a glimpse.

"Here, have a look." Sun held out the torn, square piece for her to see.

"What's written there, and why's it so important? Read it for me. You know how. I can't. My eyes are like the soles of my feet. I went to the night school, but I only learned my letters up to 'b.' My son knows how to read, of course. He even knows some Chinese. Oh, my boy! Will he get released by the high court this time?" Han-gap's mother seemed to forget all about the scrap at the thought of her son's case. She started scraping the potatoes again.

Sun took the scrap out of the kitchen and handed it to Jeong-seon, who took it quickly, nearly tossing her spoon onto the tray in her haste. On the scrap appeared a smattering of letters. Jeong-seon immediately recognized the handwriting.

3-33

"Sun," Han-gap's mother called out from the kitchen, "here's more!" Assuming that to find every scrap of the letter was somehow important for Jeong-seon, the wife of a hero, she had looked further and found some.

Stifling laughter, Sun made to return to the kitchen. Mr. Heo had never ordered her off on such unnecessary errands. Why on the earth was a scrap, finding a scrap, so important for the world?

She was met on the way by Han-gap's mother coming out of the kitchen herself and handing over two scraps of paper. "Here. Good enough? I don't know what's on them. My eyes are like the soles of a bear's feet." She rubbed her eyes, as if that could clear them enough for reading.

Glancing at the words written on the scraps found by Han-gap's mother, Sun could make out, "rumor," "love affair," and "Yeong." She could roughly gauge the trouble. Jeong-seon was rumored to be having an affair, and the letter had alerted Sung, who had ripped the letter to shreds and hurried off to Seoul. That would explain why Jeong-seon was so flustered. And her sobbing at the well, was that for the same reason? Of course it was. And why had she sent no letters for the three months after leaving for Seoul? "But how could a virtuous woman like Jeong-seon do such a thing?" Sun shook her head in wonder.

"Where is it?" called Jeong-seon. Too impatient to wait for Sun to get back, she opened the double door and held out her arm.

"There are only two pieces," announced Sun, quite boldly, openly disclosing her ill will, "with words like 'rumor' and 'affair,' written on them. The sender's name appears to be 'Yeong.' Is that enough now?"

At this, Jeong-seon blushed scarlet and abruptly slid the door closed, but she pulled it so quickly that it slipped out of its groove and didn't close well.

Jeong-seon suddenly realized that Sun was not the girl that she had imagined. The realization profoundly displeased her, and she found herself annoyed at Sun's boldness.

"Sun, come in here," she ordered, and started needling her as sharply with questions as if she were a pin cushion.

"Who does the washing for my husband? You?"

"Han-gap's mother and I take turns."

"Who cleans the bedding?"

"The bedding? Same as with the washing."

"Well, thanks for all the hard work."

Sun remained silent, puzzled.

"Who brings his food tray?"

"I do."

"Always?"

"What?"

"Oh, who else could do it? Who makes his bed?"

Sun didn't answer.

"Who else but you, right?"

"Why are you asking these questions?" Sun demanded, showing annoyance.

"Oh, I just wanted to know. Are you upset?" asked Jeong-seon, sounding regretful.

"I'm not upset," replied Sun, her face growing sad. "Mr. Heo himself makes his bed, cleans his room, fills his wash basin, removes his food tray, and even maintains the fire for heating his room. He doesn't order other people and even declines help if we offer to do things for him."

3-34

Embarrassed at Sun's response, Jeong-seon posed a different question to change the subject. "What does he do all day? Does he go out? Does he stay home?" Even in these questions, Jeong-seon remained alert to feeling out the relationship between her husband and Sun.

"He is constantly busy, with no time to rest. He gets up very early and does a lot before breakfast. He cleans his room, sweeps the yard, and tends the trees, then goes to the riverside to do exercises and wash himself. He gets back home about sunrise. At first, he was doing all that alone, but one or two villagers eventually began going along with him, and then more. For about a month now, many people have been meeting on the ridge in front of the house here to do exercises, sweep the roads, and go wash in the river or go for a run. They also gather firewood or pick up rocks from the fields. Before the land froze, they even made some new rice paddies near Rabbit Well. All that before sunrise. After sunrise, they do their own work. These days, about fifty people join in. Whenever they shout and sing, "Get up early and work for the village before the sun gets up, work for us all," we feel like rushing out and joining in. This coming spring, we women are going to join them. In the paddies and fields that the men worked on before sunrise, the women will farm in common to earn money for the children's school fees, books, and lunch. In other words, for their education."

Explaining about Heo Sung's work and project, Yu Sun felt suddenly joyful and energized. Her heart seemed eased of its earlier annoyance over the paper scraps. Moreover, she wanted to tell Jeong-seon, who seemed to have no useful thoughts, about something of use.

"When you were here before, you must have taken a road around the village instead of walking through the village on the main road. Things have changed a lot there since Mr. Heo came, and new things are added, too. We made a yard for threshing, and built a big storage shed, a barn for the oxen, and a pen for pigs. Except for a few rich families, the threshing yard is used by all the villagers. They bring stacks of grain stalks and thresh them there. Around the yard are the barn, the pen, and even a henhouse. We also built a house there for a family that takes care of the place, a family with twins, I heard, so the place is very clean. There are still people who have a barn and a henhouse on their own property, but that'll change soon. Mr. Heo walks around after breakfast to see if anybody is sick or if any family is having trouble. People tell him, "Our baby is throwing up," or "Today's the day to pay the school fee." Afterwards, he goes to the threshing yard to see after the oxen, pigs, and chickens, and evenings find him teaching at the night school and doing paperwork for the cooperative. He has no time to rest, no, not a minute. But that's not all. Since he's a lawyer, people come from all over to ask if he'll take on their lawsuit. Some bring a chicken, some a bottle of alcohol, but Mr. Heo refuses any pay. If they insist, he'll first check if the chicken's from a village without any contagious disease and then put it in the henhouse at the threshing yard."

Yu Sun grew so excited in the telling that her cheeks flushed red. As Jeong-seon listened, she felt a new apprehension over Sung, having learned something of him that she had not known before in such detail. At the same time, she found herself displeased to sit as the actual wife and have to listen to Sun speak with such excitement about Sung, as if he were her own husband.

3-35

To hear Sun tell it, Sung had been leading a busy life. He busied himself, however, for nothing of self-benefit, nothing that fed or clothed him. Serving others and the world were things that Jeong-seon knew only as ideas in books of moral exhortation or through words from a church pulpit, nothing that she would ever put into practice herself. But her own husband was doing all that, which surprised her, yet also reassured her that a man leading such a busy life would likely have no time for a lover or an affair.

When Jeong-seon later went to the village to greet people, she finally had a taste of the busy country life and its radical difference from life in the city. Most interesting for her was the threshing yard, which would be sprayed with water at night to facilitate freezing and thereby reduce the dust. In the middle was placed a large, long stone, a large mortar, or a log, and this was called a "yard stone." It was fixed in place using a number of smooth, flat, circular stones. Stocky men would then use thick straw ropes to tie a mat down tightly for grain sorting, and after covering their heads with a white cloth and binding their pants around the shinbone with a pad-like cloth, they would divide a large sheaf of rice into smaller, workable sheaves, tie up the roots of each with tough strings made of rice straw or hemp, holding each bundle tightly underfoot to do so, then raise each up high over their heads with both hands and bring the bundles smashing down upon the "yard stone" with a loud cry of "Chi!" Rice grains would tumble off with a rustling sound. After being threshed several times this way, each rice-sheaf would stretch back its bowed neck, lightened after shedding its grain, as if disburdened of life's weighty responsibility, and be thrown to the edge of the yard for ready collection. At that moment, its name would change from "rice-sheaf" to "straw bundle."

Afterwards, the old and the children would use ash-tree canes to knock away the remaining grains hanging to the straw's tops. They would then grab these tops with their hands to pull and shake them vigorously to get rid of the dry grassy part and prepare the straw for better trimming so that it could be bundled into sizes larger than an armful. The resulting straw would be twisted into ropes, mats, and shoes during the whole winter or be used to cover pits and to block the wind from play areas for children. Its color, softer and warmer than gold, would adorn the village all winter, and in the spring keep the rain out of homes as the straw thatch for farmhouse roofs.

As the sound of threshing continued—*Che! Shiruruk. Che! Suwa!*—the yard stone became covered by lovely grains of rice, exquisite in color and shape. The grains would then be brushed together using a sweeper to form a golden cone.

"Let's have a cigarette break," one might say.

"Just a little left to do," another might note.

The energetic men worked joyfully until the landowner and the supervisor of the tenant farms came out to stand nearby with arms crossed and feet shod in dress shoes that failed to match the work in progress. They had drunk alcohol and eaten meat in the warm room of a tenant farmer's house and would come out occasionally to supervise. Whenever these two emerged in this way, the joyful men's faces would cloud over.

The landowner would take half the cone with him, even have it carried by tenant farmers. He walked through the twilit village with a triumphant air, having also received other debts repaid at high interest. He took more than half of the farmers' joy and sweat that way. How pleasant life would be if the men's families could consume all that rice for themselves alone. That was Sung's vision, but Jeong-seon knew nothing of it. The scene was just an interesting spectacle for her.

3-36

Why did Sung rush off to Seoul even though the trial was not for several more days?

Around eight in the morning on the day before Jeong-seon and Gap-jin went to Oryudong, Sung received a letter from Lee Geon-yeong warning him of a rumor that Jeong-seon and Gap-jin were getting too close.

Putting little trust in Geon-yeong's words, Sung first considered the letter mere slander. Indeed, suspicions about his own wife based on someone else's words struck him as improper, and he even had ill feeling toward Geon-yeong for writing. Sung's heartfelt outpourings in his journal reflected this state of mind.

He could not, however, calm his misgivings even though he tried to act the loyal husband to his wife. He was in agony. "Jeong-seon and Gap-jin." The phrase burned in his heart like birdlime and could not be quenched.

Sung suffered all day. To doubt his wife was not right, but he tended to doubt her.

He finally decided upon going to Seoul. With a tormented heart, he took the early morning train to Seoul on the very day that Jeong-seon went to the baseball stadium with Gap-jin.

Sung first wanted to arrive without providing notice of his visit and thereby discover what Jeong-seon was doing and whom she was with. But he reconsidered, "No, that's not the right thing to do. To doubt my lovely wife isn't right. It's better to send notice."

He decided upon sending a telegram to announce, "Arriving in Seoul tonight, Sung." He even got off to do so at the stations Shinanju and Pyeongyang, but each time, in a sudden fit of anger, he decided against it, telling himself, "No, I'll just arrive unannounced."

He tried various ways to control his feelings and calm down, but found himself actually trembling no matter what he tried, incapable of calming his nerves for some time. His reason, however, eventually overcame his emotions. At Hwangju station, he sent a nice telegram: "I'm coming tonight. Your husband." He even bought three baskets of apples.

As he boarded the train again, he felt a kind of joy. Though he had passed through the scenic Daedong River region without paying much attention, he was now more relaxed and able to view the scenery around Namuritbeol and the Jeongbang Mountain Fortress. But the grey mountains there, with their gloomy tint no matter how bright the sun, seemed to reflect Sung's heart.

Shortly before ten that evening, he got off at Gyeongseong Station. As the train slowly stopped at the platform, Sung tried to spot Jeong-seon, even sticking his head out the window a bit, not so much as to be noticed, but he couldn't see her.

"She's probably looking for me in the first and second class cars," he told himself. "She wouldn't know I now ride third class like a farmer."

He picked up his baggage and got off, making his way through the crowd to the first and second class cars to search for his wife, but she was not there, either.

As he was about to climb the stairs, a little disappointed and upset, somebody clapped him on the shoulder and greeted him in English with a hearty "Hello!"

Sung set his baggage down on the ground and accepted the man's hand, shaking it. The man was Lee Geon-yeong.

3-37

Sung felt a foreboding at encountering Lee Geon-yeong rather than his own wife, along with a degree of embarrassment that she was not waiting for him.

"Ah, Dr. Lee," Sung replied, quickly controlling his feelings and attempting to express the appreciation owed. "Thank you for your letter."

"I'm sorry," Lee said, again in English. He proceeded in the subtle manner of one comforting a younger brother or a junior whispering, "I realize that it's rather forward of me to say anything about your private life, but I love and respect you deeply, so I couldn't just ignore a matter concerning your honor, especially one causing me considerable agony." He then raised his voice to its normal tone, no longer needing to speak secretively, and asked, "Did you send notice that you're coming?" He was still standing close to Sung, who smelt cigarettes and alcohol on his breath, another omen.

"I sent a telegram, but probably too late," Sung explained, unable to lie but feeling uncomfortable.

"What time did you sent it?" Geon-yeong asked, his tone implying that he had more to tell.

"Around five, from Hwangju," Sung replied.

"Oh, I see," Geon-yeong observed, again in English and giving a shrug like a Westerner. "Jeong-seon won't have gotten it, I expect." Immediately regretting that he had referred to her by name in such a familiar manner, he added, "Your wife, as far as I know, went to watch a baseball game this afternoon with Gap-jin, and then went on with him afterwards to eat dinner somewhere. That's what she does these days, almost every day, so if you go home now, your wife won't be there. If you want to catch her, you should go instead to the Cheongmokdang restaurant or Gyeongseong Hotel. Oh! It's time for me to go! Good-bye, take care of your wife!" With those parting words, Geon-yeong hurried up the steps, heading for the opposite platform, apparently, his walking stick swinging. Geon-yeong was in fact on his way to Incheon, having just left Seo-bun and downed a shot of whisky at the station restaurant to dull his conscience. He had been hanging around the station wondering if he might meet some woman stepping from the train arriving on the Gyeongui line when he had happened to encounter Sung, and he was now sauntering off truly satisfied with the revenge about to be wreaked upon Gap-jin and Jeong-seon.

Why the trip to Incheon? He never acted without purpose, and had two reasons for going to Incheon. He intended to visit a woman doctor with a practice there, but he also wanted an alibi for his whereabouts, proof that he was gone from Seoul in case there should be trouble on account of his dealings with Jeong Seo-bun. That he had run into a reliable man like Sung at the station, a man who would never lie, was an unexpected gain.

Sung, feeling almost insulted by Geon-yeong's words, rushed off for the trolley stop in a confused state, his baggage in one hand as he dodged traffic on the broad street as thick with cars as ice floes in a stormy sea. His heart, too, was turbulent with thoughts and misgivings.

Just as he had almost reached the trolley stop, he was compelled to step abruptly back, nearly struck by a car that loomed suddenly before him as it quickly passed by. The car honked loudly and sped on toward Cheongpadong, leaving Sung behind in dust and gasoline smoke.

3-38

Sung, having barely avoided being struck, took several steps after the car, though in shock, not anger. He had glimpsed his wife and Gap-jin within. Gap-jin had been sitting on the left side with his right arm around Jeong-seon's shoulder, and they were laughing, their faces turned to each other, deep in conversation.

Sung tried to doubt his eyes, but he had seen too clearly. The evening was dark, and the car interior bright. He could not have mistaken his wife, nor Gap-jin.

Reluctantly admitting the truth of Geon-yeong's words, Sung completely lost all peace of mind. He felt his own pulse beat faster, his hands and feet grow cold, and his knees begin to shake. Jealousy and rage blazed through his soul.

"Taxi!" Sung called, his hand raised high. One of the taxis lined up before the station rolled out to him. The driver stepped out and loaded Sung's baggage as Sung got in.

"Where to?" asked the driver after resuming his seat and turning around.

"Indogyo Bridge, quickly." Controlling himself to hide his emotional state, he added, "If you catch the car that just passed by—that one a couple of cars ahead—I'll pay you ten won. Drive fast!" He bent forward as if to impel the car forward by his own weight.

Reminded of a car chase in some movie, the driver was curious but wary. Ten won, however, was not a bad fare, so he sped up, though to no more than 25 miles an hour.

The taxi, moreover, was old. Despite its paint job and fancy appearance, the faster the engine revved, the more the car rattled, belching out clouds of smoke without really going much faster.

As a car overtook them, Sung grew impatient. "Can't you go any faster?" His tone was almost angry.

"You can't go over the 25 mile-an-hour limit," replied the driver. "You'd get pulled over." He even slowed down. Realizing that he would be unable to accelerate enough to get the promised bonus, he declined to waste gasoline.

Sung grew angrier but could do nothing. As more cars passed, he threw himself back in the seat, disappointed, and gave up.

Even the rattling taxi eventually arrived at the Han River's Indogyo Bridge. "Should I cross?" asked the driver, halting at the toll gate.

Sung motioned with his chin to drive further, but otherwise sat motionless though he felt like beating the driver up. He had missed the car with Jeong-seon and knew it but hoped to en- counter her and Gap-jin on the bridge somewhere.

"And what if I do catch them?" he asked himself.

3-39

After ten at night in winter on the bridge spanning the Han River, few people were to be seen beyond one or two individuals pulling loaded carts, the occasional laborer walking across, and a farmer or two heading home late. In the distance, the electric lights of Yongsan and Samgae, and the half-moon glow over a mountain—probably the one where Haengju Mountain Fortress was located—conferred a forlorn scene.

As the taxi moved along the road on the railway bridge toward Nodeul, then back again toward Seoul, re-crossing the river, Sung attentively scanned left and right, but Jeong-seon was nowhere to be seen.

"Drive inside the city gates," Sung ordered. He was so angry over the slow taxi for losing the car with Jeong-seon that he wanted to pull the driver out and pummel him, but he controlled his anger, remembering what Mr. Han would say. Mr. Han held that the common malice of Koreans was to make trouble over things that could no longer be recovered, thereby further increasing the harm for both sides.

Once, Sung and Han witnessed a bicycle delivery boy carrying a bowl of *seolleongtang* soup collide with another cyclist. The bowl went smashing to the ground, and the two men tore into each other, cursing and beating in endless argument. Observing them, Han remarked, "Our folk often do this, not only in private affairs but also at the political level. The bowl is already broken. One should move on. But people accuse each other for what's already done and can't be undone. That's really futile." Mr. Han then suggested to the fighters, "You should go to the police. Or just go home." But they didn't listen.

Although Sung could hardly suppress his anger and his desire to argue with the driver, he controlled himself out of respect for Mr. Han.

Sung checked into a hotel in Jeong-dong. He felt shame in doing so rather than going home, but to face things there threatened even greater shame, so he chose a hotel where an acquaintance had once stayed. The clock struck eleven. Sung called home, only to hear Yu-wol say that Jeong-seon was not yet back. He sat in blank silence, unmoving and ignored by the boy spreading a mattress for his bed. Upon the mattress was placed a green quilt of artificial silk, and along the top edge of its upper side, a scarlet strip seemed to shine with near brilliance.

The room was not bad but looked empty without a desk, wardrobe, or painting. He grew morose to think that this was the room of a first class hotel in downtown Seoul and recalled Mr. Han saying that Koreans idled their lives away despite the country's cultural poverty. Whenever Sung encountered trouble, he would recall Han's words, realizing anew their meaning and power. However, he was not currently in a state to reflect deeply on them. Anxious concern over his wife's whereabouts and actions pierced his heart through and through, twisting in every direction.

"Jealousy is a base feeling," Sung reproached himself, but he failed to repress that feeling.

Leaving word that he would soon return, Sung walked out of the hotel and headed for Jongno, the downtown district. Midnight in that area always brought out the drunks and rickshaw pullers, who roamed about like nocturnal animals. "I should eat something," Sung thought, noticing his hunger and recalling that he had eaten no dinner. Any husband expecting to be met at the train station by his wife would have anticipated eating at home and would naturally have skipped a meal even on a train running late.

3-40

The Jongno intersection fell silent after the trolley to Dongdaemun had rattled past with its piercing red headlights and rollicky noise. The occasional taxi loaded with drunken customers appeared and disappeared like small crabs crawling across a moonlit seashore before vanishing into the night.

"Where should I go?" Unable to decide, Sung stood blankly facing Hwashin Department Store. Ignorant of the area's restaurants, he didn't know where to go or what to eat.

At that moment, Sung heard some people coming loudly around the corner at Taseogwan Restaurant. The principal voice belonged to Gang, a lawyer whom Sung knew well. The man following him was a lawyer named Yim. Both were well known among their colleagues as being very 'heroic.' They had good incomes, but they spent too freely because they couldn't manage to put their dissolute lives behind them. They loved drinking and talking, and were strictly loyal to friends, thereby fitting the template of the old traditional Asian hero. They were also very arrogant, often behaving haughtily, yet they enjoyed social gatherings among people of various ages.

"Hah! You think I don't know? But I do. I know everything!" Gang was bragging.

"Huh! Those bastards," was the reply. Yim seemed enraged about something.

Sung doffed his hat and politely greeted these two, his seniors.

"Oh, who's this? Ah Mr. Heo, it's you." Gang laughed and took Sung's hand in greeting, shaking it gladly. He did so not only because he respected Sung, a junior, but also because Sung's humility and polite deference triggered his heroic gallantry.

"Oh, you're here, Mr. Heo." Yim also shook Sung's hand in greeting. "But what are you doing here? I heard you're doing such great work for country people. Isn't that right?"

"Oh, yes, but not yet really great work. I'm still learning."

"Well, let's talk about that a bit later," Gang intervened. His good cheer renewed, he said, "Now that we've run into Mr. Heo, we should go have a drink together." He lifted his stick and shouted in the direction of the intersection, calling for a taxi.

"Hey, mister, where to?" inquired a rickshaw puller, unwrapping a blanket from his shoulders and folding it over his arm. He left his rickshaw in the same spot and approached the three lawyers.

"What? I call a taxi, and you come? What do you want?" Gang, as if enraged, glared angrily at the man.

"We've got to earn money, too. Here, come on." He went for his rickshaw and pulled it up to Gang. Slinging his blanket back onto his shoulders, he smoothed the seat, pushing down on the cushion to flatten it, and fawning in deference, said, "Please, get in."

The other rickshaw pullers watched them, half out of interest and half out of curiosity about the outcome. A couple with more courage drew their rickshaws nearby and stood waiting as the other man had done.

Gang surveyed the scene with a drunken eye, gazing at the rickshaw men, not only the three nearby but the others in the distance, then climbed into the nearest rickshaw and said, "I'm very impressed by your devotion and passion for your job." He was directing these words to the rickshaw man whose rig he had chosen, but that man didn't seem to realize that Gang was addressing him. Gang then turned toward the other rickshaw pullers and said, "Fools! Either pull up as closely as this fellow or go to find other customers. Don't just stand around skulking. You'll starve." He made as though to swing his stick at them, raising it level with his shoulder. The other rickshaw men scattered like startled chickens in a fluttering frenzy.

Gang laughed out loud.

3-41

Sung also climbed into a rickshaw and followed Gang and Yim to a famous restaurant, the biggest in Seoul—actually in the whole of Korea. At the entrance, bright with electric lights, stood an old, bald-headed waiter dealing with a drunken customer bundled up in an Inverness overcoat and wearing glasses, while two *gisaeng* women lingered nearby, vacantly, as though in a daze. They had apparently tried hard to play the coquette, but without much effect on the man and so had lapsed into indifference.

"Oh, you're here, Father?" cried the younger of the two *gisaeng* vivaciously, noticing Gang and tugging on his hand.

"'Father,' you say?" retorted Gang, deciding to pick a fight "How am I your father? I don't even know your mother."

"Oh, you don't have to get so angry," the older *gisaeng*

interjected, humor in her tone. "Just take it to mean you're the father of your own children."

Gang laughed. "That's right." He patted the younger *gisaeng* on her shoulder. "Oh, my good daughter."

"You don't want to be called 'Father,' but you now call me your daughter," grumbled the younger *gisaeng*, now grown sullen.

"You don't like being called his daughter, do you?" Yim put in, draping his arm about the sullen *gisaeng*'s shoulders and lightly pinching her cheek. "Just understand him to mean the only daughter of his mother-in-law."

"Ow!" she screamed.

The drunkard who had been causing difficulty for the waiter drifted away quietly, overwhelmed by the imposing air of the three men. They followed the waiter along winding halls, apparently heading for a very isolated room. Unused to this sort of place, Sung looked around curiously. He noticed calligraphic writings by nobility on the walls and observed drunken customers with *gisaeng* women, their faces whitened and eyes glittering as they strutted past, dragging their long skirts. The women all seemed to know Gang and Yim because they offered greetings in passing by, joked in unmannerly ways, pinched the two, embraced or were embraced, and clutched at hands. Nobody knew Sung, however, and Sung didn't know anybody.

Some rooms were dark and empty, but from other, well-lit rooms came sounds of the *janggu* drum, the traditional harp *gayageum*, and voices singing. From one room was heard the voice of a customer singing along in an excess of mirth but constantly off key. From another room somewhere issued loud voices, as if in argument. Probably just raucous joking, thought Sung. The rooms seemed to stretch into the hundreds.

The room where Sung was led seemed the quietest. It was also well heated. Even the small antechamber for shoes and coats seemed heated. Sung felt the floor's warmth through his socks as he peered into the room. The larger room was illuminated by two bright lamps. The interior of the room further from the door was set off by three folding screens, each one about three meters long and composed of twelve sections painted in floral patterns. A fancy purple pallet with indigo stripes lay spread out on the floor, and several square pillows and cushions with embroidered bat patterns for good fortune were strewn about. In the corner nearest the antechamber stood a couple of potted plants, one like a castor-bean plant, but called *yasde* in Japanese, and the other a cycad plant. And in the middle of the room squatted a large, low rectangular table covered with a white tablecloth.

"Please, take your coats off." The two *gisaeng* had followed them from the restaurant entrance and were now helping Gang and Yim out of their Inverness coats. Sung took off his coat himself and hung it without assistance.

3-42

The waiter brought tea, and it tasted terrible. Sung was surprised that such a high-class restaurant would serve low quality tea. He looked more carefully at the pictures on the folding screen and those hanging on the walls and discovered that none had any special artistic quality. The inferior taste, however, might not be particularly the restaurant's fault. Perhaps this was simply the level of Korea's cultural standards. Sung again recalled words from Mr. Han: "As a dewdrop reveals natural law, so a floorboard reveals national culture." Han had meant that by inspecting such a floorboard, one could judge the technology and artistry of Korea for a particular time, and by analyzing even the grime on a plank, one could understand in detail the conditions of that time.

From elsewhere in the building came the strains of a Japanese song. These days, a lot of Japanese frequented Korean restaurants, and Koreans were said to sometimes visit Japanese restaurants as well. A

Japanese guest coming here would judge Korea's cultural standard based on the pictures and furniture in this room, thought Sung.

"Hey," Gang called to the waiter. "Don't bring snacks that make the stomach full. You understand? Just tasty snacks."

"Where can you find food that doesn't fill your stomach? Even water does that," cracked one of the *gisaeng*.

"What did you say? What do *you* know?" Gang gave a sidelong scowl as if threatening a child.

"You can't even feel well-prepared food once it's in your stomach," Yim said, acting as though he knew everything.

"Right. A beautiful woman's like that, too," Gang added. "Just a light thing, whether she's beside you or being embraced, or even sitting on your lap. That's how she is."

"Let her die and become a ghost, then," said a *gisaeng* sharply.

Alcohol and snacks were brought. The *gisaeng* women poured Japanese sake into small Japanese cups, setting them before the three men.

Gang lifted his cup and turned to Sung saying, "Here, Mr. Heo, let's toast." Sung had once attended a lecture by Gang, so he politely raised his cup with two hands and knelt, as was customary. The three sipped the liquor before setting their cups down again.

Then pointing to Sung, Gang asked the two *gisaeng*, "Girls, you know who this gentleman is?"

"No, not at all."

"Have we seen him before?"

Embarrassed at their own ignorance, they gazed at Sung.

"Bitches, you don't know him?"

"How can we? We've never seen him before."

"Right. We've never seen him."

"Guess."

"Well . . ." the younger of the two girls murmured.

"Maybe a schoolteacher?" the older suggested.

Still unsure what to say, the first girl refused to hazard a guess, shook her whole body impatiently, and exclaimed, "Oh, I don't know!"

"You've never heard of Mr. Heo, the lawyer?" revealed Yim, triumphantly. "You're so ignorant."

"Ah!" she exclaimed. "Mr. Yun's . . ." but was silenced by the other *gisaeng's* glance. The two of them knew Sung's name, and that he was Mr. Yun's son-in-law.

"We saw the photos in a magazine," said the older *gisaeng*. "Your wife is very beautiful."

3-43

"Pour some more," Gang ordered. "This just leaves me thirsty. Such a small cup doesn't suit a heroic man like me. Legendary Chinese heroic men used to drink directly from the jug and use swords to slice the ham haunch for eating. What's this tiny cup for?" He made as if to throw it onto the table.

"Should I order bigger cups?" one of the *gisaeng* asked.

"Of course," Gang replied. "Bring bigger ones. Whisky, too. I need to drink like a real man and forget the sorrows of a hero untimely born. You agree? Others can talk about the League of Nations or arms reduction or whatever. We've got nothing to do but drink. Real men like us, but unable to prove ourselves. How tragic! Hey, you bitches! Why do you laugh? What do you know about such things? Disgusting bitches!" he exclaimed, then laughed roughly. Gang seemed to be getting more and more drunk.

The whisky arrived, a dark, capacious bottle sporting a white horse on its label, accompanied by three high-stemmed, crystalline glasses, and yellow-brown liquor soon flowed from the dark bottle into the glasses of crystal as the *gisaeng* poured.

"Enough. Here, Mr. Heo, let's toast." Gang lifted a glass, nodding to Sung.

"Oh, I can't," Sung declined.

"What'd you say? No, none of that. Here, drink some more. A man should drink when it's time, and not drink when it's not time. Don't be so inflexible."

"Have some." Yim echoed the encouragement. "A man should be able to drink."

"Yes, have some!" urged the younger *gisaeng*, her tone endearing.

"Afraid of your wife?" the other *gisaeng* taunted lightly, smiling.

Sung already felt flushed from the sake. He hesitated, doubting that he should drink so much, but his anger and the alcohol already imbibed encouraged him to drink more and grow truly drunk. He accepted the whisky and downed it as Gang had intended.

Deciding that Sung was not interested in the two *gisaeng*, and concluding that they were also beneath his own dignity, Gang summoned another, rather more coy one, loudly ordering that San-wol be brought.

The whisky in Sung's stomach seemed to possess a magical power. It made him joyful and gregarious. He felt as if time had stopped and space had opened up without bounds. Taking initiative, he offered drinks to Gang and Yim, and even to the two *gisaeng*.

The new *gisaeng* called San-wol soon arrived. She was wearing a pink jacket and white skirt, making her look quite decent. As she crossed the threshold, she bowed lightly, placing one hand on the floor and kneeling. Her eyes twinkled.

Sung was surprised. He felt certain that he had seen her before. San-wol also started upon seeing him, but her eyes twinkled more. Unsure about the propriety of showing that she knew him, she turned to the other guests.

"So, San-wol, are you proficient at serving men these days?"

asked Gang, pulling her by the hand and placing her beside Sung. "Tonight, you should serve this gentleman. We'll see if you're qualified to be a great *gisaeng*. These other two have failed," he added, laughing.

3-44

Only then did San-wol realize that Heo Sung was the guest for her to entertain. She lifted the bottle to pour, waiting for him to raise his glass, as was the Korean style.

"Just pour it in," Yim said. "That's the way with Western drinks." He was again acting as if he knew everything.

But Sung lifted his glass, and San-wol poured the whisky. Without drinking, he set the glass back down. Who was San-wol? He remembered having seen her several times.

As Sung and San-wol looked at each other oddly, Gang said, "Well, well, the man of talent and the woman of beauty must've already recognized each other. Congratulations! Here, Mr. Heo, *gambbai*, as the Japanese say. In other words, bottoms up. San-wol, you should serve your man well, of course, but I didn't expect you to fall in love with him at first sight." Gang laughed again, exuberantly raising his glass and spilling the drink.

"The bond between a man of talent and a woman of beauty is predestined by the heavens," explained Yim, playing innocent.

"No, that's not it," responded San-wol, embarrassed. "I've seen him several times before. But that was when he was still a student. That's why I didn't recognize him at first." Then calling to mind her profession as *gisaeng*, she smiled brightly and turned toward Sung, speaking kindly in a Seoul accent, "Mister, don't you remember me? While I was in school, I sometimes visited your wife, though I never spoke to you."

Sung nodded. He remembered now. Yes, he had seen her at Mr. Yun's house. At that time, Sung had been a student living in the servants' quarters and wouldn't have dared even to glance at female guests visiting Jeong-seon, the daughter of the house.

"Oh, I didn't realize you're a *gisaeng* of noble lineage. I could see you'd attended school and were educated, but I didn't know that you're the daughter of an aristocratic family." Gang spoke joyfully, again spilling his drink. "San-wol," he added, "have a drink from me." He handed his glass to her.

"How gracious you are," she said, accepting the glass. Gang poured for her, an unusual act. She chugged the drink.

"My God! Are you crazy?" cried the younger *gisaeng*, astonished to see San-wol down the whisky in one shot.

Returning the glass to Gang and pretending to be drunk, San-wol retorted, "You know, I'd just like to get drunk tonight."

"Only half a year's passed since San-wol started her work as *gisaeng*, but she's one of the greatest in our time," Gang claimed, looking around at the others, one after another, leaving unclear whom he was addressing. "San-wol's actually a daughter of Seo, who was a well-known church elder. She went to elementary school, then middle and high school. She even went to college, but after two years' study, she had a certain realization and became a *gisaeng*. That's why she's a completely different sort than these two here." At this point, he directed his attention momentarily to the two other *gisaeng*.

He then turned to Sung and continued. "She's fluent in Japanese as well as English, can write and play the piano, can sing, and hey, girls, what else can she do? Right, right, she looks beautiful, can talk well, and has character, but what are her flaws? Do you know? Oh, right, she has no fear and is smart, a very unusual *gisaeng*." He laughed.

The night deepened as the gathering slipped further down into pools of drunkenness.

3-45

As San-wol became the center of attention, the other two *gisaeng* drew back.

Sung felt his mind become slowly detached, as though he were losing control over his thoughts and actions. He even leaned onto the square pillow and stretched out his legs as he grasped the hand of the *gisaeng*. Also drunk, San-wol lay her head upon Sung's shoulder. He turned toward her to smell her hair and brushed his hand down her back. Sung finally realized what alcohol could do.

He drank as much as Gang and Yim offered him. Almost two bottles of whisky were gone. The guests and the *gisaeng* all got drunk, and as they did, the electric lighting itself seemed inebriated, as did the glasses and the bottles. Sung felt as if not only Korea but also the whole world, and even the entire universe were falling into drunkenness. He now understood the full meaning of the Chinese expression "*Ho-Ri-Geon-Gon.*" The words "World In Drink Bottle" took on more than their literal meaning.

"Oh, my God," Sung realized, "how could I be so drunk?" He felt some shame, but his conscience was easily numbed by the strong, anesthetic whisky.

In his mind, a jumble of thoughts swirled incoherently. Thoughts of his wife, her family, his project in the countryside, Mr. Han, San-wol, and various other people and things. These drunken thoughts all seemed like unreal dreams, and even serious things became unimportant. Everything seemed amusing. Even Jeong-seon and Gap-jin. He had no idea what they were doing at that moment but found it ridiculous, whatever it might be.

"Never mind!" Sung said in English.

"Never mind?" San-wol looked at him curiously, but with eyes that also seemed to offer everything, as though pleading for him to take her. The whisky had also transformed her. She had dropped the pretense of decency and assumed the air of a coquette.

"Oh, yes, never mind!" Sung repeated. Imagining his wife flirting with Gap-jin, he drew San-wol nearer, clasping her waist. She trembled like a virgin with her first love.

Gang was talking to Yim in a self-important way, but the latter was preoccupied with one of the *gisaeng*, trying to pull her onto his lap, and not listening.

"I'm happy," San-wol whispered, more to herself than to Sung. She rubbed her cheek against his chest in excitement and clung to him, her arms stretched around him just under the armpits of his vest. "But happiness is just a moment," she added, as if near tears, and she brought her head lower, rubbing her cheek against his thigh.

"So passionate," Sung thought, gazing at the nape of her neck. Jeong-seon herself was little different. Also passionate. Was he too well-mannered toward her? Weren't all women passionate?

"What are you doing!" exclaimed the older *gisaeng*, slapping Sun-wol's rump. She had just returned from the other room, where a lucky gambler had tossed some money her way.

"Ow," cried San-wol, jumping up and giving her a sidelong scowl. San-wol carried herself with pride at the beginning, but she would be on friendly terms with other *gisaeng* over time.

Sung suddenly got up and went out, as if he had remembered something.

"Hey, where are you going?" San-wol followed him.

3-46

"Wonderful. She must be really in love with him," said the older *gisaeng*, chugging the whisky left in her glass as if annoyed.

"Who's in love?" asked the younger *gisaeng*, using the chance to shake herself loose from Yim's embrace and sitting up next to the older woman.

"Oh, I'm so hungry," the older one said, and clapped her hands emphatically.

"Are you? Then order some food," said Gang, holding his glass out for more alcohol. "Bitches, only wanting food."

"Well, you should stop drinking," the older *gisaeng* retorted, trying to hide the bottle but then reluctantly filling the glass.

Forgetting to drink, Gang mumbled, "Alcohol is really great. What else in this world is good for a man except alcohol?" He gave an abrupt, curt laugh. "Don't you girls agree?"

"You'll spill your drink," warned the older *gisaeng*, and grabbed Gang's shaking arm to stop the trembling. That didn't help, so she took the glass away from him and held it to his mouth. Gang stopped talking and drank it down.

"Oh, how nice it is." Gang blinked from the whisky's sting and struck himself on the knee.

"Yes, alcohol is really something special," the older *gisaeng* said, making a jealous face. "It can instantly transform an earnest bore like Mr. Heo and get the arrogant San-wol to fall in love with him. Seems like she'll even follow him to the outhouse."

"A man of talent and a woman of beauty. A man of talent and a woman of beauty. Yes, a man . . . of talent . . . and a woman . . . . of beauty. That's what those two are, girls. These days, *gisaeng* bitches like you two only crave money. Yes, it's true, just money. For money, *gisaeng* today would sleep even with a dog. You . . . you said that, right? You deserve to die."

"No, we didn't say it," protested one of the *gisaeng*. "Someone else must have."

"Right," agreed the other *gisaeng*. "Someone else, and she shouldn't have said it either. She misspoke."

"Oh, really? It's not true you only crave money? You're just a couple of thieves."

"Thieves? How are we thieves?" the younger *gisaeng* sharply retorted. "What about you lawyers? For money, a lawyer would even help children sue their parents, wouldn't he?"

"Right! That's right!" The older one laughed, clapping in agreement.

"What! You bitches!" Yim, feeling provoked, grew seriously angry.

"Hey friend," Gang cautioned, "don't get angry. Actually, they're right. We lawyers aren't much different from them. We'd take any lawsuit for money . . . But the *gisaeng* in old times were different, they had spirit and sophistication. Some were great personalities. Nongae from Jinju was heroic, for instance, and Hwang Jin-ee from Songdo was a very special *gisaeng*. She was beautiful, well educated, even aristocratic. Why'd she become a *gisaeng*? She wanted to meet a great man that way. She even boasted once that there were only three constants in Songdo: Bakyeon Waterfall, the scholar Seo Hwa-dam, and she herself. Even a *gisaeng*, if she has such ambition and self-respect, will be treated with respect. No young man would dare reap her with his little sickle. You girls should become like Hwang Jin-ee." He laughed and tried to chug whisky from his empty glass, without even noticing.

3-47

Sung had left abruptly at a sudden thought of Jeong-seon. Though drunken and charmed by the beautiful woman shimmering before his eyes, his heart had not forgotten Jeong-seon. With a pang of guilt, he would wonder, "What am I doing?" Quickly suppressed by: "What's wrong with it?"

San-wol caught up with him in the hall. "Where are you going?" Sung turned and looked into her pleading eyes as she clung to his arm.

"Home," he said, grasping at her hand to bid farewell. Sung didn't often drink, but he hadn't quite stumbled into oblivion despite reeling from the many shots of whisky. He felt seasick. His pulse raced, and his head ached, and his eyes wouldn't focus. He realized that he might throw up.

"Stay longer," San-wol begged. "I'll take you home later." She hung onto him in an effort to persuade him.

Sung looked and for the first time saw a drunken woman's face: the flushed cheeks, the dilated pupils. He would never have imagined such a young woman clinging to him like that. Anguished, he tried to clear his mind but could scarcely even keep from falling down. He stumbled down the hall with his coat draped over one arm and San-wol hanging onto the other. Hat askew, looking every bit a tramp, Sung felt just sober enough to know he was drunk, but too drunk to hold himself steady.

"How can you go home, stumbling like this?" asked San-wol in concern as they neared the front door.

"Drink more . . . stumble more," Sung tried to retort, and grew annoyed that his tongue wouldn't say clearly what he meant.

They had almost reached the door when the two other *gisaeng* came out after them, also drunk and bumping into one another noisily. "Come back, please!" they called. "Are you running off and leaving the other two gentlemen behind?" One took Sung's coat, the other his hat, and they went back in.

"Well," pleaded San-wol, "let's go back in, too. Otherwise, Mr. Gang and Mr. Yim will be very disappointed." She tugged at Sung, firmly holding her ground.

"All right," Sung agreed. "No place to go anyway." He turned and headed back to the room, walking in front. Knowing that his wife was not awaiting him, he felt gratitude, even intimacy toward San-wol, who was still holding him. She would surely do this for other men every day, and even several times a day, but what was wrong with that, he wondered? Who wouldn't? With such thoughts, Sung stumbled vigorously into the room, burped and said, "Mr. Gang, Mr. Yim, I'm drunk. So drunk. Whose fault? Yours. Both of you."

"Mr. Heo," laughed Gang. "Mr. Heo, somebody else is responsible for that."

Sung felt displeased. The "somebody else" could well mean "your wife." Hiding his thoughts, he said, "Yes, you're right. It's San-wol. She's responsible. Right, San-wol?"

"Yes, yes, I'm the one," she agreed, pouring him another drink.

3-48

Sung drank every drop offered as the bottle went around and around. The very stars above seemed to whirl off course, and life below grew demonic in word and deed. Ethics, ideals, diligence, responsibility, character, honor, dignity . . . all these melted away like lumps of salt in alcohol.

He lost track of how long he had been talking, nor did he recall what he had talked about. Around three in the morning, he staggered from the room, San-wol again following, never leaving him alone.

Whether Sung was heading for the outhouse or his hotel as he stumbled down the hall, he abruptly halted at the sight of cluttered slippers before the door to a room and muttered, "Huh . . . why're they drinking so late? That's how we lost our country." Shrugging off San-wol as she tried to pull him away, he slid open the double doors to the room.

Seven or eight men gazed up blankly with drunken faces at this unexpected intruder. Among them sat about the same number of *gisaeng*.

"Hey," Sung began, "I don't know you, but I've got to ask. What're you doing? Each of you born to Korea, a country with nothing. Why're you here? You should go to bed early, get up early, work hard. Not drink all night. What's wrong with you?" He wanted to give a long, indignant lecture, but his tongue wouldn't cooperate.

"He's drunk, don't mind him," San-wol apologized.

"Hey," one of them retorted, "you want to teach us a lesson, you'd better be sober first. But you're just spouting drunken nonsense, you drink-addled fool! Your own eyes already drip cheap whisky by day!" The man tried to stand up in his anger, intending to pummel Sung.

Sung felt ready for a fight even in his drunkenness. But he was also surprised. He noticed people there whom he would never have expected. A couple were teachers, another two journalists. They were all known as respectable people with honorable professions. Sung's surprise sobered him. Losing his swagger, he stood there silent, head bowed in thought.

At that moment, Gang and Yim came out into the corridor, having heard the boisterous noise.

"Mr. Heo, what's the matter?" they asked, tugging at his arm.

"Oh, Mr. Gang . . . And Mr. Yim, you're here, too." The people in the room knew both Gang and Yim, which relaxed the tension.

"This is Mr. Heo, the lawyer Heo," Gang announced, by way of introduction. Sung surmised that they were all about to have drink together, but he bowed his head toward them several times in both greeting and goodbye, then stumbled down the hallway toward the door. The waiter and San-wol helped him stay on his feet, and after getting him into a taxi, San-wol climbed in, too. Sung had already passed out.

3-49

When he finally woke up, he saw unfamiliar things: a fancy cabinet with floral patterns, a wardrobe, a bookshelf, a stationary chest, a desk, and a chair. Each unexpected. Turning his head, he found somebody lying nearby, no more than half a meter away, a young woman on a mattress.

Surprised, Sung got up. "Where am I now?" he asked himself, opening his eyes wide. He was thirsty, tasting bitterness in his mouth, and his head ached as he struggled to keep his eyes open. He noticed a burning in his throat, but felt even more discomfort at heart.

As Sung sat up briskly, the woman, who had been lightly snoring as she slept, awakened and opened her eyes. She first smiled gladly with twinkling eyes, but opened them wider when she noticed Sung sitting blankly.

She also then sat up. "I just fell asleep a few minutes ago," she explained, vaguely excusing herself.

Sung finally recognized the voice as San-wol's, realized that he was with her, and slowly recalled fragments of the previous night's drinking with Gang and Yim. As usual with nondrinkers who happen to get drunk, he could remember very little after a certain level of drunkenness. The evening seemed like something of long ago and far away, having left behind only traces of things, like words written on a chalkboard but mostly erased. He couldn't piece together what had happened but suspected that nothing honorable had. How could he know that? From the bitter taste in his mouth, the dull ache in his head, the unease in his heart.

San-wol offered Sung honey tea that she had prepared. "You didn't want to go home and were not clearheaded enough to find your hotel, so I brought you here to my place." San-wol then turned on the heater and wrapped a blanket about his shoulders. After warming her hands under the mattress for a while, she began doing her hair and spoke again. "Would you have ever come to my place if you weren't drunk? To the home of a *gisaeng*? That someone with great vision like you has come to my place and stayed for several hours is something that'll never happen to me again. I'll always treasure the memory, so don't feel displeased."

As Sung remained quiet and well-mannered, San-wol continued speaking. "The sun is up now. You can wash your face, have breakfast, and go wherever you want. Don't make such a serious face. You can stay drunk until you leave. Even if you're sober, act drunk. Men show their real selves only when they're drunk. Last night, you showed yourself, undisguised and frank as you are . . . That's why I like my job as *gisaeng*, I can sample people in their drunken honesty. I'm really sick of those men who don't drink and make a show of being moralistic. What deceit! What falsehood! Oh, abomination, abomination!" She spat the last word out in English, that harsh term from the Bible, and trembled as if gazing upon some abominable thing directly before her eyes.

3-50

San-wol's words were heated. Only a woman who herself had experienced some abomination would be so enraged about men's deceit. This made Sung curious. "Why do you curse men but praise drunkards so strongly?" he asked, now more relaxed, though not yet completely sober.

"Curse men? Oh, I don't curse them. Why should I? Without men, life would be too boring for us women. I'm not talking about how men earn money to feed us or do hard and difficult work for us. For hard work, there are oxen or horses, or machines these days, but men as toys are irreplaceable. That's why I love and praise them. Curse them? Never. I love and praise them, I fall in love with them, go through agony over them, get deceived and dumped. No, no, never mind. I'm speaking foolishness," San-wol laughed, pretending to be drunk though she was completely sober.

Taking in San-wol's words and behavior, Sung's stern heart softened, and he felt almost joyful. "Excuse me please if this sounds rude," he began, "but how did you become a *gisaeng*?"

"It's a bit embarrassing to talk about . . ." she replied, pretending to be more drunk. "I grew sick of those decent men, those gentlemen from church or school, so I became a *gisaeng* to find libertines and drunkards. Libertines have love, courage, and loyalty, and drunkards are honest. They don't fake. Truth, love, courage, loyalty. You find these in Korea only among libertines and drunkards. Religious hypocrites only become genuine if you take them to a bar and get them drunk. Of course, if they rid themselves of their whole pretense, if they utterly demolished their whited sepulchres, they might stink too much." She laughed. "Really, how many people would still smell nice without their disguise? You agree? Remember how you stopped and slid those doors open in the hall last night? The men in that room are the better sort of hypocrites. They at least go out at night to drink. Aren't I right? Mister, don't act so polite, don't sober up. What was I saying! Don't disguise yourself like that. Just be yourself. If you don't like my opinions, say so, or if you find me cute, show me. Like last night when you were drunk, oh!" San-wol played the coquette, but her voice seemed to choke back bitter tears.

"I'm not hiding myself," Sung told her. "This is me. I'm taking you seriously."

"I know. Already when you were living at Jeong-seon's place . . . I mean, your father-in-law's house. You were a topic for us. A talented and honest country bumpkin." She laughed again. "Really, but Jeong-seon . . . Oh sorry! I shouldn't call your wife by her name anymore, but what should I call her? Well, it doesn't matter now because we're drunk. Jeong-seon, I mean your wife, also called you, 'My bumpkin.' Yes, she did. At the time, that made me angry because I had . . . what should I say? A kind of respect for you, or something like that. I still do. Anyway, my wish has come true, even if just for a short time. I've managed to have a man I like over at my place." She stopped and laughed with joyful pride.

3-51

"But how," Sung felt that he had to ask, "could you become a *gisaeng* solely to meet drunkards? That's not only self-abuse, it means that you're neglecting the debt you owe society, the role you should play, from the smallest community to the entire nation. Whatever complaints and excuses you might have, for someone of your talent, education, and social status to become a *gisaeng* is inexcusable. What good is a *gisaeng* for society? Why not become a nurse? Why not a kindergarten teacher? Why not a night-school teacher in the countryside? With your talent and education, you wouldn't starve wherever you go, would you? Nurse or teacher, doesn't either serve society? But a *gisaeng* will be just a toy of tramps, drunkards, and men of certain classes, won't she? A woman without property or education, with just a body, might have no other choice than to become a *gisaeng*, whether sold by her parents or at her own initiative to earn money to feed them, but what good reason could you have for becoming a *gisaeng*?" The rebuke was earnest, entirely serious.

After listening quietly, San-wol agreed, "You're right. A *gisaeng* won't do anything for society. But listen, life isn't so simple. No *gisaeng* becomes a *gisaeng* just because she wants to be one. Some talk about Hwang Jin-ee, but I don't believe everything they say about her. Ask all the *gisaeng* in Seoul, about four or five hundred in all, why they became *gisaeng*, and you'll hear explanations from each of them. There are reasons they became *gisaeng*, reasons showing they had no other choice. Who'd choose this out of desire? Marxists say capitalism forces our hands. Fatalists say it's nothing less than fate. But things aren't so easily explained by one single theory. Some *gisaeng* might have been born to the wrong parents, some might have been filial to their parents, some might have turned their backs on society and consciously chosen a life of dissipation. Or some, like me, might have grown sick of proper gentlemen and preferred the truth, loyalty, and rash love of libertines and drunkards." She gave an ironic laugh. "Life isn't so simple to explain. The reason you gave up your social status and your beautiful wife to work for farmers isn't easy to explain with Marxist theory, fatalism, or any idealism. Same with our reasons for becoming *gisaeng*. I don't resent anyone. I wouldn't even try to blame a lothario like Lee Geon-yeong for dumping me even if that were the reason. Oops, I said something stupid again. If I keep on talking like this, I'll turn myself inside out. What's the use of all this talk! But I would like to make Lee drunk just once to tear off his the disguise and see what he's really like."

After washing his face and putting on his clothes, already brushed by San-wol, Sung left and returned to his hotel in Jeondong. The hour was already one in the afternoon. As soon as he reached his hotel room, he stretched out on the bed and reflected on what had happened the previous night and that morning. He saw a new aspect of life that he had never before known. While wondering what had happened to Jeong-seon, however, he fell asleep.

3-52

Sung still had no desire to go home, and even thinking of it as his own place left him feeling violated. He rather missed San-wol already, feeling more trust toward her than Jeong-seon. He wondered if he should go back to her. He even wondered if he should revenge himself against Jeong-seon by having an affair with San-wol. Or should he go somewhere for a drink? Should he take San-wol out for a drink? He could then get drunk and go back with her to her place. All of these thoughts flitted through his mind. San-wol was a beautiful woman, and talented. He couldn't forget her special way of dealing with him, trained *gisaeng* that she was.

As he sat lost in such obscure reflections, a light suddenly came on. "Oh my God," he realized, "I'm so corrupt." He shook his head as if to shake off something dirty. "How could I think only of sensual pleasure!" He abruptly stood up, shuddering. At that moment, he recalled Mr. Han, who had always provided strength whenever Sung grew discouraged or sensed the danger of being corrupted. Mr. Han had ever been a source of great strength for him. He grabbed his hat and rushed from the hotel, headed for Han's place.

The small gate that he had not seen for too long, the weather-darkened doorplate, these things and more, so long familiar, received him like old friends. Han's daughter opened the gate. She seemed to have grown a lot in the last six months, but still welcomed him gladly, like her own brother.

"Is your father home?"

"Yes."

"Does he have guests?"

"Yes, the usual guests."

With these words, they reached the wooden floor used as the Western room. "Don't you use this Western room any more?" Sung asked, untying his shoes.

"No, we don't," Jeong-ran admitted, head bowed as if with embarrassment. Finances had recently grown more strained, and they avoided the Western room to reduce bills for heat and light, using only the main room.

Han was there, sitting on a spot warmed by the *ondol* heating system. His wife sat nearby, and so did four or five young men. Beside Han's wife was an empty place that must have been Jeong-ran's, Sung surmised.

"Oh, Mr. Heo, you're here!" Smiling broadly, Han jumped up and shook Sung's hand. "When did you get back?" His face had gotten more emaciated, leaving his cheeks in shadows and wrinkles about his eyes and mouth. He now had the appearance of an old man, and several missing teeth made him look older still. Sung felt saddened.

"I got in last night," Sung explained, making an apologetic face for being tardy about visiting.

"We've been talking about work for farmers, and also about you. Speak of a tiger, and here one comes!" Han laughed, then recalled his courtesy. "Have a seat here, your hands are cold. I heard you were sick. I'm sorry that I couldn't visit you. Please, sit here," Han said, offering his own warm spot to Sung and taking a seat himself near the door.

3-53

Because Sung knew Han well, he didn't refuse but sat down on the spot offered. It was quite warm, and was made even more comfortable by a thin cushion Jeong-ran had knitted.

"How's your wife doing? Is she well?" Han asked, still smiling gladly.

"Yes," Sung replied, but without conviction.

"Did you come for that law case?" Han asked, his inquiry sincere. "I heard about it from your wife the other day."

"Oh," put in Han's wife, smiling at her husband but addressing Sung, "he worried so much when you were sick and wanted to visit you, but he couldn't afford a trip, unfortunately."

As Sung learned, Han had been forced into retirement from his school that year for lack of a teaching certificate. In the view of the school administration, the young dean, and the director of the school affairs' office, anyone without some official teaching qualification was worthless. Han now had no income for food. He was living on savings, and to reduce expenses had closed the Western room, his place for meeting young people, the center of his world and his life project, and had moved to the main room for that purpose.

No longer teaching, he now had nothing to fall back on to support his family as they had lived. If he sold his house and household goods, he might survive two years. He might be satisfied with that. He would be able to continue meeting young people during that time, training and organizing them further, but when the money ran out, he would have to move to the servants' quarters of a family somewhere to work as a servant. Sung suspected that Han perhaps didn't dwell on that because he was currently too busy with his life's work. Day and night, he met with young people to discuss his vision for Korea and his plans for what Koreans could do, about a mission for young people, about the hope and confidence that he had for Korea's future. He considered all this his duty but also found it his joy as he trained young people of capacity and faith. That was his way of paying his debt to Korea, saving his country and making his life worth living. He pursued all this, but not so much consciously as out of second nature.

The young people, however, hardly ever turned out as Han wished. As long as they were regularly visiting his place, they were all his students or associates, all pursuing his aims for Korea. But when they started working or went overseas for a couple years' study after graduation, they would lose their passion, even if they never quite turned against him. Why were Koreans so unreliable? Why would so few Koreans stick to a decision and pursue it throughout their lives even to the point of death? A few loyal to Mr. Han would lament or fall into disappointment, wondering if that was the cause of Korea's downfall.

The topic of that night's discussion settled upon the *Hwarangdo*, or "Way of the Flower of Youth," from the Silla Dynasty. King Jinheung had set up a new institution to promote the young and talented and thereby strengthen the country in a time of ceaseless attacks by the neighboring states Baekje and Goguryeo, raids that had enfeebled the Shilla people's security. Based on the Dangun spirit passed down from old times, the King had chosen beautiful women designated as *Wonhwa*, or "Source of the *Hwarangdo*," and about three hundred young men of talent selected for education in justice and for training in skills of music and song intended for mutual enjoyment. Through such education and training, the young men became virtuous and loyal vassals as well as skilled and courageous officers and men. They followed five rules:

1. To be loyal and serve their king
2. To be filial and serve their parents
3. To be faithful to their friends
4. To never surrender in a battle
5. To never kill without proper cause

They willingly died for justice and never swerved from a decision once made. Loyalty imbued their true character, and they took justice more seriously than their own death. Listening to the stories about various *Hwarang* individuals and their chivalry, the young men gathered in Han's place came to appreciate their ancestors' admirable actions, and each made his own personal commitment to the *Hwarang* ideals.

"Mr. Han, I was in anguish last night and came to you today for help. I feel restored, so I can leave now." Sung said his farewells to everyone, ignoring their bafflement. He felt only happiness and encouragement.

3-54

Sung's happiness and courage didn't result from the stories about the *Hwarang*. Such stories surely might encourage young Koreans, but he found courage in Han's ceaseless endeavor, in that hope never relinquished. Han didn't pursue things that were already going well and cherish hope for them, but difficult things hard to achieve, and this touched Sung deeply.

What was the sum of Mr. Han's life work? It couldn't be converted into monetary value, nor any other quantity. He met four or five young people every day and thus well over a thousand each year. Even if Han didn't meet new people every single day, his accomplishments were still amazing. But how many people would truly understand the meaning of his efforts? If they could understand it truly, there would be no doubts about their commitment to his work. Labor that brought no financial profit for the investment!

What Sung was doing was also work invested without expectation of such profit. But wasn't that what Korea needed most these days? More people should be doing this kind of work, but they viewed their own interest as the most important thing. They were too calculating to do work that brought no profit, but Korea needed people who were less calculating, people not so clever as to think only of their own interest. "Tending only one's own garden" was the art of living in a settled society. If a folk was much behind other folk and busy catching up, trying everything new, then more people were needed for tending the gardens of others, like an adult willing to care for several children. Such people would surely endure hardship. Being unappreciated, even ridiculed as crazy, they would be laughed at by the 'smart' people. Mr. Han was one of those. Sung intended to become another. Without money, power, or name, they would one day be buried in the ground, but if their efforts achieved anything, and a great house were some day built, Han and Sung would serve as bricks buried deep in the earth, supporting the foundation.

Sung envied Han's satisfaction with his unappreciated work, even his lack of concern for personal ease. "Yes," he concluded, making up his mind on the way down Gyodong Alley, "I should give up on having a family. I should never have married at all!" He had suddenly recognized how restraining marriage was, especially mentally, and how wasteful of one's energies. Some writer had said, "For the familial happiness of millions, we ought to forego having a family." Sung suddenly understood what Paul the follower of Jesus meant in saying that if a man weren't married, he should remain single, and likewise for an unmarried woman. "Yes," he repeated, "I should give up on a family. I should live my life alone and continue the work for farmers. I should consider the country my beloved, my true wife, and let Jeong-seon marry a man compatible with her."

With these thoughts, Sung swept all hatred toward Jeong-seon from his heart and headed quickly toward home, to Jeong-seon's house.

3-55

Sung stood before the gate to his house, realizing that about half a year had passed since his last time there. The nameplate with the words "Heo Sung" seemed to mock him.

Closing his eyes, he stood silent and still for a while in his thoughts. He recalled how he and Jeong-seon had come every day to direct the carpenters and the men putting up wallpaper during the renovation after his father-in-law had bought them the house. He missed those days when he had dreamt of a sweet home, but also felt embarrassed.

He then remembered how his happiness at the time had been pricked by a conscience guilty of mistreating Yu Sun, like a dart of pain piercing his heart. He felt again the embarrassment experienced in wondering if he was attracted to Jeong-seon because she was more educated, with more money and power than Yu Sun. If only he had married not Jeong-seon but Yu Sun, he wouldn't be unhappy now, nor would he be at pains to ignore the shameful rumor as "the guy who married for money." Sung felt as though he were being ineluctably punished for an act against his own conscience, an act prompted by private desire.

A beautiful wife wouldn't always make for a sweet home, nor would an educated wife. Having a nice house, money, high status, and health, having everything that people think necessary, wouldn't always add up to that. Sung as husband and Jeong-seon as wife, what did they lack? To all observers, they seemed the perfect couple, but they were unhappy. Where did the unhappiness come from? Personality differences? But what is personality? Sung couldn't come up with a ready answer.

As if to dismiss these troubled thoughts, Sung cried out loudly, "Open the gate!"

Inside, the servants had gathered in the main room to relax and chat in a house with neither master nor mistress because Jeong-seon had already left for the train to Bongcheon.

"Listen!" Yu-wol exclaimed, her eyes opened wide with astonishment. "It's the master!"

"What? You're crazy! That man wouldn't be here. The master of Jaetgol might be, but not Mr. Heo." The old maidservant's tone was condescending toward Yu-wol, and even her reference to Mr. Heo was less than respectful, unlike her more courteous allusion to the "master of Jaetgol."

Again came the cry, though decidedly louder, "Open the gate!"

"See, aren't I right?" Proudly victorious, Yu-wol made a face at the old maidservant and rushed off calling out, "I'm coming." At Yu-wol's quick exit, the old maidservant, the seamstress, and the cook instantly made to grab their things and hurry from the room.

Once unlocked, the gate creaked open at Yu-wol's touch. She stuck out her head. "Oh, Master! It really *is* you!" She felt so happy that she nearly clung to him, but stopped herself, realizing that she dare not. Of the various servants, only Yu-wol had truly missed Sung. Perhaps the others looked down on him, but she alone genuinely welcomed his return.

Sung patted her on the head, then stepped across the threshold, inquiring, "How are you?"

Yu-wol ignored the formal question. "Lady went to the countryside. Took the train just a little while ago." She trailed after him, concerned.

3-56

"To the countryside?" Sung asked, surprised. "Where? Which village?"

"Yours," Yu-wol replied, fidgeting to find the right words.

He entered his room, which looked so familiar. It yet retained the memory of a young married couple, though their time together there had been short. The pictures on the walls, the desk, and the wardrobe all remained the same as before. Jeong-seon's skirt and jacket hanging on a wall looked the same. Only one thing seemed to have changed, the smell of cigarettes. In the ashtray lay several half-smoked cigarettes. Did Jeong-seon smoke? Or a man? Or some men? Men who visited her? For a moment, Sung felt displeasure.

"To the countryside?" Sung asked again, as if not trusting his ears. He sat down on the warmest spot of the *ondol* floor without removing his coat.

"That's right."

"Took the train just a little while ago?"

"That's right."

"Which village?" he asked again. He couldn't imagine that Jeong-seon would go to his village. If she had really gone to Salyeoul to follow him, he would have to change his opinion about her.

"Yours," Yu-wol repeated. She stopped clearing the room to gaze at him, wondering if she had said something wrong.

Sung sat with closed eyes for several moments, apparently in thought. Finally opening them again, he asked, "What time did she get home last night?"

"Well . . ." Yu-wol hesitated, unsure what to say.

"You said she hadn't returned by midnight, didn't you?" Sung's tone was that of a merciless judge interrogating a witness.

"Midnight?" Yu-wol's eyes grew wide, as if she had seen something incredible. The phone call last night around midnight, the vaguely familiar voice, had that been a call from the master? Did he know that the lady had gone out with the master of Jaetgol the night before to start an affair? She felt his scary eyes, felt as if she had committed some terrible crime.

"I don't remember the time," she replied. She couldn't bring herself to admit that the hour had been past one-thirty.

Sung would have asked more questions but stopped himself, feeling it beneath his dignity. Whatever might have happened the night before, he wanted most of all to know why Jeong-seon had gone to see him. But he couldn't know the answer to that.

"Have you eaten?" Yu-wol asked, checking his face.

"I'll eat out and come back. Just prepare the bedding." Sung got up and left. Around ten, he had dinner, then went to the hotel to retrieve his baggage and return home by taxi. In the room, the bedding laid out was what had been used on the wedding day. The old maidservant may have done so with conscious intention. Perhaps the angels of her better nature had moved her to help Sung and Jeong-seon regain their first love. Sung lay there with open eyes, his thoughts preoccupied.

3-57

Was the bond between a man and wife to be so easily broken? "Free love, free divorce." These words were heard, not just in Korea, but in other civilized countries, where they were actually put into practice. For Sung, however, the marriage relationship was a knot difficult to cut. Was he influenced by old Asian tradition? Or from the teaching of Jesus? Regardless, if a man loved a woman, even if the love were only platonic, that love would leave an indelible trace. Sung experienced this in his relationship with Yu Sun. His love for Sun, though unannounced, had always struck his conscience. He thought that the trace of his love for Sun would never disappear.

Such was love, and how much more so the relationship of a married couple, a relationship based on important nuptial promises. A relationship based on their complete union, body and soul. Even if he should remain lifelong separate from Jeong-seon, she would remain forever in his heart like a shadow. Even if she should die, the joy, sadness, love that she had given him ... no, something entirely beyond all that would permeate his body, his heart, and never dissipate. As for the woman, her body would have experienced great change from absorbing her husband's seminal fluid. Jeong-seon's body and heart must therefore have been marked by Sung as though with a seal.

For Sung, marriage was not simply a legal contract. The legal part was just one aspect of the whole, but the moral law itself was also only another such aspect. Marriage had various aspects, aesthetic and biological, among others, not even to mention the religious. All these combined, however, would not possibly encompass all of a marriage.

"Something mysterious," Sung thought. If there were anything mysterious, the marriage relationship was. Setting aside the possibility of the previous lives taught by Buddhism, was there not a mystery in the way that two people who had grown up without knowing each other should marry and share a life together?

Korean belief about becoming "one body from two bodies," or Buddhist theory on couples bound together by previous lives, didn't these allude to the mystery of the conjugal bond? Sung sighed deeply, immersed in such thoughts.

"Am I too old-fashioned? People these days seem to accept free love and free divorce. Am I the only one who regards marriage as mysterious and holy? Possibly, 'I' might be sacrificed for 'us,' but how could 'I' rupture the holiness of marriage just for 'my' desire? Or am I too ethical, like Tolstoy?" Sung pondered these things.

"But perhaps our marriage is already destroyed. Or am I wrong to suspect this? Did I make a mistake trusting Dr. Lee? That car I saw in front of Gyeonseong Station, the man and woman inside, were they really Gap-jin and Jeong-seon? Or did I imagine everything? Is coming home late always proof of an affair? Or is that my hasty judgment?"

His wife's familiar skirt and jacket caught his eye.

3-58

When Sung woke up the next morning, the room was still shuttered and dark, and the only sound was a low hum from the electric heater switched on by Yu-wol earlier that morning. The room had a pleasantly mild temperature, much like early summer. Who would have imagined the season to be Korea's coldest, the time between early and mid-January, between *sohan* and *daehan*, as Koreans would call it.

Sung groped under his pillow for the light switch. It had the shape of a small eggplant with a button pale as bone. When the light was off, pressing the button would switch it on, as pressing again would switch it off. A long extension cord allowed the switch to rest under the pillow for convenience.

"How nice if every Korean home were equipped with this!" Sung exclaimed, partly as lament, but with heartfelt appreciation as he held the device in hand long after switching the light on.

The hour hand of the jade-green desk clock pointed to eight. The sun must have already risen, only to be greeted, perhaps, by wind and snow. Within the room, however, isolated by double doors, unwanted news from outside was kept at bay. If a message needed delivering, it could come by telephone, no need even to open the door and let the cold wind in. Beckoning Sung was a life where one need not get up at all, but just lie about, lingering in bed, perhaps caressing a woman, or if that grew boring, one could eventually even get up. Drapes woven of genuine Chinese silk, not some cheap substitute, hung on each of the four walls. Wedding gifts.

If Sung rang the bell at his bedside, Yu-wol would rush in with fresh water for him to wash his face, then bring a breakfast of bread, fruit, and milk. That had been his usual breakfast in Seoul after establishing himself as a married man. When Sung had finished washing his face, Yu-wol would politely offer him with both hands a big, soft, well-ironed towel that she had kept draped over one arm. And while Sung shaved or Jeong-seon combed her hair, Yu-wol would put fresh underwear and clean clothing under the bed pallets to warm them. She would do this carefully to ensure that the clothes warmed evenly and did not wrinkle. And as Sung and Jeong-seon changed into their fresh clothes, Yu-wol would assist by standing nearby, handing them their clothing piece by piece. If she mixed up the sequence, she would get a harsh reminder from Jeong-seon: "Pay attention!"

Once finished dressing, Sung and Jeong-seon would exit arm in arm for the opposite room whistling the wedding march. That room, used both for dining and for Sung's study, was equipped with Western furniture. The round table in the middle, customarily covered with a red tablecloth, would have atop that a white cloth, clean and well-ironed, upon which toast bread, milk, boiled eggs, fruit, water, and coffee would be served using fine china. Sung and Jeong-seon would embrace and kiss before blessing their breakfast when they were on good terms. Such fresh beauty, after a good night's sleep and getting dressed up so fine, would be seen by the two of them alone, the privilege of a married couple.

"I wish we could have a child," Jeong-seon might say, rubbing the tablecloth with a teaspoon. "How nice to have a baby like you here next to us," she might add, blushing shyly.

"Better one resembling you." Sung would suggest, rising to pat her head.

3-59

Jeong-seon liked having a morning bath, but even more the Western way of taking a shower, so much so that she wished to have a shower installed. But putting a Western bathroom in a traditional Korean house would not be easy.

"We should sell this damn home and build a Western one," Jeong-seon would lament when talking about the bathroom, her voice even rising in anger. "Rooms in a Korean home are too small. A piano, a table, or a bed would already fill one. The outhouse is so far away, and even to visit the reception room, you have to wear a coat and muffler and walk to another building. Why on earth did our ancestors build homes this way?" Jeong-seon didn't bother to hide her irritation, and she would pester Sung, "Even if the site is fine, let's just tear down this place and build a Western house."

When Jeong-seon went on this way, Sung often agonized over being unable to grant her wishes, but he also sometimes disliked her selfishness in thinking only of her own comfort, given the country's difficult situation.

Jeong-seon, however, seemed interested only in how fast she could get a Western-style house to furnish as extravagantly as possible for her greatest possible enjoyment. She grew frustrated at her husband's apparent inability to understand her dream for something so normal. The husband's role was to understand and fulfill a wife's normal desires, or so Jeong-seon believed. What else was a husband for but to please his wife? A husband unable to do that, she thought, would be like salt without its savor. Such a salt-free husband was not to Jeong-seon's taste.

Moreover, Sung lacked a certain skill to please his wife as a man. Jeong-seon had heard from her married friends various things about a couple's life together, particularly the sexual relationship, but Sung was different, too well-mannered. He respected his wife too much, and was too solemn. She expected more skill from him, to no avail.

Sung was not unaware of his wife's expectation, but his understanding of human dignity left him unable to respond to her demands. He tried to bring her moral views into consonance with his own by inviting Mr. Han or citing from books that she would not disdain, such as the Bible, hoping to interest her in serious issues:

1. Service
2. One's role
3. Responsibility
4. Abstinence
5. Sacrifice of oneself for the community
6. Sacrifice of desires or privacy to play a role and be responsible
7. Work for the country is primary, with work for self and family secondary
8. Equality and nonresistance

Sung discussed these topics with Jeong-seon a lot.

3-60

Jeong-seon was certainly able to follow Sung in such discussions. She knew the English terms for those topics well enough to translate Sung's Korean remarks and even amuse herself in a childlike manner by going on to agree in English, chirping, "Okay," "All right," "Good," or "Understood." Even Sung had to laugh with her.

He would, however, interpret her behavior in a way consistent with his own views. "Of course, Jeong-seon knows these things," he told himself. "She not only knows them, she also values them. An intelligent, highly educated, virtuous woman like Jeong-seon, how could she not? She is certainly the new kind of woman needed by Korea. At least, she should be." And he then found her playful, childlike manner rather lovable.

Recalling himself from these thoughts, Sung sat up in his pajamas and looked around in the room. Suddenly, he missed her. Her smile, her sullen face, her early morning face with eyes hardly open, her fits of rage, her various poses, her behavior that only a husband can see. He saw them all, reflected on the wall, the wardrobe, wherever his eyes landed, and even with his eyes closed. Her breath seemed to brush his cheek, and her fingers the nape of his neck. He could almost detect her scent.

Shaking his uncombed head, Sung realized, "Jeong-seon is inseparable from me. She has permeated my body." He felt his heart nearly explode from desire for her, and though he tried to suppress this feeling by dint of will, he failed. "A girl who betrayed," Sung reminded himself, trying to arouse his animosity, but up rose an image of poor Jeong-seon shedding regretful tears, and he felt only sympathy for her.

Was she not a cute wife? Wasn't he at fault for leaving her behind? By being cute, hadn't she already fulfilled her role as a wife? Did selfishness or selflessness matter in a cute wife any more than it mattered in a cute child? Perhaps a cute wife was like a flower. Didn't a flower have value as a flower regardless whether or not it grew into a fruit? Perhaps her self-interest complemented a selfless husband. What would happen to a family if a wife and mother also forgot herself, her home, her children, and her husband? Sung tried to reform the views that he had held concerning women and the role of a wife.

As his new views came into focus, Jeong-seon became a wife without flaws, a wife whom he powerfully missed and found lovely. Reflecting further, he even seemed to find his original idea about married couples confirmed, namely, that Jeong-seon was not an entity separate from him, for a married couple was a unity bonded as powerfully and mysteriously as elements in a chemical bond.

Sung stood abruptly up and took Jeong-seon's pillow to bury his nose in it and catch her scent. He then took her clothes from the wall to hold in his arms and again catch her scent.

3-61

"Master, are you awake?" cried Yu-wol from outside the door, furtively peering in.

"Oh, I'm up," Sung called, quickly putting his wife's clothes aside in a corner before going to open the door. Radiant sunlight poured into the room in waves.

Yu-wol handed him two letters and entered the room to open the windows and fold the bedding. Sung checked the envelopes, turning each to see both sides. Both were for Jeong-seon, one from Dr. Hyeon with the name written on the envelope, but the other with no name. With a rather unpleasant inkling, he first opened the letter lacking a sender's name. The writing was quite messy, the message messier still, and it closed with the word "Deiner," German for "Yours." The content was as follows:

> My Jeong-seon,
> Now you are *my* Jeong-seon. I caught a cold from last night's trip to Oryujang Hotel and back and am now

lying sick. I have a fever. Even in fever, I was planning to see you tonight but can't because I'm too sick. I miss your soft skin so much. Come see me as soon as you receive this letter. As Sung will come to Seoul soon, we should also talk about what to do. Should I kill him? Why didn't he die of that illness? You have to come see me! If you don't, you are not my Jeong-seon!

That was it. Sung didn't know where to begin. "It was truly Jeong-seon and Gap-jin that I saw in that car two nights ago!" he thought. "They were on their way to Oryujang Hotel!" Rage flared up in Sung's heart, and he ached for blood.

Yu-wol noticed his flushed face and trembling arms. Realizing whom the letter was from, she felt the hairs on her neck stand on end.

Feeling that Yu-wol was watching him, Sung quickly brought his emotions under control, folding the letter and returning it to its envelope. He then opened the letter from Hyeon.

My Dear Jeong-seon!

Your behavior and questions yesterday left me wondering after you were gone. I wanted to follow you, but I got a house call for a patient and came back late in the evening. That's why I write this letter. If you have any problems, come to see me as soon as you get this letter.

Sung also put this letter back into its envelope. Trying to control himself, though he felt his mind slipping its moorings, he gave Yu-wol an order: "Bring water for washing my face." To regain control over his mind, unsettled as a ship battered by storm, he brushed his teeth, shaved, and even washed his hair, taking a long time. His toothbrush several times slipped and poked the soft palate behind his upper teeth. Worse still, he twice cut himself with his razor while shaving, once under an ear and another time on the chin. He even had difficulty buttoning his collar and found that he had to knot his tie three times to get it right. When he forced himself to sit at the table, he suddenly had a nosebleed. The white tablecloth soaked bright red.

"Your nose is bleeding," Yu-wol said, trembling but not knowing what to do. She found herself resenting Jeong-seon and feeling great sympathy for Sung.

"Aaah . . ." Sung sighed, no longer able to restrain himself. Ignoring his bleeding nose, he lay his head on the table, striking a tea cup with his elbow and spilling the tea. Pink-colored tea stained the white table cloth and spread like blood.

Yu-wol quickly grabbed the rolling cup.

3-62

Sung spent the rest of the day in confusion. The next day, he was still confused, but several times thought of "revenge" and even let his thoughts dwell on how to avenge himself. He eventually reached a point where he had to decide either on revenge or on endurance and forgiveness. What if he sought revenge? That might satisfy for a moment, but he, Jeong-seon, and Gap-jin would all be shunned by society. He could gain only momentary satisfaction from vengeance. If he endured and forgave, however, he and the others would remain unharmed.

"Forgive!" he thought, remembering the teaching of Jesus.

He seemed to recall Jesus teaching that one could divorce a wife who had committed adultery. Wasn't that right? But he said that a man *could* divorce his wife, not that he *had to* do so. Even divorcing didn't mean the same as revenge.

Sung wondered what Mr. Han would do, and reflected on his principles:

1.   Boundless love and responsibility

2. Life of serving
3. Putting country before self

Shouldn't love be boundless? Shouldn't responsibility be boundless? Shouldn't love and responsibility toward wife, husband, and children, and also nation and people, be boundless? Didn't he then have to love Jeong-seon boundlessly once she had become his wife even if she did have flaws? Shouldn't he fulfill his responsibility as a husband to the end? No, not to the end, but endlessly! If a life of serving were paramount and if Sung should truly serve his country and people, he should first serve his wife, shouldn't he? If he couldn't forgive and serve her, how could he love and serve others, a large group of anonymous people, and even the abstract nation? And if he truly believed in sacrificing "self" for "community" and "nation," how could he justify destroying himself by acting in narrow self-interest instead of focusing on life's greater responsibilities? If Mr. Han were facing this choice, there would be no doubt about his decision, or so thought Sung. After three days of such agonizing, he came to the same decision.

He thus wrote a letter to Gap-jin:

> Gap-jin, I forgive you for what you have done to my wife. I also forgive my wife, who may in some way have compelled you to commit adultery, betraying our friendship. The improper letter you sent my wife, I will burn it after finishing this letter. You should reflect on your actions and not repeat them, not even in your thoughts toward my wife. You should grasp this opportunity to abandon your life of dissipation and start a new life for our country and people using your talent and ambition.

After writing these words, Sung prepared to burn the letter

from Gap-jin. But there he felt some reluctance. He reflected that he might need to show the message to Jeong-seon and ought perhaps keep it for that purpose. He struck a match and blew it out. He repeated this three times. Lamenting to himself, "Oh, my weakness, my weakness," Sung finally lit the piece of paper on his fourth attempt. As the paper burned, reducing to ashes, Sung's heart brightened after this time of darkness.

3-63

After burning Gap-jin's letter, Sung ate a relaxed dinner, quite pleased with his decision. He then went to a barber for a haircut and also visited a public bathhouse to relax. Upon returning, he lay down in delight to feel so pure, as though he had washed filth from body and mind. Some small bit was yet lodged in a corner of his heart, but he tried to ignore it. He had almost fallen asleep, exhausted from the past days' agony and weariness, when a knock at the gate and a loud cry jolted him awake: "Telegram!"

The telegram read: "Arrival in Seoul seven tomorrow morning."

After a futile wait for him in the countryside, Jeong-seon was returning to Seoul.

Sung awoke at five the next morning, but didn't feel as pleased as the day before when he had burnt Gap-jin's letter. Much as a body washed clean by bathing becomes again sticky from secretions of oil and sweat, he felt as if his soul were once more tainted by something. He tried to change his mood, washing his face and doing gymnastics in the backyard. Punishing both body and mind to remove the taint, he forced himself to the train station.

"Boundless love, boundless forgiveness, boundless responsibility, boundless love, boundless forgiveness, boundless responsibility, serving, killing the self, serving, killing the self . . . boundless love, boundless responsibility." Murmuring these things while heading for the station, he tried to dispel the cloud of jealousy and fog of hatred obscuring his heart.

Lights yet burned along the streets. Empty streetcars rushed loudly by, their headlights already off though a dark fog dimly shrouded houses and streets. Heavily burdened at heart, his shoes echoing against the empty street, Sung walked toward Namdaemun Gate to pick up his wife. His lips were dry, and his tongue was sore.

Around Namdaemun Gate were a lot of people, not only those going to the nearby market but also lines of students and clusters of people on the way to welcome the imperial army from Japan and see it off to fight in Manchuria. The train station itself was crowded with passengers and those waiting for the army.

From the vantage of platform one where Sung was waiting for Jeong-seon, he could see the people on platform two very well. Ten minutes before the train with Jeong-seon arrived, the army train heading north pulled into the station. As the train pulled in, the crowd waved flags and cried out "Victory!" Officers and soldiers wearing woolen caps responded by sticking their heads out the windows. Both crowd and soldiers were enthusiastic. Observing this dramatic scene of imperial enthusiasm, Sung felt so touched that he almost cried. Young men leaving their homes and loved ones behind to fight for the empire, the crowd welcoming and sending them off, all of them expressed loyalty, sacrifice, courage, exhilaration, making for a pathos remote from ordinary experience. Sung wished all Koreans could experience this touching moment. At the same time, he felt terribly helpless, even dishonorable for lacking the opportunity to set forth heroically for the fight.

As he stood there lost in thought for the first time over the heroic, inspiring life of a soldier, Jeong-seon's train pulled in blowing billows of cloud-white steam.

From a window flashed the image of Jeong-seon's forlorn face.

3-64

At the sight of her husband standing on the platform, Jeong-seon had an impulse to call to him loudly, the instinctive reaction of a wife toward her husband. Even if she had cried out, her voice wouldn't have reached him through the double windows, but she knew that something thicker than windows hindered her from reaching out to him with feeling. Moreover, she felt pained at heart to think that her husband was happily waiting for her without knowing her secret.

Sung boarded the train and came to her. "Didn't you take a sleeping car?" he asked, his voice glad.

"No, I didn't." Jeong-seon glanced at Sung, then avoided him by bowing her head as if looking for her bag. She felt her face flush and her heart pound.

Picking up her luggage for her, Sung got off first and followed the crowd that was still shouting, "Victory!" as it headed for the exit.

Jeong-seon grew dizzy watching his steps, but followed asking herself, "Can he be so calm if he knows my secret? Or does he not know?" She felt like a criminal taken by the police and hardly noticed going through the wicket. Yu-wol, waiting there, greeted her.

Sung set the luggage down and turned to ask, "Did you eat anything?" Gazing at him with pleading eyes, she shook her head in silence. Sung called a taxi, loaded the luggage, and sent it home with Yu-wol. He then suggested to Jeong-seon, "Let's have some tea to warm up." He proceeded, and Jeong-seon quietly followed.

Helping her out of her coat upon arriving at the tearoom, he asked, "How was it for you in Salyeoul?"

"Fine," Jeong-seon answered, taking a seat.

Sung took his seat and looked at her. For an instant, the scene of her and Gap-jin flashed before his eyes. He could see them in the car again, Gap-jin's arm around her, and he again tasted bitterness.

"*Jioshoku*," Sung called to the waiter, using the Japanese word for breakfast. He tried to suppress his emotions and calm himself down as he searched for something to say. He finally forced himself to smile. "Did you like Salyeoul better on this trip?" he asked.

Jeong-seon just nodded without saying anything. She couldn't speak for the lump in her throat.

"The people in Salyeoul are all nice," Sung volunteered. "They earn their food through working with their hands and sweating a lot, and their concern day and night is how to harvest more rice, how to find more manure, how to buy new clothes for their children on New Year's Day through weaving and selling more straw bags. Or they worry about their oxen, wondering if they're cold during the night and thinking about mixing nice feed for them in the morning by adding more beans. These are things they always think about. They don't have leisure time like the people in Seoul for thinking about how to earn money without working hard or how to get a woman or a man. I miss Salyeoul. How about you? Don't you have any wish to move there and live by honest sweat, working diligently and humbly for others?" He looked at Jeong-seon and sighed.

3-65

"What could I do in Salyeoul? Would there really be any job for someone like me?" replied Jeong-seon, also sighing.

"Of course, there would be. You could cook, wash clothes, and weed the garden. In your leisure time, you could teach the women and children how to read and write. You're also good at music, aren't you? You could play for the villagers." Sung paused.

"There would be enough to do. The bigger worry would be about having too much, not too little. Actually, Seoul is the place you have nothing to do. What's there to do in Seoul? What've you done since graduating from university? Other than eating rice harvested through the hard efforts of farmers, wearing clothes pieced together by the painstaking labor of young women factory workers, and managing your servants in their constant work for you, what else do you do? And you're not the only one living like this. But even staying in Seoul would be good if done for charitable acts. Or at least if you earned the right to food or clothes through work. That way, you wouldn't be dependent on others. You wouldn't be living off the fruits of other people's labor. If people like Lee Gyeon-yeong or Kim Gap-jin would take a hoe in hand and do some farming, injustice in the world would decrease a lot, and the burden of workers would be lightened. Don't you agree?" Sung said, looking at Jeong-seon as if in reproach.

"Don't even imagine that," Jeong-seon responded, frowning. "Whatever might happen, I won't sponge off your hard work, so don't worry. But I won't do any cooking, washing, or weeding either, not even if I have to die of starvation. My ancestors haven't done such humiliating work in five hundred years. My family's different from yours." Jeong-seon trembled as if greatly insulted, and threw her bread onto the plate.

Astonished at her reaction, Sung fell into a rage beyond self-control, and snapped back at her, "You say your family's never done low jobs like weeding and cooking? What then about betraying and disobeying a spouse? Which is lower, what you do or what I suggest? Judge with your mind and education!" With that, Sung brought his fist down hard upon the table.

Sung's words were a knife to her heart, leaving Jeong-seon momentarily breathless and dizzy. "Does he know?" she wondered, feeling suddenly paralyzed.

At the sound of Sung striking the table, the waiter rushed over and waited for an order.

"Bring black tea instead of coffee, please," Sung ordered and began smearing butter roughly onto his bread. He remembered an old saying: "Women have no soul, no reason." How unreasonable Jeong-seon's inference, how improper her moral sense, how inferior her emotions. Sung was aghast. "I can't reason with her," he thought, greatly displeased, even to the point of animosity.

Her head bowed low, Jeong-seon poked at an egg ordered from the ham-and-eggs section of the menu, and tears dropped from her eyes.

3-66

Jeong-seon's tears broke Sung's heart. She was so lovely in his eyes, for she was of course beautiful. Her face, her eyes, her nose, mouth, ears, skin, figure, voice . . . he loved every part of her. Her hands seemed made of lily flowers, her fingernails, pink and clear, gleamed with beauty. Sung ought in fact to hate such hands, so typical of the noble class who enjoyed life without labor. Only the heir of an aristocratic line stretching back more than five hundred years would have such hands. They were fit only for tuning the stringed *geomungo* or for touching piano keys, but never for holding a needle. If such hands were to work in water for even one winter, or at weeding for only one summer, they would forever lose their beauty. Sung suffered still more over Jeong-seon's beauty because he wished her heart to be as beautiful as her body.

He changed the subject. "What are you going to do in the future? Are you following me to Salyeoul or staying in Seoul?"

Jeong-seon hardly cared so long as her infidelity remained hidden. If Sung were to discover the truth and make it an issue, her life would be ruined. She would be abandoned by her family and despised by the world.

Jeong-seon remembered the life of Maria Shin. She had married an old man, but fell in love with a young man in the church choir and got pregnant by him. Her husband sued her for adultery and had her imprisoned for six months. Her family abandoned her, and she eventually had to work as a waitress in a bar. Would her life take the same course? Everything depended on Sung. Jeong-seon had faith in his character. If she confessed, she was convinced that he would forgive her, cover her faults, and love her as his wife. But she also feared him. Sung had very strong willpower and spirited courage, like the old Goguryeo people. Once he had set his mind on something, he wouldn't stop regardless of obstacles. If Sung reacted in that Goguryeo spirit at proof of his wife's affair, he might kill her on the spot rather than bother with suing her for adultery. Jeong-seon was afraid of that.

She calculated that her best interests lay in not telling him her secret, unless he was already aware. But she didn't know if he had already found out. If he did know, she saw no way out other than to change her attitude and behave more softly in appealing to his love and character. She thus tried to determine what he knew, and had been carefully observing him since her return.

After they arrived home, Sung didn't talk about her any more, nor did he ask her whether or not she would go to Salyeoul. He kept to the reception room, even sleeping over there, giving as excuse that he was writing the defense paper for final appeal at the high court. Jeong-seon sensed that he was actually waiting for her to take the initiative in saying something.

She was nervous about that, but also worried about a sudden visit from Gap-jin or a letter from him that Sung would notice. She felt constantly unsettled about these things and was looking for a chance to meet Gap-jin, not because she missed him but because she wanted to talk about keeping their secret hidden.

3-67

Jeong-seon sought opportunity to see Gap-jin but was initially unsuccessful. She wouldn't run the risk of composing a letter, which might provide written evidence. She even trembled whenever the phone rang or a letter arrived, worrying if they might be from Gap-jin.

But on the day when Sung went to court, she took her chance. She changed her clothes and went out to catch a covered rickshaw headed for Jae-dong to find Baron Kim's home. Lacking the address, she asked around for his house, but nobody knew the residence of Baron Kim. Even with his full name, Kim Gap-jin, she couldn't find anybody who knew him. Knowing Jaetgol alone was no help either, for she didn't know exactly in which part of the area he really lived, Jae-dong or Gaheo-dong.

She eventually got out of the rickshaw and tried on her own, looking for the doorplate with his name. She was ashamed of herself, but felt driven by necessity, for she had to see Gap-jin one way or another. In desperation, she braced herself to go to the police station and ask for his address. A policeman there leafed through a book listing addresses. Rudely curious that such a beautiful woman was looking for a man, he asked, "What's your business with him?"

Flushed with confusion, she replied, "He's a relative."

"A relative? And you don't know the address?" he asked, interested.

"I arrived from the countryside," she lied, "and know only that he lives in Jaetgol."

The policeman gave her the address, remarking, "Mr. Kim has so many young female relatives who don't know his address." He closed the book and scrutinized her closely.

Burning with shame under his gaze, Jeong-seon thanked him and left the police station for Gap-jin's house. It turned out to be far more derelict than expected for the son of a baron. At least, it had signs of a noble residence: a double gate and what looked like a gate to the reception room, though in a Western style. Jeong-seon entered and was looking around when a woman opened the door of the servants' quarters and stuck her head out.

"Is Mr. Kim Gap-jin home?" Jeong-seon asked, trying to sound composed.

"Oh, you're looking for the master in the reception room?" the woman responded. She pointed to the gate fixed up in the Western style, purchased somewhere or other. It indeed led to the reception room.

"Does he have guests?" Jeong-seon asked cautiously.

"I don't think so. He seemed to be sick in bed with a cold. You can go in. Women visit all the time." The woman scrutinized the strange guest, then closed the door to soothe her crying baby.

Jeong-seon pushed against the gate leading toward the reception room. It opened easily. She wondered if she should call him, but then braced herself and cried out. "Is Mr. Kim there?"

"Eh, who's there? Young-ja?" Gap-jin opened the sliding door of his room slightly. His hair was mussed, as if he had just gotten up, and he was wearing a wrinkled bathrobe. "Oh, who's this?" he said, looking very surprised to see Jeong-seon. He hadn't expected her to show up.

3-68

Gap-jin felt a bit embarrassed because Jeong-seon seemed cold, though he was also annoyed, but he was mainly worried by her serious expression. He thought quickly. "What do I care if she acts like this? If I have to, I'll just deny what happened. Maybe I can even have some more fun with her. I won't turn her down if she brings enough money to live on. Even if she doesn't, I can have my fill of her since she's finally come to see me. That won't take long. Since the night at the Oryujang Hotel, I've not had much desire for her anyway." Thinking these things and wondering how to react, Gap-jin remained silent for some time.

Jeong-seon also found herself tongue-tied, though she had come to see him. Even if she had been an unrefined woman, talking about her husband to the man with whom she had conducted an affair would still be unpleasant.

"The master has come home," Jeong-seon finally uttered.

"The master?" Gap-jin pretended not to understand.

"Lawyer Heo, my husband, is home. Today's the day for the trial in the high court." She deplored Gap-jin's pretence of ignorance.

"Oh, wonderful! Congratulations!" Gap-jin pronounced. "Is that why you came to see me, to tell the happy news? Is that all?" he asked, his tone critical.

"The point is, he's now here, so don't write or call, and don't come see me," she explained, her expression earnest. With that, she had said all that she came to say and was getting up to leave. Gap-jin pulled her on the skirt to make her sit. "Let me go!" she cried. "What are you doing?" Great anger welled up in her humiliation.

"Why are you so upset?" asked Gap-jin, unblushing, "You shouldn't get so angry at me pulling your skirt. Go ahead and act virtuously before other men, but with me—no need to get upset even if I pull on your underpants, right? Come on, sit down here." He pulled her down next to him and smiled. "So, you want to hide our love from Sung?"

"What! Our love? Ridiculous! What're you talking about?" In her fury, she wanted to deny everything.

"Oh, what's this now?" He raised his voice as though announcing to the world, "Yes, let's listen to the theory of love relationships from a modern woman. We ignorant, old-fashioned men would regard our affair one of love. Are you saying it needs more to be love? Your theory implies body and soul are separate. You seem to think that physical union doesn't mean love, that the union of our souls is also necessary. If that's what you mean, then let's have a real relationship." He laughed in mockery and peered at her from different angles, tilting his head first one way, then another.

Jeong-seon wanted to slap him a dozen times.

3-69

As Jeong-seon shot him a sharp look, Gap-jin said, "You shouldn't deceive your husband about our affair. Tell him frankly what you did. If Sung wants a divorce, be happy and accept it. You can come live with me. We'll open a bar with you as hostess, and me . . . well, what should I do? Should I be the *banddo*, as the Japanese call the manager? No, maybe not. The *banddo* just sits in a back room keeping the accounts, so how could I keep track of the scumbags holding my Jeong-seon's hands and kissing her." Gap-jin laughed at the thought. "Obviously, if I run the sort of bar I'm thinking of, I can't reject a customer's demand for my girl's hands and lips. But a woman who's betrayed her husband is an *uwakimono*, a Japanese slut, not someone her lover can trust either, don't you agree?" He laughed and quickly leaned over to Jeong-seon to hug and kiss her.

Instantly, she slapped him, very hard and loud.

Shocked and with mouth agape, he drew back. The lower part of his bathrobe fell open, revealing the hair on his swarthy leg. "I see you can hit people," he finally said, staring at her as if to see what the slap meant, an innocent aspect to his character leaving him unsure.

Jeong-seon abruptly stood up and wiped her lips on her sleeve several times, as if some dirt wouldn't come off. "How on earth did I fall in with such a devil!" She cried out, nearly in hysterics.

"Oh, I see," he said, growing sarcastic as he rubbed his cheek. "How disgusting! You want to betray me, too. First Sung, now me. Who's next? Oh, of course! Lee Geon-yeong. I'd wondered why he was seen hanging around the Jeong-dong area. Forget him. Who but me would suggest opening a bar? Geon-yeong? Never! He's just a coward who worries about his reputation. He's small-minded, mean. He's completely different from me. I wouldn't even lift a finger in my defense if Sung sued me for adultery. Fine by me if you don't want to stay with me. Go wherever you want. I won't care whether you're with Geon-yeong or some Chinese guy selling the Chinese pancake *hoddeok*. Once I've had a girl, even if she were a renowned beauty of ancient China like Xi Shi, or Yan Guifei, I don't give her a second look. If I were responsible for every girl I've had, all the hairs plucked from my body would still be too few to embroider my guilt. That sounds almost like Buddhist wisdom! But what do you plan to do? Oh, I see, you want to go on deceiving Sung. You'll visit your old school or go to church as if nothing's happened, right? You're a thoughtless piece of work, but so are all women. That's why I consider them such a low form of life. In fact, I wonder how many of the ladies at school or church are better than you, anyway. Women are made of deception and lies. I know this, at least, and treat them like they deserve. But a country bumpkin like Sung thinks women are angels from heaven. He admires them, and that's why he's so easily tricked. But don't be too smug, Jeong-seon, Sung isn't a complete fool. Should I show you something? Where did I put it, the letter from that idiot?" He then got up as if to rummage around for it.

3-70

Opening a desk drawer to search inside and pulling a jacket from its hanger to fumble through the pockets, Gap-jin took his time, putting on a big show, like a policeman searching a house, before finally producing a jade-green envelope from his bathrobe pocket. Extracting the letter, he proudly tossed it to Jeong-seon.

She instantly recognized the letter's handwriting and also glimpsed the words "Lawyer Heo-Sung Law Office" on the green envelope. Fearing the worst, she read the letter. He knew about her and Gap-jin at the Oryujang Hotel. He told Gap-jin not to see her any more. He promised to burn a letter from Gap-jin to her. There was even more, but her mind already reeled. Holding the letter in one hand, she stared blankly at Gap-jin.

He had waited for her to finish reading, and noticing her fixed stare, he said, "See? Sung isn't always a fool. He read my letter. About how I couldn't forget our night at the Oryujang. How I couldn't forget your soft skin. That we should meet once again before he returned. Stuff like that. I meant it, of course. That day after the Oryujang, I was lying around aching all over my body and missing you a lot, so I sent you that letter telling you to come see me. I waited a long time, but you didn't come. Why not?" He gave her a sidelong glace before continuing, "No matter. Sung is still a fool, though. How could anyone just forgive a man who's had an affair with his wife? I wouldn't leave a man in peace even if he'd done nothing more than just brush against my wife's wrist. What a fool! He deserves to be cuckolded. And you know why else he's a fool? All that talk about forgiving me and burning my letter. That just makes him a bigger fool. Why do that? Why destroy proof of the enemy, why lose an advantage for himself? How can a lawyer think like that? He should just eat shit and be cuckolded." Gap-jin laughed at the thought and chattered on for a while. At one point, however, he suddenly appeared to recall something. "Oh, right, what did that fool say to you?" Gap-jin's face now showed some concern.

Jeong-seon didn't answer.

"If he makes a fuss, just come to me."

She remained silent.

"I'm not sure he really burnt the letter. If he really did, great, but if he hasn't, we might face a problem. That letter alone is enough for him to sue us for adultery. We could end up in prison. As if some country bumpkin would dare sue us ... but you should still make sure it doesn't happen. I'll try not to be so jealous." Gap-jin again attempted to touch her.

"Why on earth did you write me?" Jeong-seon scolded. She brushed his hand away, but as she picked up her muffler and prepared to go, he embraced her from behind, not wanting to lose her.

At that moment, a voice was heard from the yard: "Mr. Kim! Gap-jin!" The two froze like a pair of *jangseung*, the traditional Korean totem poles that stand at the typical village entrance. The voice was that of Sung.

3-71

"Quickly, into the closet!" Gap-jin whispered, pushing Jeong-seon that way. She hurried to hide. Once she was securely hidden, Gap-jin opened the double door. Outside stood Sung, his expression somber.

"You have a guest?" Sung asked, glancing at the pair of women's shoes. He would usually recognize his wife's footwear but was paying little attention because he didn't imagine her being there. He simply assumed that Gap-jin had once again sweet-talked some woman.

"No, I don't. Come in. When did you get back?" asked a flustered Gap-jin as he greeted Sung. He was just managing to collect himself when he caught sight of Jeong-seon's shoes on the stepping stone, and even his strong heart dropped. In the next instant, however, he smiled wryly to recall the old saying, "Hiding the head but showing the tail."

The two now sat down face to face but remained silent for some time, not in an attempt to read each other's thoughts but because neither felt comfortable about breaking the ice.

Still looking somber, Sung finally opened his mouth. "I don't want to talk long. I came to hear just one thing from you, and I expect a clear answer."

"Fine with me," was Gap-jin's bold reply, leaving Sung surprised. "I don't want to talk long either. I want to hear just one thing from you, too, and I also expect a clear answer." Gap-jin chose his words to mock.

Sung felt annoyance, but ignored the insult. "First, as I explained in my letter, you shouldn't meet my wife any more. I want to have a clear statement from you on that." He paused and gazed at Gap-jin.

"All right," Gap-jin said.

"Second, if my wife turns out to be pregnant with your child, I intend to include the child in my family register without breathing a word, so you should swear to say nothing about the issue."

"I agree to that."

"I trust you'll keep your word."

"Yes, you can trust me. I'm really sorry for this," Gap-jin added, showing himself a bit embarrassed.

"In that case, I'll go now," Sung said, preparing to leave.

"Wait a moment," said Gap-jin, motioning with his hand for Sung to stop. "I told you I have something to ask, too. That letter I sent, can I trust it's really been burnt?"

"Yes, you can trust me on that."

"I appreciate that. My mind would never be at ease so long as the letter remained in your hand. I appreciate what you've done. You can go now."

3-72

Sung silently stood up and left the room. Outside, putting on his shoes, he gazed more attentively at the pair of women's shoes positioned nearby and stopped tying his laces in surprise. The lacquered shoes were one of the two pairs made for their wedding. Although he might have difficulty specifying the shoes' exact characteristics, he did remember Jeong-seon going out several times with them on. He particularly recalled telling her that the sharp toes didn't look nice, and she hadn't worn them anymore after that. They were the ones with the clover pattern.

Sung resumed tying the shoes laces and plodded away from Gap-jin's place without glancing back.

"Good-bye." Gap-jin's voice trailed along behind. "I can't go out. Thanks."

Sung picked up his pace and was soon coming upon the Jae-dong Police Station, though without noticing. He heard himself thinking, "Jeong-seon was there. She went to Gap-jin while I was off to court. Should I leave her there? Should I?" He broke into a run, trying to close his ears to such thoughts because he believed he was doing the right thing. Coming abreast the police station, however, he halted.

"My anger won't go away unless I see her, if she comes out soon or not, how she looks, and how she might react if she were to see me." This thought finally won out. He turned and ran back to the alley, making even more haste than before. Hiding where he could see Gap-jin's gate, he waited like a hunter stalking prey, but grew uncomfortable standing on one spot, so he tried pacing back and forth. When somebody passed by, he pretended as if he were looking for an address. He realized that his bearing was not very respectable, but his brain was so congested with blood that his usual judgment and willpower seemed clouded by a thick, obscuring fog.

But what of Jeong-seon herself? And Gap-jin? After Sung's steps no longer echoed in his ears, Gap-jin stood for a long time looking toward the door through which Sung had departed. He seemed at a complete loss, even utterly abashed, but he soon wiped away everything unpleasant and embarrassing, the way he always did, and recovered his normal, ebullient mood. He was good at that.

He deliberately laughed out loud for a moment, then opened the closet door, saying, "The fool is gone, come out." But even as he opened the door, he suddenly stared, mouth agape, threw his arms wide, and cried out, "Jeong-seon!"

Pale of lip, she seemed not even to draw breath, and her eyes were glazed open like those of the dead, but she was crouched down like a child avoiding punishment, trembling as if with spasms.

Ever terrified of a corpse, Gap-jin ran in horror from the room to the veranda and screamed, "Is anybody out there?"

3-73

At Gap-jin's loud cry, servants and other people from the nearby rooms all rushed out and over to him. They made a great fuss over Jeong-seon, taking her from the closet, massaging her arms and legs, and splashing water onto her face. But she didn't come to and wouldn't stop trembling.

"Jeong-seon, Jeong-seon, wake up!" Gap-jin shook her vigorously, now worried about consequences. He felt less fear with others around, but was already growing concerned about legal complications. If she died, he would have to report to the police to be investigated. That would mean answering reporters' distasteful questions, and the papers would publish gossip about the incident.

"How could I ever see Mr. Yun again?" he worried. "And what

of my prospects for that banking position?" At this thought, he almost hated Jeong-seon.

Thinking quickly of an excuse, he spoke aloud in a puzzled tone to the people gathered around. "Well, I don't understand this. She came to talk to me about something, and before we'd even finished, she suddenly dashed into the closet! Look how she is now!"

Most present only listened, but one old maidservant spoke up to show off her knowledge. "Does she have the crazy fit?"

"Right, the crazy fit. Epilepsy." Gap-jin was overjoyed to find a proper word for her condition.

In the meantime, Jeong-seon came to. Opening her eyes, she first looked around, then abruptly got up, hid her face in her hands, turned to the wall, and started crying. Her clothes were wet and wrinkled, and her hair was disheveled, as if from being pulled.

Gap-jin sighed deeply at the sight. "I was afraid you were dying," he said. The incident had left him feeling disenchanted with women, losing any further interest in them. And for at least one woman, namely Jeong-seon, he felt something like fear. He coldly informed her, "I'll call a taxi. You can go home." After a pause, he added, "I should go out and make a phone call." He put a coat on over his bathrobe and left.

At the gate outside, he ran into Sung, who had waited for some time at a distance before again walking up to the gate. Not having heard Gap-jin's cry for help, Sung had finally concluded that Jeong-seon had left sometime while he was away. He had been just about to head home when Gap-jin stepped out.

"Oh," uttered Gap-jin, startled. He stepped back and asked, "You're still here?" After wavering a little, he explained, "Jeong-seon came to see me and fell unconscious for a while, but she's now come to. I was so worried she might die. I didn't ask her to come. She came to talk to me, but when you showed up, she must have fainted. No, I mean she came after you'd left. Oh, but anyway, it's good now she's alive again. I'm on my way to call a taxi, so you can go, too. Good thing you came, you can make sure she gets home okay." He then walked off in great strides, saying, "Damn, where can I borrow a phone?"

3-74

Watching Gap-jin walk off in that striding manner and turn the corner, Sung felt an almost uncontrollable annoyance and rage. "So," he thought, "it was true that Jeong-seon had been there! Why had she come to see Gap-jin, why did she hide when I showed up, and why did she faint?" Reminding himself, however, that "Self-control is strength," he managed calm down. Even in these circumstances, he reasoned, he would save Jeong-seon more embarrassment if he went in and took her home. He braced himself and headed for the guest room.

People were still crowded on the veranda outside the room and looked surprised at the sight of Sung. Although he felt as though cold water was showering down on his head and back, he kept his composure as he opened the double door to the room slightly and looked in.

Jeong-seon was seated leaning against the wall her expression blank, but she again hid her face in her hands as soon as she saw Sung.

"I'm happy you've recovered," he said, closing the door behind him and noticing that the people on the veranda had left. Jeong-seon began crying again, her face on the floor and her shoulders shaking. From outside soon came the blare of an automobile horn. Sung again opened the double doors. "The taxi's here. Let's go." Sung's voice was gentle but shaken.

Jeong-seon sat up, wiped her tears, blew her nose, fixed her hair, and, after picking up her bag and muffler, left the room. She kept her eyes down while tying her shoes and didn't even raise them when she stood up, unable to look at her husband.

Glancing at her briefly, Sung led the way toward the gate. He heard Jeong-seon's steps behind. As they reached the corner beyond the gate and turned toward the big street, they found the taxi waiting in the alley, and there also encountered Gap-jin.

"Are you all right?" Gap-jin asked, looking at both Sung and Jeong-seon. He was pained to see her pale face wet with tears, and Sung's serious face set like stone. "Ah, what have I done?" thought Gap-jin with deep regret, an emotion seldom experienced in his life.

Sung let his wife into the car first, then got in himself. Not drawing closer to the taxi, Gap-jin could only watch as it move slowly away, its wheels turning around and around. "Mr. Heo, good bye," he finally said. No answer returned from the departing car.

Watching it roll down the narrow alley, honking to clear its way, Gap-jin reflected on Sung, and on himself. "Ah, how miserable I look!" He closed his eyes in self-reproach. "A drunkard, a skirt chaser, a cheat having an affair with the daughter of my mentor and wife of my friend, a jobless scoundrel, a heel deserving no respect, and a reprobate utterly useless for the world!" Gap-jin sighed deeply. Feeling like a fool in his dirty, wrinkled pajamas, with an unwashed face and a heart he'd filled only with lust, Gap-jin reflected on his own wretchedness as he trudged home, head bowed as if fearful of meeting anyone he might know.

3-75

Upon returning to his room, he stretched out and closed his eyes to think. He had originally possessed a healthy moral conscience, and was actually not an unintelligent person. His brilliance had been recognized in elementary school, and he had received the highest education one could get in Korea. His willpower, however, had long been paralyzed by the selfishness inherited through his ancestral bloodline and the lazy, hedonistic lifestyle of alcohol and women. He was knowledgeable, but couldn't practice what he knew, or if he ever had put it into practice, he wouldn't have kept at it for long. He lacked any passion in self-sacrifice for justice, country, scholarship, or any ideology, nor had he patience for any of that. He desired only power and pleasure, and wanted to gain them without working to discipline himself. In this, he was a victim of his own heritage, fated by birth.

Jeong-seon was the same as Gap-jin. She possessed brilliance and a moral conscience, but her own pleasure came first. Neither Gap-jin nor Jeong-seon could understand the mindset of the Japanese, who were happy to sacrifice themselves for their country. They instead considered Japanese soldiers stupid for willingly heading into battle and death. Their own hearts were hardened by their heritage of a narrow-minded selfishness that robbed them of the freedom to think differently. If they had been invited to give a talk or to write an essay, they would have been able to develop unbeatable arguments through their long experience in speaking and thinking, much as they would also have been up to the task of finding flaws in any matter or person using their sharp, critical minds. Their ethical willpower, however, was extremely weak, as they were addicted to selfishness, pleasure, and alcohol.

They were cunning enough to claim things achieved by others as their own accomplishments, though they let others do the hard work, merely watching the work and complaining if it didn't go well, boasting that they would have done it better. All these characteristics, however, were apparently inherited weaknesses, so Jeong-seon and Gap-jin perhaps deserved sympathy for being unqualified to participate in developing a new era. But might they reform anyway? A breath of renewed life might be triggered in them by being deeply moved emotionally. But if some scholars were right that an old and feeble folk couldn't regain its youthful vigor, their descendents, the heirs of an old and feeble blood, would never regain their youth, either.

Gap-jin had made well-meant resolutions several times since middle school. He had resolved to lay off drinking and smoking, to subdue his zest for lechery at the sight of a woman, to exercise daily, to hike regularly, to read good books, and to keep accounts of money spent. He had even made such far-reaching resolutions as to say, "I'll dedicate myself to Marxism," and "I'll dedicate my work as a lawyer for farmers, workers, and socialists." He sometimes even boasted about that. But it was all just talk. Such resolutions lasted no longer than a month. Only one resolve appeared binding on Gap-jin, a resolve encapsulated within a question posed and answered to himself: "What can a man achieve other than to enjoy alcohol and women? A man shouldn't bother himself with the little things." That resolution had been kept.

Therefore, Gap-jin spent a lot of time asking himself, "How can I get my hands on a hundred thousand won?" or "How can I get that girl?" Achieving something big through accumulating a little bit every day couldn't be expected from a person without willpower. "Who would do that? Maybe a fool like Sung." Such was his thinking. In this respect, Mr. Lee Geon-yeong also belonged to the same crowd as Gap-jin.

3-76

But Gap-jin was distressed. Sung, the very man toward whom he had condescended for so long, appeared to possess a power greater than he had ever felt. Sung's attitude, refusing to grow enraged over something that anybody else would fall into a rage at, marked him not as a fool but as a man possessed of uncanny strength. Gap-jin conceded how utterly wrong he had been in thinking himself the stronger and wiser. He now felt himself less 'worthy' than Sung. That caused him deep dejection and embarrassment.

"Turn over a new leaf?" he considered. "Change my direction?" He recalled Mr. Han's words, that "clean living" was the source of strong character. Mr. Han's life, led without smoking, drinking, frequenting brothels, or grasping for money, dedicated instead to guiding young people, was certainly clean. And Mr. Han had power to move people's hearts. Second to Mr. Han in leading a clean life was surely Heo Sung. Gap-jin had never previously considered Sung to have any special power, but he felt it strongly now. He could no longer help but recognize Sung as a man possessing strength beyond any that he could imagine for himself.

"Should I change my lifestyle? Live clean without smoking, drinking, or chasing women? Dedicate myself to some work in the world? Live such a pure life?" Gap-jin felt his heart beat faster at such thoughts.

As his fingers brushed the pack of cigarettes in his bathrobe pocket, however, he felt the old urge to smoke. Shaking away all thought of quitting, he abruptly rose to his feet, located a match, and lit up. He inhaled deeply, as though to draw smoke down into his belly. After an hour or two without cigarettes because of the commotion with Jeong-seon, the smoke left him feeling lightheaded.

"Does this paralyze the will?" Gap-jin wondered. He smirked once, but extinguished the cigarette, rubbing it hard against the ashtray. He took the entire pack from his pocket and twisted it with both hands until it ripped in two, then opened the double doors and threw the pieces out into the yard. He spoke to himself out loud, resolving, "I'll stop smoking. I'll never smoke again!" To mark his resolve, he clenched both fists and shook them in the air.

"But what about my drinking?" he reflected. He imagined the amber whisky burbling into a glass before his eyes. That was the alcohol that he loved most. He imagined himself drunk after several glasses of whisky and holding a young woman's hand as he whispered lascivious words. That was so delightful to recall that he encountered genuine difficulty giving it up. But he also recalled his embarrassment at having to see doctors for treatment of the syphilis and gonorrhea contracted from such women. An acquaintance of his chased only virgins or married women for that very reason, and Gap-jin had considered doing the same. But he found himself imagining a pack of male dogs chasing female dogs in springtime. "Shouldn't a human being aim a bit higher than that?" he thought, and spat into the spittoon.

3-77

"Damn it, should I just become a Marxist?" Gap-jin scratched his head vigorously with all his fingers. "I'd be hundred times better at it than the Korean Marxists these days," he thought, proud of his knowledge and talent. He recalled words from the *Communist Manifesto*:

> A specter is haunting Europe . . . Workers of the world, unite!

True to his legal training, however, the Maintenance of Public Order Act came to mind:

> Anyone belonging to an association conspiring toward overturning property relations or overthrowing the state shall be sentenced to a legal penalty ranging in severity from three years incarceration to capital punishment . . .

In his mind's eye, he imagined incarceration. He had once visited a prison led by a teacher in criminal law. The gloomy room with the cold floor, the dark-blue uniform of prisoners on trial, the red-clay colored uniform of the prisoners, the iron chains, above all, the *yongsu*, that straw hood covering the head of a criminal. None of these offered a particularly pleasant vision. Moreover, the place of execution! Gap-jin had previously believed that being present at an execution would provide more enjoyment than summating legal arguments as a prosecutor at court, which would itself be fun. He had once even enjoyed laughing and clapping his hands while imagining a detested journalist being executed. But he had absolutely no desire to become a death-row convict and stand before the executioner.

"I wouldn't like being a Marxist. I don't like anything that might lead to imprisonment or execution." He shuddered at the thought. "Damn it, should I become a Christian instead? Maybe even a pastor?" He imagined church:

> To God be all praise,
> He washed my sins away . . .

Just listening and letting others sing such hymns would be tolerable, but singing along himself? Mingling so closely with those fools? That would be discomfiting! He couldn't carry a tune and actually didn't much care for music, anyway.

"Hey, is making such sounds a *real* job?" he would say to ridicule friends working as professional musicians. In Gap-jin's mind, law was the worthiest field of study, and to be a public official, especially a man of the judiciary, was the highest of attainments, prosecutor being the summit. Other than prosecutor, college professor or lawyer was the only profession he considered appropriate. But not just any college professor, not merely some position at one of those colleges in Korea! Only a professorship at Tokyo Imperial University would be good enough. Such an arrogant character as Gap-jin could hardly conceive of going to church and singing hymns or praying with bowed head alongside every Kim, Lee, and Choe.

Of course, he didn't believe in God, anyway. He would be a materialist. Besides, that Jewish God Yahweh was certainly just a figure of myth. The man Jesus, on the other hand, was more appealing. But Gap-jin didn't want to go hungry, walk around barefoot, get struck by stones, or be crowned with thorns and pierced in his side while slowly dying on a cross. He would be willing to follow Jesus if that meant living a long, comfortable life and wearing a real crown. For a life like that, he would need to find himself a beautiful, wealthy wife and aim at passing the National Exam for Government Offices.

But whether or not God existed and had a son named Jesus didn't much matter. He could still believe in Jesus. And if he went to church every Sunday, sang hymns like everybody else, and prayed to God, the Son Jesus, and the Holy Spirit, he would encounter no barrier to becoming a Sunday school teacher and then an elder.

"Well, I could do it, but what would I get in return?" As he reflected on this, he noticed a cigarette still in the ashtray, so he lit it, inhaled the smoke deeply, and exhaled rings and various other shapes.

3-78

"What should I do?" Gap-jin swirled his arms about as if for exercise, then knelt at his desk. "If I continue like this," he told himself, "I'll become nothing but a rotten egg." He blinked at the prospect.

"Damn it. Should I start a mining business?" He thought of Choe Chang-hak and Bang Eung-mo, those successful men in the mining industry. "If I struck it rich like them, I could have a cool one or two million won in my hand. Some man named Bak Yong-un became a quick millionaire, I heard. If I went into the business, I'd do even better. I'd put my money in Siksan Bank, Joseon Bank, Jaeil Bank . . . in the Japanese banks, too. But these days, people talk about the economic blockade and the war in Manchuria . . . Right, I should invest instead. Go in big with the one or two million won, make it ten times that within a year. Up to twenty million won! Wow, that'd be great!" Gap-jin's eyes widened at the vision of twenty million.

"With twenty million, one could do anything. Should I go into politics? Get the Japanese parties like Jeonguhoe and Minjeongdang under my influence? Or buy land? Oh, if only I had that twenty million. Ah, how I'd spend such money. I could call in all the *gisaeng* in Seoul for myself . . . What a banal thought. I could do better. I could buy the house of Viscount Yun on Mt. Inwang, have 20 young pretty concubines . . ."

As he indulged in his delusions of grandeur, imagining the twenty million won, he was informed that lunch was ready. That cut short his vain imaginings, but the thought of money distracted him from the agony brought on by his dalliance with Jeong-seon.

"*Yo-o-si,*" he sighed, agreeing with himself in Japanese. "I should do the mining thing. Does it need capital?" The idea had taken deep root in his mind, but wouldn't mining require capital? And wouldn't finding a new mine take a lot of work? He'd rather be handed a rich mine that someone had already found, but who would give a good one away freely? He began to suspect the mining business would not be so easy. "Damn it. Too much trouble!" He found yet another surviving cigarette and lit up. It was easier just to smoke.

After lunch, he continued to dwell on thoughts of money, but came to no solid conclusions. "Well, I should at least pass the law exam this year," he mused, and pulled from his shelf the textbook for criminal law, his weakest point. "Yes, I should first become a prosecutor . . . Right, right, a prosecutor is the best thing." He started to study the book, but after six months off, starting again proved difficult. He hurled the book away. "Getting married to the daughter of wealthy family is surely quicker! But I've undoubtedly lost my reputation by now."

Gap-jin ground his teeth and reflected. "If Sung hadn't burnt my letter, I'd still be worried he might sue me for adultery. I must have been crazy to write that!" A moment later, he thought, "Go somewhere to drink?" He looked at his watch. Only three in the afternoon! "Bars aren't open yet," he muttered, annoyed.

3-79

As Sung was riding away with Jeong-seon, he suddenly wondered if she had taken poison. "Do you need a doctor?" he asked.

She looked at him, eyes pleading. "No," she said.

Relieved, he remained silent.

"Where to?" the taxi driver asked, glancing in the rearview mirror as he exited Jae-dong alley.

Sung turned toward Jeong-seon. "Home," she whispered, barely audible.

He understood and ordered the driver, "To Jeongdong. Go by way of Gyeongseong Radio Station." On the ride home, neither Sung nor Jeong-seon spoke another word. Upon arrival, he ordered Yu-wol to make a bed for her in the main room. He then left the house.

Jeong-seon lay in bed suffering in body and heart. She didn't know what would happen to her body, and her mind was a torrent of thoughts. She realized that Sung must have known everything that had happened. She now understood why he hadn't shared a bed with her in the days since her return. Yet . . . he had come to the station to pick her up. He had treated her normally since, though not as warmly as before. He had handled her adultery without showing any sign of rage or hatred. Most husbands would curse and threaten their wives, perhaps even kill them. Sung's behavior made her wonder what was on his mind.

"Did he forgive me with that boundless love?" she wondered. "Could a husband forgive such a wife? If my husband had committed adultery, would I be able to forgive him? Or perhaps his love for me has cooled so much he doesn't care? Or are his anger and sadness unbearable, but suppressed by masculine willpower? Like the hard, thick crust of the earth pressing down the molten fire beneath? Does my husband's strong character suppress an immeasurably hot fire of jealousy and rage?" This final thought made her see Sung as huge and fearsome, filling the whole world.

Until that moment, Jeong-seon had never imagined Sung higher, better, more powerful than herself. She had always considered him a country bumpkin, but his capacity to endure the unendurable compelled her to recognize him as possessing more than ordinary strength. Gap-jin had always spoken of Sung as a dupe or a fool, but she saw that this wasn't necessarily so.

But if Sung were suppressing anger and sadness beyond the usual limit of the bearable, might he not suddenly erupt like a volcano, shaking and burning everything? Wouldn't such great force grind her to dust or reduce her to ashes?

3-80

For such a respectable, powerful man like Sung, she should have been a faithful wife. She also realized that she underestimated his value. Many other men, including Gap-jin, had desired her beauty and property, but Sung had repeatedly declined her father's offer of her hand. She had previously assumed that his refusal stemmed from a sense of personal or familial unworthiness. But she now understood that he had greater ambitions than marrying a woman of property and connections or beauty and education. She had been proud of herself as a beautiful woman, a daughter of a noble family, a woman of high education and property worth some 100,000 won, believing all these to be the best recommendations for a good marriage, but these were all irrelevant to Sung.

If only she had felt respect for Sung from the beginning, she wouldn't have betrayed him. But that jar was already spilt upon the ground, and there could be no filling it up again with the same water. She felt a deep, longing regret. "I didn't see him clearly," she cried. "I must have been blind. How could I have thought Gap-jin better than Sung. How could I have judged so wrong?" She struggled in heartfelt anguish. Then with a sudden thought, she called out, "Yu-wol."

Yu-wol rushed into the room. "Yes, ma'am?"

Jeong-seon closed her eyes, too embarrassed to look directly at Yu-wol. "Did master inquire about me?" she asked.

Yu-wol remained silent.

"I mean before I came back?" Jeong-seon added, opening her eyes. Yu-wol looked very virtuous and beautiful.

"No, not much," Yu-wol replied, uncertain of the question.

"Which room did he sleep in before I came back?"

"The main room," she replied, bowing her head to stifle a giggle. "When I went to him before breakfast . . . sorry, it's so funny." She couldn't speak for giggling.

Jeong-seon was surprised at Yu-wol's giggling and suddenly felt jealous, imagining that Sung might have wanted to seduce her. "Brat!" she said, her voice sharp. "Why are you laughing like that? Tell the truth!"

Yu-wol stopped giggling. "Master was hugging your skirt, the one that hangs on the wall, but he quickly tossed it in the corner when I knocked." She gazed at Jeong-seon almost in fear.

Jeong-seon listened with eyes again closed. She felt shame at her own ignorance of her husband and asked a different question. "Did the master of Jaetgol come to visit often while I was gone to Salyeoul for those two months?" She was seeking clues from Yu-wol's response.

"Oh, yes, he came day and night," she answered, then hesitated.

3-81

"Did he? What did he do when he came?" asked Jeong-seon, though she feared to hear the answer.

"Whenever he came, he went to the main room . . ." Yu-wol stopped, uncertain about revealing all the details.

Noticing Yu-wol's hesitant gaze, Jeong-seon urged her, "Tell me everything you saw."

"In the main room, he'd order the old maidservant to make him a bed. He'd just be wearing underwear, and he'd hug her. It's hard to talk about. He'd get up late and order water brought for him to wash himself, then drink alcohol and get angry during breakfast over having nothing to eat. It was so embarrassing." Yo-wol's face revealed indignation.

Jeong-seon again closed her eyes. She had no heart to insist on hearing more. Feeling dirtied that her bed had been touched by Gap-jin's body, she abruptly got up. "Take the mattress away," she said.

Yu-wol folded the mattress to put into the bedding closet.

"Take the sheets, the mattress cover, and the pillowcase. Wash them clean. I don't know if I'll ever use them again, though."

Yu-wol worried about having angered Jeong-seon, but she felt that her words concerning her master and mistress, and even Mr. Kim, were blameless. She bustled about with the bedding, putting it out on the veranda, and called loudly toward the servants' quarters, "Hey, Granny, you should take these sheets!" Yu-wol suddenly felt like an important person, and she muttered to herself about Jeong-seon, "How embarrassing that woman is."

Back in the room, Jeong-seon felt a growing suspicion that Yu-wol had divulged every detail of recent events to her husband. She scowled as Yu-wol returned. "Bitch, did you tattle everything to the master?"

"No," replied Yu-wol, confused. Humbling herself, she asked, "What could your servant tattle to the master?" Then more firmly, "I didn't tell him anything."

"You told him I got home late after going to the Oryujang Hotel with Mr. Kim of Jaetgol, didn't you, bitch?" Jeong-seon's voice grew sharp.

"I even don't know what 'Orijang' is," Yu-wol said, beginning to sulk.

Jeong-seon quickly turned away, dashed off a letter at her desk, and said, "Take this to the doctor in Dabanggol. She should come immediately!" As Yu-wol left, Jeong-seon looked at herself in the full-length mirror. Her hair was disheveled, and her clothes wrinkled, as if she had spent a night in jail. She gazed at her face. It was that of an invalid who had just crawled out of bed.

3-82

"What I have become!" exclaimed Jeong-seon, staring with dejection into a mirror. "What will I yet become?" Reflecting on this, she wondered if she ought to enter a Buddhist nunnery, something that Korean women used to consider when they were upset.

When she visited Mt. Geumgang once on a school field trip, she had felt something about the nuns, poetic though, not religious. She recalled that feeling. But she was too lively and passionate to waste her years living the cold and forlorn life of a nun.

"Should I kill myself?" she wondered. As a woman born to fortune, she had never considered that before. She had even laughed at the rash actions of her classmates, Miss Hong and Miss Kim, who had thrown themselves onto the train tracks in Oryudong. "Why did they do that?" she had asked. "They were young, like flowers in the spring of life!" For Jeong-seon herself, life was like springtime, her youth like a flower, and daily life a concert. She considered herself an otherworldly fairy, born to a charmed life, not one of suffering. She lacked nothing. She had a good family background, property, beauty, talent, and high education. The only thing she had to do was just enjoy it, and if that got boring, she could just sleep. Even ineluctable death seemed not to touch her. She was a queen beyond mortality, a celestial, immortal queen, a queen enjoying beauty and love forever like the moon goddess Diana.

But now, before even a second year of marriage had passed, she had come to think of death. "What shame, what humiliation!" She saw only these in her future, and for one who had never experienced such feelings, these were worse than death. Believing she could no longer live after being pointed at and ridiculed by the world, she muttered, "I should kill myself." She drew away from the mirror and flopped listlessly onto the floor.

She considered various ways of committing suicide. Throwing herself onto train tracks. Drinking lye. Overdosing on sleeping pills. She recalled reports of suicide in novels and newspapers. Drowning. Hanging. Slitting wrists. Bodies drowned, choked, torn apart by trains. All these were conjured up before her eyes. None looked good.

"Should I work for farmers my whole life, following my husband?" She recalled Salyeoul. To dedicate herself for the education of farmers' children, winning their adoration like a mother . . . she imagined herself in that picture.

Would her husband, however, really forgive her? No, what if he had actually gone out to buy a knife or a pistol to kill her? Such thoughts raised goose bumps over her entire body. "My husband can do anything he sets his mind to!" The thought seemed to confirm a real possibility of being murdered. "Where did he go?" Jeong-seon looked around the room, as if to see him in every corner holding a bloody knife and glaring at her. She felt again that turbulence of her nerves before her breakdown earlier. "Yu-wol!" she cried out in fear. At that scream, her old nanny rushed in. Jeong-seon's lips were pale.

3-83

After the patients were gone, Dr. Hyeon took off her medical gown, went to the Western room in her home's inner quarters, and settled onto the sofa to light a cigarette. Crossing her legs like a man and leaning her head back, she allowed her mind to wander. From a teacup on the table, steam rose in thin lines.

She found herself missing a man in her life. Though she usually adopted an air of tough independence, she felt lonely. As a woman over thirty, perhaps she felt that her youth was almost behind her.

"Should I get married?" she wondered. She sometimes considered the possibility these days, and since Jeong-seon's visit, she somehow felt the desire even more strongly. Though one might expect that seeing Jeong-seon's bloom fade from the drought of conjugal harmony would dissuade Hyeon from thinking of marriage, precisely the opposite had transpired. Hyeon felt an abstract longing to suffer as a young wife. She wanted the actual experience of that suffering, and also the suffering of a young mother.

"Suffering is the spice of life," a friend had once said, and it didn't sound like a joke. Arguments between husband and wife. Worries about sick children through sleepless nights. As a gynecologist and pediatrician, Hyeon had heard a lot about these in her daily work. Every woman who grew close enough to open her heart admitted to having problems and sufferings. Any woman claiming to have no problems and boasting of plentiful money, a beautiful home, and a great relationship with her wonderful husband would likely be telling vainglorious lies.

"Why on earth do they get married?" Hyeon would ask, and even sneer at them, presenting herself like cooled ashes after instinct and emotion have burnt away. But much like water flows beneath ice on a winter stream, desire for love was flaring deep within her still-young heart.

"But whom could I possibly marry?" she sighed. She had high expectations that she didn't hide. "There's no worthy man in Korea," she would often say, thinking of the men who had written those letters kept stored in the box. Dr. Lee. That banker Kim. A young literary man. A tramp. A teacher. The list went on and on. But with none of them did she want to share her life.

"How can you get everything from just one man? You should be satisfied with the looks of one man, the talent of another, the body of still another, the sophistication of another still, the money of yet another, and so on. You cannot expect everything from only one man," a *gisaeng* friend had once told her. Hyeon also thought about the similar views of the Russian Communist revolutionary Alexandra Kollontai concerning "red love."

"Actually, the real problem is in living together with a man for the rest of your life after marriage! That's what makes finding a husband so difficult. But to have a husband for a couple of days, any of those guys who write me letters, including Dr. Lee, would be good enough ..." She laughed out loud at her ridiculous musings.

A young maid rushed in at the sound, concerned that something had happened. "What's wrong?" she asked.

"Oh, nothing. I just laughed to myself." As the girl turned to leave, Hyeon asked, "By the way, are you going to marry anyone when you grow up?"

"No, I won't do that," she replied, shyly twisting her body, "I want to stay here with you forever."

"What if I get married?"

"What?" The maid's eyes grew wide in alarm, as if she had heard something dreadful.

3-84

At that moment, Yu-wol arrived with the letter from Jeong-seon and was admitted.

"Oh, it's you." Accepting the letter from Yu-wol's hand and opening it, Hyeon asked, "When did the young lady get back? She'd gone to the countryside, hadn't she?"

"You mean Mrs. Yun?" said Yu-wol, correcting from "young lady" to a title with more respect. "It's been some time. Maybe three or four days? Anyway, she wants you to come quickly." Yu-wol then greeted the other maid, her friend, grasping her hand.

"Has Mr. Heo come back, too?" Hyeon asked.

"Yes, but earlier. The same day madam left for the countryside."

Hyeon nodded, but asked herself, "What does Jeong-seon have that's so urgent?" She lit another cigarette and closed her eyes, like Sherlock Homes reflecting on the solution to a problem. Jeong-seon had asked about abortion. She had been so nervous. She had gone to the countryside immediately after leaving Hyeon's place. All these facts seemed like clues to a riddle. "Is marriage really something disgusting?" she wondered. "Is living alone the best solution?"

Hyeon extinguished the cigarette. "Call a taxi," she ordered.

Ten minutes later, an elegant and cool Hyeon sat face to face with Jeong-seon. "Now, it depends on you." These were her first words after hearing Jeong-seon's confession. "If you regret your actions and want to become Mr. Heo's faithful and obedient wife, you should simply become that kind of wife. But if you don't want to continue this marriage, then leave it. Whatever you decide, just remember you're the one who made mistakes. Even by the standard of 'red love,' your actions were probably wrong. There's no way you can make excuses for what you did. Apart from the issue of chastity, it's about faithfulness. There might be bourgeois or communist chastity, but there's no such distinction for faithfulness. As long as we have life in a society, faithfulness is essential. By your actions, you broke faith. You betrayed a person you shouldn't have and did what you shouldn't have done. What you have to do now is confess everything to your husband and beg forgiveness. After that, as I said earlier, you should choose what you want, either continue your marriage or dissolve it. By the same token, you should ask your husband to do something. Or demand something from him. That's why I want to know your opinion now. Stay married, or get divorced? You've got to decide first." Hyeon gave a piercing look, as if to peer into Jeong-seon's thoughts, but felt sad to see her confused, haggard face. Against the heaviness of marriage, Hyeon felt the lightness of being single.

Jeong-seon burst into tears and lay down prostrate on the floor. "What should I do?" she wailed. To confess *everything* about her affair with Gap-jin, to hear Sung's response afterwards, and to face an uncertain future . . . Jeong-seon saw only darkness everywhere. Where had she found courage to accompany Gap-jin to the Oryujang Hotel? She now couldn't make up her mind what to do, but only wept in frustrated silence.

Hyeon sat and watched Jeong-seon weep soundlessly. In that silence, the hands of the clock slowly turned.

3-85

"You can't solve the problem with tears," Dr. Hyeon finally said, touching Jeong-seon's shoulder. "Isn't it time that women gave up crying, anyway? Tears are just the weapon of the weak. Hot emotions won't solve difficult problems; cold intellect alone does that. You should cool your heart, make it cold as ice. You'll then be able to think straight. If you'd kept your heart cold, things wouldn't have turned out like this. Your passion messed you up . . . Jeong-seon, every engine has a cooling device. Engines run on heat, but without being cooled, they'll stop running or even break down. That's why cars and planes have radiators. A passionate individual also needs something like a radiator. What's a person's radiator? You really don't know? It's the intellect, *intelligence*. Jeong-seon, you're naturally *intelligent*, but your *intelligence* and *emotion* aren't in good harmony. They don't communicate well. You should cool your heart for your head's sake, and reflect well."

In her confusion, Jeong-seon couldn't catch Dr. Hyeon's every word. She realized, however, that her actions had been not *intelligent*. Recognizing that, she grew even more disappointed. She had believed herself a shrewd person but now saw that her shrewdness possessed little value. She pitied her intelligence for going bankrupt so easily.

Judging herself this way, she admired and feared her husband's intelligence and willpower even more. He could control himself. Dr. Hyeon was a person of cold intellect, but her husband had more than that. He had strong willpower and hot passion as well. For the first time, Jeong-seon was analyzing her husband's character psychologically, something only possible due to Dr. Hyeon's help.

"Couldn't I live on my own?" Jeong-seon asked, feeling helpless to decide.

"Alone?" Hyeon shot back. "After getting divorced?"

"That's one possibility."

"You could live on your own. You've got property, and you can live on that. At least, you'd have no problems about food and clothing."

"Should I work as a teacher?"

"Unlikely. Who would hire a woman divorced over an affair?" was Dr. Hyeon's merciless response.

That pricked Jeong-seon's conscience, but she knew it was true. With tears in her eyes, she again asked, "Then, what can I do with my life?

"You want to do something?" Dr. Hyeon still spoke coldly. "You mean you want to do something even though you have enough food and clothes?"

"Yes. Tell me what to do. I can't think of anything on my own. I've even thought of killing myself. I still think about it. But isn't there some other way than killing myself?" Jeong-seon gazed at Dr. Hyeon with eyes wet from tears.

"Suicide is also a solution," Dr. Hyeon acknowledged. "The world always sympathizes with the dead." She then closed her eyes in thought.

3-86

"However," Hyeon observed, opening her eyes and rearranging her crossed legs, "suicide is the most dishonorable way of solving a problem. People who commit suicide either feel responsibility without power or want to escape dishonor through death after failing to solve their problems. What sorts of people kill themselves? Spurned lovers. Penniless bums. The mentally ill, who might appeal to plausible philosophical motives, but who actually suffer mental problems, as a bit of common sense would make clear. Regardless the reason offered, only the weak commit suicide. Dying is the easiest thing in the world. Even the good-for-nothing who never succeeds in life can manage to die."

Dr. Hyeon paused, then spoke with a different tone. "Dying for one's country on the field of battle, or for serving and saving mankind like Jesus, Peter, and Paul, or for the truth like Giordano Bruno, such deaths deserve respect but are beyond most of us. But do any of us have the right to take our own lives out of agony or shame? That's actually a sin. The weakness itself isn't sinful. Sin might be committed out of weakness, but to kill yourself? You could still do something of value. Comfort and tend the sick as a nurse, or teach poor children to read and write, or even just do cleaning work wherever it's needed. There are so many things you could do. Why die? Your husband might even forgive you if you speak with him sincerely, and you could have a second chance at a happy family. Listen, there aren't many men like your husband in all of Korea. Most men these days chase money and skirts and just want a comfortable life, but your husband didn't care about money, beauty, or the city's pleasures. He went to the Korean countryside instead, the poorest place in the world, a place without pleasures. That, my dear, is heroism. Not everybody can do that. If I had such a husband, I would wash his feet with my hair and kiss their soles every day. I really don't understand what more you needed beyond that." On that earnest note, Dr. Hyeon ended her remarks, sighing with deep sincerity.

Jeong-seon now listened with a cooler head. Hyeon's statements were entirely reasonable, even logical. She understood two main things:

1. Don't be self-centered.
2. Sung is a man of great character.

Not only did she understand these two, she felt greatly pressured by them both. To lighten the mood, she abruptly threw out a surprising question. "Should I become a *gisaeng* like Seon-hi?"

"What?!" Dr. Hyeon was astonished.

"A *gisaeng* like Seon-hi. Her *gisaeng* name is said to be San-wol." Jeong-seon smiled as she spoke.

Pleased to see Jeong-seon again relaxed and smiling, Dr. Hyeon broke into loud, mannish laughter.

3-87

As Dr. Hyeon was preparing to leave, Sung came in. He had just returned home and been heading for the guest room when Yu-wol told him about Hyeon's visit. "Ah, you're here," Sung noted, shaking her outstretched hand.

"I didn't know you had come back. You should've called me at least!" Hyeon admonished, pretending to be aggrieved and abruptly withdrawing her hand from his.

"I'm sorry," he responded, smiling.

They all sat down.

"Well, how is the work in the county going?" Hyeon asked, attempting to lighten the mood, "I really have no idea of the country life. I've visited Seokwangsa Temple for a couple of weeks, but that's all. The most inconvenient thing is having no electric lights. Don't you agree?"

"What? The temple has no electric lights? I think it does," Jeong-seon interjected, cheering up.

"Everything in the country is inconvenient," replied Sung, in a lighter tone. "The city is designed for convenience, but nobody's concerned about the country. If only a tenth of the city's facilities were provided to the countryside, it'd be a better place to live than the city. The blue sky, clear water, beautiful mountains, green grass, wild birds, fresh air, simple lifestyle . . . where else can we enjoy all these than in the country?" Sung spoke with passion.

"But we doctors have no other choice than living in the city, do we?"

"Why? The country needs doctors, too. There are also diseases there."

"True, but could poor farmers ever afford house calls?" Hyeon insisted, but her tone was uncertain, betraying the weakness of her argument.

"Country people don't need doctors who come only by car. They need lots of doctors willing to walk to make house calls. When I went to Salyeoul, that village alone had over ten patients suffering dysentery or typhoid. I went to the district town to find a doctor. He insisted on travel expenses and extra pay for a house call in addition to taxi fair. But he wouldn't come when needed, so I got a thermometer and some medicine to take on the role of nurse practitioner ..."

"I see," Hyeon interrupted. "So that's how you got typhoid! Nearly dying in the line of duty, you might say." She gave a loud laugh.

"Farmers don't know the meaning of infection, quarantine, or disinfection. Why do doctors want to stay only in Seoul? Why isn't even one doctor out of ten thousand willing to go to the countryside, where doctors are needed? Doctors in the city are willing to offer medical treatment to the scoundrels and concubines, much as they would for their own parents, even serving throughout the night if necessary. But they're unwilling to make house calls to farmers, the very people who labor to feed and clothe our nation. Dr. Hyeon, why don't you help the poor rural women and children who work so hard day and night, instead of treating rich people here in Seoul? The city already has enough doctors and hospitals. It's got plenty of university hospitals as well as medical college hospitals like Severance Hospital. Why are you here? To earn money to live? If you go to the countryside, you won't have any worries about food and firewood. Open a practice in Salyeoul, and you'll get a house, food, firewood, and side dishes. Whenever a family makes rice cakes or slaughters a chicken, they'll share the food with you. And you'll spend the rest of your life respected and loved like a mother by the farmers." Sung's eyes glittered with passion.

"I don't want to be called a mother!" retorted Dr. Hyeon, laughing. But her face then turned serious, showing respect at Sung's words.

3-88

Night deepened over Seoul as snow quietly fell. By ten that evening as the snow was thickening atop the wall around an empty Deoksu Palace, the tinkling keys of pianos at Ewha College had fallen silent, and the grounds of the Soviet and American consulates were still as a forest, their trees heavily laden with the white snow.

The city hadn't seen much snow this winter, but when the flakes came falling, they created beautiful scenes. Tonight was one of those beautiful snowy times. Snowflakes didn't whirl down broken in a cold, swirling wind but fell steadily, retaining their perfect shape. They were not the angry shards of hard-bitten snow, but wet flakes bringing tears and smiles. These fell gently onto roofs, branches, stones, and even oxen dung scattered in the streets. Unless they scattered like startled birds to the earth from the leaves of branches too thin to bear their weight, the flakes remained unmoved where they had fallen, awaiting a second command from God so long as they could.

The earth was white, the sky grey, but the entire world seemed imbued with special light, the luster of a snowy evening. A soft, pure, silent world. One of the loveliest scenes on earth. Was anyone looking? People were sleeping, also birds and other animals. The moon and stars slept behind clouds. Only God and dreaming poets looked upon the peaceful scene. Or young lovers meeting secretly. Or those with worries keeping them from sleep.

Under roofs covered with the peaceful snow, some failed to find sweet sleep. These entered no warm beds of pleasure, but endured pain, quarrels, and tears.

Toward the hilltop where a hall connected the American and Russian consulates --Jeongdong Palace and West Palace in earlier times—a dark shadow hurried up from the direction of Yeongseon Gate. It ran stumbling like a young deer chased by a hunter.

The shadow stopped at the hillcrest, standing upright and glancing about as if to ask, "Where am I going?" Onto its obscured head and shoulders, the wet flakes of snow gently fell. After reluctant indecision, the dark figure hurried down toward Jeongdong Church. Leaving small footsteps behind in its descent, almost running down the slope, the figure drew quickly near the front of the main entrance to the courtyard, looked around again, then moved toward the church as if drawn there. Reaching the entrance, it stood holding onto the gate pillar as if to support itself from collapse. Its head and shoulders were now entirely white with snow that fell like pear blossoms from grey skies.

It was Jeong-seon.

"God," she wondered, "where should I go?" She looked up to the church roof with its spire. Some time had passed since Jeong-seon had lost her faith in God or Jesus. Perhaps she had never truly possessed any though she had gone to church, read the Bible, and prayed the entire fifteen years of her schooling. Since graduating from Ewha College, she had not once reopened the Bible or prayed. The religious service on graduation day had been her last. Why, then, had she hurried to this place so deep in the night to hold onto the pillar of its gate and weep?

3-89

Why had she come here?

After Dr. Hyeon had left upon learning that a patient was waiting to see her, Sung and Jeong-seon had eaten dinner without exchanging a single word. The silence was so heavy and painful, almost unendurable.

Jeong-seon expected her husband to open his mouth first. She believed that he would surely break the heavy, painful silence and offer her some words of comfort. She tried to eat even though she couldn't taste the food, but Sung not only said nothing, he also kept his eyes on the rice bowl and the dishes, never even glancing at Jeong-seon.

Jeong-seon tried to gauge his mood by glancing sideways and raising her eyes for a sharp look, but she failed to catch even a fleeting expression on his face, he was so reserved. Occasionally, though, she noticed him holding his spoon with rice and looking ahead blankly as if caught in some painful thought.

Dinner went on that way until it was over, and even before the small table was taken away, Sung left for the reception room. Jeong-seon went to her desk and bowed her head in tears, unable to control her sadness.

She had wanted to ask her husband for forgiveness, confessing all her faults as Dr. Hyeon had advised. And if her husband were willing, she now would have followed him to the end of the world. She believed herself capable of going to Salyeoul to draw water and cook rice, even wear clothes of rough hemp cloth. But all throughout dinner, she found no chance to tell him so.

She had expected that "limitless love of a husband" from him. She even felt deserving of it since he had studied with the help of her family and had even gained a dowry of nearly 100,000 won through her.

She nervously waited for him to return. Upon hearing some

sound from the yard, she wondered—like a young woman waiting for her lover—if he were coming. Had her husband come then, she would have clung to him in tears.

But he didn't come, not even when the clock pointed to nine. Jeong-seon became impatient and ordered Yu-wol to go see if he were still in the reception room and what he was doing. The girl returned to report that her husband was packing his things.

Was he then planning to go back to Salyeoul? Did he intend to leave her and go to Salyeoul? Jeong-seon stood up and left for the reception room. She intentionally made audible sounds in stepping onto the veranda, and waited a while outside the door. All remained quiet in the room. She then knocked at the door twice, as in the Western way, and waited. Some ten seconds passed before she heard Sung get up and open the door. He looked at her blankly, then gave way and made a sign for her to enter.

She had imagined that she would throw herself into his arms as soon as she saw him, but his indifference discouraged her. She also felt annoyance at the sight of his traveling bags set about in the room.

She looked around at the bags and asked, "Where are you going?"

"I'm leaving for Salyeoul," he replied.

"If you want to leave, you should first settle the issue." She spoke sharply, her voice trembling with anger.

3-90

When Jeong-seon turned on him demanding resolution, Sung was initially at a loss for words and sought to fathom her intentions from the look in her eyes. They looked poisonous, and her lips trembled. She was furious at Sung for preparing to leave, but her reaction stemmed from disappointment over not receiving the boundless love expected from her husband.

"Settle the issue?" Sung coolly replied, satisfied that he had sufficiently read her meaning.

"Exactly. You should settle the issue first. You can't leave without doing that." She kicked over a suitcase in her anger and flopped down to sit on the floor with an attitude of challenge that he settle things then and there.

"Isn't everything already settled? Since things *are* settled, I'm going my way. But there is one thing still to be settled." Sung pulled a document from the inner pocket of his jacket. "Here are the divorce papers. I've already stamped them, so whenever you're ready, you can stamp it, get your father's stamp as well, and take it all to the Gyeongseong office. I've already given your father an official certificate formally turning the property in my name over to him. So isn't everything already settled? What else is there? Oh, right, one more thing. I included in the certificate an official statement that this house also goes to your father." Sung then pulled the key for the safe from his key ring and tossed it to her.

Jeong-seon nearly fainted at Sung's response. Was that what he had been up while he was out all day? At her husband's decision to leave, she felt as though the rope from which she was dangling had just been cut, leaving her to plunge onto the rocks below.

"I already knew about your relationship with Gap-jin," Sung told her, softening his tone. "Somebody sent me a letter about that. I didn't want to believe it, but I was so distressed I returned to Seoul earlier than planned. If I'd come back only a day earlier, our situation wouldn't have been so bad, but this must be how it's supposed to be. I sent a telegram from Hwangju and expected you to meet me at the station, but when I got off there, you must have just finished eating at a restaurant with Gap-jin. That means my telegram must have arrived while you were with him at the stadium watching a baseball game. As I was coming out of the station, I saw the two of you in a taxi, probably on the way to Oryujang Hotel. At home the next day, I intercepted a letter to you from Gap-jin and found out what happened at the Oryujang Hotel. I waited until today for you to say something. I can guess why you sought me in Salyeoul, but I wanted to hear everything directly from your lips. I believed you would regret what you did and confess to me, so I waited. My belief was in vain. I realized today that everything is over. What else could I do but settle things in our relationship, as you said, and return by night train to the place waiting for me?" Sung finished speaking and gazed at Jeong-seon, whose face had turned dark.

3-91

Even while packing his things, Sung had still waited for Jeong-seon's repentance. When she entered the guest room, he expected her finally to confess and regret, but he had only found her sounding rather sulky and annoyed. He felt his last hope cut off.

"Did you tell Father everything about me?" She was going on the offensive.

Sung remained silent.

"What did you tell my father?" she repeated, pressing for an answer. She had felt shame at Sung's detailed account of her transgression, but any possible tears of regret were blocked by the blaze of rage and resentment over his apparent revelation of her secret misdeeds to her father.

Sung was displeased by her reaction. It swept away even the last residue of sympathy and feeling toward her in his heart. He took more offense at her behavior now than when he had found her at Gap-jin's place earlier.

Sung had told Mr. Yun about neither the divorce nor her affair. He only told him that he wanted to lead a poor life among farmers in the country and therefore wanted to give his property back to him. Jeong-seon's abrupt reaction, however, had left him little opportunity to relate these details, and he was now even doubtful of her ability to distinguish between good and evil. He picked up the phone and called a taxi. He saw no reason to wait any longer.

Jeong-seon spewed forth at Sung every last profanity-littered, curse-laden expression that she could dredge up, almost as though she had lost her mind. She first insisted that he stay, then told him to get out. She dumped his bags outside the gate, then screamed that he take nothing because everything belonged to her. Sung left the house deprived of coat and suit jacket, with even his vest torn off, and with no baggage at all, bearing only the mockery of the servants. Just as he was climbing into the taxi, Yu-wol secretly brought his jacket and coat. They had been tossed out by Jeong-seon with the words, "Clothes worn by that mean bastard!" Yu-wol had picked them up and followed him.

"Oh, thank you." Sung accepted the jacket and coat and put them on, then patted Yu-wol on the head.

"Gyeongseong Station," Sung told the driver. The engine revved in response.

Yu-wol knocked on the window and called, "Master, please take me with you. I want to follow you."

Sung refused several times but finally opened the door and asked, "Where do you think I'm going?"

"I want to follow you, Master. Please take me with you, I can do anything." She attempted to crawl into the taxi.

"All right." Sung made room for her. From inside the house was heard Jeong-seon's angry screaming, punctuated by sobs.

As the taxi drove off with a loud roar, heading toward Daehan Gate of Deoksu Palace, Sung straightened his collar and noticed that he was hatless. He glanced at the driver in the front seat in embarrassment over his improper attire.

3-92

Arriving at the station, Sung learned that the train's departure was not for an hour. He took Yu-wol to a restaurant and seated himself in a corner behind a folding screen for privacy.

Not daring to sit with him, Yu-wol stood at attention nearby. He turned to look up at her and said, "Yu-wol, you should go back."

"No," she insisted. "I don't want to. I will follow you." She shook her entire body in refusal and chewed on the ribbon of her outfit. She was wearing a pink skirt with a traditional yellow jacket, a white apron, and a violet ribbon, or *daenggi*. These typical colors of a young Korean girl's clothing drew people's attention. Yu-wol was small for her age of sixteen, but her physique revealed a mature young woman.

"What could you do in the country?" Sung asked her, his tone solemn.

"I want to go anyway. I'll do whatever you tell me to." Her response bespoke firm resolve.

The train for Bongcheon left Gyeongseong Station at 10:40 and pressed through the heavy snowfall. Its third-class car was crowded with standing passengers even though many were packed three to a seat. There were also the usual cases of some lying on seats pretending to sleep or leaning on their bags in adjoining seats. These were more likely Japanese than Korean, and looked more educated.

Sung finally located a seat and let Yu-wol sit down, then hunted through the train for a car less crowded, but found no place to sit. Leaning against the side of a seat in an effort to rest his legs, he was surprised by a youthful female voice from behind him. "Aren't you Mr. Heo, the lawyer?"

He turned around. A young woman stood there wearing a *jobawi* hat of jade and gold and a Korean traditional overcoat, the *durumagi*, lined with black sable.

"Sir, don't you remember me? I'm San-wol, Baek San-wol."
The woman gladly moved closer, almost as if to cling to him.

Hearing the name, he recognized her. "Ah!" Sung nodded,
smiling to greet her.

"Where are you going?" she asked, but thought better and
withdrew her query. "Oh, I'm sorry to ask such a question."

But Sung replied honestly, "I'm going to the country," and
asked in turn, "Where are *you* going?"

"Oh, just a moment . . ." She paused in consternation at
noticing a number of people staring at her. But recovering and
calming down, she said, "Don't you have a seat? I have some
questions, so let's go find a place to sit." She took a step first and
turned to look back. Seeing him follow, she continued toward the
door. The next car held a restaurant. Grasping the doorknob, she
looked at Sung with coquettish eyes. Putting one hand on his
chest, she said, "If it's too embarrassing to go in with me, we don't
have to. Will you lose face?"

"Not at all," Sung demurred.

"I appreciate it." San-wol let him take the doorknob, and she
made as to follow him.

Wondering why she was there and what she wanted to talk
about, he opened the door, went in, and took a seat.

3-93

San-wol took off her overcoat and draped it over a nearby chair.
Dressed in a light pink skirt of fine silk and a traditional jacket of
white, with navy-blue hem along the sleeve and set off by a dark purple
ribbon tied at the breast, she looked like a newlywed. Moreover, her
face, lightly flushed with alcohol, looked very beautiful.

Sung spoke first. "Where are you going?"

"I'm following you." San-wol spoke in normal tone, no longer the *gisaeng* coquette. To the waiter standing beside the table awaiting the order, San-wol said, "Whisky and soda," her English perfectly accented. She then turned to Sung, "What would you like to have?"

"It does not matter," he replied, speaking in polite tones, as to a married woman.

"Ham salad?" she suggested. Turning to the waiter, she ordered, "All right! Ham salad!" She was about to turn back to Sung, but her eyes suddenly widened. She leaned close to Sung, whispering, "Dr. Lee is here, with two women!" She spoke in English and stuck her tongue out slightly, mocking Lee.

Without turning to look, Sung simply nodded.

"Should I go tease him a bit?" She had again adopted the tone of a *gisaeng*.

"Do you know Dr. Lee?" Sung asked, curious.

"Every woman in Seoul knows him. All the pretty ones must have each received at least two letters from him," she replied, her face and neck shaking lightly with restrained laughter.

"Where did you meet him?" Sung asked.

"At a gathering. He wanted me to write down my work address. I did, and he's been sending me letters ever since, telling me that he feels for me, has respect for me, loves me, stuff like that. He's even come to see me three or four times. I just had the doormen request his calling card, and he would leave. What point was there in him showing up at all?" She raised her head and looked in the direction of Dr. Lee.

"He's about to leave now, is he afraid of me? Wait here a moment, I'll go tease him." San-wol stood up and walked toward Dr. Lee with the gait of a *gisaeng*.

Sung turned his head slightly to watch.

"How are you doing, Dr. Lee?" San-wol, holding out her hand, addressed Dr. Lee in English as he was just about to get up.

Reddening, he took her hand with reluctance.

In perfect English, she said, "I'm very sorry," then continued in Korean. "I apologize for not answering your letters. I also apologize that the doormen didn't admit you on any of your three visits. Forgive me." Looking him directly in the face and smiling in delight at his loss for words, she asked, "Are these your sisters?" with emphasis on the word sisters. She turned to the two women. "Forgive me. I'm Han San-wol, a *gisaeng*. Dr. Lee has been a good teacher for me." She held her hand out for them to shake.

The two women reluctantly stretched their hands forth.

3-94

After standing nearby rubbing his hands nervously, Dr. Lee finally braced himself, gathering all the fragments of his scattered courage, and hazarded an excuse. "I haven't visited your place, maybe your servants are mistaken."

She laughed. Her voice rang with a clear, high tone accomplished through years of singing lessons. "Oh, did I say something wrong? I apologize." She then switched into English, "I thought these ladies were your sisters, or friends. I heard some time ago that you're engaged to Shim Sun-rye." She laughed again.

"No, I had contact with Shim Sun-rye for a while, but it's just rumor that we were engaged. Also, I didn't go to your place, your servants were mistaken." Lee's voice was solemn, as though sincere.

"That may well be. When I glanced out the window, I saw a man who looked like you and had the same voice. He didn't leave a business card when the servants asked for one. Maybe he was just someone who looked exactly like you. Pardon me if I'm mistaken." San-wol laughed in delight, nodding her head.

In the meantime, the two women had moved away. Dr. Lee bowed his head slightly to San-wol in the Western way and also left.

Watching him disappear, San-wol laughed once more and returned to the table with Sung.

"How was that? Aren't I an *excellent* actress?" She downed her whisky and laughed loudly, resting her forehead on one hand as though amused beyond restraint.

Sung laughed with her. As he did, San-wol laughed even more, her shoulders shaking violently.

After her fill of laughter, she took a cup and offered it, "Here, take this. Just three drinks, no more. You'll need some whisky to hear what I've got to say. I don't want you to be quite so serious. Here, take it please."

At her offer, he accepted the cup but set it aside. "I don't want to drink any alcohol. I'm the one who advises the farmers in Salyeoul not to drink. Even without drinking, I can hear what you have to say." He smiled to make his refusal polite.

"Just one cup. Otherwise, I'll feel so embarrassed." San-wol tried to take the cup back, intending to fill it, but Sung grasped her arm and refused. "No! Please don't try to force me. I'll feel uncomfortable turning you down several times. If you want to do me a favor, don't make me feel uncomfortable." He moved the cup beyond her reach.

San-wol felt momentarily embarrassed, but quickly recovered. "Do you know why I got on this train?" she asked. Her voice sounded earnest, but Sung didn't know what to say and ignored the question. "Oh, it's already Susaek," she said, looking out the window. The train stopped, and the signalman could be heard announcing the station in Japanese: "Suisioku."

3-95

"It doesn't matter if it's Susaek. I'll follow you wherever you go," San-wol said. "This evening, a regular guest of mine called me in. You'd recognize his name if I told you, but that's unnecessary.

Anyway, he's called me the last five or six days in a row, and he must have spent quite a lot money doing so. He's expressed a desire to come to my place, but I've made excuses to forestall that. I may live as a *gisaeng*, but no one other than you has come to my place and stayed overnight. *Believe me.* I don't know what'll happen tomorrow, but it's true so far.

Anyway, this fellow insisted today on taking me somewhere. Baecheon Hot Springs, or Pyeongyang, or Oryongbae Hot Springs. I once wanted to go to China and see Harbin. He suggested going there. Another time, I wanted to see the Great Wall. He suggested a trip through Sanhuaiguan and Yeolha on the way, he was so eager. He's about fifty, but age doesn't really matter much. I finally persuaded him to postpone the trip till next time, and I came to the station to see him off. He then gave me this." She showed a glittering diamond on her ring finger and said, "This is supposed to be an *engagement ring*." She laughed in amusement. "He told me he'd go first to find a good place and send me a telegram. I'm supposed to put on a tailored, Western-style dress then and go to him. He gave me an envelope for the suit. Oh, I haven't seen what's in it yet."

She took a Western envelope from her handbag. It was from a certain hotel, and on the outside was written her name, "Baek San-wol," in both Korean and Chinese. The handwriting was quite good. San-wol opened it, and a check fell out. "One thousand won," it said, and bore the signature of a name beginning with Kim, along with an official, square stamp. She quickly hid the name with her hand.

At the sight of that, she stuck out her tongue and returned the check to its envelope as if of no importance, leaving it on the table like a used tissue. Again smiling, she said, "As I was standing on the platform, I noticed a young girl following someone who turned out to be you. But I couldn't follow you and leave my client alone, so I just watched, following you with my eyes and wondering if you had come to send somebody off or to go somewhere yourself. But you got on the train. From where I was standing at first class to where you got on was quite some distance, so I almost lost you. I made an effort to keep my eye on a man without a hat and a young girl wearing a pink skirt. My client noticed my distraction and asked why I was looking only in that direction. I said that I was just enjoying watching people. He was quite disappointed.

As soon as I saw you board the train, I resolved to follow you. Of course, I first had to please my client by seeing him off, but after the train started to roll, I did what the Japanese call *dobinori* to get on the accelerating train. The signalman made a big fuss about that, but I'm not bad at *dobinori*. I played tennis and basketball in school and am quite fast. Anyway, that's how I followed you, Mr. Heo . . . or should I say 'Sir.'" At those words, she sighed, looking forlorn and sad.

3-96

Sung was startled, scarcely able to believe that she'd boarded the train to follow him. "What about the ticket?" Sung asked, still doubtful.

"I didn't buy one, I had no time," San-wol smiled to realize her predicament. "I'll probably have to pay for a ticket from Busan. That's no big deal." She picked up Sung's cup and downed what he had simply left untouched.

"Where are you planning to go?" Sung was somewhat worried.

"If I'm trouble for you, I'll get off at the next stop, but if you're fond of me, I'll follow you anywhere. Am I trouble? Do you feel embarrassed being with a *gisaeng*? But what can I do? Should I kill this love that blazes up in my heart like a flame? If I have to choose between killing this love and killing my body, I'll kill my body." She was about to say more when three men who looked Korean but wore Western suits entered the dining car and looked at San-wol. "Let's get out of here," she said, rising first.

Sung also stood up and called the waiter for the bill. He kept his back to the three as he paid, then went out with San-wol toward the first and second cars. Neither of them wanted to face the men. As they passed from the dining car, cold wind blew against their warm faces. The next car would be second class, followed by the first class, so they waited in the cold space between for the next stop.

Leaning against the wall, Sung looked blankly out the window. Snow was falling, and the world outside was white.

Staggering suddenly and trying to balance herself, San-wol placed her hands onto Sung's shoulders and leaned closely upon his breast, almost as if without forethought. With a whiff of alcohol on her breath, she begged, "Mister, please hold me and kiss me at least once. I know I'm doing your wife wrong, but I've lost all power to control my passion after several months as a *gisaeng*. I've known you since I was in college. I knew you when I dropped by to see Jeong-seon. Even if you kiss me for my passion, your wife will forgive you. Don't think of me as just some *gisaeng* lusting after you. Is that what you think? Please don't." She stretched her arms around his neck and clung to him.

Sung was still gazing out the window. He felt no desire for his wife or any other woman, but wished only to become a farmer forever in Salyeoul. He didn't think of San-wol as a lust-driven *gisaeng*, as she feared, nor did he dislike her. Quite the contrary, he considered San-wol to have depth beyond what he could find in Jeong-seon. Never having been passionately loved by a woman, and having been mistreated by his own wife, he was moved, even flattered by San-wol's committed, passionate love. But he had no desire to marry again, or love a woman anew.

"I left my wife. I've decided never to fall in love and marry again," Sung explained, tilting his head up toward the ceiling to avoid San-wol's eyes.

3-97

"You left your wife?" San-wol drew back, surprised.

"Yes," Sung nodded.

At that word, she clung to him again. "Just once, just one time. Please put your arms around me and kiss me at least once." She sprang up with surprising athleticism and kissed him.

At that moment, the train's long, sharp whistle was heard, followed by several short ones, and the train shook fiercely in an abrupt attempt to stop. San-wol pressed her head against Sung's chest like a child terrified at the overwhelming noise. The train shuddered to a halt.

Sung managed to shake her off and opened the door to see. The world was buried in snow. To the right, a mountain slope was visible. Pine trees stood with branches weighed down by snow. The crew came running from the locomotive with lights in their hands.

"What happened?" Sung called out, leaning from the train.

"*Raekisides*," they responded in curt Japanese and hurried on.

"*Raekisi*? Run over?" Sung said to himself and jumped off the train. San-wol followed, as did a few other passengers. Snow was falling heavily.

Sung caught up to one of the running crewmen and asked where the body lay. "*Dokodes*?"

"*Seugu sokodes*," replied the crewman, indicating a place just ahead, and added as he rushed on that the body seemed still living, "*Mada sindewa inaiyoudes*."

Sung ran toward the locomotive, oddly alert. Only a couple of meters to the front of the locomotive lay a body stretched across the snowy tracks. Blood had sprayed in lines and spots on the snow.

Sung was about to pass the locomotive and approach the body when a crewman restrained him, warning him against going closer, "*Ittja ikemasen!*"

Startled, Sung stopped. In the headlight of the locomotive, Sung could see the body, a woman clad in a Western coat. The black enamel tops of her shoes glittered in the brilliant light. Sung felt unreasonable agitation and couldn't calm down. He experienced an overwhelming desire to know what had happened, and not just out of professional interest as a lawyer intent on determining the legal ramifications.

"Oh my God!" cried San-wol. She had caught up with him and stood clutching his arm.

The head conductor walked in dignity to the scene, glanced about with the attitude of a policeman in charge, briefly lifted the woman's bleeding head, then opened the coat and put his ear to her chest like a doctor. After listening, he signaled to the other crewmen with a wave of his hand.

The others rushed forward like soldiers at their officer's command, carefully lifted the woman according to the head conductor's directions, and carried her past where Sung was standing.

"Oh my God!" he cried out at the sight of the face dangling limply from the crewmen's arms. "Jeong-seon!"

"Jeong-seon!" screamed San-wol.

3-98

"Do you know this person?" The head conductor had stopped and turned around upon hearing Sung cry out.

"It's my wife!" Sung exclaimed, drawing quickly near.

At this unexpected response, not only the conductor but the others around looked at Sung and San-wol with undisguised curiosity.

Sung negotiated with the head conductor to put Jeong-seon into a bed in a first-class car instead of laying her out in the conductor's compartment since she was still alive. The man agreed on condition that they get off in Gaeseong. After about a ten-minute delay, the train started rolling once more.

Sung obtained a first-aid kit from the conductor, gave Jeong-seon an injection of heart stimulant and wrapped the bleeding part of the head and legs with gauze and bandages, leaving her in San-wol's charge as he went to find a doctor. In the first- and second-class compartments, most passengers were already in bed. Among those still up, there was no doctor.

In the third class, Sung found a man who introduced himself as a doctor, but was carrying no doctor's bag. Sung brought him to Jeong-seon's side anyway. The doctor checked her pulse, listened to her heartbeat, and said, "She's in no danger." He then left.

Around one in the morning, the train arrived in Gaeseong. Sung got off carrying Jeong-seon the way that nurses did with patients immediately after an operation. San-wol and Yu-wol followed. Jeong-seon was borne in his arms to Namseong Hospital. Already alerted by telegram, the hospital staff, working under a Dr. Kim, was waiting for Jeong-seon, ready to operate.

She was first laid on the operating table and given another shot of heart stimulant before undergoing surgery. Her head and legs were the parts most gravely injured. Her head bore an injury from the left ear to the crown, with a cut six centimeters deep, into the meninges, and her right knee was dislocated, its kneecap broken. Additionally, her shoulders and the back had inner bleeding and abrasions.

As Jeong-seon underwent surgery, Sung waited outside with San-wol and Yu-wol, straining to hear the slightest sound, but nothing from Jeong-seon was audible.

After she had been moved to a ward, Dr. Kim responded to Sung's inquiry, "We have to wait and see overnight. She's had a concussion." He expressed this with the typical indifference of a doctor, then gave instructions to a nurse and left the room. Sung followed and requested permission to stay overnight in the hospital. The doctor agreed, and Sung was even allowed to help care for Jeong-seon while staying with her.

The hour was already three in the morning, but Jeong-seon hadn't awakened even once. She seemed as if in a sound sleep, but sometimes had convulsions. The nurse came in every hour, checked Jeong-seon's pulse, and gave an injection.

Seated next to his wife, Sung held her wrist and checked her pulse. He sometimes counted the beats, which at times dropped to seventy, at times rose to a hundred and twenty or thirty. She felt a little warm but seemed to have no fever. The pulse slowly stabilized to between ninety and a hundred around five in the morning.

San-wol and Yu-wol both remained sleepless in the next room, looking in several times an hour.

Sung sometimes cried at the sight of Jeong-seon's head wrapped with bandages, and whenever her pale lips seemed to move slightly, as if to speak, he called softly, "Darling, darling, it's me." If her eyes seemed to blink, he would whisper with a lump in his throat, "Jeong-seon, darling."

But she didn't open her eyes until dawn.

3-99

By nine the next morning, the bright sunlight that follows a hard snow shone through the window of the hospital ward. Jeong-seon's pallid face had regained some of its color as her body temperature recovered somewhat and her circulation stabilized. They put her on IV now instead of injecting heart stimulant. The doctor reassured Sung that 38 degrees Celsius was not a dangerous body temperature. When Sung had first arrived, hatless, accompanied by a *gisaeng*, and bearing a nearly dead woman hit by a train, he was not so welcome. But his well-mannered behavior softened the staff's resistance, and as he went through the procedure to authorize his wife's hospitalization, filling in the forms with their names, their address in Seoul, and his profession as lawyer, the doctor and nurses realized that he was not a tramp and ceased to worry. Nobody dared to ask what had happened, however, or how Jeong-seon had come to be hit by a train.

An older nurse whose surname was Ivey, and who was said to have been living in Korea for twenty years, came into the ward and was surprised to recognize the patient. Mrs. Ivey had previously worked at Severance Hospital and had known Jeong-seon when she was attending university nearby. Even after moving to Gaeseong, she would visit Jeong-seon whenever she happened to be in Seoul. Widowed, her children off in her home country for university, Mrs. Ivey worked in the hospital as the head nurse.

She had first looked in on the patient in the manner of a nurse, but at the sight of Jeong-seon, she was startled and turned to Sung. "Isn't she Yun Jeong-seon? Am I right?"

"Yes, you are right," Sung politely replied. "She is Yun Jeong-seon."

"Are you her husband?" Mrs. Ivey looked him and Jeong-seon in turn.

"Yes, I am Heo Sung."

"The lawyer Heo?"

"Yes."

"What happened to your wife?" she asked, both surprised and concerned.

Sung didn't know what to say and remained silent, but anybody confronted with such a scene would infer a love triangle. The people on the train the previous night would have thought so, and the same was true of the hospital staff. Noticing San-wol's presence, even Mrs. Ivey must have drawn an identical conclusion, for she shook her head a couple of times in dismay.

Knowing that her presence would only continue to make Sung uncomfortable, San-wol soon left the hospital. Her heart was so full of things to say, but she just bade Sung good-bye and left.

Around midday, Jeong-seon regained consciousness. Her eyes focused upon Sung and showed surprise, but with consciousness came pain that made her frown. Her eyes closed again, but she reopened them to see if her husband really was there.

"It's me, it's me." Sung brought his face close to hers.

She opened her mouth, showing that she recognized him, but could utter no sound. She then frowned again, apparently in pain.

"Darling, don't worry, the doctor says you're fine." Sung took her hand, and she trembled at his touch.

3-100

She didn't easily emerge from this dangerous state. Her concussion and the broken bones in her right knee were severe injuries. She was sometimes lucid, but at times relapsed into a coma, and this continued for a while.

Having received a telegram from Sung, Jeong-seon's father came despite his illness, accompanied by Dr. Lee of Severance Hospital, and they stayed one night before departing the next day, entrusting her care to Sung and Yu-wol. Before leaving, Dr. Lee informed Sung that the concussion would require time to stabilize before any attempt to diagnose its severity. As for the broken knee, it would need x-rays to assess its seriousness, and if the bones were damaged so severely as to fester, the leg might have to be cut off above the knee. The patient couldn't be moved in her current state, he added, so they would have to wait another two or three days.

Sung stayed in the hospital every night, caring for Jeong-seon and only dozing off in a chair for ten or twenty minutes while she slept. At nighttime, her pain seemed to increase. Unable to endure the ache in her head and leg, she would groan repeatedly, the only sound to come from her lips. If Sung tried to speak to her, she would briefly open her eyes and mouth, but her only expression was a pained frown.

A week passed in much this way.

Dr. Lee was again to come from Seoul. A decision had been made to cut off Jeong-seon's right leg.

Before his return, on the fifth day of her hospitalization, she finally spoke her first words, crying out to her husband, "I'm dying!"

"No, you're not," Sung comforted. "The doctor says you're fine, so don't worry."

"I'm dying, why didn't I die? I jumped in front of the locomotive to die, why didn't I die? Did even the locomotive push me away because I was dirty?" She began to cry.

"No. God saved you because you have a lot to do in the world. Remember what they say? The one who won't work is truly low, but the worker is worth more than an entire country. Don't think about dying. Have peace in your heart and get better. The doctor says the danger is now over." Sung took a bandage and wiped her tears away.

Thereafter, whenever she regained consciousness, she spoke in tearful despair, but Sung always comforted her with kindness.

At times, she worried more about living than dying. "If I survive, will you forgive me?" she would say.

"I've already forgiven you. It's your turn now to forgive me," was his reply. He felt vaguely uncomfortable saying this, but sympathy for her overwhelmed his reluctance.

"How could I go on living after being crippled like this and ridiculed by others? Are there any newspaper reports about me?" she would ask. In her uncertain state between life and death, she still worried about being handicapped, being laughed at, and being reported on.

Mystified by the feminine mind but empathizing with her, Sung said, "Being crippled doesn't matter, though naturally, you won't be. Why care about newspaper reports or ridicule? Isn't it enough that I love you and you love me, that we work together loving each other? Work will prove victorious over everything," he said, comforting her.

3-101

Despite his words, Sung had been displeased by a particular newspaper article. This article, published in a Seoul newspaper, was undoubtedly based on statements made by Dr. Lee Geon-yeong. Sung felt sure of this because the reporter knew well the area where they lived, possessed photos of him and his wife, and gave a "full account of the incident" with details that only Dr. Lee would know.

According to the article, behind Sung's public image as a patriot and man of virtue was hidden a secret obsession with sex. While living in Mr. Yun's home, he had seduced Jeong-seon, and even after their wedding, he had continued his affairs with other women despite the damage to his marriage, such as an affair with a certain female doctor in Dabanggol. He also went to Salyeoul, pretending to work for the farmers there, but his real reason for going less than a year into his marriage was his secret relationship with a young woman, "Yu Sun." After the death of this young woman's father, he openly took her into his Salyeoul home, making her in principle a *cheop*, a second wife, but without letting her tie her hair up in the manner of a woman who is no longer single. When he briefly visited Seoul to pursue a lawsuit on behalf of some farmers, he neglected his wife and went to see a young *gisaeng* instead. Jeong-seon sought revenge through an affair with a certain Kim, son of a baron in Jae-dong and graduate of the Law College of Imperial University, a man also famous for his sexual affairs. In such a manner had the marriage of patriot Heo Sung been marred on both sides through immoral love affairs. On the very day when Jeong-seon threw herself in front of the train, Sung was underway on that same train in the first class section with the *gisaeng* San-wol. Jeong-seon had known of this, and in jealousy and despair had determined to die by throwing herself onto the tracks before the train bearing her husband and his lover as they enjoyed their immoral pleasures. She had taken a taxi and followed them to Susaek, where she attempted the planned suicide, but the thick snow had softened the blow and saved her life even though she had been struck hard and knocked some distance by the impact. According to witnesses, when Sung attempted to carry Jeong-seon to the hospital, the *gisaeng* San-wol was enraged and had made a big scene at the Gaeseong station.

The editor of the newspaper, expressing his concern and public indignation, added such headings as "Sex Maniac Disguised as a Patriot" and "Quartet of an Immoral Love Affair." Sung had not shown the article to Jeong-seon, but had affirmed the existence of a report when she asked. The hospital staff, however, had seen the paper, and their respect for Sung and his wife had instantly vanished, leaving only sneers on their faces and contempt in their eyes. Sung ignored them and consoled himself by reflecting that the tragedy might turn out well for their marriage if Jeong-seon became more committed as a result. Even if she were to retain a scar on her head and lose a leg, he would be happy with her.

But he felt sorrow over Yu Sun. He hated that the reporter had used her real name, although presenting it in quotes as if it were an alias. What a great blow this would be for her life. He regretted having taken her into his home, for the people in Salyeoul would probably believe the newspaper report. He had planned to urge a marriage between Yu Sun and Maeng Han-gap if the latter were found innocent and released from jail, but he knew now that his lawsuit would fail, and he was worried about Yu Sun. He hoped that if Jeong-seon recovered and accompanied him to Salyeoul, everything could be resolved.

Sung expressed none of this to Jeong-seon, but he did tell her, "Don't worry. It doesn't matter what they say now if we love each other for life and have a happy family. Use the garbage others throw as compost for happiness." But his words of comfort didn't seem to calm her anxieties.

3-102

Sung knew that Jeong-seon would feel crippled to know just of the scar on her head, would even wish to die, so how could he tell her of the impending operation? How might she react upon learning that her leg would soon be cut off? How shocked or sad? He thought the better course not to tell her beforehand.

The doctor would normally have discussed the operation, but he lacked respect for her, believing that she and Sung were even beneath his contempt, so he didn't bother to raise the subject with either of them.

The scheduled operation approached. Mr. Yun was informed by Sung but didn't reply. He had seen the newspaper article and vented his rage at his servants, wanting to know nothing more of his daughter or son-in-law. Cared for by only one person, one alone in the whole world, she was wheeled to the operating room on a roller stretcher.

She lay quietly on the operating table, expecting merely a small incision to her injured knee, but grew anxious at lying on such a place for the first time. As the nurse wrapped white cloth around her head to cover he eyes, the white ceiling above and the several people standing around disappeared from view, Jeong-seon felt a chill creep down her spine, as though a shadow of death had fallen across her body.

As the nurses worked to undress her, she instinctively attempted to bend her legs, but couldn't. Naked, she felt humiliated to think of the doctors who had scrubbed their hands earlier and were now standing nearby in their white gowns and waterproof aprons. But as her ankles were being tied, her sense of humiliation decreased, replaced by dull despair as she slipped into near oblivion under anesthesia from a pantopon injection.

A chill, moist sensation, as unpleasant as the brush of a cold-blooded animal against her skin, spread across her naked body. "God!" Jeong-seon silently cried. Feeling as if she were floating through boundless space, cold and dark, she felt that she could only call out helplessly to God.

Clattering could be heard. Were they arranging scalpels on the glass plates? The sharp edges of those nickel-coated knives! Jeong-seon felt the hairs on her neck rise in fear. "What are these people about to do to me?" She began to have doubts, but recognized her powerlessness to resist whatever they might intend.

Someone approached and placed something like a cup on her nose. A chill, whether of fluid or air, flowed through her mouth, nose, throat, and even, it seemed, into her heart. She detected a certain odor. "Chloroform? Ether?" She tried to dredge up names for anesthetics. She was very fearful of the anesthesia and disliked it intensely, but she could not resist. Surrendering, she breathed in deeply. If she died this way, then fine, she decided.

"One, two, three, four . . . count like that," said a voice. Coming from Dr. Kim, it expressed no sympathy, but she had little time to reflect on that.

She counted as told: "One, two, three, four . . ."

She felt anguish and sadness. She wished to hear her husband's voice, to touch his hand, but the hand holding hers was not her husband's. It was of a doctor checking her pulse.

3-103

"One, two, three, four ..." Jeong-seon's counting pierced Sung's heart. Her voice, trembling and tearful, nearly moved him to storm the operating room and bear her away.

"Boundless love! Ah! Why couldn't I have expressed it?" With an intense agony of regret, Sung blamed himself for the impending amputation. Jeong-seon hated to be crippled, and she was now to have a leg cut off! What despair she would suffer upon awakening, what shame she would endure in public as an amputee. Such painful thoughts pierced him to the marrow. "I should love her with all my heart. From now on, I should love her without bound," he vowed.

"One, two, three, four ..." and her voice was no longer audible, only an obscure rustling sound.

Slightly above the knee joint, the nickel-edged knife held by Dr. Lee made a single incision. Bright red blood welled from the wound, only to be quickly sopped up with gauze in the hands of a nurse, preventing its further flow onto Jeong-seon's white skin.

The cut flesh was then held open right and left by nickel-coated forceps, the blood vessels were ligatured, the periosteum was scraped and opened, and the bone was finally cut into by a saw. Loud rasping filled the room as the saw worked to and fro. Jeong-seon's leg trembled, as though with stifled convulsions, and her lips moved with unarticulated words, whether in pain or complaint unclear.

She occasionally managed a scream, but didn't seem to feel conscious pain.

One doctor constantly checked her pulse, his lips moving to the count. Nurses were kept busy wiping sweat from the surgeon's forehead and continuously providing gauze. But all carried on their tasks silently.

The doctors at times seemed to have only eyes and hands, and the nurses only ears and eyes. The latter moved swiftly, like well-oiled machines, alert to the doctors' signals and curt commands. "No mistakes, work quickly," seemed their common motto.

Crack. With an eerie sound, Jeong-seon's leg was suddenly broken in two. The part cut off lay soft and still warm. A nurse lifted it like a piece of wood and set it on a large metal plate. The toes of the amputated limb quivered as if struggling to live. But they would never again revive.

Dr. Lee wrapped the bones of Jeong-seon's stump with the flesh and skin that had been held open using forceps, stitching the mass together using a crescent-shaped needle threaded with white silk. He then coated the stump with medicine, applied gauze and cotton, and wrapped it in a bandage. The operation was over.

"Look at this!" Dr. Lee showed the now dead, amputated leg. He turned it over twice with his hand, then stabbed it with the scalpel. Pus mixed with blood gushed out. The other doctors took turns touching the leg and turning it around, as though playing with a toy.

Jeong-seon was washed clean and dressed in clothes. The cup on her nose was removed. Nurses wiped sweat from her forehead, moved her again onto the roller stretcher, and covered her with a sheet and blanket.

3-104

As the door creaked opened, and Jeong-seon was rolled into view on the stretcher, her dark-haired head still wrapped in the bandage, Sung initially stepped aside, his heart pounding with an inexplicable mix of emotions. But he then joined in and helped pull the stretcher. He tried to calm down despite feeling overwhelmed.

In the ward, when the nurses transferred her from the stretcher to her bed, Sung was aghast to see a leg missing and reacted as if this were unexpected. "Jeong-seon's lost a leg!" was his shocked thought.

Very soon after her return to the ward, she opened her eyes. "Is the operation over?" she asked her husband, who was seated at the bedside.

"Yes," he said, nodding.

"Did they do the surgery?" she asked again, curious.

"Yes." Sung was reluctant to speak at length.

Jeong-seon smiled. "It doesn't hurt."

"That's what the operation was for," he told her, and also smiled.

"You haven't slept for several days, have you? Let Yu-wol take care of me while you get some sleep," she advised, concerned at his haggard face.

"Don't worry about me," he said, offering her a sip of lemonade from a bottle nearby. She accepted with pleasure.

Jeong-seon spent the day ignorant of her amputation. The next day was the same. She even felt an itch on the knee and foot of her missing leg and asked Sung to scratch them, never noticing that her leg had been cut off.

"Won't my leg still be crippled?" she would ask, worried.

Whenever she asked him to scratch, he would pretend to do so, making as if to touch her leg. She would then rest quietly, satisfied that her itch was being scratched.

Having neither high fever nor pain after the operation, she was able to spend most of the daylight hours awake and talking to her husband. She was always in a good mood.

On the morning of the third day, however, the doctor had to change the bandage on the wound. Sung couldn't stay in the room, and she finally discovered that her leg had been cut off.

When the doctor had finished and Sung went back in, wondering if she had found out, she was crying, her face hidden in her hands. He understood but remained awkwardly aside at first, uncertain what to say.

"Ah, don't cry," he finally told her, "You're alive and safe now, don't cry." He took her arms and tried to draw her hands from her face. But she resisted, like a stubborn child, and held her hands there with more force. The more he attempted comfort, the more she shook her head in tears.

"Darling," Sung whispered, embracing her with one arm in another attempt at comfort, "I agreed to the amputation. Don't worry. You have lost a leg, but you are here, and I will love you more than before, so don't worry."

3-105

"Why didn't you ask me before letting them cut my leg off?" Jeong-seon took her hands from her face and showed her anger.

"If your leg hadn't been amputated," explained Sung, "gangrene would have set in, and more would've had to be removed. The doctors said that even your life could have been in danger. I didn't want to see you suffer and maybe die. There was no other real choice."

Jeong-seon grew more agitated. "No! I don't like this. I'd rather die than live as a cripple."

"If you get too upset and move a lot, you might start bleeding. That would be very dangerous," Sung cautioned, appealing to her and holding her hands.

But she didn't easily overcome her resentment over losing a leg, and she sometimes berated Sung. Whenever this happened, he either remained silent or tried to comfort her.

With the passing of a week or two, she came to be touched by his devotion, noticing that he even neglected to eat and sleep from caring for her. She came to truly appreciate her husband, a man who actually had every right to hate her, but instead took heartfelt care of her when her own family would do nothing and the whole world had abandoned her, ignoring whether she lived or died.

"Forgive me," she would sometimes say upon awakening and holding her husband's hands close.

In one of those moments, he told her, "In a few days, you'll be discharged, and we can stop in Seoul to have a prosthetic leg made before going on to Salyeoul."

"No, I don't want to go to Seoul. How can I go looking like this?" She smiled, but her face clouded as the smile faded away.

"What about the prosthetic leg?"

"Can't we have somebody come here to make it?"

"That would cost a lot, and we now have nothing but the work of our hands to live by. From now on, we have to earn money to live."

This statement frightened her. It was true. They had no money. Sung had returned the property, worth nearly one hundred thousand won, to her father, who would pointedly refuse to see her in her current state. Earning money to eat, working for food and clothing, had never before occurred to Jeong-seon. Manual labor was something for the lower classes. Lacking property now, she felt helpless as an infant with no place to suckle. Without even a notion how to face the future, she didn't know what to say. After a long pause, she finally asked, "How can we possibly earn money?"

"Why can't we?" Sung responded, but with confidence.

"Well, if you work as a lawyer, you can, but in Salyeoul, what can you do?" Jeong-seon gazed at the ceiling, utterly at a loss.

Her husband smiled. "I've bought some land, and between the two of us, we can make enough to feed ourselves. I can farm, you can mend clothes."

Having always had a seamstress at home, she had never once worked to mend her own clothes. In Jeong-dong, she kept both seamstress and cook, but she now lacked courage to show up in Seoul as an amputee with a reputation blackened through newspaper reports. She felt ashamed about going to Salyeoul as well, but who other than her husband would now take care of her? Into whose hands could she entrust her crippled body except his? At these thoughts, tears welled up in her eyes.

"When I recover, I'll go to Salyeoul. I'll mend clothes and cook for you," she cried, her face creased with emotion.

3-106

One day during Jeong-seon's convalescence, Sung received a call from Seoul. He wondered if it were from his father-in-law, who had not yet sent a telegram, not even in the name of him and his young son. But when he heard a woman's voice from the other end of the line, he immediately recognized San-wol, even before she introduced herself. Her voice was low, like an alto's, and gentle.

"It's Seon-hi," she said. "You might know me better by the name 'Baek San-wol.'" Her voice no longer sounded like a *gisaeng*'s.

"Yes." Sung didn't know what more to say.

"How's your wife doing? Is she up?"

"She's still in bed."

"Is she all right?"

"She's now out of danger."

"What about the leg?"

"It had to be cut off."

"What?" Seon-hi seemed very surprised.

"Yes, it's amputated. But she's alive, I'm thankful about that." Sung offered a diffident laugh.

"Oh! Yes, you're right. She's fortunate to have survived!" Seon-hi fell silent for a moment, then asked, "Well, is it okay for me to come see her?"

"See her? Well . . ." Sung hedged. He wasn't sure how a visit from Seon-hi would affect his wife.

"I know you're not comfortable with my visit, but I'll come by the day train. I have something to discuss with you, but nothing that might cause you any problems. You can tell Jeong-seon I'm coming. See you later." Seon-hi hung up without waiting for Sung's response.

Sung returned to Jeong-seon's room. "Was it from my father?" she asked, impatient for details.

"No, it was from Miss Baek Seon-hi. She's coming by the day train," Sung replied, trying to sound casual. But he felt uneasy.

That same day, the technician for Jeong-seon's prosthetic leg came from Seoul. He had come a couple of days earlier to make a plaster mold of her intact leg as a model, and he now brought the finished product, a hard rubber prosthesis. Worn with silk stockings and shoes, it looked no different than her natural leg.

Jeong-seon sat up on the bed, supported by Sung under her armpits, but she didn't want to put on the prosthesis in the technician's presence. Sung asked him to step out and leave them to attach it themselves.

The stump was not yet completely healed, so it ached when the prosthesis was attached. Jeong-seon clung to Sung's chest and cried, not so much from the pain as from the fact that she had to put on a rubber leg.

"I don't want it, throw it away!" she cried, drawing the bed cover to hide her face in her aversion.

Sung rewrapped the leg and placed it out of view.

"I don't want to wear a rubber leg," she insisted.

"You can leave it for whenever you want," he said, attempting to comfort her.

Despite her words, Jeong-seon tried it on once a day. She even tested walking several steps, but would cry hysterically each time.

The prosthetic leg occupied her mind day and night. From awaking in the morning to closing her eyes for sleep in the evening, it appeared in her mind. Each time it came to mind, she felt depressed.

3-107

About the time that Seon-hi was to show up, Sung decided that he should talk to Jeong-seon about his connection to her. But he had to think hard on how to broach the delicate issue.

"Seon-hi stayed here overnight when I brought you to the hospital," he began.

"She did? Here?" Jeong-seon showed surprise.

"Yes. After I got on the train at the Gyeongseong Station, I looked around for a seat and ran into her. That's how she ended up following me here and staying overnight."

Jeong-seon looked at him in wonder. But recalling that Seon-hi had known him since college from visits to her house and assuming that her husband would have nothing improper to do with a *gisaeng*, she remained relaxed.

"I spent a night at Seon-hi's place. Mr. Gang, a lawyer you've heard of, once took me to a drinking place. I got completely drunk there, and when I woke up the next morning, I was in a stranger's room. Seon-hi sleeping beside me. She had been called in by Mr. Gang for entertainment. That's how I happened to spend a night at her place," Sung spoke somewhat awkwardly, but he felt better for having confessed.

Listening to him, Jeong-seon felt great emotional turmoil. Her respect for Sung fell away, replaced by a powerful surge of jealousy, but she was in no position to criticize. She lay on her hospital bed, eyes closed, fury mounting, unable to breathe. Grinding her teeth and turning pale, she felt as if her blood had frozen.

"Go away!" she finally yelled.

Sung didn't reply and went out to the next room. Finding Yu-wol there, he motioned her to Jeong-seon.

"You bitch!" yelled Jeong-seon. "What do you want here? Get out!" Her voice carried over to where Sung waited. Driven out by Jeong-seon, Yu-wol returned to Sung.

Jeong-seon cried out, "I'm the one without a leg. Seon-hi has everything!" She thought of Seon-hi as a terrible enemy and would have knifed her on the spot if given a chance. After that outburst, the door opened as a nurse entered, and Seon-hi slipped in behind her. Jeong-seon quelled her tears and pretended to be sleeping.

Seeing her apparently asleep and taking care not to awaken her, Seon-hi tiptoed to the bedside and stood there. Two or three minutes passed with Seon-hi standing nearby sighing and looking into the gaunt face of her friend.

Seon-hi no longer looked like San-wol. With her hair styled again like a student's, wearing a simple serge skirt and a Chinese silk jacket, she held the coat that she had once worn in her student days. She was wearing dark glasses with a glittering, turtle-shell frame, seemingly to hide her identity. No one in the hospital recognized her as San-wol. She seemed to be waiting for Jeong-seon to wake up.

Sung sat in the next room like a criminal awaiting judgment. He had expected an unpleasant scene as soon as Seon-hi arrived, but felt that it had to be gotten through. Regardless whether there would be rain or hail, it had to be gotten through. His sole hope was that Jeong-seon's fragile health would not be harmed.

3-108

Pretending to sleep, Jeong-seon reflected on how to deal with Seon-hi. Initially, she had been very upset, but as Seon-hi stood there waiting, her anger dissipated, replaced by sympathy. Seon-hi had been standing there for some thirty minutes, waiting for her to awaken without once leaving the bedside to look for Sung. Jeong-seon began to sense Seon-hi's sincerity and regard her more favorably, remembering their student years as good friends. Steeping herself in this mood, Jeong-seon slowly opened her eyes, stretching herself as if waking up.

"Jeong-seon," whispered Seon-hi, at the sight of her awakening. She threw herself into Jeong-seon's arms, rubbed her cheek against hers, and kissed her. That was an old habit from the time when they had played at being in love. Looking into Jeong-seon's eyes so closely that their noses almost touched, Seon-hi cried out, "You're alive!" She again rubbed her cheek against Jeong-seon's and kissed her as a mother might kiss a daughter.

"Yes, I'm alive. I couldn't die like I wanted to," Jeong-seon said, moved by Seon-hi's warm embrace.

"You shouldn't say that," protested Seon-hi, drawing back and sitting down on a chair. "Why die? You should live. I happened to be on the same train, and just after passing Susaek Station, it suddenly stopped. Mr. Heo must have had a hunch. He got off the train as if he had suspected what had happened. Snow was falling heavily. Some crewmen running past cried out, '*Raekisi*,' that someone had been run over. They said it was a young woman. When I heard that, I felt strange, too. I'd have felt differently about a man. A woman feels closer to a woman, it seems . . ."

"A woman also feels more hatred toward another woman," Jeong-seon smiled.

"Yes. So when I ran following . . ." Seon-hi paused. "Or did you hear the whole story from Mr. Heo?" she asked.

"Why on earth would he tell me? How could I ask him about that?" Jeong-seon replied, showing genuine interest in Seon-hi's report.

"Yes, I see," Seon-hi agreed, and continued her story, prompted by Jeong-seon's interest. "So when I ran following Mr. Heo close to the spot—though not so close, they didn't let us get very close—I could see in the beam of the locomotive's headlight the body of a young woman lying across the tracks, covered with snow and blood. I recall how her enamel shoes glittered, and how I felt suddenly sad, imagining I might also die that way some day. But I never imagined the woman was you. The body—I thought it was a dead body—was being carried away in front of us when Mr. Heo cried out in shock, "Oh my God! Jeong-seon!" He reached out for the dead body. It was *you*. I saw you, too. Half your face was covered with blood, and your skirt was all . . . oh, I can't tell any more. How could I?" Tears flowed from her eyes.

Jeong-seon also cried to see her weeping. The tears washed away all bitter thoughts and feelings from their hearts.

3-109

"Then . . ." Seon-hi forced an embarrassed laugh through her tears. She wrapped a handkerchief around two fingers and wiped her eyes without removing her glasses. "Then I saw you were alive, and Mr. Heo negotiated with the conductor to carry you to a first-class bed. Your husband also went looking for a doctor in the other cars and soon returned with one, or at least somebody who claimed to be one. We weren't sure. Anyway, that's how you came to be here and how I ended up staying overnight. That's what really happened, but oh, the things people said about us!" Seon-hi was about to switch to that topic when Sung opened the door and came in.

"Oh, you're in here," noted Sung, finally having the chance to greet her.

"It must be very exhausting for you to take care of your wife," Seon-hi remarked. "But it's wonderful she's recovered so much." She looked at Sung and Jeong-seon in turn.

"Who's recovering?" Jeong-seon retorted. "I've lost a leg! How can I recover?"

Sung felt alarm at these words, but was relieved to see that Jeong-seon was not truly upset. He also looked at Seon-hi, curiously, for she was no longer dressed like a *gisaeng* but was wearing the clothes of a student. He noted scarcely any trace of a *gisaeng* in her bearing, and even found himself wondering if she had ever been San-wol. But she was also no longer the Seon-hi who used to visit Jeong-seon.

"Why are you staring at me?" she asked. "Are you trying to find traces of the *gisaeng*?" She shyly hid her face behind both hands. There was no trace of a *gisaeng* in that.

"Jeong-seon," she said, dropping her hands from her face, "you've never seen me as a *gisaeng*, have you? There's a kind of beauty in the *gisaeng* style. It might be one of the beauties Korea offers. The bearing, the manner of walking, everything has to be relearned to become a *gisaeng*. Oh, why am I talking about such needless things!" Seon-hi turned to straighten Jeong-seon's covers and pillow, then offered Sung a chair, the only one in the room.

"No, you sit there. I can sit here." He sat down on the edge of the bed.

"Well, why did you become a *gisaeng*?" Jeong-seon asked, suppressing the unpleasant thought that her husband had stayed overnight at San-wol's place.

"What's the use of telling that old story?" Seon-hi sat down on the chair and addressed Sung, "I've stopped working as a *gisaeng*. I closed my business immediately when I got back to Seoul from here. I'm no longer a *gisaeng*." She turned to Jeong-seon and said, "I'm out of that profession. From now on, I'd like to work as a kindergarten teacher in the countryside. I could also teach there at a night school." She turned to Sung. "I'm serious. Please find a job for me. Is there a kindergarten in Salyeoul? Jeong-seon, are you going to Salyeoul?"

"I don't know," Jeong-seon replied, going against the truth of her heart.

"Jeong-seon, I want to go where you go. It's okay for me to follow you, isn't it?" Seon-hi looked nervous with excitement.

Jeong-seon observed her, with cold, sharp eyes, as if to pierce her heart for the truth. She even felt some agitation, wondering if Seon-hi wanted to steal Sung away out of love for him. Why else would she suddenly stop working as a *gisaeng* and want to follow her?

3-110

"Why follow me?" asked Jeong-seon, her tone ironic. But she smiled, and stopped herself from saying, "Don't you actually want to follow my husband?"

Seon-hi glanced at Jeong-seon. Relieved by her joyful smile, she reminded Jeong-seon. "I'd been famous for my disobedience since childhood. I wouldn't listen to my father and mother when they were still living. Even if I suffered punishment or had to skip meals, I wouldn't obey. I don't know why I was so stubborn. In school, I was the same. When the adults told me what was right to do, I didn't trust them. They tried to pressure me with their authority as adults and teachers, but I could tell when they were wrong. I didn't want to obey them if they were wrong. Jeong-seon, you saw me being punished several times by teachers, didn't you?" she asked, checking for agreement.

"Of course I saw it! And I remember what that teacher called Dolbae said to you, 'This girl wouldn't be hurt even by a straw cutter, wouldn't burn even in a fire!' Remember that?" Jeong-seon laughed aloud with joy.

Sung was happy about Jeong-seon's good mood, and Seon-hi felt the same. Jeong-seon had relaxed to see in Seon-hi's attitude and words the truth that she was not just following a man, but had recovered a source of self-esteem beyond just being a woman for men.

"I grew up that way, not readily obedient. I was the same with my paternal uncle, the one I stayed with after my parents died. Besides, I knew he was against me, so why trust him? I defied him and wouldn't even listen to him. My uncle hated me, but his wife was even worse. I was close to my maternal grandmother and aunts, but my uncle didn't want me to visit them. One reason was that they had left Seoul. My uncle wasn't interested in taking care of me. He didn't care about his niece, he just wanted to have the property left by my father. When I graduated from high school—I was eighteen then—he made a big fuss about marrying me off to some scoundrel. I insisted on going to college. 'Why college? What for? I won't pay for that,' he said. He was as stubborn as me. We had a big fight, but my aunt and uncle wouldn't give in. How could an eighteen-year-old girl defeat an uncle? I finally told him he could have all the property if he supported me for college, and he agreed to that condition. The property? It wasn't much, my parents owned some rice paddies in Yangju, Goyang, and Siheung. All together, it'd bring about sixteen or seventeen thousand won a year, about eighteen bushels. I regretted my decision later, but I'd already agreed and couldn't change it. Anyway, I signed the documents, like they wanted, and let them have everything. What could I do afterwards? When I graduated from college, I was penniless. I couldn't ask my uncle to feed me any longer, so I left his house the day after graduation. But why am I telling you all this? I started off telling how I was a disobedient girl and ended up complaining about my life. I'm so ashamed," Seon-hi hid her eyes behind her hands.

3-111

"I see. That's how your uncle took your property," said Jeong-seon, showing sympathy, "I didn't know all this. You never told me."

"Why should I have? You're the daughter of a wealthy family. If you'd known I'd become penniless, you might've looked down on me."

"No! How could I?" Jeong-seon protested.

"Sure you would've. You wouldn't have liked me to come see you as a *gisaeng*, would you?" Seon-hi indicated Jeong-seon with a twist of the chin.

Jeong-seon's face suddenly clouded.

"We don't have to argue about this any longer. Besides, I stopped being a *gisaeng* the day after leaving this hospital. Not because I cared about newspaper reports. I just decided not to work as a *gisaeng*. People make a lot of fuss over the news reports, as if something scandalous had happened. I couldn't stay home without being bothered. People would come over to call me in for work or come by to visit me. I told the cooperative office for *gisaeng* I was out of the business, but people didn't believe it. They thought I was avoiding them because of the papers. They tried to comfort me, telling me I'd be all right. I didn't know what to say!" Seon-hi abruptly changed her tone, seeming to recall something. "By the way, Mr. Heo, we met Dr. Lee on the train the other day, didn't we?"

"Yes, we did," Sung confirmed, recalling the scene.

"I had a bit of fun with that, didn't I? Did you overhear what I said? I apologized for not writing back after getting several letters from him. I even apologized that my servants had turned him away at the gate those three times he'd come to see me. That's what I said to him. I heard later that he was about to get engaged to one of the two women there with him. She probably graduated from some college of education in Japan and didn't know about

Dr. Lee. She must have left him the next day. Hey Jeong-seon," she said, looking again at her friend. "I've even heard a rumor Dr. Lee might try to get Shim Sun-rye back."

"What about Miss Jeong?" asked Jeong-seon, referring to Jeong Seo-bun.

"Miss Jeong Seo-bun?" scoffed Seon-hi. "No way. You think that Dr. Lee has any interest in her? If he's rejected by Shim now, he might go to Miss Jeong for a couple of days, just for fun. She'd be so appreciative over his cultivated manners, she'd make a fuss about welcoming him. Miss Jeong's exactly the right victim for men like Dr. Lee. You and I are too experienced to fall for him, and Sun-rye was just a rookie. Poor Dr. Lee's not got many chances left now. If he can't get Sun-rye this time, he's finished. Well, he's also interested in Dr. Hyeon, but does he have even an inkling who she is? Time for him to pack up and leave."

Sung listened in surprise to Seon-hi, who grew more and more talkative. San-wol had not been a particularly talkative *gisaeng*. Her appeal was in being coy, like a lady. She had even been somewhat reticent, appearing to reflect before speaking. That had especially attracted men's interest. The decency. The coyness. Yet Seon-hi was now so talkative, she seemed as if she had taken ephedrine and gone into a manic state. The woman with the low, alto voice now spoke in lovely, joyous tones.

"Sun-rye's problem is she gives herself too easily," added Seon-hi. "Dr. Lee would say my problem is in not giving myself at all. People claim holding back has its charm. That's so true. If a woman seems to give herself, but not completely, men will die for her. A *gisaeng* uses the same strategy. But I don't disobey for that reason," Seon-hi added, laughing. "I was nurtured into disobedience from having to live with people out to do me wrong. I disobeyed because obedience would've been to my disadvantage. A woman like Sun-rye, who grew up with loving parents, lacks experience in disobedience, wouldn't you say? But self-protection sometimes demands it." She looked at Sung.

Sung nodded agreement.

3-112

"As for obeying or disobeying," Seon-hi continued, "I learned enough from my *gisaeng* time to graduate with a degree in the field, so to speak. If you're a *gisaeng*, every guest seems to favor you, they all seemed willing to sacrifice themselves for me, as far as promises go. But if you believe them all, you'll end up in more than trouble. You learn to stay firm inside, telling yourself, 'All right, I don't believe you, I don't want to listen to you.' But to them, you say, 'Yes, yes, you're right. Oh, how generous you are! Certainly, of course.' That's the business. Doesn't it work like that? Aren't I right, Mr. Heo?" Seon-hi laughed.

"But living like that is worse than dying," she added. "A life without believing anybody, without listening to anybody, just rejecting everybody in cynical skepticism, that's very hard. It's really terrible, Jeong-seon. I need to place my trust in some heart somewhere, even if just the heart of a cat or dog. Without that, life is just a desert. What's the point having millions of people around if you can't trust any of them. If you can't, they're no better than enemies, and you're caught behind enemy lines, right? Taking pride in disobeying, in closing one's ears to others, can be kept up for just a little while. I can't live that way. That's why I stopped being a *gisaeng* and decided to listen to people. Don't laugh, Jeong-seon. Someone like you, born to good fortune, wouldn't understand the psychology of a woman like me."

"Decided to listen to people? To whom?" Jeong-seon asked.

"Well, to Mr. Heo. To listen to him, and also to believe him. But he's your husband, so I need your agreement. You won't object, will you?" Seon-hi looked at Jeong-seon.

"Why should I object? Everyone's free." Jeong-seon seemed to grant permission, but her words held reservation.

"If I go to the countryside," Seon-hi wondered, "will I have any work to do? Like a nanny in a kindergarten or a teacher at an elementary school, or whatever is available. I've saved about five thousand won from my work as a *gisaeng*, so I don't need a salary. I just want to do some 'useful work' now. I don't want to be a toy for men any longer. I'd rather become a useful person and do useful work. But I can't farm, and I have more ambition than to work in a textile factory. If having somebody like me as a teacher is shameful, maybe I could just teach the basics, like the alphabet and numbers. If I'm not allowed to do that, I'll go do factory work. That might be useful anyway. Mr. Heo, do you think I could do something? I don't want to be utterly useless anymore, I want to be useful with every fiber of my being. Could you help me do that? Like in the Bible story, you can think of me as a lost lamb returned to the shepherd." Seon-hi's voice had altered now, from excited to somber, even depressed.

Realizing that she had expressed most of what she had wanted to say, she felt empty, and she also worried that her words had not only been insipid but had exposed her weakness to ridicule and herself to embarrassment. Having emptied her heart, not an easy thing to do after keeping so many secrets hidden there, she felt as hollowed out as a mother who'd just given birth.

4-1

Spring came to Salyeoul. The Dalnae River flowed gently and joyfully, as spring in the countryside returns with water. Between the fifth and twentieth of April, in the third of the twenty-four traditional seasons, the one called *Cheongmyeong*, the land was plowed. Wet earth, broken and turned up by plowshares, promised a plentiful harvest in the fall.

The plowers, who bore a long-stemmed tobacco pipe askew on their backs for smoking breaks, held a lengthy, stiff whip for lightly tapping an ox on its left or its right as guidance. Oxen adjusted to these taps as they ambled along, swaying in their gait as froth dribbled slowly from their mouths. Arriving at a field's end, they turned either right or left according to the plowman's command, like soldiers obeying the orders of an officer. A young ox yoked for the first time never listened well and would get the lash, but those oxen with three or four years' experience knew exactly what to do. Part of the grain and straw from the fields that they plowed would serve as their feed during winter.

An ox was a member of the farmer's family, and farmers could recognize an ox from far away. They knew the strength and weakness of each ox. If an ox developed a limp or fell ill, the entire village grew concerned, not just the owner. They would call in a vet, but also visit a shaman and have a ceremony performed to drive out the malicious spirit.

As the plowman's whirling whip caught the spring light, the land itself seemed to revel in pleasure. "*Irya, irya tsheut tsheut!*" cried the plowman, encouraging his ox. The way broken by the ox was followed by a farmer who would begin leveling the ridges.

Holding a thick, tough stick in one hand, he would advance while using one foot to smooth down the top of a ridge. Following him was a farmer who applied ashes. He carried the ashes in a basket and scattered them by tipping the basket at an angle and shaking it lightly and skillfully to make the ashes spread evenly, dusting the earth with a dark trace.

Different crops called for different measures. Barley and wheat didn't require ridges to be leveled, but millet and cotton demanded leveling and even tamping. Tamping was done by the youngest farmer, the least trained man. He would level the ridges and tamp there, moving his foot from side to side in preparing the ground for sowing. Afterwards, an older man, the one with the most experience of plow time, carried out the most important work, the sowing itself.

To rise to the honorable position of "sower," one needed at least thirty years' plowing experience, along with proper skill. Sung's field in Salyeoul was plowed by an older man, known as the Old Man of Dolmorut House. He was in his mid-fifties and had worked hard and lived frugally his entire life, so he had come to own some paddies and fields as well as a clean house, though made of straw, and was well respected by the villagers. He was a man of silence, almost like a deaf person, and he was industrious as an ant. In his home, he was ever found busy at something. Under his influence, his daughter, son, and daughter-in-law were all like him, silent and diligent. His family only worked. In sowing, the man would grab a handful of seeds from a gourd hanging at his side and walk along, scattering them silently. Head tilted to one side and with one shoulder lowered, he sowed as if he could continue forever walking the length of the field and back.

If the young man tamping asked, "Aren't you hungry?" he would just reply, "Not yet time," and keep on working.

4-2

The Old Man of Dolmorut House, so busy scattering the yellow seeds, was followed by another old man, called "Father of Twins," who was famous for his humor and constantly cracked jokes to make others laugh as he covered the seeds. He still had something of a topknot, though merely a hint of one, and a shaggy mane tumbled about his ears and neck, graying hair that tangled and stuck out. No comb seemed ever to have touched his head.

Although he was called Father of Twins, none among the younger generation knew when the twins had been born and died. Only a rumor that his daughter-in-law had lived quite long as a widow and then run off led villagers to conclude that at least one of the twins had been a son and had even gotten married. But the old man now lived only with his wife, a contrast to him in her closed reticence. Probably waiting to die more than trying to live, one would say.

"How can you young folk be hungry already? When I was young, we could walk six hundred kilometers a day on water alone, but still not . . ."

With such words, the Father of Twins scolded the young men who craved lunch as soon as the sun slipped past its zenith, and he kept on covering seeds, first with one foot, then the other. The younger men laughed out loud even at such characteristic remarks by the old man, finding them funny.

"Why'd you walk just six hundred kilometers instead of six thousand?" asked a young man, humor in his voice.

"Because the day was short, not because I didn't want to," he retorted, opening his eyes wide. At this, the young men again burst into laughter. "Hey," the old man added, "you're hungry because you laugh too much."

Sung himself could hardly keep from laughing.

From the distance came the plowman's command. "Left, left!

Tsheut tsheut!" The workers raised their eyes and saw the oxen plowing the last furrow under the mulberry tree. One low-hanging branch was struck by an ox. It broke off with a sharp crack.

Five minutes later, the old man of Dolmorut House finished scattering all the seeds, shook the dirt from his feet, and walked to the edge of the field. He had perfectly matched the measure of seeds to the field, a point of honor for him since he regarded as shameful dereliction of duty any seeds left over in the gourd. A hand experienced at sowing should know how much seed a field required, not only the total, but also for each handful scattered.

The Father of Twins was the last to shake the dirt from his feet and leave the field. The younger men had already lit their pipes. "Give me some," he said, stretching forth a sun-darkened hand.

"I'd like to, but I'm afraid of the officials at the government tobacco company," explained a young farmer, moving his half-emptied tobacco pouch safely out of reach.

"Old man, you just carry your mouth?" asked another young man, laughing.

"You bastards!" he cried. He then boasted how he had grown tobacco himself in the past and how his had been the only tobacco in the whole village. This yarn always got unwound whenever he begged tobacco off others.

"You mean once upon a time, back when tigers smoked?" retorted the man with the tobacco pouch, handing that and the pipe to the old man.

The old man blew against the bowl of the still hot pipe, cooling it down, then stuffed tobacco in and lit that with some glowing ash fallen to the ground. His hollow cheeks quivered as he drew the smoke in.

4-3

Spring twilight was especially brief and dark. Already as the sun had set halfway behind Siru Peak, the darkness was growing, as if rising from the moist earth. Only upon hearing voices from within the shadow of the mountain could one begin to make out the people returning to the village from plowing.

Light purple smoke rising from one of the chimneys had now vanished in the gloom, but the evening meal steamed from old bowls on a cracked table. A woman's voice called out from the kitchen, "Go see if Daddy's here!" The children raced as barefooted as dogs to the gate outside. Clinging to their father, they pulled him into the house.

The father shook himself loose. "My back aches!" he said, but at their embarrassment, he took their hands.

His wife asked, "Are you finished plowing?"

"There's a bit left. The ox started limping." The husband took some of the boiled millet into his mouth as if it were tasty.

Yet how tasty it was! The parents and their children all silently ate the boiled Manchurian millet and the bitter soy paste stew in the darkening room. They could scarcely see each other, but the food tasted sweet to their hunger. Previously, they had been constrained by circumstances to borrow half a bushel of Manchurian millet on condition of repaying later with a bushel of rice, but they could now expect to repay with just half a bushel through the cooperative set up by Sung.

The meal was silent, with not even the sound of chewing. There was nothing to chew on. Lacking starch, the soft, boiled millet flowed instantly from spoon to throat. Emptying the bowls took only about five minutes, and when they had filled the rest of their stomachs with scorched-rice water, the head of the family sat briefly in the room's warm spot, leaning against the wall and reflecting as he listened to the clatter of his wife washing dishes.

This moment was his only moment of leisure.

The children had meanwhile fallen asleep elsewhere in the room. They had played the whole day to exhaustion, and no sooner were their hungry bellies filled than they collapsed in sleep.

The bedbugs came out on schedule. Though these pests would sting on neck and waist, neither husband nor wife had time or energy to deal with them. From plowing all day, as well as from malnutrition and overwork his entire life, the head of the family felt as though his body were falling down deep into the earth as soon as he stretched himself out on the floor.

"How's your back?" his wife asked, worried about her husband, who was rapidly getting old and feeble. Rubbing his back, she also fell asleep. Whichever of the two first woke up would take down the covers for the rest of the family and then also lie down, uncovered save for the feet, stuck under a corner of someone else's blanket.

When the head of the family woke up again, he heard his wife already making fire and cooking in the kitchen. The damp straw of sorghum and millet allowed only a weak fire, but popped loudly and produced a lot of smoke.

"Where do you work today?"

"Mr. Heo's field."

"You'll get a good lunch."

"You should go to his house, too. Draw some water for them at least. The wife is alone and unable to do anything without that leg. Of course, Han-gap's mother will surely come, and Yu-wol."

So went the couple's breakfast conversation till the children got up.

"I want breakfast."

"I want to pee."

After putting on the traditional *mokdal* socks that covered only the top of the feet, and before leaving to plow, the man opened the henhouse door. The morning was yet dark, but chickens ventured out, clucking *kideuk, kideuk.*

4-4

The plan for the day was to get Sung's field plowed. After Sung had followed the plowers to the field, Jeong-seon joined Seon-hi, Yu Sun, and Han-gap's mother in preparing them lunch.

Because Jeong-seon's stump still had not hardened enough, she couldn't yet wear the prosthetic leg and could only manage to move from her room to the balcony by awkwardly crawling on her hands and single knee. Upon reaching the balcony, she sat there on the floor helping with the food preparation. She sometimes occupied herself in pulling the flesh of dried fish from its bones, along with helping Seon-hi try to make various side dishes, though neither of them had skilled hands. Jeong-seon cut her finger once, Seon-hi twice.

"Oh my, hurting such fine hands!" Han-gap's mother felt sympathy for them.

"How well you cut radish!" Jeong-seon praised Han-gap's mother as she cut the radish for the salty pancake flavored with tiny shrimp.

Actually, Han-gap's mother was not especially good at cutting things thin and fine. That wasn't necessary in the countryside. Jeong-seon and Seon-hi were nonetheless very impressed to see her cut slices of radish, her dark, boney fingers coming slowly closer to the knife as it crunched down.

"May I have that, please?" Seon-hi reached for the cutting board. "I'd like to try."

"No," said Han-gap's mother, "you might cut your finger again, how terrible to cut such a nice hand." But she relinquished the board with a wrinkled smile.

Moving her fingertips slowly, like Han-gap's mother, Seon-hi tried to cut the radish evenly, but that proved harder than expected. After only a few slices of the knife, her wrist ached as if afflicted with arthritis.

"Does your arm already hurt?" Jeong-seon asked, showing herself the senior in this matter.

"No, not at all," Seon-hi replied and continued cutting, enduring the pain, but the knife didn't move quite as she wanted, and—with a cry of "Ow!"—red blood suddenly spurted from her left hand. The brand-new Japanese knife, honed sharp by Sung on a whetstone, had easily sliced into the tip of Seon-hi's middle finger, including the fingernail.

"Oh goodness! What should we do?" Han-gap's mother looked quickly about for something to wrap the finger with.

Jeong-seon also cried out in alarm and made as though to get up, but recalling her missing leg, she cried out for Sun, who was making a fire in the kitchen.

Sun rushed forth, brushing ashes from her hair with one hand and wielding a smoking wooden poker in the other because Jeong-seon's voice had been so urgent.

"Quickly!" ordered Jeong-seon. "To the room. Bring gauze, sterile cotton, bandages, and disinfectant from the medicine cabinet."

At her order, Yu Sun ground the poker into the dirt to quell the smoke, tossed it back into the kitchen, and ran to the room opposite the main room. In that room were a simple bookcase and a medicine cabinet with glass doors. The cabinet contained several kinds of emergency medicine along with various medicaments that could be administered by people other than doctors. Yu Sun knew exactly what was where and also their application because she had put them in order and used them. In a manner of speaking, if Sung were the doctor, Sun was the nurse. She brought out everything asked for.

Jeong-seon was speaking to Seon-hi. "Here," she said, holding out her hand. "Show me your finger."

Seon-hi held her hand up and showed the bleeding.

Jeong-seon took some sterile cotton with a pair of tweezers

and cleaned the cut with disinfectant, then wrapped the finger with gauze, added some cotton, and wound a bandage around that. She seemed almost like a trained nurse.

"What did I tell you?" she scolded. "You should have rested your arm when you felt pain."

"Ouch! It hurts!" Seon-hi took the wounded finger carefully in her other hand and held it closely against her chest.

4-5

The sun rose high. The day was warm, almost like summer. In Sung's field, about three kilometers north of the village, and also by the Dalnae River, oxen and farmers were sweating. A young man named Botdol, stripped of his shirt in the heat, was spreading ashes.

"The weather's suddenly got so warm," murmured the Old Man of Dolmorut House, wiping sweat from his forehead with the same hand that had scattered seeds.

"When it's time to get warm, it gets warm, and when it's time for the sap to rise, it rises," said the Father of Twins, who was trailing along behind. He looked around for nods of agreement, but the younger men pretended not to have heard.

One of the young tampers laughed, though, and mimicked his tone. "When it's time to get hungry, you get hungry."

"You fool!" cried the Father of Twins. "Mock an older man, and your balls fall off! Ill-mannered idiot!" He stamped his foot loudly in covering the seeds.

People laughed, but they all felt that gnawing hollow in their stomachs. They dreamed of the tasty food expected from the hand of Sung's wife. She was from Seoul, after all, and people from the capital were supposed to prepare better food than country folk did.

When a band of women bearing food atop their heads was seen approaching along the riverside, the workers' mouths watered as their taste was whetted and their hunger sharpened. Even the oxen seemed to drool more.

Glancing at the women, they tried to distinguish Yu Sun from Seon-hi, that *gisaeng* San-wol whom the newspapers had reported on. Identifying Han-gap's mother was simple, for she was such a familiar person, like their own mothers.

Sun bore a basket of rice and dry side dishes, while Han-gap's mother bore a jar of soup, Seon-hi a jar of scorched-rice water, and Yu-wol a jar of *makgeolli*, the traditional raw rice wine. Yu Sun and Han-gap's mother moved gracefully, just touching their burdens with a single hand, but Seon-hi and Yu-wol stepped awkwardly despite supporting their jars firmly with both hands.

They set the food down on grass near the front of the field, spilling a bit of the scorched-rice water and *makgeolli*. Sung stopped tamping and hurried to help the women arrange the dishes. The other young men envied him.

Sung smiled to see Seon-hi wearing farm clothes, and with a towel wrapped about her head like the other village women. She smiled back.

Yu-wol drew close to Seon-hi and took her hand to show Sung the bandaged finger. "Look here. She cut her finger slicing the radish. Even her fingernail!"

"Yes," Han-gap's mother added, clucking her tongue. "Such a nice hand, and she tried to cut like me. What a pity!"

"Did you put some antiseptic on it?" Sung asked.

"Yes," Seon-hi said. "That's how I can learn things." She smiled.

"School doesn't teach such *useful* arts, does it?" Sung returned to the field satisfied.

As the men ate, Seon-hi and Yu-wol served them from their hearts. The men politely refrained from looking at Seon-hi, but they were pleased to be in the presence of such a beautiful woman. The same old radish soup and the same old salty pancake with tiny shrimp seemed more flavorful than usual. The seven or eight men ate up all the rice, as well as the side dishes, and emptied the jars of soup, *makgeolli*, and scorched-rice water. Afterwards, they enjoyed tobacco offered by Sung.

The world was full of light. The Dalnae River appeared to flow more joyfully. Oxen nearby chewed on their fodder of bean and millet hay, seeming to enjoy it deeply.

4-6

"It was good."

"It was really tasty."

The men praised the food, wanting Seon-hi to hear them. They seemed to have genuinely enjoyed the meal.

The women collected the empty dishes and left for home, bearing them again on their heads. Along the way, Han-gap's mother and Sun plucked wild chive and Japanese hyacinth, and grubbed up yams along the roadside, which Seon-hi found interesting. She had seen pickled wild chives, but never the leaves, nor the entire plant growing in the soil. She quickly recognized shepherd's purse, however, though she had never seen its stem or its yellow flowers, but Japanese hyacinth was something entirely unfamiliar.

"Wow, there are so many kinds of edible plants," Seon-hi said, amazed.

"Yes," Han-gap's mother explained, "people say all plants can be eaten until Dano. They don't have poison before the fifth day of the fifth month."

"Do you live just on plants?" Seon-hi asked.

"Of course not, but some people make porridge these days by mixing plants and millet, half and half. Some folks can't even afford that. In Bangameori, some people gathering plants passed out because they didn't have anything to eat. They were found nearly dead with plants in their mouths. That's what they were doing just to survive! It's so hard even to survive these days." Han-gap's mother pulled mugwort out of the ground, shook the dirt off, and set them carefully in her basket, like precious gems. She looked at Seon-hi. "Even the poorest people in Seoul don't just eat plants, do they?"

"No, naturally not," Seon-hi agreed. "People in Seoul don't live on plants alone. Even dogs and cats get rice and meat in some families." Seon-hi reflected on life in the capital. More than five months had already passed since leaving Seoul, the city of prosperity and pleasure. What did Seoul and Salyeoul have in common? She was suddenly struck by the thought that people in Seoul ate rice without knowing how the plant looked, whereas the farmers who planted it could not even have any in their mouths.

"Good Lord!" cried Han-gap's mother. "How could they give such food to dogs and cats when some people don't have anything to eat? Wouldn't they get struck by lightning?" Her eyes widened in surprise, and she looked at Seon-hi in disbelief.

Yu-wol joined in. "People often threw leftover food in garbage cans. Beggars would come to pick it up."

Han-gap's mother was even more surprised. "What a waste! They should give it to poor people. Not a grain of rice should be wasted." She had scarcely had a meal entirely of rice in her life, and she had never lost a single grain while preparing it. She always made sure of cooking every grain, and eating each one. She had often heard her mother and grandmother say, "You sin if you waste even one grain of rice."

The plants picked and gathered as they walked along the road were more than enough for preparing side dishes. Seon-hi realized how generous the land was.

Jeong-seon was sitting alone on the balcony as they returned. "Did the plowers enjoy the meal?" she asked, sad about being a cripple stuck at home, but trying to put her mind on other things.

"Oh, yes!" replied Han-gap's mother setting down her jar. "They all ate very well. See, they ate and drank everything up. Rice, soup, and *makgeolli*. Even licked the side dishes clean." Han-gap's mother was greatly satisfied. "They never had such tasty food," she added.

"They really ate well!" Seon-hi confirmed, though if she had been alone with Jeong-seon, she would have joked about the farmers' table manners.

"Wow, really?" Jeong-seon smiled in satisfaction, looking at the empty dishes displayed by Sun and Yu-wol.

4-7

Spring in the countryside was peaceful though busy, but Jeong-seon didn't always have peace of mind.

They had come to Salyeoul a week before Christmas on a day with heavy snow. Arriving by automobile at the village entrance, Sung carried Jeong-seon from there on his back. She felt ashamed to be seen that way by the villagers and inwardly complained to God, who had saved her from the train, resenting him for not letting her die and preserving her from such shame.

From the time of their arrival, Sung had treated her as a father might treat a precious little daughter. He always cleaned up after her when she had used a bedpan, emptying and washing the bowl himself. With such concern, he took care of her.

But the more he did, the more she suffered. Her betrayal weighed upon her conscience, and she felt sorrow toward her husband over her crippled body, but that was not all. She was pregnant. She imagined the birth of the baby to be the day of her death sentence. Struck by a train and missing a leg, yet she had still kept the seed of new life within her body, and it was growing. She hoped that the baby would at least resemble her husband, but that would surely not happen. If the baby were to look like Kim Gap-jin, she wouldn't know what to do.

If only she had both legs, she could have fled long ago. But where? No place was left but the land of death.

When her morning sickness began, she maintained silence and explained away her lack of appetite, her nausea, and her occasional flushed appearance as consequences of poor digestion from being often bedridden.

But after five months, her belly showed, though most people didn't notice since she generally stayed home. Her husband had obviously noticed, but he never said anything, and remained silent. Jeong-seon thought that she would feel better if he would make a big issue about it, if he would just say, "You bitch! Whose child are you carrying?"

Whenever the baby moved in her womb, her mothering instinct brought happiness, but the very next moment brought fear. The baby moved powerfully in play regardless of Jeong-seon's emotions.

"Does the baby take after its father, Gap-jin, in such powerful movements?" She grew saddened at this thought, regretting that she couldn't talk about the problem with her mother, who had died long ago.

Moreover, she was anxious over Seon-hi and Sun. For the first month after Jeong-seon's arrival, Seon-hi and Sun lived in her place, but then Sung, out of thoughtfulness for Jeong-seon, fixed up the place where Han-gap's mother lived and let her take in the two women. He planned on building a house to double as a kindergarten for Seon-hi to run as soon as the land thawed and the plowing was finished.

Jeong-seon initially appreciated him having Seon-hi and Sun live in another place, but her gratitude was brief. As the baby grew in her belly, she imagined the two young women as enemies scheming to steal her husband.

"Ah, what should I do?" Jeong-seon often cried out in her solitude.

4-8

Jeong-seon practiced walking with the rubber leg, usually when nobody was around. She felt embarrassed even when her husband helped her stand, and also didn't like putting on the prosthesis in Yu-wol's presence. Realizing that she had to depend on it for the rest of her life, she felt as if both heaven and earth had vanished.

But Sung's newfound love for Jeong-seon was truly astonishing. One warm Sunday morning, he helped her put on the leg and took her for a walk to the riverside, supporting her with one arm, and in the other carrying the crutches, the kind called *matsubazue* by the Japanese. They were alone, without even Yu-wol. The day was a day of rest for the whole village, one of only two days each month when the farmers and oxen rested, a day when the farmers could sleep late and spend time with their children. Other days, they came home late, often long after their children had gone to bed, though even if they were to come earlier, they wouldn't be able to see their children in the dark, for their homes had no light. They would only have been voices in the darkness. On this day alone, once every two weeks, the village families were able to experience the joy of being together in the light.

Sung arranged to have no visitors on these off days and to spend time only with Jeong-seon, taking her out to show her the fields and their colors.

"Does the leg hurt?" he asked as they reached the bottom of a hill.

"It doesn't hurt, but I feel a little dizzy." She leaned against him, resting, one arm upon his shoulder.

"That's because you've just stayed in the room, not getting enough exercise, but if it's too much, we can go back home." He gripped her waist to ease the pressure on her stump.

As his fingers touched her belly, he noticed its fullness. No sooner had his hand touched her belly than Jeong-seon instinctively drew back. She flushed and said, "My belly is big, isn't it?" She smiled bitterly, as if she'd just tasted mugwort juice.

Sung quickly withdrew his hand from her waist, but also tugged at her arm. "Let's walk a bit more."

Jeong-seon, looking down at the river with bowed head, walked as her husband led her. The prosthetic leg, unlike her real one, didn't move as she wanted. She felt the baby turn roughly about in her womb.

"This is the place we sat down last year. Let's have a seat here." Sung took off his jacket and spread it upon the grass. Among the dried leaves, bright green blades of new grass protruded, and ants crawled from the earth to scurry along. In the river, fish swam about, propelled by a flick of their tails. On the opposite side of the river, farmers of another village half-led, half-pulled a heavily burdened ox, and from further away, a voice shouting "Left, left!" was heard, apparently a plowman crying out commands to his ox. In the further distance, a long train pulled its load along the rails.

4-9

Sung and Jeong-seon sat silently looking upon the river, flowing quietly, joyfully in the spring season. Youth was flowing. Life was flowing.

An apricot flower floated upon the river's surface, borne downstream by its current. Small fry gathered around to nibble, but darted away upon finding it inedible. The flower, like some messenger of spring, had paused and then gone on. Sung's and Jeong-seon's eyes joined in following its journey. But their hearts could not so readily follow the flower.

The baby in Jeong-seon's womb again moved strongly. "Why didn't I die?" she asked, turning to her husband.

"Why do you say that?" Sung looked into her eyes, now welling with tears.

"I want to die. What's the point of my life? The future will bring only unhappiness to me and a burden to you. I wish I could die right now." Tears rolled down her cheeks.

"Don't say that. You can have a good life here. Enjoy the arrival of spring, and likewise summer when it comes. When you're strong again, you can do whatever you like. Teach children, or women. Play music or write. Whatever you want. You'll enjoy it, whatever you do, don't you think? And there's something else important for you to do." Sung smiled to comfort her.

"What?" she asked, blowing her nose.

"Love me and help me," he said, drawing aside the veil of hair that had fallen across her face.

"How can I?" she cried.

"What do you mean?"

"Do I have right to love you?"

"Of course you do. No one else under heaven has that right."

"Do I? Even a cripple like me?"

"Does that matter? You can love me regardless of that, don't you think? Actually, you're such a beautiful woman, far too beautiful for me. But perhaps you need me more now, someone you can lean on and belong to. That would make me happy."

Jeong-seon cried even more. His words offered no comfort. They were painful instead. Why? She felt sorrow not over her missing leg but for having shamed him before the world. Worse still was the seed of Gap-jin in her womb. But worst of all was that her heart had allowed a man other than her husband to plant a seed in her belly. She couldn't confess this to him, not even if he already knew. Or even because he already knew. If she confessed, she would have to die on the spot. How could she ever face him again?

Jeong-seon had once entertained liberal views on chastity. Perhaps she had been influenced by the fashion of her times. But the more she reflected on her action as she lay nearly bedridden for months after the operation, the stronger became her belief that she had sinned. To be intimate with a man other than her husband was clearly wrong in her awakened conscience. As evidence of that sin grew month by month within her womb, she came to consider it punishment from God. Or if not God, then nature.

4-10

Several changes occurred in Salyeoul after the plowing was finished. These were necessary for the village to grow more healthy.

The first big change was the construction of a kindergarten. Seon-hi met the cost. The villagers didn't quite understand a kindergarten's purpose. Some thought it a *seodang*, a traditional school, when they heard that children were gathered there and taught. Nobody opposed it, of course, since Seon-hi paid for it to help the villagers.

The kindergarten site was located on a hillside between the village and Sung's house. Seon-hi bought the land from a Mr. Yu San-jang. Although a man of some wealth in the village, Mr. Yu showed little interest in Sung's work and rather resented that Sung was "spoiling" the farmers. The actual reason for his resentment was that he could no longer profit from interest on money lent to the farmers on long- and short-term loans ever since Sung had set up the cooperative. Until the year before, the villagers had been forced by circumstances to beg him for loans of money or food, but they no longer had to do that now and didn't go to see him any more. Worse still, they were less humble than before whenever they met him on the road. That was what really bothered Mr. Yu.

But he couldn't resist selling the hillside property, which was useless for farming and therefore worthless. He got a much better price than its agricultural value as it was to be used for a kindergarten. Profit proved greater than resentment.

The site was on land a bit higher than Sung's house, and one could thus see not only the river but also the field and the railroad quite well from there. The kindergarten itself comprised two rooms of sixteen square meters, to which was added a room of eight square meters for Seon-hi's place, including a kitchen, a toilet, and a washroom. A level yard of about 300 hundred square meters surrounded the place, which was also fronted by another 1000 square meters, all to be planted with grass. Construction took about three weeks, and the tin roof glittered in sunlight even from a distance when all was finished. The villagers praised the structure.

Seon-hi conferred with Sung about hosting a party to celebrate the building's completion. They invited every family with a child over four who couldn't go to elementary school and treated the families to rice cakes, beef-rib soup, and watery kimchi made of sliced radishes.

Some among the invited didn't attend. Mr. Yu San-jang was surely one of them. A notorious gambler nicknamed Itja and a man nicknamed Nari who frequented the district offices didn't come either. Itja often spoke badly of people even if without ill intent and eagerly sought out places to gamble through the night for as many as five to ten days in a row. He would go far out of his way to gamble, but showed no interest in useful things. He rarely brushed his teeth or washed his face, and after being widowed, he never tried to remarry, but just lived on as a burden to his three sons, an utterly useless man. The man called Nari was entirely different, the kind of gentleman scarcely found in a village. He was well-spoken, well-kept, and well-behaved. He wore a hat and dressed in a suit, though it was a bit rough. His manner and appearance earned him the title Nari, or sometimes Jusa, expressions for a person with a certain position. He had ability and was sly, as shown by his ceaselessly glittering eyes, and he maintained the lifestyle of a nobleman able to afford clothes of artificial silk for his wife, apparently by cheating people for whatever he could get, for he did no farming and had no property. Such a man was clearly not one to find Sung's work agreeable. While the man called Itja was endlessly spreading ill rumors about Sung and Seon-hi, the man known as Nari was undoubtedly crafting some malicious plot in secret.

4-11

On the kindergarten's opening day, about twelve children came. Although beginning time for schools would ordinarily be nine in the morning, the children's homes lacked clocks for keeping time, nor did their parents have the mental habit of precise time. The exact time for their arrival was thus not fixed. They set out for kindergarten whenever they finished breakfast.

On the first day, Seon-hi boiled water in the washroom and bathed the children. How their bodies were covered with dead skin and dirt! They hadn't washed since playing in water the previous summer. The boys wore their hair short, but the girls' long hair swarmed with lice, except for a few. By lifting the hair behind their ears, Seon-hi could see the white nits.

She tried to clean the first couple of children by soaping them down from tip to toe, but the dead skin on their knees and elbows had hardened and wouldn't easily wash off without scrubbing. The children liked playing and splashing in the water, but they disliked being washed, especially their hair. They wriggled and struggled to resist, crying out loudly when soap got in their eyes. Seon-hi continued by washing the rest of the children less thoroughly, taking care not to make the experience unpleasant.

Despite going easy with most of them, she was sweating all over when she finished, and her wrists ached as if with arthritis. After clothing the last child, she looked at the dirty water, as grey now as soupwater with salted oysters. Her kindergarten lacked plumbing, and she felt sorry for the children washed in dirty water at the end. But each washed child proudly told the others in turn, "Hey, I had a bath!"

After wondering how she could run a kindergarten without a musical instrument, Seon-hi discussed the issue with Jeong-seon and was able to get her piano for the kindergarten. She taught playing and singing to the children using methods observed in the Department of Children's Education at her university. She strove to teach them with as much devotion as possible.

Observing the children daily, she learned step by step what was important. Her findings were based on what the children of Salyeoul lacked. These were as follows:

1. They didn't recognize the difference between clean and dirty.
2. They had no concept of time and order.
3. They were not disciplined to listen to adults; they didn't respect authority.
4. They were untrained in collective life and thus extremely individualistic and selfish.
5. They were mostly unskilled in their talents.
6. They were not well-developed physically.

Seon-hi decided to do her utmost to help the children develop what they lacked.

Over the next ten days, the children increased to twenty in number. This occurred as word spread from child to child about the bean porridge for lunch and as parents recognized the opportunity for ridding themselves of troublemakers at home.

As the children changed, learning to brush their teeth and wash their faces every day, wipe their runny noses on something other than their hands, organize themselves for collective activities, and settle issues through means other than fighting, Seon-hi grew ever happier, for their transformation was the result of her efforts. Though the work left her worn out, she enjoyed what she did, feeling its value and usefulness. Most of all, she was happy that through the bustle and exhaustion, she could take her mind off the agonized young woman that she once had been and at times still imagined herself to be.

4-12

Her life of volunteer work, however, didn't always provide pleasure. Living alone in a large building, she had to endure agonizing loneliness as a young woman. The more she suppressed her love and desire for Sung, the fiercer blazed her heart.

Whenever she saw him, she felt drawn into a world of dreams, and her heart fluttered as she experienced such things for the first time in her life. She wrote down in her journal:

> On the way to seek my beloved,
> I perspire.
> On my back and brow, so acutely,
> I perspire.
> Sitting face to face before my beloved
> With bowed head,
> I only wiped the moisture from my brow.
> Unable to speak, a poor woman,
> Ah, I only wiped away the moisture.

Only wiping away the moisture,
I stood up and said, "Good bye."

She also wrote:

Seeing you, what did
I say?
Nothing.
Leaving decently, saying, "Good bye,"
I thought of turning around,
Of adding another word,
But I couldn't.
Twice, three times,
But I couldn't.

And there was also written:

My beloved lies across the sea,
A sea impossible to cross.
My beloved flies the high-arched sky,
A sky impossible to reach!
Ah, to see my beloved, though I should not.
Ah, my life!

Seon-hi also penned a letter in English late at night under the lamplight, thinking of Sung:

My beloved "somebody"!
When the children are gone, and I am alone, "somebody" walks in my heart, filling it completely. Has he been waiting outside, peering through the lattice, entering upon seeing me alone?
Wherever I go, "somebody" follows. I want to speak

my heart to "somebody." But I know I shouldn't. I want to kneel down and kiss the foot of "somebody." But a voice behind draws me back, warning, "Don't!"

Desire often overpowers me. I long to embrace "somebody" tightly and flee with him to a freer world where nobody will trouble me if I embrace him or pour out my heart to him. Ah, I so want, just once, to pour forth all the words weltered in my heart. But oh, I cannot!"

With such fervor did Seon-hi love Sung. But though she had once kissed him on that train in her drunkenness under a *gisaeng* mask, she now chose not to reveal her heart or speak about her love. She never visited Sung's home without reason, though she lived so close by, and if she needed to visit, she tried to avoid times when he might be home. But she longed in her heart for him to be there, so poignant was her love. She even longed for him to visit her. Such a contradictory heart left her in torment.

4-13

On a day in late August, when the summer was almost past, the weather was very hot, almost like the heat of *malbok*, the last of Korea's dog days. During the daytime, a sudden thundershower released torrents of rain, but as night fell, the heat returned.

After the children were gone, the kindergarten was quiet, with no soul around but Seon-hi. She was playing the piano in darkness, having chosen not to light a lamp after dinner. She played whatever came to mind, music for her alone to hear.

Having refused any assistance, she did everything herself, cooking meals, washing clothes, and cleaning the room and yard, everything as though it were her job. But she had Yu-wol stay over at night to prevent any rumors spreading about the nighttime activities of a woman living alone, and she was expecting Yu-wol to arrive.

Tiring of the piano, she stepped out, carrying a fan against the heat. She could hear the flowing waters of the Dalnae River, deepened by the day's rain. Harmonizing with the baritone of the Dalnae were the tenor of the narrow-mouthed toad, the broken-hearted alto of the cuckoo from a further mountain, and the various sopranos of mosquitoes in the air and other insects in the grass.

An eerie wind moaned once, and rain fell again, in drops heavy as beans. Closer to the ground, the wind was not strong, but its power seemed to grow more intense higher up. The clouds rushed along on a westward wind, but as that dark layer occasionally broke open, higher, northward-moving clouds were unveiled, only to change their direction a moment later. The sky vacillated, like the heart of a troubled, indecisive lover. Obscure moonlight confused Seon-hi's own heart even more.

The world grew suddenly darker. Lightning then flashed silently across the sky from distant Namseom Island in the east toward the far western horizon, appearing to inscribe the Chinese character for heart as it flashed overhead. Like neon illuminating the heavens, yet also like some secret code of love, this "mute lightning" perplexed Seon-hi and intensified her suffering. The turmoil of sound, light, and motion in the heavens and on the earth seemed to express the anguish of her great, painful love. Heaven and earth couldn't communicate, not even by adjusting the speed and direction of the clouds and emending the length and inscription of the lightning. Unable to communicate, the heavens darkened as lightning faded, and raindrops fell more thickly. Were they the teardrops of a broken-hearted love?

Seon-hi stood in that poignant darkness, alone and sad. Her love and longing for Sung had grown only stronger, and her suffering as well, for she would no longer reveal her heart.

"I saw my beloved in one I shouldn't love." That was the whole truth of her suffering. The love had to be quelled. It had to be quelled forever.

She looked to the north, toward Sung's house. Though it was half hidden by the hill slope, she could see light from one of the rooms. Sung might be there reading books, making project plans, or writing documents about the cooperative or some other community projects. Would he spare even a shadow of a thought for Seon-hi, she wondered. She couldn't imagine that his heart, firm as stone and cool as ice, had been touched by even the passing of her shadow.

"I saw my lover in one I shouldn't love." She turned and looked off in another direction. The clouds were still a whirl of confusion, and lightning from Namseom Island repeatedly sketched and erased its broken-hearted code.

> Ah, this broken-hearted lightning!
> An endlessly painful code,
> A code none can break,
> Timelessly written and unwritten.
> Ah, nothing but my heart-love's desire.

She murmured this like a poem, but the words and rhythm failed to calm her. She wished to run to Sung and cling to his chest, to speak her heart, regardless of consequences. But as she had taught herself to do, she let her rebellious heart be struck again and again, like being caned hard on her legs till they freely bled, all the while being commanded, "You shall not do that!" Since coming to Salyeoul, she had shed much blood in her heart, but had still not exhausted the wellsprings of her love.

"I can't block my feelings for him," she thought, "but I can make it my life's work to see the springs of this love run dry." She began to pace quickly, her eyes on the confused course of the clouds above and the code written and unwritten by the lightning. "Why is Yu-wol not here yet?" she fretted.

4-14

Seon-hi was surprised to find herself still innocent at heart, though she had entertained so many men as a *gisaeng*. She wondered if a woman's love couldn't be felt for just any man but solely for that man specifically intended for her love. She had always been cool toward men. There were a handful to whom she had felt attracted, but she could always control herself if she tried. With Sung, however, her heart and body were utterly shaken, and she could not calm herself in either body or heart any more than one could calm a storm-tossed ship.

> My love was meant for my beloved alone.
> Before I met him, it was not there,
> But since first seeing him, it burns my whole body.
> It is like
> A flower that cannot but bloom because spring has come.

Such were her circumstances. Or even like this:

> This is just the Creator's practical joke.
> Why did He make me love the one forbidden?

At that moment, Yu-wol came running, accompanied by a dog. "Miss, come quickly," she panted.

"Why? Who wants me to come?" asked Seon-hi, rousing herself from painful thoughts.

"Mr. Heo wants you. Mrs. Heo is going into labor." Yu-wol preferred not to call them "Master" and "Madam," but she also felt the awkwardness of referring to them using different terms. She had in fact served her mistress Jeong-seon since childhood, and calling her just Mrs. Heo seemed a great wrong.

"Mrs. Heo is in pain?"

"Yes, she felt unwell at dinnertime and now has a lot of pain," she explained. Yu-wol, or Ul-lan as she was now called, glanced continually in the direction of Sung's house, her expression worried.

Like a doctor, Seon-hi picked up her bag with various medicaments, including some for injection, retrieved her umbrella, locked the building securely, and followed Ul-lan. Even in these circumstances, her heart pounded more quickly as she neared Sung's house.

The dog that had accompanied Ul-lan ran before them and barked. Sung was sitting on the edge of the balcony looking across the dark yard. With the light glowing from behind him, Sung seemed like a statue to Seon-hi's eyes.

"Is Jeong-seon going into labor?" Seon-hi asked, trying to calm herself. She stepped up onto the balcony, brushing against Sung's strong arm in doing so.

"Yes, she seems in a lot of pain." Sung followed Seon-hi into the room.

"Are you here, Seon-hi?" asked Jeong-seon from within the mosquito netting draped over her pallet. Her voice sounded relieved.

"Yes, I'm here. Are you in a lot of pain?" Seon-hi knelt beside the mosquito netting and looked in to see Jeong-seon.

"Ow, ow, ow!" cried Jeong-seon before she could even answer. Feeling that sharp pain again, Jeong-seon frowned and tried to endure. Though the pain lasted under a minute, her forehead dripped sweat.

"It hurts so much, what should I do?" Jeong-seon asked, grasping Seon-hi's hand when the pain had stopped. She sounded sad.

"It's the pain of giving birth to joy, isn't it? Try to endure. That's a mother's responsibility, isn't it?" Seon-hi offered this as comfort, but no sooner had she uttered these words than she regretted them. Was Jeong-seon really giving birth to joy? Was she rather bearing a curse? Seon-hi felt sorry for her.

4-15

Jeong-seon felt the pain more often, and it grew stronger as the night deepened. She pulled the mosquito netting down and kicked the cover off with no shame at revealing her body. Screaming with pain, she twisted her body, disclosing the stump that she kept hidden even alone at night with Sung, and him sleeping.

Seon-hi had never experienced such a scene. "I should go for a doctor," she told Sung.

"A doctor?" Jeong-seon overheard in a moment of lucidity. "No, no doctor." She resisted, again wanting to keep her stump hidden. But she also felt too ashamed over her adulterous pregnancy to deserve a doctor, or even a midwife. "If you call a doctor, I'll die!" she cried, hysterical.

The pain returned. Jeong-seon grabbed Seon-hi's hand and screamed. Her friend gripped back, tensing her entire body in response. When Jeong-seon's pain stopped, both were dripping with sweat. She pulled Seon-hi's hand to her chest in desperate love and cried out, "Seon-hi! I'll die!"

"Don't say that. Pain in childbirth is normal. That's why they talk about birth pangs, isn't it? In an hour or two, the baby'll come out. When that happens," promised Seon-hi, offering words of comfort, "you'll feel wonderful, completely pure and healed."

Sung came in at that moment, but Jeong-seon waved him away. "You should go to bed in the other room," she said.

At this, he turned and silently left the room. Sung understood her. He understood his wife's heart, her pain in giving birth to another man's child, not his. Sung was unsure of his own feelings, uncertain of his own heart. He lay down in the other room, but when the screams came again from the main room, he automatically rose and went to see. At the sight of such a tragic scene, his wife writhing in pain and thrusting with the stump of her leg, he felt his heart constrict.

"Don't come in," pleaded Jeong-seon. At his wife's frantic plea, Sung rushed out to the yard, unable to endure any more. Lightning flashed, and big drops of rain fell as a gloomy wind whirled the clouds about. The entire world seemed in great pain.

The night deepened, and with the rumble of more thunder came a downpour of rain. Jeong-seon seemed in greater pain. She twisted Seon-hi's hands powerfully and screamed, wishing herself dead, but as the pain receded, she drifted into unconsciousness. Seon-hi grew concerned, wondering if this was that critical state called *jagan*, considered dangerous for giving birth. "Jeong-seon, Jeong-seon," she called, trying to rouse her friend, but thinking, "This must be the worst pain in life." Would Jeong-seon live? Her suffering seemed unbearable.

4-16

"Seon-hi, please forgive me," Jeong-seon said, holding Seon-hi's hand on her chest as the pain momentarily decreased.

"Forgive you? Why? You've done nothing to me." Seon-hi wiped the sweat from Jeong-seon's brow.

Jeong-seon seemed about to say more but stopped talking as the pain subsided. After another surge of pain had come and gone, a weakened Jeong-seon opened her eyes and said, "Seon-hi, forgive me. I've hated you, though I didn't show it. I hated you in my heart because"—pulling her friend more closely and whispering in her ear—"because I didn't like for you to love Sung. Yes, I know your heart very well, and that's why I hated you. But I now think there's nobody except you I can talk to openly. I can't rely on the heavens, the earth, a tree, or a stone, can I? If I die, please close my eyes and clean and shroud my corpse. Would you? I don't want anyone else to touch my body. I don't want them even to see my body. Only you understand my filthy heart and body, so you alone can touch me! Will you?" Jeong-seon implored, nearly crying out the words into Seon-hi's ear.

"Don't say that!" Seon-hi protested, more to calm herself than Jeong-seon. "If my presence here in Salyeoul makes you unhappy, I'll leave. I'm sorry if I made you suffer. Actually, I'm the one with nothing to rely upon, not even a tree or a stone. That's why I came here to live, to rely on you. I'll leave." She wiped away her tears.

Again came the pain, this time lasting nearly half an hour. Outside rumbled loud, rolling thunder as rain poured down. The hour was about three in the morning.

"Seon-hi," Jeong-seon managed to ask, despite her pain, "what medicine did you bring in your bag?"

"Pituitrin injection for stimulating contractions, sterile water for rinsing the baby's eyes, and special oil for washing the baby's mouth and body. Things like that." Seon-hi opened the bag and showed her.

"Give me the injection," Jeong-seon said, stretching out her arm.

"No, that can wait."

"I can't wait"

"Endure a bit longer."

"How can I?"

"You'll give birth early this morning."

"But I can't stand any more. Please do something. I can't stand it. Just kill me. I don't deserve to live anyway."

"Don't say that! Just try to endure a little more. Stay strong in your heart."

"It hurts too much. My back is breaking. What did I do wrong?"

"You've done nothing wrong. Adam and Eve are the ones who

sinned and brought on this pain."

"When the baby's born, who'll raise it? If I die, who'll raise it?"

"Don't talk like that! You won't die, but if you did, Mr. Heo would raise it, of course!"

"No, no. If I die, I'll take the baby, too. Wherever death takes me, even to the sulfur pit of hell, the baby comes with me." Jeong-seon suddenly blacked out.

"Jeong-seon, Jeong-seon!" Seon-hi tried to shake her alert, but to no avail.

Hearing Seon-hi cry out Jeong-seon's name, Sung rushed back into the room. Seon-hi quickly covered Jeong-seon's nakedness, remembering her words.

4-17

"I think we should send for a doctor," she advised Sung, making room for him.

"But she won't have that, and we can't get an obstetrician anyway." Sung rubbed his forehead, seemingly embarrassed, and looked into Jeong-seon's face. She appeared to be sleeping now, for she was breathing heavily, spittle dribbling from her mouth, like a child exhausted from play and lying asleep with limbs splayed out. Unendurable pain had sapped her self-control.

"I heard it's not good to fall asleep giving birth," Seon-hi said, checking Jeong-seon's pulse. It seemed weak, fluttery. "We really need a doctor," she insisted. "We don't know what's going to happen. I'm very worried." She looked at him, wondering what to do.

"No, not that, no doctor," murmured Jeong-seon, coming to, though still drained.

"The birth will go faster with a doctor," Seon-hi gently scolded, like a mother to a difficult daughter.

"No, no doctor," Jeong-seon again murmured. "You don't want to see me die, go away. I see mama. Telling me come with her. Telling me get dressed. Take the baby. Mama, wait. Let's go. Want to go with you," Jeong-seon mumbled, tearful and only half conscious, then frowned, again in pain, twisted her body, and opened her eyes.

Sung and Seon-hi both shivered at her words. Sung was shocked by Jeong-seon's desire to take the baby into death.

"Darling," Jeong-seon whispered, and sought Sung's hand. He took hers. "Forgive me, please," she pleaded, her hand trembling in his. When he remained silent, she continued, more strongly now, "Forgive me. Just have sympathy for me, a poor woman. Forgive me. I didn't do right by such a nice husband as you. I've betrayed you badly. I can't give birth to this child and face you after. I'll just go away now with this fruit of my sin inside. Just say, 'Jeong-seon, I forgive everything. Die in peace.' Please say it," she implored, now sobbing.

"Don't think that way. I forgave you long ago. Don't think that, don't grieve over it, be at peace . . ."

Sung was not finished when she covered her face with both hands and said, "No, no, you haven't forgiven me yet! You only have sympathy for me because you are a nice man, you feel sorry for me, a poor woman, but you haven't forgiven me. You don't truly love me. You have a strong will, you can will yourself to love me for the rest of your life, but you can't *really* forgive and love me," she cried, burying her face in her pillow and finally realizing how much she had wronged Sung. She considered herself worthless and even envied Seon-hi, whom she had looked down on as a *gisaeng* but who was now a woman respected by the people of Salyeoul for her work. In comparison, Jeong-seon felt utterly without worth.

Sung was silenced. Jeong-seon had spoken the truth, and he could make no excuses or deny it. Reflecting in his heart, he realized that, comfort her as he might for the rest of his life, he did not truly love her. He had resolved to try to love her for the rest of his life, and hoped that by immersing himself deeply in his work, he might forget about real love or affection. All that was true, and it cast a dark shadow across his heart. Or was it like a dark cloud on the horizon, a distantly looming, obscurely threatening storm?

4-18

Pain again rendered Jeong-seon unconscious and silent, but her countenance showed a confused mix of grief, fear, and desperation. Her physical and mental agony was too great not to show, and the changing expressions on her face and the twisting motions of her body joined in a quietly unconscious, miserable dance of suffering.

When she again came to, she took Seon-hi's hand. "Seon-hi, I'd forgive everything if I could. If somebody wronged me or even tried to kill me, I'd forgive them. I only wish there were somebody to forgive all my wrongs. I've sinned against my father, my husband, and my friends, even against the life in my womb. What've I done since I came into the world, what've I done with my twenty-three years? What've I done for the world? I've only caused trouble and fallen in debt to others. Nothing else. Even if I asked God to forgive me, He wouldn't, would He?" Jeong-seon grimaced as the pain returned. "It hurts again!" she cried. "When's it going to stop?"

When the pain subsided and Jeong-seon fell into exhausted sleep, Seon-hi turned to Sung. "Mr. Heo, tell her that you forgive everything. She's suffering so much. When she reawakens, tell her you've forgiven her and will love her like before. How terrible if she should die without hearing these words from you. And if she survives this ordeal and recovers, please love her with all your heart. I know you're a man of character, generous enough to do these things. Don't you have sympathy for her?" Seon-hi's words ended in low sobs.

Sung suppressed a cry surging up inside but could not stop his tears seeping through eyes shut tight. They flowed down his cheeks and dropped to the floor. "I'll forgive," he finally said. "I'll . . ." He paused to scoop water from the bowl near Jeong-seon's head and put his hand to her mouth. Though still unconscious, she accepted the water and swallowed. Her lips were parched, as if from high fever.

"Forgive me," she murmured, revived by the water and grasping his hand tightly.

Sung drew near and whispered, "Jeong-seon, I've already forgiven everything. A husband's love is boundless. Just stand the pain a little longer, it'll go away."

A rooster crowed. The storm had since stopped, and only the intermittent sound of water dropping from the eaves broke the early morning tranquility.

"Thank you," whispered Jeong-seon. "I can die without resentment. No one else could love and forgive me. Forgive me completely. Pity me, a poor woman. If I die, bury me somewhere easy to visit. I want a small tombstone. It should say, 'Jeong-seon, Wife of Heo Sung.' And . . . and . . . marry Seon-hi." She cried again, but no longer with tears of pain and resentment. They were of gratitude, satisfaction, and love.

Seon-hi was stunned at Jeong-seon's words. Sung said nothing.

The sun rose above the horizon. Where had the storm and clouds gone? The heavens had cleared completely, not even a cloud remaining, and the sky shone with bright, clean light, like early autumn.

In the house of Sung, a tiny cry was heard. Jeong-seon had given birth to a daughter.

4-19

As autumn soon arrived, then winter, the old year ended and a new one began. On a day in April after the Buddha's birthday had passed and the apricot flowers had all fallen from their branches, a car was heard loudly approaching Salyeoul, soon appearing as a taxi that abruptly halted.

From the taxi emerged a man in an elegant suit sporting a soft gray hat tipped down in front in the jaunty English way and wearing tortoise shell glasses. A spring coat was draped over one arm, and he carried a stick with a handle of water buffalo horn. He was smoking a cigarette.

The driver took a suitcase and bag from the car, along with something that looked like a guitar, closed the car door, and stood before the young man, awaiting payment.

The young man looked with displeasure at the village and muttered in broken, poorly accented Japanese, "Damn it! What's going on? I sent a telegram."

"I have to go," said the driver at last, unable to wait any longer. "Please pay me."

"How much?" The young man still spoke in Japanese.

"Four won, eighty jeon," answered the driver in Korean.

"Four won, eighty jeon? So expensive! Too expensive!" shouted the young man, even more agitated.

"You agreed to the fare before you climbed in, didn't you?" The driver's voice also rose.

"In this thing? In this old clunker!" cried the young man, poking at the car with his stick. Glaring with angry eyes, he added, "It costs at most fifty jeon in Tokyo."

"Tokyo is Japan. This is Korea. You can't renege after agreeing to the fare." The driver had become less polite.

"What did you say? Say it again." The young man pushed the driver.

"Are you going to strike me next?" protested the driver. "We don't have to fight, let's just go to the police!" He grabbed the young man's arm.

The young man stumbled forward a couple of steps, pulled along by the driver, but then shook off his grip, exclaiming, "Let go my arm!" He rummaged feebly through his pocket, drew forth not a wallet but a bundle of folded notes, picked out a five-won bill, and tossed it to the ground. "Take it, you bastard!" he snapped, still using Japanese, and spat out his cigarette.

The driver silently picked up the money and climbed back into the car. Sticking his head out the window, he turned to face the young man. "What sort of cheapskate are you? Carrying on like that over so little money! Go eat straw soup if you're so cheap. Your parents are too poor to buy cotton clothes, but you're special if you wear a high-collared suit?" He started the car and cursed at the young man as he slowly pulled away. He had the money, was again in his car, and could safely have his revenge.

The children of the village had meanwhile gathered around at the sight of the car and the high-collared suit. "It's Jeong-geun, son of San-jang," they whispered to one another.

Jeong-geun, son of Salyeoul's wealthiest man, Mr. Yu San-jang, had gone to study in Tokyo and was now back.

4-20

Hardly any among the children were glad to see Jeong-geun. They had often heard their parents complain about his father, Mr. Yu, but had also heard that Mr. Yu was angry at his son, who had gone to study in Japan but wasted money. They remembered their parents gloating over Mr. Yu having to sell some of his rice paddies to support his son. Yu San-jang's family had earned little money from interest on loans ever since the cooperative had been set up the previous year. The children's interest in Jeong-geun thus lay only in gawking at his outfit, which they could not but admire. "Wow," they thought, "he looks nice. He's wearing a high-collared suit."

"Hey," Jeong-geun shouted. "Carry these things!" He pointed his stick at the taller among the children. The others, afraid of being included, stepped back, but those pointed to automatically obeyed the order.

As the bigger children began carrying the suitcase and guitar, the others trailed along behind. Jeong-geun lit a cigarette and started toward the village whirling his stick.

At the moment, a man bearing an A-frame came into view, saw Jeong-geun with surprise but gladly greeted him, took the children's awkward burden, and loaded it onto his A-frame. "Did you just arrive by that taxi?" asked the man, a distant uncle to Jeong-geun.

Jeong-geun exploded in anger. "Why didn't anyone come pick me up at the station? They knew I'd be arriving today! Are they all dead?"

"We had no idea you were coming. Your father didn't let on." The poor man staggered up under the burden of his nephew's baggage.

"I send a telegram to my family, and the village doesn't even know?" Jeong-geun's tone was improper, particularly for addressing an uncle, but he felt provoked. Scarcely three years earlier, whenever he returned for vacation from his studies in Pyeongyang, the whole village would emerge to greet him, alerted by telegram to his arrival. But not a single soul had come out this time, and that was a radical change.

The older man bore everything in silence.

Some of the children ran ahead to report his arrival, and except for Mr. Yu, his family came out to meet him on his way. A servant named Miryeok ran fourth to greet Jeong-geun, bowing deeply like a child.

"Bastard, what good are you to me now?" He struck Miryeok across the back with his stick.

Ignorant of Jeong-geun's reason for striking him and shocked into wordlessness, Miryeok took the A-frame from the older man and hefted it onto his back. The frame pressed hard where he had been struck, increasing his pain.

His family was glad to see him, but he didn't bother to doff his hat for them, not even upon encountering his mother, who was ailing. When they reached the family house, he asked her rather curtly, "Why isn't Father out here to see me?"

His mother frowned. "He's in the reception room, of course. Go see him."

"I sent a telegram saying I'd arrive today!" he shouted, seating himself on the threshold of the side door rather than going to his father. "Why didn't anyone pick me up?"

"How should we know a telegram came?" she retorted. "These days, your father says nothing to anyone. He doesn't even show his face to eat. He's upset and says the world is coming to an end because the villagers and distant family members don't come by. Ever since Heo Sung set up a cooperative, or whatever it's called, people don't borrow money or grain. They don't drop by any more. How we've survived this long, I don't know! That's why your father's so upset and won't talk to anyone, not even family members."

4-21

While Jeong-geun was sitting on the threshold, his wife had changed her clothes and now stood in front of the kitchen with a boy of about four or five, patting him on the head, and advising him in whispers, "Go say 'Daddy'!"

The boy sucked on a finger soiled with dead skin and dirt and glanced sideways at Jeong-geun with big eyes. He shook his body, resisting.

But his mother poked his side in urging him to say hello to his father, hoping to draw attention to herself through the child. "Go say 'Daddy.' He's your father. Go hug him!" she whispered.

Jeong-geun's wife looked older than he did. Her complexion was poor, as if from some internal condition. Perhaps she had suffered as a young married woman left alone and missing her husband, but the Yu family was known for generations to treat its women badly. They survived only on leftover rice with soybeans, and weren't allowed to see a doctor when ill. Even the mother-in-law received hardly any medication despite being sick, so what could the daughter-in-law expect?

"Jang-son, go to your father. Greet him," she repeated, shaking her son.

Finally, he reluctantly started toward his father, but when he noticed his father look him over indifferently, then gaze in the other direction, he was discouraged and returned to his mother's skirt.

"You say that Sung spoke ill of us?" Jeong-geun asked, upset at a remark by his mother. "And who is he? Just a man who couldn't keep his wife satisfied. She had an affair and tried to kill herself when he found out, but she survived. How dare he walk around so shamelessly? He was booted from his lawyer job!" Jeong-geun spat his contempt.

"His wife had an affair?" Jeong-geun's mother drew closer, ears itching to hear more.

"Sure, it was in all the papers, and you slept through it?" Jeong-geun's frown broke into amusement, and he continued, "Not only that, but he couldn't bear to separate himself from a *gisaeng* named San-wol, so she quit that profession and followed him here to run a kindergarten. Do our kids go there, too?"

"Of course not. They don't even go near the place. Your father looks at Sung as his deadly enemy. He wouldn't stand under the same sky with that man, so how could we possibly send the kids there? So, she's a *gisaeng*, is she? I heard she graduated from a university."

"A university! No, just a college. After that, she worked as a *gisaeng*. Everybody in Seoul knows about her. Humph, that crazy fool! Bringing a *gisaeng* here and having her run a kindergarten! He makes himself look so good on the outside, but I read in the newspaper that he even deflowered Sun, the daughter of that *chosi* family!" Jeong-geun grew more enraged as he spoke.

"Is that really true?" she asked, surprised to hear the news about Sun. But she nodded as she considered it. "It must be true. Keeping that young woman in his house for six months, he couldn't have left her alone! And to think, he arranged to have her married off to Han-gap after he'd had his fun!"

"Sun married Maeng Han-gap?" Jeong-geun was surprised.

"That's right. As soon as he got out of prison two months ago. The wedding took place in that kindergarten."

"Humph," he said. "I guess he can't handle two concubines. But Han-gap must be crazy if he's happy about marrying a deflowered girl." Jeong-geun seemed quite amused again. At that moment, Jang-son, urged on by his mother, ran to him crying, "Daddy," and hung onto his knees.

4-22

"Go away," said Jeong-geun, brushing his son off like an insect.

Thrown off balance, Jang-son burst into tears and rushed back to his mother, sobbing as if snapped at by a dog.

"What are you doing?" Jeong-geun's mother scolded. "How could you do that to your own child when he was hugging your knees in joy at seeing you, his dear father? Don't you have any feelings for your son? Are you going to be as cold to your own child as your father was to you? The Yu family must be naturally coldblooded!"

"My son? Who's my son? My son wouldn't be so filthy or have huge eyes like a cat." Jeong-geun abruptly stood up, as if to emphasize the point.

"Whose son is he, then?" demanded his wife, ordinarily not one to protest even at being stabbed with a knife. "I've never heard such nonsense."

"Oh, shut your trap. You want to be kicked out of this house and get nothing to eat? I won't forgive you this time." He spoke with complete confidence.

"You should talk! I've heard you had fun in Japan with a girl called Nam or whatever her name is. What sort of bitch would run after a married man with a child? If she can't keep her hands off a married man, let her live as a concubine, second or third one, I don't care. But what did she want? You to divorce me? What've I ever done wrong? Ever since I came to this family, I've worked hard, even given birth to a son. Was that all wrong? Who'll kick me out? Go ahead, just try to kick me out!" With courage impelled by female jealousy, Jeong-geun's wife gave word to her protest.

"Call her a bitch, will you?" Jeong-geun turned toward his wife, stepping aggressively and hurling his stick. "Listen, you bitch. Open your trap again, I'll kill you without a second thought."

Jang-son panicked and tugged his mother toward the kitchen, wailing loudly.

"Kill me! Just try to kill me! Do it! What'd I do wrong? Tell me! Did I ever serve your parents badly? Was I ever unfaithful? What'd I do wrong? Just tell me! You got nothing to say! When I married you and joined this family, I brought rice paddies that produce five bushels a year and a field that takes two days to plow! And whose money supported your studies in Seoul and Japan? Now, you want to kick me out because you've fallen for that girl called Nam. Fine, but how are you going to kick out a woman who's produced a son?"

Distracted by her son, who was continually pulling at her skirt and calling for her to come, she suddenly slapped his face and cried out, "Little bastard! What are you crying about? Why are you crying?" The boy released her skirt and ran into the kitchen to avoid a second slap, but stopped there without seeking further escape through the back door. He stood trembling and calling his mother.

Unable to endure any more, the mother-in-law rushed to her. "Stop, my daughter, that's no way to speak. How dare you address your husband that way! When I was young, I just listened to my husband no matter what he said. And why slap the little one? Stop it!" After scolding the daughter-in-law, she turned to her son and tried to calm him down, speaking as a mother with experience. "You shouldn't act like that. You should greet your wife and child with joy when you come home after a long absence. A young man can have ten concubines, as people say, so when a man's young, he can have affairs and concubines. But he shouldn't abandon the wife he married, the one whose hair he let down on their wedding day! It's clear your wife's been unhappy ever since you threatened divorce and other unpleasant things in your letters from Japan. Try to make her feel better, try to resolve things."

"Not when this bitch talks badly about Nam and gets everything wrong. Nam In-suk's pure and virtuous. Concubine? She's not the sort to be anyone's concubine. And she doesn't have any relations with me, either. I've got the highest respect for her. And this bitch here talks . . ."

"What's going on over there? Why's it so loud?" Out from the back door of the reception room stuck Mr. Yu San-jang's head, hatless, his topknot exposed. "What a scoundrel, to come home from wandering around Japan on the excuse of studying and not even to greet your father first but just cause some big commotion in the house! Is that all you've learned in Japan? Scandalous, having such a son!" He slapped the door.

Jeong-geun had been loud and boisterous, but he couldn't dispute his father's words, and cried out in anger, "Why did I come here?" He left the house, heading who knew where.

4-23

Jeong-geun's appearance in Salyeoul gravely disrupted peace in the village. From the time of his return, he spared no effort in spreading the rumor that Seon-hi was a *gisaeng*, that Jeong-seon had lost her leg through an affair, and that Sung and Seon-hi had a relationship.

The villagers initially believed none of it because they trusted Sung and Seon-hi rather Jeong-geun, but just as no tree remains without a cut after ten chops of an axe, so trust and loyalty prove as easy to tear away as thin paper.

"Look, we can't put our children under the charge of a *gisaeng*," people started to say, and some children attending the kindergarten even taunted Seon-hi to her face, pointing at her and chanting, "She's a *gisaeng*, a *gisaeng*."

And when the villagers heard Jeong-geun quote newspapers claiming that Seon-hi was Sung's concubine and that Sung had even deflowered Sun, the villagers treated Sung as somebody to be shunned.

The rumor about Sung and Seon-hi caused trouble to every project undertaken by Sung in the village. Fewer and fewer people attended the weekly meetings to discuss village issues, even fewer who did attend brought rice, straw, and straw rope for storage, and even fewer families welcomed Sung, previously an honored guest.

What caused Sung the most trouble, however, was Han-gap's attitude, first of distance and then even of enmity. Jeong-geun was clearly working on making Han-gap the kingpin of Sung's opponents.

"Have you been to his house again?" complained Han-gap in great annoyance one day when Sun had just returned from Sung's place.

Surprised by her husband's statement, Sun stared at him with eyes wide open, as though he had uttered blasphemy. Doubting her ears, but finding her voice, she asked, "What's wrong?"

"You don't know what's wrong?" Han-gap retorted, more agitated. "I know everything. I know why you go to Sung's house so often. You think I don't know anything? Go to his place again, and I'll kill you." His tone echoed that of the prisoners with whom he had done time, particularly of one man imprisoned for killing his wife over an affair.

"What are you talking about?" Sun asked, nearly in tears. "How can you speak of Mr. Heo like that? You know we couldn't survive without his help!"

"I know everything," he insisted. "I'm telling you now, don't go to his place again. Better listen to me." He took a few steps to head out, but turned abruptly back and demanded, "Whose baby's in your belly? Tell the truth!" He glared with the suspicious eyes of a police interrogator or government prosecutor.

"What are you talking about now?" asked Sun, so confused that she didn't know what to think.

"What am I talking about? I'm asking whose baby's in your belly!" He spat in disgust, his body trembling from the rage and jealousy blazing up in his heart.

4-24

Han-gap's words were a bolt from the blue for Sun. She even wondered if he were of sound mind.

"Where did you stay while I was in prison?" he pressed.

Heavy of heart and resentful at the question, Sun couldn't bring herself to answer.

"I know everything," he repeated, a sarcastic smile on his angry face, "I heard you lived with Sung while I was in prison. You slept in his room, using the excuse of having to care for him when he was sick. Humph. And he now pretends as if nothing happened. Right, nothing at all. That bastard Sung turned you over to me after he'd had enough fun with you. But also because that bitch San-wol showed up! Damn him, I'll break his legs! That bastard tries out all the pretty girls and pretends to be well-mannered. You know why I had to stay so long in prison? That bastard arranged it in the guise of defending me. I know everything. You think I don't know anything? It's infuriating!" He ground his teeth in anger.

After this argument, Han-gap was completely altered in behavior. He no longer worked, but continually drank instead. At home, he would cast accusations at Sun. She tried several times to explain things, speaking earnestly, but the more she explained, the stronger became his suspicions. She finally just endured the abuse, actually suffering more for Sung than herself because he was treated badly now, and his work suffered from it. Sun worried more about how to clear him of the false charges.

Late one night, Han-gap came home drunk. He had been at the market, drinking with Jeong-geun, a common habit recently. Fumbling for the door handle, a simple loop of rope, he shouted, "You bitch, did you go to Sung again for fun?"

Sun quickly got up and undid the loop. Even through the door, Han-gap stank of liquor.

"Bitch! Slut!" he cried. Setting one foot in the room, he grabbed her hair and jerked her toward him. Sun crashed her head and shoulder on the door frame and fell against her husband. He stepped aside and pulled again at her hair. She stumbled to the ground outside holding onto her belly, pregnant five months with their baby.

"Bitch! Slut!" Again and again, Han-gap kicked her back, shoulder, and face.

Sun didn't even gasp at the pain, but endured the kicks, giving way with each blow.

"Die! Just die!" he screamed, enraged and heady with alcohol.

Han-gap's mother at first remained in bed, regarding the noise as just the night's usual drunken behavior and thinking it normal, but eventually noticing an unusual sound even with her poor hearing, she opened the door of her room.

"What's going on? Why do you carry on drunken like this every night? Where do you get the money to drink every day?" She then spied something pale stretched out on the dark ground and hurried out in surprise, wearing only her bloomers without the upper part. "What's this?" she screamed.

4-25

Han-gap's mother groped her way toward where Sun was lying, and at a closer look cried out again in shock, "Oh, what've you done to her? She's not alone, she's carrying your child!" She bent down and took Sun's arms to pull her up, but found to her even greater shock that Sun had no strength to stand. She called Sun by name and gently touched her head. "She's bleeding! Oh, my baby, my baby!" Sun didn't respond.

"Leave the bitch alone. Let her die." Han-gap kicked Sun once more in the side and staggered out.

"My baby, my baby," repeated Han-gap's mother. She again tried to grasp hold and lift Sun, but found this beyond her strength. Returning to her room to light a lamp and bring it out, she saw Sun clearly, head drenched scarlet with blood and body shaking as though racked by silent sobs. "What should I do?" Han-gap's mother wondered. She loudly called her son. "Han-gap!" No answer. She called again. "Han-gap!" Silence.

"Oh, what should I do?" she worried. "That damned boy is becoming just like his father. Why does he drink so much these days?" She turned again to Sun. "Baby, my baby, get up off the dirt and go lie down in the room. I can't carry you with my weak arms. Oh, what should I do? What if she loses her baby? What should I do? Oh, her skirt is soaked with blood, too! She's bleeding from her womb! What should I do? Where'd that damned boy strike her? Oh, something dreadful has happened! My baby, my baby!"

Han-gap's mother sat flustered for a time, not knowing what to do. She finally returned the lamp to her room, put on some clothes, and left the place.

The dogs in the village barked.

Han-gap's mother hurried as best she could to Sung's house. There was no one else to turn to when things went wrong. But as she approached his place, she heard an uproar. Stopping for a moment, she listened. Someone was yelling. It was Han-gap!

"What's that damned boy doing there?" she wondered and walked faster. As she drew near, she saw Han-gap in the yard flailing at Sung. He had grabbed him by the collar and was striking at him. Sung was trying to block Han-gap's kicks and punches, but returning none.

"You bastard! Keeping me in prison. Having fun with my wife! You bastard! One of us will die today!" He struck at Sung again and again, all the while calling him a bastard and repeating his threats. Even angrier at being unable to land a blow, for Sung was quite strong, Han-gap cursed and cursed with a tongue thickened from alcohol.

Han-gap's mother took her son by the shoulders. "You wretched boy, how can you do this? So ungrateful! How can *you* do this to Mr. Heo? How could I have survived without him while you were in prison? Mr. Heo supported me like his own mother. You damned boy, how can you do this? Come with me! Get back home!" She pulled him away and said to Sung, "Please come, too. This boy beat Sun, and she's losing blood. What should we do? I had to leave her alone on the ground bleeding from her womb. Please don't be upset by this drunkard, please come to help." Pulling Han-gap, she disappeared into the darkness.

4-26

Drained of energy from drink and fighting, Han-gap allowed himself to be dragged away by his mother.

"My son," she reproached, "you must have been listening to Jeong-geun, but why trust him? He's a scoundrel. Ever since Mr. Heo came to our village, Jeong-geun's father hasn't been able to gouge profits through usury. That family hates Mr. Heo deeply, but you still believe what Jeong-geun whispers to you about Mr. Heo and your wife? As for your wife, she always slept in my room with me. There's nothing to doubt about her integrity and virtue. I would know if there were, not you or Jeong-geun. Besides, Mr. Heo isn't that sort of person. Since Jeong-geun returned, the villagers've changed their attitude toward Mr. Heo. That's wrong, really wrong. Mr. Heo and that kindergarten teacher both spent their own money to do something good for the village, and people should know that. I told you all about this, but you didn't listen to me. You believe that scoundrel instead, and look what you've done now! Your wife's bleeding from her womb, and I'm worried about the baby she's carrying. Oh, why am I fated to this! I thought I could hold my grandchild before I die, but look what's happened! I should have died sooner so I wouldn't have to see this. Your father killed a man when he was young. He got drunk and struck a friend too hard. Your father was a good man sober but a violent drunk. Whenever he drank, he lost his self-control. You're just like him. After killing his friend that way, your father never touched another drop and spoke even less than he drank." Han-gap's mother talked like this the whole way home, also lamenting, "What'll we do if the baby's hurt?" Her overwhelming desire was to hold a grandchild, and she imagined the little one moving in her arms. She even put the grandchild's safety above that of her daughter-in-law.

They arrived home to find Sun still lying face down on the ground. Han-gap didn't seem to notice, but he hadn't responded to his mother's words either in staggering along after her. His head ached, and his body was heavy. He tried to collect his thoughts but couldn't, like trying to put a broken pot back together. His chin would sink again and again, his eyelids droop, and his legs wobble. Jeong-geun had invited him to drink at a brothel in the district town, and he had even fallen asleep there before coming home. But he'd heard there that Sung was a bastard who still sometimes met Sun in secret, that the baby in Sun's belly was not his own. Drunkenly believing these things, he had rushed home, a distance of more than eight kilometers from the town. A mere simple-minded man, he lost control in his rage at hearing the rumors from Jeong-geun and had set out for home intending to follow the example of the prisoner who had killed his wife.

As he now found himself sobering up, he grew even more weary. He was beginning to worry, half realizing that he had done something terrible, but he also felt as if he had not finished the business. He would briefly raise his head all of a sudden, mutter something, then quickly fade out. He had managed to hear only some of his mother's words.

At one point, he stared blankly at his wife lying on the ground, then suddenly lifted his head and proudly shouted, "Die, bitch!" before being dragged inside by his mother.

4-27

Sung headed for Han-gap's place with the first aid kit, accompanied by Seon-hi. As they approached, he noticed Han-gap's shoes lying in the dirt outside the gate, apparently having slipped off his feet there and been forgotten. Seon-hi widened her eyes, glancing about in fear.

Sung wasted no time squatting beside Sun and checking her pulse, initially finding nothing, but as he awkwardly sought the right spot on her wrist, he finally located a faint beat. Seon-hi was watching him closely and understood at his nodding that Sun still lived.

"We should move her into the house," Sung told Han-gap's mother, gently touching Sun's bleeding head.

Han-gap's mother, who had been trembling and looking first at Sung and then at Seon-hi, visibly relaxed at this suggestion. "Let's put her in my room," she said, going on ahead to prepare a mattress and pillow. "Bring her in. Will she be all right?" The old woman's dark, wrinkled face, with grey hair in torn disarray and tired eyes wearied by the years, appeared in the lamplight almost like a death mask. Having suffered worry and poverty her entire life, she seemed without energy even for sadness or despair. Resignation alone was set in her face.

Slipping one arm under Sun's neck and the other under her knees, Sung carefully lifted her in his arms. He felt saddened to think that this woman who had so strongly desired to be held in his embrace was now held by him in such a terrible state. As he was laying her down in the room, she briefly opened her eyes and seemed surprised to find his arms around her, but her eyes again soon closed. In standing up once more, Sung saw that Sun's blood had stained his arms and chest red.

He looked down at her and recalled her words the previous fall when he had advised her to marry Han-gap. "I don't want to marry," she had told him. "Just let me stay in your house." But as he tried to persuade her, she had finally relented with a sad face, nearly in tears, "I'll do as you suggest because I know you're saying all this for me."

She had not wanted to marry Han-gap, but did so because

Sung wished her to, and because she realized that her love for Sung was just an impossible dream. She also knew that she could not possibly live her life alone, so she married Han-gap though she still loved Sung in her heart, as he well knew.

Gazing at Sun lying there with bleeding forehead, hair disheveled from being pulled at, and nether parts soaked with blood, Sung felt such intense pain that tears welled up in his eyes. "Ah, you poor, lovely girl," he silently lamented.

Sung and Seon-hi, like doctor and nurse, washed and wrapped Sun's injured forehead. Sung then discreetly exited the room, leaving Seon-hi in charge.

Stars twinkled in the sky high above, as the clouds of the early morning hours had all now vanished. Under that limitless space and within unbound time, a life comes forth to suffer and die. Sung sorrowed over such a life. He looked vacantly up at the sky and sighed.

4-28

After doing the best that she knew to staunch Sun's bleeding, Seon-hi went out looking for Sung. She found him gazing at the sky and approached, wiping sweat from her brow. "We should call a doctor," she said.

"Is she bleeding a lot?" asked Sung, as if waking from a dream.

Seon-hi sighed. "It's quite serious," she said.

"I'll go get a doctor. You stay here and take care of her. She's a poor woman." Sung started off for the district town.

Watching him disappear into darkness, Seon-hi sighed again and looked up to the sky that Sung had gazed at. The stars were twinkling their eternal cold light.

Seon-hi tried to care for Sun by administering doses of salt, something that she had learned from a book. From the neighboring room, Han-gap could be heard snoring. He sometimes muttered.

Han-gap's mother was crouching in a corner, her mind half gone. She now seemed to lack even the energy to repeat, "Oh, what should we do?" or "How is she doing?"

Seon-hi wondered if she might have become indifferent to any further thoughts from ceaseless worries and sadness her entire life.

"Mother," Sun called, opening her eyes.

"Yes?" Han-gap's mother crawled to her daughter-in-law and sat close by.

"Mother, I didn't do anything wrong," Sun said, her tears flowing.

"I know, you did nothing wrong. It's all because of Jeong-geun," she affirmed.

"If you understand me, I won't have any resentment when I die," Sun sobbed. She had recovered sufficient consciousness to understand what had happened to her.

"Die? What would I do without you? No, you won't die." Han-gap's mother adopted a tone of confidence, trying to comfort her dying daughter-in-law.

Sun fell silent again, her eyes closed. Only the tears flowing and glittering in the dim light showed that she was still conscious.

Seon-hi sensed the sad thoughts that Sun could not express, and felt pain for her.

"Mr. Heo!" Sun called after a while, opening her eyes again.

"Mr. Heo left for the district town," Seon-hi explained, whispering close to Sun's face, as if with a sick sister.

"Why?" Sun asked.

"To fetch a doctor," Seon-hi said, wiping Sun's tears with her palm.

"In this night?"

Seon-hi didn't respond.

"I don't want to live," Sun confessed, grasping Seon-hi's hand. "Will Mr. Heo get back before I die?" Tears again flowed from Sun's eyes.

"He'll be here soon. He's coming back by car," Seon-hi replied, checking Sun's pulse. It was scarcely beating, and Sun's lips were very pale.

4-29

Sun opened her eyes again and weakly called out to Seon-hi.

"Yes, what is it?" asked Seon-hi. "But take it easy, don't think too much." She touched Sun's shoulder.

"I feel my mind growing weak," Sun continued, speaking with difficulty. "I want to say something while my mind is still clear, before it gets too weak."

"Don't say that. You've just lost some blood and feel weak because of that. You'll recover as soon as the bleeding stops. Blood is quickly regenerated. Don't worry."

"But if I don't bear this child, how can I prove the rumors false? I have to give birth to do that. Even if I die, I should bear the child, which will look like Han-gap. But the baby in my belly is probably already dead, Miss, so how can I get rid of the false charges? Not just the false witness against me, but also against Mr. Heo's honor? He was so kind to me, even more than my parents and brother. He's done nothing wrong, but . . ." She broke off in tears.

"Water!" came the sudden voice of Han-gap from the next room. "Give me some water! Where is she?" He was already shouting. An hour's sleep, and he must have imagined his wife sleeping beside him.

"Sobered up now?" Han-gap's mother asked, sliding open the door between the two rooms. "Damn you! Maybe you were drunk, but how could you do such a thing? Take a look if you're not still blind. Look!" She pinched him.

"What, what, what?" He sat abruptly up, opening his eyes with difficulty, and looked into the other room. Seeing his wife with her head bandaged and bloody, he vaguely recalled what he had done. He remembered pulling her hair and hurling her through the door and hard against the ground because Jeong-geun had told him that she and Sung had slept together. He remembered those unbearable words about their affair, and how he had dashed all the long way home to kill them. He remembered rushing to Sung's house but not precisely what he did there. He also remembered that he had enjoyed a bit of time in the district town with a voluptuous *gisaeng*, urged on by Jeong-geun. But all that was nebulous as fog. The whole world was murky, as if he were trying to see with eyes wide open but couldn't. He tried to recall more exactly, but failed. "What happened?" he asked, half lost in confusion.

"What happened?" his mother retorted. "Can't you see? Your wife's head is bleeding and she's losing blood from the womb. Oh, what if she's lost the baby? You damn boy!" In tears, she struck her son on the shoulder. But remembering that he was thirsty, she went to the kitchen and brought back a bowl filled with water.

He gulped it all down, fell back into bed, then sat up again. "Why make such a big fuss about losing the baby? Let it die, yes, let it die!" He spoke the words proudly and fell back onto the bed. Even in his half-conscious state, he was still jealous. Or was he simply driven by vanity to justify his actions and not lose face as a man?

4-30

Seeing Han-gap drunk and talking in such a way, Sun felt a surge of animosity. She hadn't married him for love. She would have preferred to live her life cherishing only her love for Sung, her first and last love. Sun didn't believe in a second love. Her Korean blood rejected such a thing. She had already devoted her true love to Sung and had married Han-gap only on Sung's advice. That was her sole reason. Realizing that her sacrificial love hadn't spared Sung dishonor, she regretted the marriage. But she didn't complain about her husband. She would remain true to the end in her sacrifice for Sung.

Han-gap again was snoring, defeated by alcohol and weariness. A rooster crowed, and the eastern edge of the sky began to brighten.

When Sung returned with the doctor, accompanied by a nurse, Sun had fallen unconscious. She sometimes came to, complaining of pain in her belly, but each time again blacked out. The doctor informed Sung, speaking half in Japanese, that the fetus was dead. Shaking his head, he added that the mother was also in danger from excessive bleeding.

Only after the doctor had arrived to examine Sun did Han-gap reawaken, to a splitting headache like being chopped at with an axe and burning eyes as if poked by hot needles. That pain was nothing, however, compared to what he now felt at the sight of his half-dead wife lying before his eyes.

"There's no other way than to operate, but even that won't guarantee anything. It's just the only thing to try," the doctor said, seemingly reluctant to operate.

"Can't you save the baby?" Han-gap's mother asked the doctor, trembling and not understanding his Japanese words.

He glanced at her briefly but didn't answer.

"What should we do?" Sung asked Han-gap.

"Whatever we can to save her," gasped Han-gap, weakened by his hangover.

"You agree to an operation? The doctor says the baby's already dead," Sung said, giving Han-gap a long, serious look.

"We should do whatever we can to save her," repeated Han-gap, avoiding Sung's eyes by lowering his head. He released a long sigh.

The doctor turned to Han-gap. "For an abortion, we need the parents' agreement, or at least that of the family head."

"Please save her, whatever you have to do," agreed Han-gap, pleading. Tears had filled his eyes.

"You mean you agree to the operation?" repeated the doctor, certain that Sung would pay.

"Yes, we should save her. She must be saved," insisted Han-gap. "Will she survive if she has this operation?" He looked at the doctor.

"Please save the baby," implored Han-gap's mother, praying with her palms pressed together.

"The baby's already dead. I can't guarantee the mother will survive, either. She's bled a lot, and her heart is now very weak. I really don't know if her heart can sustain the trauma." The doctor then grasped Sun's wrist, squatting carefully so as to prevent his clothes from brushing the dirty floor.

4-31

"Her pulse is very weak," the doctor said and ordered the nurse to prepare an injection. After rolling up Sun's white sleeve, he injected a colorless liquid. Holding her wrist, he waited for the pulse to strengthen as he opened her eyes and peered into them with the aid of a flashlight.

Leaving Han-gap alone in attendance for the operation, Sung quit the room with Seon-hi as well as with Han-gap's mother, who shook off his hand several times intending to go back, but Sung dissuaded her. "It's better not to go in."

She started to cry, as if her frozen emotions had melted and were now pouring forth. "O God, take me, but let my grandchild live. How could I live if the baby dies?"

"Hey, mister!" the doctor called, opening the door and coming out.

"Yes? What happened?" asked Sung in surprise.

The doctor approached closely and spoke in Japanese. "It's impossible to operate now. She's lost too much blood, and her heart is too weak. She'd need a blood transfusion first, but we don't have the equipment for that, and I can't do it by myself anyway." He took out a cigarette and lit it.

"What should we do then?" Sung asked, anxiety in his voice.

"Well, it's not good to move a bleeding patient, not all the way to the district town," he explained, then added in Japanese, "*Gomari-masidana*," meaning it was a problem.

"Should I call another doctor to help you? I can go quickly."

"She's in serious condition. Even if we operate . . . well, I'm not sure."

"If things go wrong even if you try your best, we have to accept it. But we should do whatever we can."

The doctor seemed almost to gloat over Sun in her state, as if pleased at having power over a woman whom he had desired but who had humiliated him by rejecting his offer that she be his concubine, yet his face also betrayed embarrassment at his inability to save her life.

They finally decided to bring in an additional doctor. Han-gap left with the doctor and nurse for the district town to fetch a second doctor and the equipment needed, while Sung and Seon-hi stayed with Sun, administering a shot of heart stimulant every half hour and keeping an eye on her.

Some three hours later, the doctor returned with a young doctor and the essential medical equipment. He had been delayed by having to treat some urgent patients, and the young doctor that he brought had graduated only the year before and had just opened a practice. The first thing to do was a blood transfusion. As it turned out, only Sung's blood type fit Sun.

"Is it all right for me to offer my blood?" Sung asked Han-gap.

"Yes. I'm so sorry. Please save her. Do whatever you can. I won't forget your kindness," Han-gap said, looking at him.

Without reply, Sung lay down as the doctor directed and had blood taken from his left arm.

Sun opened her eyes as her arm was being rubbed with antiseptic for the transfusion. She showed surprise at the unfamiliar people.

Seon-hi touched her shoulder. "We're doing a blood transfusion," she explained. "We're giving you some of Mr. Heo's blood. You'll feel better when you receive the blood."

Sun rolled her eyes to look for Sung, then closed them again.

4-32

The young doctor was inexperienced and had difficulty finding Sun's vein. He eventually had to cut through the skin to find the vein before poking the needle in. Sung's blood flowed into Sun's vein through the hole as everyone watched breathlessly. When the transfusion was over, his blood must already have circulated several times around Sun's body and through her heart.

Ten minutes later, Sun's cheek glowed pink. Seon-hi pressed a finger to her wrist and felt a clearly stronger beat. "The pulse is getting stronger," she said and moved to make room for the older doctor.

Brushing his hand across Seon-hi's body, the older doctor crouched next to Sun and checked her pulse. "It's quite strong now," he murmured in Japanese, then turned to the young doctor. "Should we start?"

The young doctor made no reply.

"*Gomatdana*," muttered the older doctor, falling again into a Japanese expression for a difficult situation. He got up and closed his eyes in thought. He was reluctant to attempt an operation that he had never performed before. "Dr. Son, do you want to try?" he asked the young doctor.

The doctor called Son reflected that the department of gynecology had offered to demonstrate the operation during his time in medical school. He now regretted having spent his intern years only in internal medicine and surgery, never in gynecology. He would like to try now but lacked sufficient courage. "You can do it," he said, declining the honor. "I'll assist you."

Sung trusted neither doctor. He didn't want them to try an operation that they had no training in.

The senior doctor touched Sun's belly. He moved his hand in various directions as if searching for the position of the fetus. But he gave no impression of knowing what he was doing. The others watched him put his ear to her belly as though he were hoping to hear the fetus. He changed ears and repeated the action. Seon-hi observed all of this carefully and despite her ignorance of surgery doubted the wisdom of attempting the operation.

"Did the uterus break?" he murmured in Japanese. "But even after excessive bleeding, the patient can make a surprising recovery," he added, speaking more clearly, but contradicting his earlier diagnosis on the consequences of the fetus being dead. He put his ear to Sun's belly again. He then placed his hands on her belly and felt around as if to determine the shape of things inside. After trying that, he covered her belly and looked into her eyes with the flashlight, grasped her wrists to check her pulse, inspected the nails of her fingers and toes, and felt about on her legs. He finally cleaned his hands with some alcohol-soaked cotton from the nickel-plated container. Drawing back from Sun, he closed his eyes and remarked in Japanese, "Her pulse is still problematic."

Sun moved her lips as if wanting to speak. Seon-hi quickly offered thin rice gruel, but Sun had too little strength to swallow, and her forehead and chest were beginning to perspire heavily. Seon-hi carefully wiped the sweat away, but it returned again and again.

The young doctor shook his head as if suddenly grasping something.

Sun's body convulsed once, and she suddenly opened her eyes. "Hey, Sun!" cried Seon-hi, gently shaking her. She had a sense of foreboding.

4-33

"It's not possible to operate," the doctor announced after again checking Sun's pulse.

"Can't you keep her alive?" Han-gap's mother pleaded, crying loudly.

"What about another blood transfusion?" Sung asked.

"We can't do that twice in one day. She's too weak, and I really don't think I could manage." The doctor ordered the nurse to gather the equipment.

"Darling, darling!" cried Han-gap. He had stood silently nearby, but now sat down beside his wife and shook her shoulders.

No response.

"Darling, darling, speak just one word, please!" he begged, still shaking her shoulders. "I've killed you. I've killed you and the baby. Darling! Open your eyes just one more time and listen to me, please!" He shook her, ignoring others' efforts to stop him, but Sun neither opened her eyes nor spoke a single word.

"Sun!" Seon-hi also called, wiping the sweat dotting her forehead.

Sun's eyes half-opened, and her lips moved slightly, as if to speak. Sung, standing behind Han-gap, looked down at her, trying to swallow the tears welling up within. In his heart, he wanted to embrace her before she died. But he couldn't, he shouldn't do so. Sung seemed to want to say something before she died. But he couldn't, and perhaps shouldn't, either.

"Aren't I the one who's killed Sun?" Sung asked himself. The thought pierced his heart. "Yes, it's my guilt. If I'd married her, this girl who followed me from her heart, she wouldn't be dying this tragic way. If I'd stayed loyal to that love and faith, Jeong-seon's tragedy could've been avoided. She'd still have her leg. All this suffering is my fault." Sung turned pale at the thought.

The doctor injected Sun with one more shot of heart stimulant, then quietly absented himself from the room, leaving the nurse to make out the receipt for Sung. "Total: Fifty won," it read.

Upon receiving the bill, Sung stirred from his dark reflections.

Han-gap was again shaking his wife and crying, "Darling, darling!"

"Oh my God!" cried Han-gap's mother, thinking of her unborn grandchild. "What should we do?"

Seon-hi tried to scoop water into Sun's mouth, but it just ran down her cheeks.

Sun's eyelids abruptly opened, perhaps an effect of the injection, for her eyes didn't move. Han-gap lowered his head to hers, trying to find himself reflected in her eyes. He spoke loudly, "It's me, me! Do you see? It's me."

Sun's facial muscles moved as though to smile, but whether from a smile or death twitch was unclear. Han-gap's mother, Seon-hi, and Sung all drew near. Sun again seemed to smile, or twitch, then closed her eyes. A rattling sound came phlegm-like from her throat, and her eyes half-opened once more. As they watched, her breathing took longer and longer, until she finally breathed her last.

Her half-opened eyes seemed to gaze off into the far distance.

4-34

"Darling, darling!" Han-gap shook Sun with a crazed frenzy, but her face no longer even twitched.

The others looked in silence as Han-gap wept and wept. Sung finally grabbed his arm. "Listen, your wife has passed away. Before her face is covered, confess you wronged her. Your wife was innocent. She never wronged you. If souls survive death, your wife's soul is here right now, waiting for you to say you're sorry, that you accept her innocence."

"Sung, I'm so ashamed. My father once killed a man, and I've now killed someone, too. My father killed a friend, but I've killed my own wife and child. How can I live any longer in such shame? And how dare I even address her soul to say I accept her innocence? I've even wronged you. How could I have been so stupid to believe that bastard?" He sighed heavily, shaking his head, fists clenched and trembling all over. Han-gap ordinarily seemed a man of mild disposition, but under that apparent meekness hid a man of wild passion. His sun-darkened, rough skin, offset by the whites of his eyes, revealed fierce character.

Clenching and unclenching his fists, his entire body trembling, he laid his face upon his dead wife's chest and loudly cried, "I was wrong, terribly wrong. I don't ask your forgiveness. How could you forgive me? I'm unforgivable. If you hold any resentment in your heart, let it be released. Go into heaven in peace."

Seon-hi and Sung cried together. Han-gap's mother remained silent, as though her mind were gone, and stared straight ahead, as if to see her tiny, wriggling grandchild.

The rumor that Han-gap had kicked Sun to death spread quickly through the village. Hearing it, young members of the Yu clan fell into a rage and spoke of revenge. Even as Sun's unlined summer jacket fluttered on the roof, calling out to her soul, young men of the Yu clan, enraged, thronged to Han-gap's place.

"Han-gap!" their leader called in a loud, furious voice.

Han-gap came out.

"We've heard that our sister died," he said, glaring in anger.

Han-gap nodded in silence.

"How could she die so suddenly?" the man pressed, rage in his voice barely controlled. "She was healthy."

"I'm sorry," Han-gap said, dropping his head.

"Sorry?" cried another young man, stepping abruptly out from behind the first.

"I kicked her to death. That's why I say sorry." He lifted his head, revealing a face full of pathos and bitter resolution.

"You bastard!" cried another man. "You think we'll let you live after you killed your wife?" He quickly stepped forth and slapped Han-gap hard on the cheek.

Han-gap remained silent, unresisting.

"You bastard, you know who she is?" said another young man. "A daughter of the Yu clan. She was never one meant for a commoner like you in the first place. That bastard Sung made her marry you. We were already angered about that. You son of bitch, how dare you kick her to death?" He quickly descended upon Han-gap and began beating his fists against Han-gap's head.

Han-gap simply remained silent, unresisting.

4-35

"Wait!" cried the first man, intervening. He turned and rebuked Han-gap, "Well, tell us. Why did you kill our sister? What wrong had she done? If she deserved to die, we will be shamed, but what did she do? Tell us, did she have an affair, or did she neglect her duty toward your mother?"

"Your sister was innocent. I was completely mistaken, crazy to believe somebody passing along rumors, and I deserve death. Do whatever you want with me. Beat me or take me to the police. I'll accept any judgment, but wait just one day. I need to do something first to avenge your sister." Han-gap spat out the blood that had dripped into his mouth from his battered nose.

The young men of Yu clan grew dispirited at Han-gap's calm

reply, but another group of young men from the same clan arrived. "You've left him still alive?" cried one of the group, dashing to Han-gap and grabbing him by the collar. "You bastard, you think you're safe after killing your wife?"

"Beat him!" shouted others.

When the man grabbing him by the collar had slapped him in the face twice, Han-gap no longer endured the abuse, but grabbed the man by the nape of his neck and kicked him in the side. The man fell down on the ground.

"All right, you bastards, come on! You dogs, did you ever care for Sun when she had no place and no food? You swine, did you ever care for my mother when she had nothing to eat? You bastards deserve death yourselves! Bastards, you yourselves mouthed the rumors that Sun had an affair with Sung! You bastards! Didn't you say that with your own double tongues? And listen to you now, the bullshit you're saying!" Han-gap spoke with such fury that bloody froth bubbled from his mouth.

"What! You son of bitch! Beat him!" cried the young men of the Yu clan in rage, and they rushed Han-gap.

Han-gap defended himself adroitly at first, kicking and beating five or six men to the ground. But his strength was lessened from overdrinking the previous night without eating. He was eventually beaten to the ground, where he lay face down.

His mother came out screaming, and cried, "Help! Please help!" But people only stood by, mere onlookers.

At this point, Sung was on his way from his house to Han-gap's place and happened upon Jeong-geun, who was standing on a hillside with his back to Sung and gazing further off, watching the turmoil at Han-gap's place. Whatever might happen there, any decline in Sung's power meant an increase of his own. Since returning to the village, he had never visited Sung. If he anticipated an encounter with Sung on the road, he would avoid him by going the other way.

At the sight of Jeong-geun, Sung forced himself to restrain his explosive anger, but knowing that the entire tragedy had been crafted by Jeong-geun, he could scarcely control his rage. "Hey, Jeong-geun," he called out. The man was startled from his absorption in the spectacle and turned in surprise to find Sung there. After a couple of inadvertent steps backward, he braced himself and stood firm.

"Are you happy to see this tragedy you yourself crafted? Are you just going to watch after conspiring in the death of an innocent person?" Sung approached Jeong-geun, glaring at him.

4-36

"What are you talking about?" Jeong-geun turned brazen, his round eyes poisonous, and he lashed out at Sung. "Who really crafted the tragedy and killed an innocent person? Who's actually the one disturbing the peace of Salyeoul Village?"

"What are you saying?" Sung took a step toward Jeong-geun.

"Think about it! You know better than me. You're the cause of all this tragedy, and you still ask me? As if you don't know?" Jeong-geun offered a cynical smile and left for the village.

Sung sighed and blankly watched him walk away. He wondered what tricks and intrigues Jeong-geun had in mind, but realized that all his own plans for the village had been shattered. After gazing for a while toward Han-gap's house, from which came the cries of angry voices and weeping, he turned his back on the scene and went home.

Upon arriving, he found Jeong-seon and Seon-hi seated face to face in the main room. He glanced briefly about the scene, then went to his own room. He couldn't calm down, feeling that something worse could yet happen that day.

He sat down at his desk, supporting his forehead in his hand, and immersed himself in thought. "I have to leave Salyeoul," he told himself. "But where should I go? And if I leave, who'll continue the project I've started?"

Sung thought of Little Gap. He was a young man who worked as a clerk at the cooperative. A son of the Old Man of Dolmorut House, he was like his father, quiet and poised, and worked for the village as if at his own business. He didn't have the most acumen among the villagers, but he was second to none in responsibility and faithfulness. Han-gap had more acumen, for instance, but he could hardly control his passion and wildness. Little Gap didn't have that problem.

"Ul-lan," Sung called. "Go tell Mr. Little Gap of Dolmorut House to come see me. He should come quickly. If he's not home, ask where he went and find him. Tell him I need to see him. Say it's urgent."

"Yes," answered Ul-lan, her Seoul accent still strong, and rushed out quickly, her ponytail swinging.

"What should I do with Ul-lan?" he considered after sending her off. "And what of Seon-hi?" he continued, thinking of other unfortunate people dependent upon him. He sighed.

"Why do you want to see Mr. Little Gap?"

Surprised at the voice, Sung turned to find Jeong-seon standing behind him. She had entered his room because she had noticed something odd in her husband's bearing and tone. He had not noticed her, so immersed was he in his thoughts and worries.

"Oh, I have something to tell him about the cooperative," he said with a smile to comfort his wife, feeling sympathy at seeing her stand precariously balanced on her prosthetic leg.

"Let's go back to Seoul," Jeong-seon suggested, trying to sit down next to him.

Sung put his arms around her to help her sit.

4-37

"To Seoul?" Sung echoed, taken aback.

"Yes, let's go back to Seoul. Why should we suffer hardship here? You tried so hard, but the villagers just don't appreciate it. Let's go back to Seoul," she pleaded. "If you work as hard there as you have here, you'll be successful at whatever you do, don't you think?"

"We didn't come here for people's appreciation. We came because the work needs to be done." Sung paused. "Actually, Jeong-seon, I'm also thinking of leaving . . ." His voice trailed off.

"Really? Good. Humph, we ought to leave this terrible place. We can go immediately, even take tonight's train."

"Well, we'll definitely leave, but I want to go to a place even worse than Salyeoul."

"Worse than Salyeoul?" Jeong-seon eyes grew wide with astonishment.

"The people of Salyeoul still have too much. For that reason, their eyes aren't fully opened. I want to go to Pyeong-gang. You remember Geombullang and Saepo on the Gyeongwon Line, just after Pyeong-gang and Bokgae? That no man's land? There's a big farm there owned by a Japanese man, and farmers are thronging to cultivate the land, so we can go there, too. We can settle on a piece of unused land and farm it. And we can find out how to help the poor farmers. I think we'll have more to accomplish there than here in Salyeoul, where people still have enough to eat and are satisfied with their lives. Salyeoul is too beautiful, its soil is too fertile, and its people are too well fed. They need to have their marrow sucked out more by the rich before they'll wake up. Even our life in this house is too comfortable. Let's live and eat like the poorest Koreans. We can experiment with ways that even the poorest of the poor can have enough to eat. If we can do that, it'll be a great way to save Korea, won't it? Let's do that. Yes, let's leave everything we've started here in Little Gap's charge and head for Geombullang with nothing but our labor power. People who go to Geombullang have nothing, so we should go there under the same conditions. We've got too much money. That's why the poor people don't trust us."

"You mean," asked Jeong-seon in surprise, "we should go penniless? Give everything away?"

"Yes, give everything away to fund the cooperative so farmers can still borrow money for farming. We'll leave with nothing but our bodies and find out if we starve or not," Sung said, smiling to make his suggestion easier for Jeong-seon to accept.

But his smile did nothing to lighten the shock. "No," she said. "No, I can't go there without a penny to my name. How could we possibly live like that? I'd rather die first." Despite her doubt and confusion, she was certain of her decision and firmly rejected his suggestion.

Knowing that more talk was useless, Sung fell silent.

They remained silent until Ul-lan returned with Little Gap. He must have been working in the rice paddy because a wet hoe was in his hand, and mud had splattered his nose and brow. He had his pants rolled up above the knees and wet straw shoes on his bare feet.

"I wonder what the problem is," he murmured, laying aside the hoe, and he politely greeted Jeong-seon.

4-38

"You wanted to see me, Mr. Heo?" Little Gap stepped out of his shoes and up onto the veranda. Though only three or four years younger than Sung, he called him "Mr. Heo" and used the honorific form of address. He was the only one among the village young people who truly understood Sung's plan and character well.

"Come in." Sung got up to greet him.

"My feet are wet, I had to work on the seedbed." Little Gap rubbed his soles on the floor.

"Come in anyway," Jeong-seon seconded, to put him at ease.

In the main room, the baby suddenly started crying loudly, as if startled. "The baby's crying," called Seon-hi from where she was pacing with the infant in her arms. She felt a subtle mothering instinct, but with her uncertain future wondered if she herself would ever become a mother.

Jeong-seon, preferring to hide her limp, crawled away into the main room. "What's wrong, baby?" She clapped her palms before the baby's eyes. The little one, now ten months old, stopped crying and held out her hands.

"She was lying on the floor playing well, but must have remembered her mother because she suddenly got upset. She threw her toys away and started to cry." Seon-hi smiled and patted the little girl's fat cheeks as she explained.

"Baby wants milk?" Jeong-seon asked, offering her breast and arranging her knees, making room for Seon-hi to sit nearby. "Come here, have a seat. Do you know what Mr. Heo told me? He suggested we move to a place called Geombullang or Saepo. I'm already sick of country life here, and he wants to go to a place even worse! What should I do? Seon-hi, you talk to him. Please convince him to take us back to Seoul. He's so stubborn, I can't do anything."

"Geombullang?" Seon-hi repeated, surprised.

"Right. You remember the place? On the way to Sambang, a real no man's land. He wants to live there. But I don't want to. He can go alone if he wants. I won't, even if I have to die!" Jeong-seon ended in anger.

"Wherever he wants to go, you should follow, shouldn't you? If he's doing something wrong, you should resist, of course, but he's doing the right thing. You should help as much as you can." Seon-hi sighed and closed her eyes.

"Where does a husband get the right to make his wife unhappy? Whatever a husband might want, if his wife says no, he should give up. Does a man own his wife?" Jeong-seon's tone grew angrier.

Seon-hi realized that more talk wouldn't help. She fell silent and quietly rose to leave for her place.

In the lonely house, nobody awaited her. For a young woman, that was hard to suffer. Sitting on the edge of the balcony and gazing down onto the Dalnae River and its riverside fields, she felt sad enough to weep. She might as well be dead, she thought. Her decision to live for the children of the village and for Sung's work had brought her to a dead end.

"Ah, where should I go?" She dropped her head.

4-39

"Little Gap, I'm leaving Salyeoul," Sung explained, his voice sad. "I've tried to stay, but that doesn't seem possible anymore. When I go, you should take charge of the cooperative and kindergarten and everything."

"What are you saying? You can't leave." Little Gap opposed him directly.

"I don't want to, either. I came here to live and die, but that's not possible, it seems."

"Why not possible? We should just kick that bastard Jeong-geun out of the village. If he stays, the village will go to ruin. Han-gap was incited by him, I know that. We need to teach that bastard a lesson." As Little Gap spoke, he grew so enraged that he appeared ready to strike the man down in that instant.

"If Jeong-geun alone opposed me, I could endure it, but the whole village seems set against me . . ." Sung's voice trailed off, as sad and discouraged as his countenance.

"You mean the old people?"

"The younger are the same, aren't they?"

"Some of the young ones are against you after being treated to drinks by Jeong-geun, but they're just a few. Even if the mature ones are few in number, they know the village won't survive without you. Jeong-geun's clever and has his tricks. He's put his father up to one of them. Mr. Yu San-jang's using special occasions like his birthday or ancestor's memorial days treat the old people of the village to alcohol and dog meat. The stupid old men think it's good for their health and are tempted by that, but it won't last long. Yu's greedy and stingy. He never treated the villagers with such generosity before, never, not even when he invited people from other villages. Really never. And he now imagines to win the people over with this trick? Humph, he shouldn't even try."

Little Gap, ordinarily a quiet person, had unexpectedly waxed eloquent. Sung was surprised. Little Gap had never seemed so observant, but he knew exactly what was going on. Recognizing that made Sung feel more relaxed about leaving him in charge of everything. He took out the documents and papers that he had put together and gave them to Little Gap. "If Salyeoul wants me back, I'll return. But for now, I have no other choice than to leave, so you should take everything over. You can use this house, too, Mr. Little Gap." Sung used "Mr." for the first time, showing his respect for Little Gap.

At that moment, a dark-faced police officer named Han appeared. "Is Mr. Heo at home?" he asked, looking directly at Sung.

"Yes, here I am," Sung answered and got up.

"How are you, Mr. Han?" Little Gap greeted, also rising.

Ignoring Little Gap, Han ordered Sung, "Get dressed for outdoors and come with me."

"What's the matter?" Sung asked.

Han's response was harsh. "You'll find out when you come with me."

Sung simply fastened his pants at the ankles and put on his farming hat. Looking into the main room, he said, "I'm going to the police station. They want to see me for something. Talk to Little Gap for anything you need done." Sung stepped down from the veranda.

Jeong-seon put the baby down and hobbled out to the veranda. "What's the matter?" she asked the policeman.

"He's being taken away because he deserves it," the man said, using a rope to bind Sung's hands and waist in front of Jeong-seon.

4-40

All along the roadside, villagers watched Sung roped and being pulled away. Sung himself could see Seon-hi further ahead, also being led away, though unroped.

As they neared the police station, Sung saw Jeong-geun coming from that direction. Jeong-geun waved to Sung gaily, smiling as if to offer him best wishes, and Sung realized that everything happening had been crafted by Jeong-geun, whose only activities since returning to the village had been to get the young people drunk and try to seduce men's wives and daughters, though he had also been seen frequenting the police station.

The station lacked a jail, so Seon-hi, Han-gap, and two from the group who had been beating Han-gap were all sitting roped except for Seon-hi. Sung was placed along with them, and they sat together bearing the reproaches of the various policemen.

"What are you looking at?"

"Why all that squirming?"

"Stop moving!"

"Don't try anything!"

Sung remained calm with bowed head. About half an hour later, Han-gap was taken to the police chief in another room. The others except for Sung trembled and dared not move their heads, but only glanced sideways.

After some twenty minutes, Han-gap, looking agitated, was dragged back by the policeman, and the two men who had earlier beaten him were taken into the room. Only Sung, Seon-hi, and Han-gap remained. Han-gap gave Sung a regretful look and bowed his head.

The two men were brought out again nearly twenty minutes later. Seon-hi was then called and led into the room by the same policeman, but not roped, a courtesy to her as a woman. In the room were a table and two chairs. The police chief was freshly shaven, his cheeks a pale, bluish tint, and his hair was long in front, nearly covering his eyebrows. He was sitting in one chair and ordered her to sit on the other.

He then asked in Japanese, "Can you speak Japanese?" This was quickly followed by several further questions, "You're a *gisaeng*, right? The concubine of Heo Sung?"

Seon-hi responded to these with a brief yes or no.

"Why did you come to Salyeoul?" he asked.

"I came to run a kindergarten," she replied.

"Why run a kindergarten?" he asked.

"I wanted to devote myself to teaching children."

The chief raised his voice. "Is the reason for running a kindergarten and night school not for Korea's independence?"

Seon-hi didn't reply.

"Aren't I right?" he demanded. "Heo Sung had the plan, and you agreed to it and came along to set up the kindergarten and night school, investing your own money, right?"

Seon-hi was quick a sharp rebuke. "And what's wrong with helping poor Koreans have a better life? Why's it wrong to run a kindergarten and a night school?"

Provoked by Seon-hi's answer, he struck the table and cried, "How fresh you are!"

4-41

Annoyed by the police chief's haughty attitude and denigrating tone, Seon-hi grew agitated and spoke very sharply. "What on earth have I done illegal? I've done nothing but teach writing to illiterate women and children!" She surprised herself by her own tone.

The chief was provoked even more by the challenge, and a policeman standing nearby slapped her. "Bitch!" he shouted. "Don't you know where you are now?"

Also enraged, the police chief ordered, "Rope the bitch!"

The policeman took out a rope and tied her up, then wrote up a report of the investigation: "The accused was very aggressive, rude in behavior and language, even using extremely abusive language in her replies to the investigator."

Seon-hi, now terribly pale, was dragged back to the others by the policeman. "How rude you are!" he said, glaring at her.

"Oh?" Seon-hi turned on him. "Is the job of a policeman to hit an innocent person?"

"You fresh bitch! You want to get a real one?" He threatened her with his fist, then loudly announced, "Heo Sung!" He pulled harshly on the rope wrapped about Sung's waist and wrists.

Sung offered no resistance, allowing himself to be dragged by the policeman into the room. The chief was puffing away on a cigarette as though still upset over Seon-hi. Without finishing the cigarette, he rubbed it out in the ashtray and skipped the formal questions about address and name. Nor did he invite Sung to sit, but abruptly posed a brusque question: "Why did you incite a killing?"

"I didn't incite a killing," Sung calmly replied.

"You didn't?" the chief retorted.

"I didn't." Sung remained calm.

"Then why did Yu Sun, wife of Maeng Han-gap, die?" The police chief raised his voice.

"Yu Sun's death has nothing to do with me."

"Nothing?"

"Nothing."

"Maeng Han-gap told me you incited him to kill her."

"That's nonsense. Maeng Han-gap can't possibly have said that."

The chief changed the subject. "Yu Sun was your concubine, right?" He glared at Sung.

"You shouldn't say such an impudent thing," Sung retorted, his voice raised. "Yu Sun was the wife of Maeng Han-gap. I arranged their marriage." He spoke firmly.

"I know everything. You had fun with Yu Sun as a concubine for about a year, but when she got pregnant, you married her off to Han-gap to hide it. As the day approached for her to give birth, you worried about what you'd done. You abused Han-gap's trust to convince him Yu Sun had hidden an affair from him, that the baby was not his own, and you incited him to kill her so you could hide what you'd done wrong. Han-gap has already confessed everything, and the other witnesses all said the same. How can you deny it?" The police chief struck the table in anger.

4-42

Sung was aghast. What the chief said echoed the rumors being spread by Jeong-geun, who had now obviously passed them on to the police. His own hillside encounter with Jeong-geun, along with the later glimpse of the man on the way to the police station, led him to understand very well what was going on.

The police chief's accusations, however, could be taken in an ethical sense. Sung himself had killed Yu Sun. Jeong-geun's hillside retort that Sung bore responsibility for the tragedies seemed a reproach from the heavens for Sung's conscience. Jeong-geun had merely been heaven's messenger.

Noticing Sung in deep thought, the police chief used the opportunity to soften his tone in an attempt to extract a confession. "Think about it. You are a gentleman who received a higher education and even passed the National Exam for Government Offices. You, as a gentleman, should admit what you have done."

"Yes, I also did something wrong" Sung responded. "But what I did was simply a wrong against my conscience, a moral failing, not a crime for which I bear legal responsibility."

"Right, right!" the chief said, speaking Japanese and writing down what Sung had told him. "Tell me everything," he added, his face brightening with pleasure. "Come," he urged, "if you confess everything, I can help you when I report to the main police station. I can report that you confessed all."

Sung felt morally responsible for the tragedy of Yu Sun and Han-gap, and he thus reasoned less sharply than usual in legal terms. He could have made clear that he was not responsible. He could have made clear that he hadn't had an affair with Yu Sun and hadn't incited Han-gap to kill her. That would have been enough. But his conscience didn't allow him to speak so decisively. He couldn't accept that Han-gap alone bore responsibility for Sun's death. He considered himself a morally culpable accomplice to Han-gap and therefore to be justifiably punished along with him. Immersed in such thoughts, Sung remained silent.

"Come on!" The police chief again raised his voice, and initiated a detailed inquiry. "Isn't it clear you incited Han-gap to kill Yu Sun?"

"I never incited Han-gap to kill her," Sung replied.

The police chief grew angry "You've just confessed you did, and a minute later, you deny it!"

"I deny because I didn't do it," Sung responded, firm and resolute.

"Oh, really?" The chief was skeptical. "What'd you mean when you admitted you did wrong? Lie, and you'll find trouble!" he threatened.

Sung patiently explained how he got involved in the incident. "Yu Sun was very nice and innocent, a faithful woman, and I cannot believe she was ever in any way untrue. Han-gap was misled by someone's false charges to believe Yu Sun was pregnant by another man. In a drunken state, he kicked her to death. I hadn't heard the rumors, either from Han-gap or Yu Sun, and I was not there when the attack took place. I went to their place only after Han-gap's mother came for help, telling me that her daughter-in-law was bleeding. The only thing I have to do with this incident is that I rushed to their place with sterilized cotton and bandages, emergency medicine, and other things used in first aid, then went to the district town for a doctor."

4-43

The police chief changed the subject. "Why on earth did you come here to live? You studied so hard to become a lawyer. Why waste your skills in the countryside?"

"Salyeoul's my home village. I came here to help people as much as I can." Sung's tone was casual.

"Help how?"

"By teaching people to read and write, by setting up a farmers' cooperative to rationalize production, distribution, and consumption, and by encouraging hygiene and improving living conditions. That's how I try to make their lives better."

"Don't you have some ulterior motive? What you're doing is already being done by the government. If you do the same work, doesn't that mean you're rejecting the government's work and rebelling out of dissatisfaction?"

Sung didn't answer.

"Aren't I right? You're dissatisfied with the governor-general's policy and rebelling against it, right? I heard you're gathering people and teaching them that Koreans have lost their rights. They're forced to depend on other people's products because they're ignorant, which makes them poorer. You tell them Koreans should wake up and become self-reliant. That's why you had them set up a cooperative, run a kindergarten, and attend a night school. To be united, right?" The police chief spoke with firmness and glared at Sung.

"I've never gathered an assembly to talk about any of these things," Sung insisted.

"Have you ever had any of these thoughts?"

"Of course. But even if I've thought such things, and even if I had spoken such thoughts aloud, neither of these would warrant criminal charges," Sung responded, adopting the careful tone of a legal argument.

"Okay, fine!" the chief replied in Japanese. He copied down what Sung had said, then spoke again. "During a recent general meeting of the cooperative this year, you talked about how to revive Koreans, about setting up a cooperative to be self-reliant, and about being unified for the common purpose of survival, right?"

"It's true that I spoke in that sense."

"All right." The police chief again copied down Sung's words. "You know the law," he added. "Surely you realize such words are criminal?" He tapped the table once with the metal head of the pencil.

"Why's it a crime for Koreans to improve their lives by their own efforts?" Sung looked directly into the police chief's eyes.

Angered, he shouted, "Because it means you're ultimately rebelling against the governor-general's policy!"

"You're wrong to think that way. Opening a night school and setting up a farmers' cooperative is purely cultural and economic. It doesn't imply anything political. Country people have no political aims anyway. But if the government forbids cultural and economic improvement as political acts, farmers would then surely be driven to rebellion."

"Don't mouth such impudence!" yelled the police chief. "If you have something to say, tell it to the investigators!" He abruptly stood up and took out a cigarette, striking a match to light it. "You're an impudent bastard anyway," he added. "Saying that you work for the people, but all the while enjoying yourself with several women. You ought to just settle down and do your job!"

After forty minutes of questioning, Sung signed the document, as ordered, and was led back out. He saw Jeong-geun march into the room with a triumphant air.

4-44

Around evening, Heo Sung, Baek Seon-hi, Maeng Han-gap, and the other two men were taken from the Muneomi police station and transferred to the main police station in the district town. As they were leaving Muneomi, a number of farmers were gathered on the street to see them off, but whether in sad support or only as curious onlookers was hard to tell. Little Gap alone followed them a bit further, sorrow furrowing his brow, and he turned back in tears when Sung told him, "I entrust everything at home to you. I entrust Sun's funeral to you."

Han-gap's mother, having now lost Han-gap as well as Sung, could only cry. Some of the older villagers dropped by her place to offer comfort, but none of the young seemed to care about her at all.

The next day, the police chief arrived with a community doctor and a warrant granted by a prosecutor, and Sun's corpse was moved to the kindergarten, where an autopsy was carried out. The doctor whispered to the chief that the cause of death was womb rupture. After an on-the-spot inspection of the kindergarten premises and Seon-hi's living quarters, the police investigated Sung's place as well, leaving only after confiscating some of the cooperative's papers and some letters.

Members of the Yu clan gathered again and made a big fuss, but nobody offered to assume responsibility for the funeral. Some even scoffed, "No funeral for her! A bitch who's had an affair doesn't deserve one!"

On a gray, overcast day of drizzle from morning on, the father and son of Dolmorut House, the "Father of Twins," Han-gap's friends, and some villagers who respected Sung gathered to wrap Sun's torn dead body in a straw mat and bury her in the cemetery.

Han-gap's mother and Jeong-seon followed the funeral procession as far as to where the flat bottomland ended. Watching Sun's body covered with a sheet and being carried away, Jeong-seon stood in tears on the road. She agonized in guilt over having made the poor woman suffer more, and recited short lines of bereavement:

A virtuous woman in truth,
A kindhearted woman, with principles and beliefs,
She leaves forever bearing the sorrow of unrequited love.

Jeong-seon murmured these words, grieving to herself in tears.

After the arrest of Sung and Seon-hi, the kindergarten was closed. Children who had attended there no longer had a place to gather and play, so they scattered over the hills and fields. Whenever they glimpsed the kindergarten building, they would scream, "The corpse was cut open there! The town doctor cut up the corpse! A ghost with her hair hanging down haunts that place!" They would then run away terrified.

Two houses of the village were now haunted. One was Han-gap's house and the other was Seon-hi's place, the kindergarten.

Even Jeong-seon felt uneasy at the sight of the kindergarten, a feeling even stronger in the early morning or at twilight. Despite her unease, she asked Little Gap to retrieve her piano and to move Seon-hi's household goods to her house. She had the piano placed on the open floor and piled Seon-hi's things together in the opposite room.

More than a week later after her husband's arrest, she received a telegram from him explaining, "I'm being transferred to the investigation department in a larger town. If you can't remain in Salyeoul, return to Seoul. You can discuss the household affairs with Little Gap."

If she had known when and what time he was to be transferred, she would at least have liked to see him off from the police station. But she heard from Little Gap that the two men who had beaten up Han-gap had been released and had informed him that Sung, Seon-hi, and Han-gap had already been transferred the previous morning.

"Return to Seoul? I don't want to!" she cried, biting her thumb. For the first time in her life, she had to decide things for herself. She herself had to take the wheel of her ship of fate and steer it with her own hands.

4-45

Jeong-seon called in Ul-lan, who grew even sadder at the sight of Jeon-seon's sorrowful face. "What's happened to Mr. Heo?" she asked.

"He's been transferred to the investigation department of a larger town."

"When can he come back?"

"I really don't know. But I need to know what you want.

Do you want to stay with me or go back to Seoul? You can do whatever you want."

"I want to stay wherever ma'am is," Ul-lan answered, referring to Jeong-seon. She had recently come to feel less ill will toward her mistress and begun rather to have sympathy for her.

"If you stay here, you'll have to farm. We should continue working the farm Mr. Heo has started. We have to weed the fields and paddies and bring in the harvest. Do you think you can do these things?"

"Why not? I actually wanted to start farming this year," Ul-lan replied, imagining herself weeding a paddy or field with her skirt and sleeves rolled up. She felt a surge of joy at the image.

"Weeding a hot field's not easy work."

"I know. But I can do it! I don't want to return alone to Seoul. I want to live in Salyeoul forever," Ul-lan said, bowing her head and wiping tears away.

"I appreciate your decision. All right, let's do it. We can live here farming the land until my husband comes back." Jeong-seon was also now in tears. "I could do anything if I still had my leg, but maybe I can weed. If not, I can cook and feed the oxen." Jeong-seon bit her lips with resolution. "Ul-lan, you've seen how they feed oxen, haven't you?"

"Sure. You just take them to the river side and let them eat grass. When they get full, you lead them to the river for water. Nothing difficult, right?"

"Who'll cut the grass for the oxen?" Jeong-seon recalled her husband returning at twilight with the oxen, toting a mesh bag full of grass that he had cut.

"Would people laugh at me if I did?" asked Ul-lan with a smile.

"How could a big girl like you cut grass? Shouldn't we hire a boy to do the work?" Jeong-seon also smiled.

At the moment, Little Gap came running. "Han-gap's mother

drowned," he announced, wiping sweat from his forehead.

"What?" cried a shocked Jeong-seon. "Where? When?"

"This morning, I went to her place, but she wasn't there. I looked around but couldn't find her. I was puzzled, but on the way back home after checking here with you, I was passing by the riverside and saw something whitish in the rapids. It was Han-gap's mother! I pulled her out and rushed to the police station. I'm just coming back from there now."

"Oh my God! What should we do?" Jeong-seon frowned in grief and worry. "What did you do with her body?" She got up and looked down toward the rapids, leaning against the door frame. She glimpsed dark figures moving there, probably the police.

"We can bury the body only when the police give permission. We don't have money for a funeral, but we should wrap and bury her somehow," Little Gap said, his tone worried.

4-46

Jeong-seon gave ten won to Little Gap to buy a coffin and a roll of hemp cloth from Yu San-jang, and the Old Man of Dolmorut House and the Father of Twins cleaned and shrouded the body of Han-gap's mother before burying her in the cemetery. Most villagers wanted to tear down Han-gap's house to prevent its being haunted, but some opposed its destruction, saying that everyone should wait for the owner, Han-gap, to decide. So they left it standing. People were reluctant to pass the house even during the daytime, so they went out of their way to avoid it.

Little Gap informed the jailhouse authorities where Maeng Han-gap was being held that Han-gap's mother had passed away and that the funeral had taken place, but he didn't tell how she had died. Nobody wanted the dog that had lived at Han-gap's house, so Jeong-seon took it in. It was a handsome dog with flat ears, but not well nourished and thus bony with a rough coat.

Han-gap's dog soon got used to Jeong-seon and Ul-lan and liked them, but it was dominated by Sung's dog, Baduk. Han-gap's dog had no name, so Ul-lan called it Seopseop, meaning "sorry," because she felt sorry for what had happened to its owner's family.

Stability returned to Sung's household. Jeong-seon was finished with weeping, having determined to rely on her own judgment and willpower to deal with things.

Waking up in the morning, she thought of the work in the field and paddies and of feeding the ox. She managed things through talking with Little Gap, who came by every morning.

She was initially unsure of her own judgment and willpower, but gaining experience over time, she grew more sure of herself and became confident. She learned to live like a widow, managing the household herself. Her education proved a great help, and within a month, she had grown very confident in dealing with household affairs.

Every morning, she sent Ul-lan off to the fields and cooked for herself with the water fetched by Ul-lan from the well. Wearing an apron and limping, she was in and out of the kitchen. Jeong-seon also learned to clean the rooms and wash clothes. She led the ox to the riverside to let it eat grass, and whenever she found a fine grassy spot for making hay, she would return the next day with a sickle to cut there.

As her powder-like hands hardened and pale face tanned, she grew more firm and energetic of mind. Work and weariness whetted her appetite, and she soon had no more need of medicine for digestion. Nor did she suffer sleeplessness, for no sooner did she put her head on the pillow, than she fell asleep. Jeong-seon had discovered a new life, a way to live without depending on others, a fulfilled life of labor and tiredness, making every day pass almost unnoticed.

In her yard, white clothes washed by her hung on the line

to dry. She learned how to moisten, tread, and iron clothes, no longer even noticing the sweat on her back that soaked her unlined summer jacket. Jeong-seon put away all her cosmetic things. She needed no powder on her dark, tanned face, nor did she need her hair styled. She discovered new beauty in simply being strong and plain.

The villagers were all surprised by her transformation into a country woman willing to take on farming and other unpleasant tasks, because returning to Seoul rather than remaining to endure country life without her husband had seemed more likely. The women of Salyeoul found in her a woman like themselves. She no longer put on cosmetics or silk clothing, and she cooked meals in the morning and evening and washed her own clothes. They thus dropped by her place to chat, eventually discovering her to be neither bad, arrogant, nor disgusting, but a nice, polite, and knowledgeable person, a normal woman whom they came to love and respect. Though the women of Salyeoul initially dropped by to observe her, they later came to learn from her and trust her for advice.

"The mother of the riverside house is a very fine person," the old women of the village remarked in her praise, and they visited with food to share.

4-47

Charged with instigating villagers to organize a cooperative and night school aimed at Korean independence, Heo Sung was found guilty and given a five-year sentence for violation of public peace. Baek Seon-hi was sentenced to three years as an accomplice, as also was Little Gap, who had been arrested during the investigation. As for Maeng Han-gap, he was sentenced to five years for injury and killing and for violating the public peace. The sentences were handed down after the preliminary time of one year and three months had passed by. All four decided to serve their sentences and gave up their right of appeal.

They had been given five minutes by the judge to discuss with each other whether or not to appeal the decision, among other possibilities. In those few minutes, Han-gap told Sung, "Forgive me. Now, I know who you are. In five years when I am free, I will devote my life to you." He tried to take Sung's hands but was prevented by the guard.

Sung nodded and turned to Seon-hi. "Do you wish to appeal?" he asked.

"I'll follow your decision," Seon-hi answered, looking at the haggard Sung.

"I'm giving up the right of appeal," Sung said.

"I'll do the same," Seon-hi said, looking at the judge.

"I won't appeal, either," Little Gap said, dropping his head.

"How about you, Han-gap?" Sung asked.

"We'll follow you regardless of whether we live or die," Han-gap responded, bowing toward Sung.

Thus was the sentence confirmed, and the accused were dragged from the courtroom by the guard. Jeong-seon cried at her place in the public gallery when she saw her husband smile at her. Sung's old teacher Han Min-gyo was there with Jeong-seon, and as he helped her from the courtroom, tears were also visible in his eyes.

Jeong-seon and Mr. Han were allowed to visit Sung one final time. They arrived at the prison by nine in the morning, confronted there by its high brick wall and dark iron gate, the fierce eyes of the armed guard staring through the small window, and individuals gathered there to visit imprisoned relatives: a few old people, a young woman, a country woman holding a baby, and a man wearing a suit. About seven or eight people stood before the gate.

After turning in their visitor's application forms, filled in by a scrivener, they had to hang around and wait their turn for admission. The large iron gate remained shut, but whenever a small iron gate opened with a screeching sound, the armed guard would appear and call a name, and everyone would move a couple of steps toward the gate, as if they had been called, but then draw back and return to pacing before the entrance after enviously watching someone else go in. From time to time, merchants on bicycles and lawyers in rickshaws were admitted.

After nearly an hour of this, the guard called "Han Min-gyo, Yun Jeong-seon." Mr. Han had Jeong-seon go first, and he followed her through the iron gate after receiving a small wooden card.

Entering through the gate, they saw prisoners wearing red clay-colored uniforms carrying burdens and moving around in a group like ants. They crossed the yard and passed through a door to the prison's general affairs office. People were working and fanning themselves in the heat. The officer in charge of visitors would draw out a paper from among many and ask, "Reason for visit?" or "Less than two months, and you're here again?" He seemed reluctant to approve visits, as if finding them tiresome, but the visitors would plead, explaining that they had come from far away or that they had to solve some debt issues.

4-48

Mr. Han and Jeong-seon had to wait outside for another hour. Only when the clock indicated eleven did their turn finally come. Looking at the judge's letter that Jeong-seon had brought, the officer in charge immediately created problems for her. "The trial's over. What's the use of this letter?" He stared at Jeong-seon, but asked at large, "Is Yun Jeong-seon the official wife of Heo Sung?" Jeong-seon was an unusual visitor for a country prison. Her beauty and bearing drew people's attention.

"That's right," Jeong-seon answered in a submissive tone, despite feeling offended.

"Why is Han Min-gyo here?" the officer asked, turning to Mr. Han.

"I'm Heo Sung's friend. I'm the only person who can handle his household affairs while he's in prison. The same goes for Baek Seon-hi. She was one of my students and has no parents and siblings, so I'm taking care of her property. That's why I've come from Seoul," Mr. Han explained, looking straight into the officer's face.

The officer was annoyed. "You're not a family member. How could you apply for a visit?" But he eventually relented. "Go down to the basement and wait!" he ordered, picking up the next application.

Mr. Han and Jeong-seon first stopped at an office where things could be sent to prisoners. They presented what they had brought and underwent a procedure to receive the used, unwashed clothes and other things provided earlier, then went on to the basement, where visitors were already waiting.

The month was June, so the basement was hot. People were quietly awaiting their turn. All appeared lost in reflection on the person they were going to see.

Whenever the guard appeared, an old woman would place her hands flat together as though standing before a Buddha statue, bow to him, and plead, "Officer, officer, please let me see my son. I'm an old woman who's walked 60 kilometers to see him."

The guard ignored her and selected the next person.

"What crime did your son commit?" asked a young man in a suit.

The old woman also bowed to him. "My son," she begged, "please let me see my son." She was deaf. Several people tried shouting into her ears or making signs with their hands, partly to kill time, but she only continued seeking permission to see her son.

The guard finally ordered her out. "No, go away!" he shouted, shaking his head and signaling with his hand. She continued putting her hands together and bowing but was pushed outside by the guard. Her son had joined a strike by tenant farmers and had set fire to the landowner's house out of anger at losing his paddies.

Jeong-seon's turn finally came. "Yun Jeong-seon, Han Min-gyo," came the announcement, calling them together. They went to the window indicated by the guard. Two or three minutes passed before the shutter in front of Jeong-seon rattled up to reveal Sung.

"Oh, you're here," he said, smiling gladly.

"How are you?" Jeong-seon asked, trying to remain calm. She nearly cried but managed to suppress her emotions by recalling an earlier warning from the guard.

4-49

"I'm all right. How is Seon?" Sung asked his wife. Seon was the daughter whom Jeong-seon had given birth to. She was recorded as the first child in Sung's family register.

"She's fine," Jeong-seon answered in a voice suffused with tears.

Sung tried to make conversation easier. "What are you going to do? Are you going back to Seoul? You can do whatever easy for you."

"I won't go back to Seoul. I'll live in Salyeoul and farm. Last year, Ul-lan and I farmed and harvested 100 bushels of rice, 50 bushels of millet, and 10 bushels of beans. This year, we're farming again, and half the crops have already produced . . . I cook. I feed the cattle. Look at my hands." She placed her dark, rough hands side by side

"Really?" Sung looked down at her hands. They were still

small, but the skin had turned very rough.

"Yes. I've learned a lot about farming. I know when to plant cotton and when to plant rice seedlings," she said, smiling.

"All right, then look after Salyeoul until I get out of prison!" Sung exclaimed in joy. "And the rice you farmed and cooked with your own hands? How does it taste? Different from the rice you ate in Seoul?" He laughed at his own questions.

"It tastes really good. But it'd taste better if we ate together. Soybean stew with pumpkin leaves is very good. I even ate beside the rice paddy during a break from weeding. Food's really tasty that way. I've got no problem with digestion now. None at all." Jeong-seon spoke as though her life were carefree.

"That's good," Sung said. "What about problems with the village?"

Ignoring the question, she asked, "Why didn't you appeal? You should have tried. Why spend five years in prison?" The brief moment of joy had disappeared from Jeong-seon's face.

"I didn't because it wouldn't have helped much."

"But five years is too long."

"I have to accept it. I'll study these five years. I'm still young. Don't worry. Keep learning about farming. Did you tell your father about the sentencing?"

"No, but he'd surely already know from the newspaper. What difference does it make? He's forgotten us, and we've forgotten him, too."

"Is Jeong-geun still in the village?"

"Yes. He's set up a cooperative and lends farmers money if they'll put up their house or land as collateral. The villagers spend the money on drinking and parties. Those with nothing for collateral can borrow five bushels of rice in the early summer on a promise to pay back ten come fall. Several couldn't pay back last year and still owe this year."

At Jeong-seon's explanation, Sung simply nodded.

"Talk only about family issues, nothing else!" the guard admonished.

"What happened to our cooperative's property?" Sung asked.

"After the police closed down our cooperative, people got back what they'd invested. We had to divide it in the presence of the police. The kindergarten had to close, too. I could've run it myself, but the villagers had changed. Recently, though, the village women have been coming by to discuss things with me, complaining about people drinking a lot without hope and falling into debt. They seem to remember the good days when you were there."

Sung thought of Salyeoul, its future, and the future of Korea.

4-50

Three years passed. The farmers of Salyeoul were suffering their worst plight since the village had been formed. Most of their houses, rice paddies, and fields were either being auctioned off, placed under provisional attachment, or subjected to order of payment because of debt owed to Yu Jeong-geun's Shiksan Cooperative. The ease of borrowing money combined with the new method of collateral borrowing, rather than the old way of borrowing based on credibility, had tightened a noose around the necks of poor farmers. The farmers had resented Sung's cooperative because it lent only for food during the lean time before harvest, for cost of medical treatment, or for buying farming tools, and they had welcomed Yu's new cooperative that lent money for anything, even parties or gambling, as long as there was collateral. The poor farmers had not foreseen that this would lead to utter ruin.

"If you sign, you get money," they fancied, but within fewer than two years, they were unable to borrow for food during the lean, preharvest times and could borrow only rice seedlings on condition of repaying twice the amount at harvest.

Jeong-geun's father was very impressed by his son's ability and placed him in charge of all his property in spring that year. Rumor had it that Yu San-jang's property had increased three- or fourfold during Sung's imprisonment. At the very least, it had surely doubled.

North of Sung's property, Jeong-geun built his own place, something of a villa, and set up house with a concubine, a young woman who had finished high school in Seoul. The Yu family's sole failure was that Jeong-geun fruitlessly spent several thousand won running for a seat in the provincial parliament. But rumors went around that he would soon become the county head, and would certainly become a provincial parliamentarian in the next election, or that he would soon become the district head through the help of a powerful connection in Tokyo. In any case, the Yu San-jang family seemed to prosper without limit.

For Salyeoul's farmers, however, who had to watch their own property taken away, their few household goods bound by slips of legal paper for sale in auction or placed under provisional attachment, the pain was enormous, a pain never previously felt. Such resentment was regarded as mere sentimentalism by Jeong-geun, who dealt with everything only in legal terms. Whenever somebody trapped in tenant farming or fallen into debt complained, he was blunt. "That's the excuse of the lazy. A cry of the weak. I lent you money in an emergency. You should appreciate it, not complain." Such were his words. He had studied law, hadn't he? He avoided breaking the law in whatever he did, considering law the most powerful force in the world. He feared law far more than he feared people. Awed by law, he never strayed from legality and always concentrated his mind on "accumulating wealth while avoiding the dragnet of the law."

But Jeong-geun did have something else to worry about, the release of Little Gap from prison.

4-51

The reason for Jeong-geun's fear at Little Gap's return was not so simple, though Jeong-geun would obviously feel uncomfortable about his tyranny in Little Gap's presence. Little Gap had only an elementary school education and was not especially clever, but he was an individual who had no fear in doing the right thing. His character could be neither bought nor cowed. Simply put, Little Gap might not be quick, but he was persistent and incorruptible. Sung had recognized these same qualities in Little Gap. Jeong-geun knew these qualities very well because he and Little Gap had been childhood playmates. He didn't like Little Gap's character and even feared it, particularly now that Little Gap had endured three years of hardship in prison. He could have gone free during the investigation or in the courtroom if he had only said, "I don't know anything, I just did what Heo Sung ordered" or "I don't know anything about Korea's welfare, I was only in it for the money." But naïve, honest Little Gap insisted that he was Sung's accomplice. He never let himself be swayed by prosecutor or judge in the preliminaries to the trial, but remained unyielding. That made him the village laughingstock. He even got the nickname "Crazy." But Jeong-geun couldn't just laugh at him as crazy.

He also had another reason for disliking Little Gap, the matter of Little Gap's wife. When Little Gap had left for prison, his wife was only sixteen. At the age of twelve, she had gone to live in Little Gap's house with the prospect of marrying him, and she did so at fifteen, but within a year of their marriage, he went to prison.

While in prison and visited by his father, Little Gap asked him to have his wife go to Sung's house to help Jeong-seon. She did so for a couple of years, but after Jeong-geun built his own house and started to live with his young concubine, he managed to persuade Little Gap's wife to wait on his concubine from morning to evening for the monthly salary of two won. She worked like a maid or servant, cooking, drawing water, preparing bathwater, washing clothes, and making beds. At the end of each month, she was given rolls of artificial silk for skirts and traditional jackets in addition to her salary.

Everyone clearly understood that Jeong-geun had taken her on not only with an eye to her service as a maid. He was undoubtedly more interested in the soft body of an eighteen- or nineteen-year-old girl. In less than a month, a rumor spread through the village that he was having an affair with Little Gap's wife. People assumed that whenever he and his concubine argued, it was because of Little Gap's wife, and that was probably so.

"Child, don't go to the concubine's house," Little Gap's father would tell her. "If you do go, come back before sunset."

"Two won isn't a small amount of money," she would reply, her tone somewhat sullen.

The nice Old Man of Dolmorut House, unlike his son, could say nothing more. Although he didn't wish to see his daughter-in-law wearing clothes of artificial silk and powdering her face, a rare sight in the countryside, he couldn't scold her since he could not afford to have clothes made for her to wear on special holidays. He was, moreover, rather touched by her manner of setting out before him the two banknotes, tightly bound together, at the end of every month.

Into this situation, Little Gap was fated to return. The Old Man of Dolmorut House went to the prison to meet his son, taking along a new suit of clothes made by his daughter-in-law and provisioned with the money earned by her to pay the travel fare.

4-52

On the day of Little Gap's homecoming, Seon-hi was also returning, and six or seven young men of the village with a day off
from work headed for the train station. Jeong-seon also started
off, taking Ul-lan with her, and went as far as the well, where
she and Ul-lan waited. Although neither of them was aware, the
well was the very place where Yu Sun had encountered Sung
five or six years earlier as she was carefully using a bowl to draw
water in the early morning for breakfast without disturbing the
dew-drenched spiderweb. By odd coincidence, her grave was
located nearby, from where it looked down on the well. The
grave no longer looked new, but like an old grave was covered
with grass. Jeong-seon had Ul-lan tend to the graves of Yu Sun
and Han-gap's mother twice a year, at Cheong-myeong in the
spring and at Chuseok in the fall. Otherwise, they were tended
by nobody. Jeong-seon didn't have the ritual ceremony with
food and drink carried out, for she had grown up Christian in
the mission school, but she let Ul-lan weed the spot and plant
some flowers.

Jeong-seon stood at the well, looking at Sun's grave. Ul-lan
doing the same, asked with deep emotion, "How long have you
lived here now?"

"Five years. We've harvested crops four times, haven't we?"
Jeong-seon replied, gazing off toward Seoul. She thought of her
father and home in Seoul. Her family had sent no message in the
last four or five years! She still missed home. But she turned reso-
lutely toward the town where the prison was located. She recalled
that her husband was wearing an earth-colored uniform there.
She had visited him four or five times and occasionally received
letters, but she felt that the two years remaining were still a long
time to wait until her husband should return.

The sun was going down, casting its faltering rays to the

heights of clouds above the horizon as they took on various shapes and colors. Farmers working the fields in the setting sun's glow seemed to rise up huge, as if in a mirage.

"*Eu-eo-heo, heo-eu-heo,*" came the farmer's chant, its words indistinguishable to their ears, no more than a sound squeezed from the stomachs of young farmers trying to overcome hunger and exhaustion. Also discernable was the clanging of bells on donkeys returning with itinerant vendors who wore handkerchiefs upon their heads under straw hats and fanned themselves with new fans as they chatted.

Finally visible was the group with Little Gap and Seon-hi coming over Muneomi Hill. Seon-hi was following behind wearing clothes that Jeong-seon had worn earlier in Seoul and carrying a parasol that Jeong-seon had asked the Old Man of Dolmorut House to take to her.

"They're coming!" Ul-lan cried, gladly running to meet them. She was now a big girl with her hair braided long. Jeong-seon took a few limping steps.

The young men were escorting Little Gap and Seon-hi with a triumphant air, laughing audibly, talking loudly, and pointing at the two freed prisoners as if they had personally liberated them. They again spoke loudly and laughed.

"Oh, Jeong-seon!" cried Seon-hi when she saw her limping toward them. She tossed her parasol aside on the grassy field and ran to hug her. The two held each other and cried.

When Little Gap greeted Jeong-seon, she wiped her tears away and bowed, but could utter not a word for the lump in her throat. He and the young men passed on by, probably to give the three women opportunity to cry freely. Jeong-seon and Seon-hi cried long, hugging each other tightly. Beside them cried Ul-lan, hiding her face with a part of her skirt, her braided length of hair undulating like a wave.

4-53

After embracing Jeong-seon and crying for a while, Seon-hi drew back and gazed at her tanned face and her skirt made of crumpled cotton cloth and her rough ramie summer jacket. She then hugged her fervently around the neck and kissed her lips before again drawing back.

"You've become more beautiful," Seon-hi said, and laughed freely. "I visited Mr. Heo before leaving the prison. He's fine. Looks to have put on weight. He told me you shouldn't worry about him, his life hasn't changed much. It's like being home, and he can study more than during his school years. Just imagine he went overseas to study and will graduate in two years. He'll be able to use the extra knowledge in his work, so you should strengthen your courage and health. Think of a bright future instead of dwelling on sad, dark thoughts. Let's see, what else did he say? Oh yes! You should go see your family. He told me your father wrote him in prison. You should see him soon because he seems to be aging, shaky handwriting and all."

"No, I won't go see him." Jeong-seon shook her head like a child, gazing toward Seoul and blinking her eyes.

Seon-hi continued. "And . . . and," trying to remember. "Oh, right!" She took Ul-lan's hands. "He said Ul-lan is now old enough to get married. Jeong-seon, you should find a good man for her. Whether you marry her to somebody from Seoul or Salyeoul, you should be a mother to her and find her a nice man."

"No," Ul-lan broke in. "I won't marry. I'll stay here," She bowed her head and touched the hem of Jeong-seon's skirt.

Taking a cricket from Ul-lan's shoulder and tossing it away, Jeong-seon quietly sighed.

"Oh, um . . ." Seon-hi again struggled to recall more. "What else?"

While the three women were crying and talking, the sun sank

completely below the horizon, and a darkness of indigo blue covered the Dalnae fields.

"Ul-lan, the meal!" Jeong-seon suddenly recalled.

"Oh goodness!" Ul-lan cried, and dashed for home.

Jeong-seon and Seon-hi also started toward home, but after a few steps, Jeong-seon abruptly stopped and pointed to the hillside beginnings of Siru Peak. "Seon-hi, there's Sun's grave."

Startled, Seon-hi looked in the direction indicated by Jeong-seon, but darkness had completely hidden the spot.

"The grave of Han-gap's mother is also there." Jeong-seon again pointed in the same direction.

Seon-hi gazed in silent contemplation toward where the graves lay. The top of Siru Peak rose against the sky like an enormous grave mound and seemed to glimmer in the dim light. Above the peak twinkled a star as if newborn.

> There lies poor Sun in rest,
> Her grave unseen.
> A lonely star twinkles in the evening sky.

Reciting to herself, Seon-hi wondered if she should compose a poem of her thoughts and inscribe it in stone for the gravesite.

Seon-hi and Jeong-seon walked on, skirting the village to avoid the villagers, and went home.

4-54

Little Gap had one thought alone in mind for his homecoming, to be once more with his wife, and he looked forward to seeing her as soon as he returned. Without question, he missed her most, for three years had passed since he had left for prison after only three months of married life. She had been just sixteen, but was now a mature woman of nineteen.

"I miss her!" he would cry out in his prison cell. He was once even scolded by the guard.

As Little Gap first glimpsed his house again, he saw that it was more decrepit than before. The rotting straw fence and gate, now fallen over, the roof with gaps because the straw thatch had not been redone for several years . . . all that disrepair brought great bitterness. But most disappointing of all was that he did not see his wife. He even feared for her decease. Greeted only by his thin younger siblings, he felt his mood sour despite their warm welcome. In his shyness, Little Gap lacked courage to ask where his wife was, but questions from everyone gathered, both family and friends, came quickly.

"Didn't you get sick?"

"Gosh, didn't your hands and feet freeze in the winter?"

"Ah, why such suffering for innocence?"

To all these queries from his mother, relatives, and older villagers, Little Gap answered, with formal courtesy, "Yes," or "No, not at all." But the entire time, he was looking for his wife and attentive to each new footstep heard from the yard, wondering if it was her. Already, the children of the village had gathered to their own homes, the chickens that had delayed climbing onto their perch had finally roosted, and even the dogs of the village had returned, but his wife hadn't yet shown up.

"You must be hungry," his mother said. "I'll see what we have." From the kitchen, she brought a portable table prepared with a meal and set it down in front of him.

Unable to contain himself any longer, he finally inquired, "Where is she?"

"Who?" asked his mother, startled. "Oh, your wife? She went to work. She'll soon be back . . ." Her voice trailed off.

Little Gap relaxed. "She's not dead. She's not gone away," he thought. He nonetheless felt disappointment at her being out so late even on the day that he had returned from a three-year prison sentence.

The Old Man of Dolmorut House said nothing, like one half dead, and ate his own meal with a face that betrayed no expression.

Even after dinner, his wife didn't return. The room with its low ceiling had grown dark. His wife was not yet back. His mother was in the kitchen washing dishes. His father, the Old Man of Dolmorut House, was crouched on the balcony, smoking.

Little Gap now walked in anger about the yard. Finally looking into the kitchen, he asked, "Where is she? Why's she not back? It's dark outside." He was no longer too shy to ask.

"You're so impatient. She's alive and will come back. If you can't wait to see her, go find her yourself." His mother raised her voice and angrily threw the dipper into the cauldron.

His father intervened. "You can go meet her on her way home."

"Where is she? Is she this late every day?" Little Gap was growing suspicious, a feeling natural in a husband toward his wife after long absence.

"We've been able to have some money in our pockets because she has a job. She works for Jeong-geun's concubine for two won a month. There's no other job like that these days," explained the Old Man of Dolmorut House, defending his daughter-in-law.

4-55

"What?" Little Gap felt an almost uncontrollable rage. "How could she work for the enemy even if you faced starvation?"

"But for two won a month," stressed the Old Man, though he sounded nervous. "Where could you earn as much?"

Little Gap left home abruptly, breathing no word where he was headed. He walked quickly toward the house of Jeong-geon's concubine. Despite his rapid pace and great anger, he couldn't help but notice how rundown the village had become. The roads were in disrepair, their middle no longer slightly elevated but low, more like a ditch. The houses had gotten shabbier as well. Jeong-geun had succeeded in destroying all the benefits of civilization that Sung had so painstakingly wrought for the village.

Little Gap was stopped in his tracks at the sight of Han-gap's house looming like a specter in the dusk. All the tragedies that had struck that home came to mind, and he gnashed his teeth to think that everything was due to Jeong-geun's scheming. Leaving Han-gap's house behind, he passed between a barley field and a ginseng field and made for a ridge further ahead. He noticed the *buyeopsong* trees that had been planted there under Sung's direction. They were dried out and dead.

Just before reaching the ridge, he suddenly stopped. Something was moving. He made out two people atop the ridge and hid by lowering himself and creeping into a field of tall grass along the roadside. He then stealthily ascended the ridge like a hunter. The features of the two were obscured, but their embrace was precisely etched in silhouette against the background of the sky. As the two kissed and embraced one another with passion, Little Gap felt the muscles in his arms and legs stiffen. His breath bated.

"You should let me go." The voice was feminine, and clearly that of Little Gap's wife.

"You're coming again tomorrow, right?" It was the voice of Jeong-geun.

"Of course."

"What if Little Gap detains you?"

"Oh, let me go." The woman tried to pull free. "Somebody might see us."

"Humph," muttered Jeong-geun. "You'll have fun tonight with Little Gap after your long separation, won't you?" He tried to press her to the ground.

"What if Little Gap finds us?" she pleaded.

"Nothing to worry about. If I report him to the police, he'll go back to prison. If that happens, we can live together. What do you think?" Jeong-geun then lifted her in his arms and placed her down on the ground.

"You bastard!" cried Little Gap. He jumped out of his hiding place and dashed toward them.

Jeong-geun managed to run a few steps away but was quickly overtaken. Little Gap grabbed him by his collar and dragged him back to where his wife sat in shock. She was trembling, hiding her face with both hands, before falling prone upon the ground.

"Bastard!" Little Gap lifted his fist high.

"I didn't do anything wrong!" cried Jeong-geun, deflecting Little Gap's fist with one of his upraised arms.

"I saw everything! I saw it all!" Little Gap struck Jeong-geun in the face again and again.

"Ow! Ow! Stop! Ow!" cried Jeong-geun, trying to avoid the pummeling. "No, stop! You saw wrong! Ow! Listen to me! Ow! Just listen to me once! Ow!"

"Bastard! You'd have nothing to say even if you had ten mouths! Damn you, I should kill you now." Little Gap threw Jeong-geun to the ground and set into him.

4-56

As Little Gap and Jeong-geun were grappling, Little Gap's wife, fearing that one might kill the other, dashed home and breathlessly cried out to her father-in-law, the Old Man of Dolmorut House, "Father! Terrible thing! They're fighting!"

The Old Man knew instantly who she meant and why they were fighting. Grabbing his walking stick, he rushed to where the two were still violently grappling. With difficulty, he pulled them apart. Freed from Little Gap's grip, Jeong-geun hurried off for his place, but Little Gap had to be dragged home by his father. The Old Man worried that something worse could soon happen, and he grieved in his heart, thinking, "I should just die." He felt shame at being unable to control his son and daughter-in-law, and all because he had made no fortune in life.

Once home, Little Gap's injuries were visible. His neck and face showed bruises, and his nose had bled onto the front of his summer jacket.

That night, Little Gap's wife walked on eggshells around her husband, frightened and wondering what he would do. Before his return from prison, she had resolved to rebuff him, tell him off, ask him, "What do you want?" if he should approach her. But she now lacked all courage to resist her husband, having witnessed his ferocity in beating up Jeong-geun. The whole night, however, Little Gap seemed oblivious to her. She felt rather insulted.

Little Gap got up early the next morning and went to see Jeong-geun. He now felt pain all over, especially on his shoulders and sides. Outside the gate to the house of Jeong-geun's "student concubine," a quite bourgeois place in whose yard were plants and flowers, a Western breed of hunting dog, and a tethered horse, Little Gap halted and twice called out Jeong-geun's name in a strong voice, all the while threatening to kick the now barking dog.

"Who's there?" asked a woman, apparently the "student concubine," as she peeked out, gradually sliding open the door of the opposite room.

Little Gap ignored her and continued to call Jeong-geun: "Hey Jeong-geun! It's me, Little Gap. I've come to have a word with you." He took off his shoes and stepped up onto the balcony. The house was built in the Seoul style.

Upon hearing Little Gap's name, the woman was frightened out of her wits. She trembled as if encountering a messenger from hell.

Without waiting for an answer from the main room, Little Gap entered. A Japanese mosquito net blocked the way, but he drew it aside with one hand and sat down beside Jeong-geun, who lay there as if unconscious. "Jeong-geun!" he again called loudly.

Only then did Jeong-geun seem to wake up, slowly opening his crushed eyes and looking at him. He remembered his official stamp and his money and touched them to reassure himself, then closed his eyes again.

"Jeong-geun," said Little Gap. "I'm here for a reason. Because of you, Mr. Heo, Baek Seon-hi, and I went to prison even though we were innocent. Even worse, because of you, the villagers who tried to improve their lives have now gone broke. I've thought about things and come to the conclusion that only if I kill you can the village survive. That's why I'm here."

4-57

"Help!" screamed Jeong-geun, struggling to get up. But seeing the hard look in Little Gap's eyes, he was utterly cowed and bowed with his face to the floor. "Spare me!" he begged. "I admit I've done wrong, but spare me. Remember our friendship, growing up together. Please spare my life." He called out to his concubine, "Darling, darling, come here and greet someone. A childhood friend has come to visit. Darling, come, make some tea. But come here first to greet him." Jeong-geun was flustered, half witless, but he focused on one thing. The police chief was scheduled to drop by after nine, so Jeong-geun figured on three hours of crafty tactics needed for staying safe.

"You think I'll enjoy killing?" Little Gap began, but was interrupted.

"Of course not. I understand your anger. But there's a misunderstanding. After your arrest, your father asked me for help.

I had just finished this house, so I asked your wife to do some work here. That was three years ago, and she not only received two won a month, but also extra money, clothes, and food, and so probably a hundred won all together per year if you include everything. I don't begrudge any of that because I understood your family's situation. Okay, I did something wrong, but just forget all that and understand me, please. Yes, you must be angry. There's nothing complicated. No, it's all just a misunderstanding."

Not batting an eye, Little Gap stared at Jeong-geun's eyes, mouth, and hands, looking for what Jeong-geun was really saying. Finally, he spoke. "I know what you're up to. I'm not going to talk about my wife. My father was at fault for sending a young daughter-in-law to a skirt chaser like you. If my wife were a woman of strict virtue, she wouldn't have been so easily swayed. I'm not going to make an issue about my wife. Judging who's right and wrong is as hard as telling a male crow from a female one. Of course, I'm angry enough as a wronged husband to kill her with the same knife that I'll use to kill you, but my reason for killing you is to save the village. If you live even three more years, this village will become an utter wasteland. Before that happens, the angry villagers themselves will attack you and your family. You'll all be beaten up, burned out of house and home, or stabbed to death, and that'll destroy the village completely. But if you and I die together, the village will survive. You don't want to die? Neither do I. But I have to kill you, there's no other way." Little Gap then drew out from under a towel a Japanese knife with a blade longer than twelve centimeters.

"Friend, please spare me!" he begged. "Little Gap, please! I'll do whatever you want. Just spare me." He called to his concubine. "Darling, come here." Jeong-geun was about to open the sliding door, but was prevented by Little Gap, who grabbed his arm and held him fast in place. As though stabbed by the knife, Jeong-geun rolled his eyes and screamed, "Ahaaah!" Then noticing the knife in Little Gap's hand was not smeared with blood, he stopped screaming, and quickly caught his breath.

The concubine, who had been eavesdropping, rushed in terror for the gate, intent on heading for the police station.

"I can guess where she's headed," said Little Gap, threatening Jeong-geun with the knife, "but you'll be dead before the police arrive."

4-58

Jeong-geun called out, "Darling, don't go! Come back!" He then knelt before Little Gap, his palms folded together in a gesture requesting mercy. His concubine turned back upon hearing his call and joined him on her knees in also pleading for mercy. Struck dumb by fear, she simply bowed again and again without uttering a word.

"You bastard! You think the law the only thing to fear, do you? But there's something even more frightening in the world," Little Gap said, waving the knife threateningly.

"Yes, I know, I understand. I'll do whatever you want. Listen, I'll take pen and paper to write down whatever you tell me. Whatever you want, I'll write. Just be careful with that knife, please. It makes my hand shake." Jeong-geun took a sheet of paper and picked up his pen.

After a brief hesitation, Little Gap agreed. "All right. Write down how you fabricated all the rumors about Heo Sung and his cooperative. Understand? Write it down."

Jeong-geun wrote with trembling hand.

"Now, write answers to my questions. Don't try to add even a small lie!" Little Gap ordered, again waving the knife.

"Of course," Jeong-geun agreed, preparing to write out the answers.

"Why did you lie?"

"Because the cooperative ruined our family business," explained Jeong-geun, speaking as he wrote, "and I hated Heo Sung for being respected by the villagers."

"How much did you get from loan-sharking and other shady dealings after you got Sung sent to prison?" asked Little Gap.

"Fifty or sixty thousand won."

"That all?"

"That's all. You expected more?" Jeong-geun asked, his writing hand stopped.

"How much debt owed by the farmers?"

"About eighteen thousand won."

"The rest's already paid off?"

"Yes. Some with house and land, some through confiscation."

"Write it down!"

Jeong-geun wrote.

"Now, write that you'll give up the eighteen thousand debt and contribute half the sixty thousand to educating the villagers and the other half to funding the cooperative."

"And how'll I live?" complained Jeong-geun.

"You already have property. If you need money, you can work at the cooperative."

Jeong-geun wrote down his agreement to donate thirty-thousand won for education and another thirty thousand for the villagers' Shiksan Cooperative. He then wrote his name and the date and stamped the document with his official stamp. The concubine and Little Gap likewise stamped as witnesses.

Little Gap was unsure whether the document would be accepted as legal, but he had often observed that a stamp guaranteed legal responsibility.

Jeong-geun, however, knew that the stamp would mean nothing as soon as he reported that he had stamped only under threat to his life.

Taking the document from Jeong-geun's hand and returning

the knife to his vest pocket after wrapping it again in the towel, Little Gap reached out to shake Jeong-geun's hand in a friendly manner and said, "My friend, if you do as you wrote, the village will build a shrine and a statue for you even while you're alive. Not only your family but also the whole village will then flourish. Please keep the promise."

4-59

Jeong-geun was surprised. He had first imagined that Little Gap was there to kill him out of marital vengeance or to demand money because of the affair. He would have offered a fifteen-acre rice paddy for that. But Little Gap didn't even mention the incident. His demand concerned only the welfare of the village, of Salyeoul. Jeong-geun would never have imagined such an exceptional thing. He himself would have used the opportunity to demand several thousand won. To fund thirty thousand won for the cooperative and another thirty thousand to set up an educational institute didn't seem such a difficult condition. He even concluded that it might be a good thing to do.

But Jeong-geun was still a little worried and wanted confirmation from Little Gap. "You won't report me to the police for false accusation?" he asked.

"If you do what you've promised, of course not. I'd even run errands for you."

"And you won't make an issue about me and your wife? There was nothing between us, but you might have misunderstood."

"Do as you've promised, and the issue will never come up."

"All right. I appreciate this. I'll keep my promise. I'm human, too, and I'm touched by you and your spirit of sacrifice for the village." Jeong-geun, his fears now calmed and his lips no longer pale, finally accepted Little Gap's hand.

Little Gap gladly shook it. "But just in case you break your promise," he added, "I'll keep the document. We should gather the villagers today and tell them your decision. Strike while the iron is hot. I'll go tell the people to gather at the kindergarten before they head for the fields. I'll tell them that you want to see them, that I'm running errands for you." Jeong-geun had no courage to oppose the suggestion.

Little Gap got up and left Jeong-geun's house. From there, he visited each house in the village to make known the general terms of Jeong-geun's decision and to ask everyone to gather at the kindergarten. The villagers were skeptical, doubtful as to what was going on. Still suspicious about a money-grubbing Jeong-geun, wondering if he were trying to trick them, they headed for the kindergarten. Within less than an hour, Little Gap returned to Jeong-geun's house and found him just finishing his breakfast. "They are all gathered, and praising you highly."

"Have a seat," Jeong-geun offered, looking nervously at Little Gap.

"No time for that. Come on, let's go," Little Gap urged, still standing.

Jeong-geun put on the traditional Korean overcoat and hat and followed Little Gap out the door.

When they reached the kindergarten grounds, they found the people gathering and talking noisily. All looked pale, even malnourished, and their legs were thin. They appeared too haggard to survive longer than three more days. Some had skipped breakfast. Others had discussed breaking into Jeong-geun's millet storage to plunder the grain if he should refuse to open it that day. They had resolved not to starve with all that food just staring them in the face.

"Let's go inside." Little Gap motioned the people toward the room. Glancing at Jeong-geun, they went in.

4-60

It was the first gathering in four years. When Sung was still around, they had come together to discuss village issues, but since his arrest, no meeting had been held. The kindergarten showed neglect. Its walls were partly fallen, and the roof had leaked. Dust covered everything inside, and the yard outside was overgrown with weeds. On her return from prison the day before, Seon-hi had cried to see it.

After waiting for people to take their seats, Little Gap stood up at the front. Beside him, two policemen wearing caps sat in vigilance. "Today is a very special day," Little Gap began. The village children peeped in, wondering what was going on. Their hair had grown long, and they were dirty, almost like the ghosts of Korean folk belief. They looked so different than earlier, when Sung and Seon-hi were living in the village.

"Mr. Yu Jeong-geun," Little Gap continued, briefly turning to indicate Jeong-geun, seated behind him, "has decided to donate sixty thousand won for Salyeoul Village. Thirty thousand won for education, and the other thirty thousand for the cooperative. This morning, he called me in and wrote out his decision in his own hand." Little Gap held the document up for the people to see, and he then read it aloud before adding, "Mr. Yu has also decided to write off the debt, eighteen thousand won, owed to him by some of you. Here are the contracts he cancelled. After the meeting, you should come up to thank him and retrieve your cancelled contract. It's true that Mr. Yu has so far been resented by us villagers. But today, we can rinse away those unpleasant memories in the Dalnae River and welcome him now as a hero who has saved our village."

Taking out another piece of paper, he said, "Mr. Yu Jeong-geun has also expressed regret for what he did to Mr. Heo Sung, Miss Baek Seon-hi, and Mr. Maeng Han-gap. But let's drop all that now. We should joyfully forget such unpleasant memories. Mr. Heo has two more years to serve in prison, but I'm sure he'll be very happy to hear about Mr. Yu's great contribution. Ladies and gentlemen, we should stand and give a hand for Mr. Yu to express our appreciation." As he raised his hands, the people all got up and applauded.

"Oh, how generous he is," murmured an old man, starting to weep.

"Now, take your seats again." Little Gap said, before nodding at Jeong-geun to get up and speak.

Jeong-geun stood up and politely greeted the assembly, folding his hands together and bowing. "I've done a lot of bad things in the past," he admitted. "I slandered innocent people and did other bad things. But Little Gap has awakened my conscience. Even though I wronged him terribly, he forgave me. Through his gesture, I've been saved from myself and given a new chance at life. I've also wronged many of you. I was immature. From now on, I'll do my best for our village. I'll do everything in my power to make Salyeoul the richest and most civilized village in Korea." He stopped briefly to quell the tears welling up in him.

4-61

After choking back his tears, he continued, "I want to confess here in front of you all. Yu Sun was innocent of any affair. Out of hatred toward Heo Sung and to get him in trouble, I told lies to Han-gap. I'm the one to blame for Yu Sun's death." He pointed to his chest. "As for Heo Sung, Han-gap, and Baek Seon-hi, as well as Little Gap here, they are all innocent. When I got back from Japan, I didn't like seeing Sung in charge of the village. I hated him because he ruined my family's business. I'm just a small-minded man who slandered good, innocent people. I'm at fault. I deserve death many times over. If Mr. Heo Sung or Han-gap had insisted on their innocence during the investigation or at the courtroom, they could have been freed, and I would have been charged with slander. But Mr. Heo Sung didn't try to prove my accusations false. I was relieved about that, but I also have a conscience, and it plagued me day and night. Sun haunted my dreams and pressed her resentment. She's family, isn't she, a distant cousin? I want to confess everything I've done wrong. I've wronged Little Gap terribly. I won't tell you how, though I deserve death for that. But Little Gap forgave me. I've now confessed everything. I won't mind if I'm arrested and go to prison. Maybe that'd be better. I haven't lived even one day free and unburdened. My burden of guilt drove me to even more wrongs. But I've confessed everything today. You can do whatever you want with me, beat me up or kill me. I deserve death more than once. If I survive, I'll continue what Heo Sung started. But I'm such a scoundrel, too ashamed to show my face." He choked up, weeping.

The policemen looked at each other, their eyes blinking. The villagers were roiled in complicated emotions.

Wiping away tears, Jeong-geun added, "What Little Gap told you before is exactly what I want to do." With those words, he left the room, too emotional to say more.

In the room, people three times cried out, "Hurrah, Jeong-geun."

Extremely agitated, Jeong-geun felt that he was almost losing his mind. He at first insisted on confessing Heo Sung's innocence at the police station to free him, but Little Gap eventually dissuaded him and took him to Sung's house. Bowing to Jeong-seon and Seon-hi, he there repeated, "Forgive me, forgive me," and pressed his forehead to the floor like a Japanese samurai.

Little Gap briefly explained to Jeong-seon and Seon-hi about Jeong-geun's change of heart, his donation of sixty thousand won for the village, and his decision to waive the villagers' debt of eighteen thousand won.

Jeong-geun repeated in tears his confession of having lied about an affair between Sung and Sun and of having spread rumors of a sexual relationship between Sung and Seon-hi, and he admitted his feelings of guilt that Sung hadn't insisted on his own innocence despite knowing all about the lies. He also offered to confess Sung's innocence as well as that of Seon-hi, Han-gap, Sun, and Little Gap at the police station.

Jeong-seon and Seon-hi took his hands and comforted him, saying, "Thank you. Thank you." He was again so agitated that he almost lost control of himself.

4-62

The next day, Jeong-geun went to visit Sung in the prison. Heo Sung was weaving a net when he was informed that someone named Yu Jeong-geun had come to visit him. Surprised and puzzled, he was taken out of his cell and led off by the guard to the visitation area, where his unexpected visitor awaited. Jeong-geun, his head bowed, explained himself directly. "I'm too ashamed to look you in the eyes. I've come today to apologize in person and discuss what to do from now on."

Speechless, Sung gazed at him without expression.

"I've come to realize my faults and confessed them to the villagers. I now need to do the same before you and Han-gap." He told Sung of his decision to donate sixty thousand won to the village for the cooperative and the education, as well as to relinquish the villagers' eighteen thousand won debt. "I realize this won't undo what I've done wrong, and I'm willing to approach the department of investigation and confess your innocence. But I'm not sure if that would free you. Maybe I can do something right, though. I can try to continue what you've started and maybe accomplish something before you get out of prison. You wouldn't mind that, would you?"

Sung still couldn't speak, unable to believe his ears. He suspected Jeong-geun of a trick.

"I know you don't trust me, but just listen. I hated you and considered you an enemy, but I was always touched by your character. I want to become a new person. I want to be your loyal follower. Please believe me," Jeong-geun implored, putting his palms together and bowing. "I know you could have been freed and gotten me imprisoned if you'd defended yourself at the police station or in the courtroom. But you didn't drag me in. Instead, you accepted the sentence despite your innocence. I'm also human and have a heart. It's taken me three years, but I can finally admit my guilt. Friend, please believe me. Can't you trust me now?" Jeong-geun bowed again, his palms pressed together.

"Jeong-geun, I believe you now. I'm pleased and grateful. If Salyeoul Village can survive and flourish, I have nothing more to wish for. I can die in prison," Sung said, sighing long and bowing.

"Get to the point! Now!" the guard demanded.

"All right. I'll get to the point," Jeong-geun replied, then turned again to address Sung. "Tell me how I should spend the sixty thousand. I'll do whatever you want ."

Sung thought a moment and said, "Go to Seoul to see Mr. Han Min-gyo. Ask him to come to Salyeoul. Do whatever he advises. You know Mr. Han, don't you?"

"By name. I've never met him."

"Mr. Han knows Korea best," Sung explained, reminiscing about Mr. Han. "He knows what Korea lacks and what Korea needs. Consult with him about what to do."

"You think he'll come to Salyeoul?"

"He will."

"All right. I'll go to Seoul immediately. I'll see him and tell him what you said," agreed Jeong-geun. After a moment's reflection, he added, "Your wife and daughter are both fine, don't worry."

The guard then slammed the window shut, blocking further communication.

Jeong-geun left the prison greatly moved at heart, an experience that he had never had before.

4-63

Dr. Hyeon in Dabanggol was lying on a couch after an early dinner, enjoying the cooling draft of a fan as it circulated the air. She had grown heavier than four or five years earlier, but still retained her virginal looks in middle age, having never borne a child, nor yet even slept with a man.

As usual, she was sipping her favorite oolong tea in a cup set on a nearby table and smoking a Westminster, a new cigarette that she had recently developed a fondness for.

Hearing a noise outside, Hyeon didn't bother to raise even her head, but simply called out, "Hey Gil, somebody must be here."

At her call, out rushed a young handsome boy of about seventeen, wearing a white Western suit. Dr. Hyeon had hired a boy because girls left her quickly as they got older, often as soon as they found a lover. Gil was the boy's name. Dr. Hyeon had chosen the boy like selecting a work of art, scrutinizing such things as his skin tone, physique, hands and feet, eyes, nose, mouth, even his voice.

"What, ma'am?" he asked.

As he drew near, Dr. Hyeon blew smoke into his face. "Are you deaf?" she asked. "Somebody is calling at the gate." She lightly slapped his hip.

"Oh, Dr. Lee is here again," Gil observed, moving away gracefully, as if with a dance step.

He was right, Dr. Lee was there, tipping his Panama hat and offering first greetings. "Good evening, Dr. Hyeon!" His walking stick was hanging from the other hand.

"Well," replied Dr. Hyeon with her typical abruptness and without bothering to get up, "why did you ever leave a woman like Sun-rye? See, you're not even worthy now to tie her shoe laces. Humph, Bodhisattva must have punished you! How on earth could you reject such a woman? And what's happened since? First one girl, then another. You even chased married women! Humph, so how are you doing now?" Hyeon made as if to complain and argue in the Western manner.

"Dr. Hyeon, you're too cruel," responded Dr. Lee, smiling. He had also grown heavier, and his face displayed the brazenness of a drunkard or a good-for-nothing. The apparent quietness and decency of five or six years ago was now entirely gone. Not troubling himself to remove his shoes, he rested one foot on the veranda and picked up Hyeon's pack of cigarettes from the table, tapping one loose and observing it. "A Westminster! Wouldn't a thinner smoke be more appropriate for a woman?"

"None of your business," retorted Dr. Hyeon, offering a light as she gazed upon his face. "You must've already had a drink again today."

"What else can a failure like me live on but alcohol? You and I are both failed generals in life," he said, inhaling deeply and enjoying the smoke.

"You're the failed general, not me. I'm an onlooker of a failed general like you."

"Gil!" Dr. Lee called to the boy, taking his hand and smiling. "I envy you."

"Why's that?" Gil asked, as if ingenuous, but taking on a conceited air.

"You can stay close to such a beauty like your mistress day and night, that's why." He nudged the boy on the shoulder and laughed before turning to Dr. Hyeon. "Come with me," he urged. "Let's go!"

"Go where?"

"To the concert."

"The Shim Sun-rye concert?"

"Of course! See, I've bought two tickets." He showed her.

4-64

"You're really going to her concert?" Dr. Hyeon raised herself on one elbow, half-smiling but uncertain.

"Why not? Somebody I love comes back from studying overseas and gives a concert, who should go if not me?" he boasted.

"Somebody you love? Humph. Dr. Lee loves anything with a skirt, doesn't he? He'd even love a broom if it had a skirt wrapped around it. Pretty cheap love. In heaven's name, how many women have you loved since you got back from America? How many have you left, and how many scoldings have you had?"

"What are you talking about?" asked Dr. Lee, embarrassed.

"You have to ask? Grow up, Dr. Lee. You don't want to lose your new job. Oh yes, I've heard you're now interested in a secretary there. But don't start that sort of thing again. Grow up and be an adult in the short time left before you get old and die. Wouldn't it be a pity to waste your entire time on earth without even once acting like a grown-up?" Dr. Hyeon took a sip from her tea and lay down again as if finished with him.

Dr. Lee remained silent with bowed head, seemingly wounded by her sharp words. He had left the church. His decent friends no longer spoke to him, and women avoided him entirely. Magazines that had previously reported his exploits with indulgence now mentioned him no more. He was quite isolated, and little could be done to repair his ruined reputation. Not even returning to the church would help much. No one took any interest even when he tried his hand at some social work. As for making his fortune, he had neither talent nor seed money. He relied on a monthly income of one hundred won from his job, but that was too little to live on and save for the future, a dreary fact of life as he approached forty. He felt so abandoned by the world, and lonely. Whenever he visited Dr. Hyeon, she would tease and criticize him, but she was at least kind enough to take him as he was. Despite her sharp tongue, she was a balm for his loneliness, so he always returned. At the beginning, he had chased her in hope of winning her heart, but he had long given up that ambition. She was now like a flower blooming in an unattainable heaven, but he couldn't stop seeing her.

As for Dr. Hyeon, she allowed him to visit, though she found him tiresome. She didn't formally receive him, she just let him drop by. When he did, she would tease him, as one might tease a cat, but he was more like a pleasant toy, never reacting with anger. She sometimes felt sorry for him, and in those moments allowed him to take her hand. Whenever that happened, Dr. Lee would be moved almost to tears. When she smiled and held out her hand, he took it, bowing like a vassal before a queen. Once he even received a slap on his cheek for trying to kiss on the back of her hand.

"What's he good for?" Dr. Hyeon sometimes thought at the sight of him. At times, she even voiced her opinion in his presence. "Good for nothing," she'd say.

Dr. Lee must have thought the same of himself.

"Maybe you can teach English," Dr. Hyeon said, trying to find a use for him.

At this, he merely laughed.

4-65

The concert hall was nearly full. Some Westerners, teachers of Sun-rye's old school, were to be seen, and also elegant women, her school friends, were gathered in a group waiting for the start. Sun-rye's father and mother were seated in the front row, excited to see their daughter's glorious return performance. Sun-rye's mother looked young, but her father had a head full of gray hair and a wrinkled face. Although a month had passed since their daughter's return from her four-year study abroad, they still sometimes awoke at night worrying over their daughter in far-off America.

Dr. Lee and Dr. Hyeon were also present.

When the clock showed a couple of minutes past eight, a professor of Ewha College, a small man in coattails appeared on the stage representing the Korean Association of Music, which had organized the concert. The audience clapped.

The professor introduced Shim Sun-rye. "I am honored to have the opportunity of introducing to you a gifted musician of Korea." He spoke briefly about the course of her career and also described with great feeling what a wonderful person she was and how hard she had studied despite possessing great talent, before adding, "But Miss Shim has an even greater virtue than these just mentioned, her love for things Korean. Her character already shows the values of a typical Korean, a Korean woman, and this is most clearly noticeable in her art. Among the pieces she is going to play tonight, *Ah, the Country* and *Sorrow of a Lover*, her own compositions, certainly express these values, but even when she plays pieces composed by Westerners, she makes them sound Korean through her fingers. In short, Miss Shim is a pianist whose playing remains uniquely Korean even on this Western instrument, the piano. She is truly a daughter of Korea and an artist of Korea." His introduction finished, he called her out onto the stage.

Shim Sun-rye, appearing flushed at the loud applause, looked thinner than five years earlier. She was wearing a traditional Korean jacket and skirt, both of ramie cloth, along with black shoes. She looked not like a modern woman who had lived in

America, but like a traditional Korean woman, modest, humble, and shy.

Sun-rye felt overwhelmed with excitement for a brief moment at her old teacher's enthusiastic compliments and the audience's thunderous applause. Almost dizzy, she had to sit at the piano with head bowed for a couple of minutes as if in prayer. With a sudden movement, her hands lifted as her ten fingers flew across the piano keys. The audience was rapt and silent, as if far away, leaving only the piano and her alone making music in the great room.

Each time a piece was finished, the audience broke into applause.

When she went back to the waiting room for a break, Miss Hall was there to hug her in tears and call her a daughter, and the school friends who loved her joyously joined in.

As she was playing *Ah, the Country* after the break, the audience could scarcely breathe, and when she had finished, the people were so moved that they even forgot to applaud. Only upon leaving the stage for her second break did they begin to clap and shout. But she could not suppress the sorrow in her heart at hearing the applause. She felt utterly weak and dispirited, as if about to faint. Her school friends fanned her face to help her revive and wiped away the sweat, but Sun-rye felt such a lonely sadness, almost beyond her control. When Mr. Han came into the waiting room and held her hands as he praised her, Sun-rye burst into tears, no longer able to control herself.

The last piece to be played was *Sorrow of a Lover*. It had first been composed when Dr. Lee had jilted her, and corrected afterwards in America in only a few parts. Sun-rye had originally not wanted to include it in the program but had been persuaded by Miss Hall. Sun-rye sat at the piano, finally playing the lovely, melodious piece, and as she finished, the audience could only sit and sigh.

As Sun-rye was about to rise from the seat, some man jumped onto the stage with a flower bouquet and held it out to her. Absentmindedly, she accepted the gift, but in the next instant stepped back in shock. The man was Dr. Lee! She let the bouquet drop to the floor and, feeling faint, hid her face with her hands.

4-66

She was caught by the professor as she fell and was carried off into the room behind the stage. Some people in the audience stood up. A voice cried out, "Kick him off the stage! It's that skirt chaser, Lee Geon-yeong! Grab him!"

As Dr. Lee stood there at a loss for what to do, an old man from the audience jumped onto the stage, grabbed his collar, and slapped him several times. It was Sun-rye's father.

"You bastard!" he shouted. "You'll die by my hand now!"

People hurried to pull them apart. The police who had been posted in the concert hall rushed forward and ordered people to leave. They then arrested Sun-rye's father and Dr. Lee.

Sun-rye was attended to by Dr. Hyeon. Some ten minutes later, the hall was empty and quiet, but in the room behind the stage were Sun-rye's mother, Miss Hall, Dr. Hyeon, Mr. Han, and a few of Sun-rye's friends, all waiting for her to regain consciousness.

"That awful man! How dare he show up again!" exclaimed Sun-rye's mother. "That devil deserves to die!" She wept as she said these things.

Another twenty minutes passed before Sun-rye came out of her faint. Accompanied by Dr. Hyeon, Sun-rye was driven home in a taxi. She fell asleep upon reaching home and slept soundly, as if nothing had happened, until she suddenly awakened and heard the clock on the veranda strike two. The moon was shining outside, and she could hear her father snoring. Sun-rye got up and opened the window quietly so as not to awaken her parents in the main room. The night revealed scattered fragments of cloud floating across the sky, but the summer moon glowed with clear light. Leaning on the window frame, she stared blankly into the sky. Her father's snoring could be heard from the main room. While she had been sleeping, he had returned home, set free by the police.

"That bastard jilted my daughter. He went on to toy with several other women. If he's not locked up, he'll come after my daughter again and then go running after a lot of other men's daughters. Don't let him out! Keep him locked away! Watch him carefully!" Sun-rye's father had said these things with such innocence that he was freed after merely being admonished not to hit people.

Returning home, he had checked to see that his daughter was sleeping soundly, then had spoken with his wife until late in the night and had just fallen asleep, still muttering, "I should've killed that bastard." Though Sun-rye had been the one jilted, her father had actually been more powerfully affected, and he seemed to have aged ten years. He wasn't the sort to speak openly about his anger, unlike the current fashion among many people, but he sometimes couldn't control his rage in calling to mind all that had happened. Sorrow was settling into his heart and making him melancholy.

Sun-rye turned her attention to the moon. It was the same moon that she had seen from her childhood to her school years, the same one that she had gazed at in longing for Lee Geon-young after their engagement. Whenever she saw the moon, she thought of him, for on the night of their first date, they had sworn eternal love in Namsan Park while gazing at the moon. He had whispered into her ear in English, three times promising, "As long as the moon shines, as long as the sky remains above!"

At the time, Sun-rye had believed his words, but she felt such shame in retrospect.

She tried to forget him while studying in America, and also upon her return to Korea, but forgetting him was as difficult as erasing the moon from the sky. This was not necessarily because she still loved him. She felt so disgusted about his character that she would just as soon spit in his face, but she also remembered various things between them. Such memories had grown unpleasant, leaving her in agony.

"Why am I so weak?" she asked herself and lay back down to bed.

4-67

Mr. Han came to see her the next day. He first comforted her parents for what had happened the day before and then turned to Sun-rye to ask, "Would you like to take a trip? You've spent time in America, the richest and the most civilized place in the world. How about going to a Korean village, the world's poorest and the least civilized place?"

The incident at the concert must have generated a lot of rumors about her. Her prospects were uncertain, although she would likely be teaching at her old school the next semester. Sun-rye wanted to get out of Seoul for a while, and her parents also thought that a trip would be good for her. All were agreed that accompanying Mr. Han was a good idea.

She already felt better to think of leaving Seoul.

"In Salyeoul, you can see Jeong-seon and Seon-hi. You know them, right?" Mr. Han asked, trying to cheer her up.

"Yes, I do." She was happy at the thought of seeing them again after such a long time.

Her mother encouraged her, speaking as if to a very young daughter. "Yes, you should go. Go with Mr. Han. Have some fun. You should listen to him."

On the station platform for the north train, about forty or

fifty men and women were gathered to see Mr. Han off. Among them were Mr. Han-eun, Miss Hall, Jeong Seo-bun, and Dr. Hyeon. Mr. Han was dressed in a hemp suit styled after the Japanese student uniform and wore on his head a cap made of lacquered horsehair, only a few of which remained in Korea. He was overjoyed at his opportunity to work for the country and promote its development. Yu Jeong-geun was also present, and Mr. Han introduced him to everyone there.

"This is Mr. Yu Jeong-geun. He's donated all his property to promote his home village. I wish we had even ten supporters like him in Korea," he said, laughing cheerfully. After introducing Yu to Han-eun, he added, "According to Mr. Yu, Jeong-seon is now a real country woman. She wears the traditional jacket and skirt made of rough hemp."

As the bell rang announcing the departure, people shook hands one last time with Mr. Han. When he was just about to board the train, a young man wearing a straw hat and only the thin, traditional summer clothes came up and said, "Mr. Han!"

He stopped and looked at the young man.

"It's me, Gap-jin," the young man announced, removing his hat.

"Oh, you're Gap-jin," Mr. Han said in surprise, putting his hand on the young man's shoulder. He looked Gap-jin over.

"We can board the train. I'll accompany you as far as Shinchon," Gap-jin said. He got on after Mr. Han.

The people gathered there stood in surprise at hearing the name Gap-jin and seeing his humble appearance.

As the train started to move, Mr. Han stood on the door step next to the third-class car and waved to the people, bowing his head several times. Sun-rye stood behind him and tried to avoid people's eyes as much as possible.

When they had entered the car, Mr. Han turned to Gap-jin. "Come here and have a seat. Where on earth have you been for so long? I've heard nothing from you for two or three years." He looked at Gap-jin's tanned and haggard face.

"Let me catch you up. I've been doing farm work in Geombullang."

"In Geombullang?" Han was again surprised.

"Right. Geombullang in Pyeong-gang. When I heard about the sentence handed down to Sung, I decided to go to Geombullang. I've lived there for two years with the farmers. I came to Seoul to buy something for the consumer's cooperative and heard about you leaving for Salyeoul. I hesitated at first, but I've come to see you, though only briefly." Gap-jin laughed cheerfully.

"Why didn't you drop by my house?" Mr. Han asked, lightly tapping Gap-jin on the knee.

"Because I wasn't ready yet. I hadn't grown up. I was waiting to see you after I'd matured." He then laughed and said, "Mr. Han, it's like a dream for me." In his laughter, he seemed like the old Gap-jin.

When the train was slowing down to stop at Shinchon Station, Gap-jin shook Mr. Han's hand. "Mr. Han," he said, "I was the most stubborn of your students but I came to follow your way. Come visit us in Geombullang next year." He then jumped off the train.

Epilogue: Finishing *The Soil*

I didn't know that *The Soil* would end here. I thought that the novel would go on, but I think that I have written all that needed to be written for now. A photographer can take a picture of "what is there." To take a picture of "what is not there" would be magic.

I believe that I might be able to write the sequel of *The Soil* in a few years. After watching how Salyeoul develops into a great village, I will report back to you about it. I truly hope that it becomes rich and civilized. I also hope that Geombullang, where Gap-jin is pursuing his new life, will become like Salyeoul. I hope and even believe that there are many such villages throughout Korea.

I also pray that Dr. Lee Geon-yeong will turn over a new leaf and contribute to Korea with his knowledge and talent. Everybody makes mistakes, but one can always change. We Koreans all have flaws. That's why our living conditions are so poor. If we only change, our lives will become better. That's our hope, isn't it?

As I was writing installments on *The Soil*, I received hundreds of letters from you. They were so encouraging that I felt almost embarrassed. I am thankful, happy, and honored through the interest shown by your letters.

I am ashamed that I didn't reflect more and write better. I wrote the novel in brief moments of spare time while working and doing other things. But I wrote what was truly in my heart.

I want to dedicate *The Soil* to Choe Su-ban, imprisoned in Sineuiju jail on charges of disturbing public order. Choe Su-ban is similar to Heo Sung in many ways. Mr. Choe still has three more years to serve, rather a long time to wait for him to read this book.

Finally, I confess that *The Soil* is unfinished. Perhaps it is fated to remain unfinished because Salyeoul is yet unfinished. It's also unfinished because I only foresaw Mr. Han going to Salyeoul. Heo Sung is still in prison, and I don't know what such people as Yu Jeong-geun, Kim Gap-jin, Baek Seon-hi, Yun Jeong-seon, Shim Sun-rye, Lee Geon-yeong, and Dr. Hyeon will do in the future. I believe that I have glimpsed only the direction of their journeys. You must wait for the sequel to see what they attempt, and only after I've observed them further, as I've already admitted, will I be able to write the sequel to *The Soil*.

Yi Kwang-su was born in 1892 during the twilight years of the Korean monarchy, which ended in 1910 with the annexation of Korea by Japan. Recognized as one of modern Korea's best novelists, especially for his 1917 novel *The Heartless*, he died in disfavor in 1950, accused of collaboration with the Japanese.

Hwang Sun-Ae and Horace Jeffery Hodges live in Seoul, Korea, and have co-translated several works of Korean literature together. Hwang Sun-Ae has a doctorate in German literature from the University of Munich, and works as a freelance translator. Horace Jeffery Hodges has a doctorate in history from UC Berkeley, and works as a professor at Ewha Womans University and as an editor.

THE LIBRARY OF KOREAN LITERATURE

The Library of Korean Literature, published by Dalkey Archive Press in collaboration with the Literature Translation Institute of Korea, presents modern classics of Korean literature in translation, featuring the best Korean authors from the late modern period through to the present day. The Library aims to introduce the intellectual and aesthetic diversity of contemporary Korean writing to English-language readers. The Library of Korean Literature is unprecedented in its scope, with Dalkey Archive Press publishing 25 Korean novels and short story collections in a single year.

The series is published in cooperation with the Literature Translation Institute of Korea, a center that promotes the cultural translation and worldwide dissemination of Korean language and culture.

MICHAL AJVAZ, *The Golden Age.*
 The Other City.
PIERRE ALBERT-BIROT, *Grabinoulor.*
YUZ ALESHKOVSKY, *Kangaroo.*
FELIPE ALFAU, *Chromos.*
 Locos.
IVAN ÂNGELO, *The Celebration.*
 The Tower of Glass.
ANTÓNIO LOBO ANTUNES, *Knowledge of Hell.*
 The Splendor of Portugal.
ALAIN ARIAS-MISSON, *Theatre of Incest.*
JOHN ASHBERY AND JAMES SCHUYLER,
 A Nest of Ninnies.
ROBERT ASHLEY, *Perfect Lives.*
GABRIELA AVIGUR-ROTEM, *Heatwave and Crazy Birds.*
DJUNA BARNES, *Ladies Almanack.*
 Ryder.
JOHN BARTH, *LETTERS.*
 Sabbatical.
DONALD BARTHELME, *The King.*
 Paradise.
SVETISLAV BASARA, *Chinese Letter.*
MIQUEL BAUÇÀ, *The Siege in the Room.*
RENÉ BELLETTO, *Dying.*
MAREK BIEŃCZYK, *Transparency.*
ANDREI BITOV, *Pushkin House.*
ANDREJ BLATNIK, *You Do Understand.*
LOUIS PAUL BOON, *Chapel Road.*
 My Little War.
 Summer in Termuren.
ROGER BOYLAN, *Killoyle.*
IGNÁCIO DE LOYOLA BRANDÃO,
 Anonymous Celebrity.
 Zero.
BONNIE BREMSER, *Troia: Mexican Memoirs.*
CHRISTINE BROOKE-ROSE, *Amalgamemnon.*
BRIGID BROPHY, *In Transit.*
GERALD L. BRUNS, *Modern Poetry and the Idea of Language.*
GABRIELLE BURTON, *Heartbreak Hotel.*
MICHEL BUTOR, *Degrees.*
 Mobile.
G. CABRERA INFANTE, *Infante's Inferno.*
 Three Trapped Tigers.
JULIETA CAMPOS,
 The Fear of Losing Eurydice.
ANNE CARSON, *Eros the Bittersweet.*
ORLY CASTEL-BLOOM, *Dolly City.*
LOUIS-FERDINAND CÉLINE, *Castle to Castle.*
 Conversations with Professor Y.
 London Bridge.
 Normance.
 North.
 Rigadoon.
MARIE CHAIX, *The Laurels of Lake Constance.*
HUGO CHARTERIS, *The Tide Is Right.*
ERIC CHEVILLARD, *Demolishing Nisard.*

MARC CHOLODENKO, *Mordechai Schamz.*
JOSHUA COHEN, *Witz.*
EMILY HOLMES COLEMAN, *The Shutter of Snow.*
ROBERT COOVER, *A Night at the Movies.*
STANLEY CRAWFORD, *Log of the S.S. The Mrs Unguentine.*
 Some Instructions to My Wife.
RENÉ CREVEL, *Putting My Foot in It.*
RALPH CUSACK, *Cadenza.*
NICHOLAS DELBANCO, *The Count of Concord.*
 Sherbrookes.
NIGEL DENNIS, *Cards of Identity.*
PETER DIMOCK, *A Short Rhetoric for Leaving the Family.*
ARIEL DORFMAN, *Konfidenz.*
COLEMAN DOWELL,
 Island People.
 Too Much Flesh and Jabez.
ARKADII DRAGOMOSHCHENKO, *Dust.*
RIKKI DUCORNET, *The Complete Butcher's Tales.*
 The Fountains of Neptune.
 The Jade Cabinet.
 Phosphor in Dreamland.
WILLIAM EASTLAKE, *The Bamboo Bed.*
 Castle Keep.
 Lyric of the Circle Heart.
JEAN ECHENOZ, *Chopin's Move.*
STANLEY ELKIN, *A Bad Man.*
 Criers and Kibitzers, Kibitzers and Criers.
 The Dick Gibson Show.
 The Franchiser.
 The Living End.
 Mrs. Ted Bliss.
FRANÇOIS EMMANUEL, *Invitation to a Voyage.*
SALVADOR ESPRIU, *Ariadne in the Grotesque Labyrinth.*
LESLIE A. FIEDLER, *Love and Death in the American Novel.*
JUAN FILLOY, *Op Oloop.*
ANDY FITCH, *Pop Poetics.*
GUSTAVE FLAUBERT, *Bouvard and Pécuchet.*
KASS FLEISHER, *Talking out of School.*
FORD MADOX FORD,
 The March of Literature.
JON FOSSE, *Aliss at the Fire.*
 Melancholy.
MAX FRISCH, *I'm Not Stiller.*
 Man in the Holocene.
CARLOS FUENTES, *Christopher Unborn.*
 Distant Relations.
 Terra Nostra.
 Where the Air Is Clear.
TAKEHIKO FUKUNAGA, *Flowers of Grass.*
WILLIAM GADDIS, *J R.*
 The Recognitions.

Janice Galloway, *Foreign Parts*.
The Trick Is to Keep Breathing.
William H. Gass, *Cartesian Sonata and Other Novellas*.
Finding a Form.
A Temple of Texts.
The Tunnel.
Willie Masters' Lonesome Wife.
Gérard Gavarry, *Hoppla! 1 2 3*.
Etienne Gilson,
The Arts of the Beautiful.
Forms and Substances in the Arts.
C. S. Giscombe, *Giscome Road*.
Here.
Douglas Glover, *Bad News of the Heart*.
Witold Gombrowicz,
A Kind of Testament.
Paulo Emílio Sales Gomes, *P's Three Women*.
Georgi Gospodinov, *Natural Novel*.
Juan Goytisolo, *Count Julian*.
Juan the Landless.
Makbara.
Marks of Identity.
Henry Green, *Back*.
Blindness.
Concluding.
Doting.
Nothing.
Jack Green, *Fire the Bastards!*
Jiří Gruša, *The Questionnaire*.
Mela Hartwig, *Am I a Redundant Human Being?*
John Hawkes, *The Passion Artist*.
Whistlejacket.
Elizabeth Heighway, ed., *Contemporary Georgian Fiction*.
Aleksandar Hemon, ed.,
Best European Fiction.
Aidan Higgins, *Balcony of Europe*.
Blind Man's Bluff
Bornholm Night-Ferry.
Flotsam and Jetsam.
Langrishe, Go Down.
Scenes from a Receding Past.
Keizo Hino, *Isle of Dreams*.
Kazushi Hosaka, *Plainsong*.
Aldous Huxley, *Antic Hay*.
Crome Yellow.
Point Counter Point.
Those Barren Leaves.
Time Must Have a Stop.
Naoyuki Ii, *The Shadow of a Blue Cat*.
Gert Jonke, *The Distant Sound*.
Geometric Regional Novel.
Homage to Czerny.
The System of Vienna.
Jacques Jouet, *Mountain R*.
Savage.
Upstaged.

Mieko Kanai, *The Word Book*.
Yoram Kaniuk, *Life on Sandpaper*.
Hugh Kenner, *Flaubert*.
Joyce and Beckett: The Stoic Comedians.
Joyce's Voices.
Danilo Kiš, *The Attic*.
Garden, Ashes.
The Lute and the Scars
Psalm 44.
A Tomb for Boris Davidovich.
Anita Konkka, *A Fool's Paradise*.
George Konrád, *The City Builder*.
Tadeusz Konwicki, *A Minor Apocalypse*.
The Polish Complex.
Menis Koumandareas, *Koula*.
Elaine Kraf, *The Princess of 72nd Street*.
Jim Krusoe, *Iceland*.
Ayşe Kulin, *Farewell: A Mansion in Occupied Istanbul*.
Emilio Lascano Tegui, *On Elegance While Sleeping*.
Eric Laurrent, *Do Not Touch*.
Violette Leduc, *La Bâtarde*.
Edouard Levé, *Autoportrait*.
Suicide.
Mario Levi, *Istanbul Was a Fairy Tale*.
Deborah Levy, *Billy and Girl*.
José Lezama Lima, *Paradiso*.
Rosa Liksom, *Dark Paradise*.
Osman Lins, *Avalovara*.
The Queen of the Prisons of Greece.
Alf Mac Lochlainn,
The Corpus in the Library.
Out of Focus.
Ron Loewinsohn, *Magnetic Field(s)*.
Mina Loy, *Stories and Essays of Mina Loy*.
D. Keith Mano, *Take Five*.
Micheline Aharonian Marcom,
The Mirror in the Well.
Ben Marcus,
The Age of Wire and String.
Wallace Markfield,
Teitlebaum's Window.
To an Early Grave.
David Markson, *Reader's Block*.
Wittgenstein's Mistress.
Carole Maso, *AVA*.
Ladislav Matejka and Krystyna Pomorska, eds.,
Readings in Russian Poetics: Formalist and Structuralist Views.
Harry Mathews, *Cigarettes*.
The Conversions.
The Human Country: New and Collected Stories.
The Journalist.
My Life in CIA.
Singular Pleasures.
The Sinking of the Odradek Stadium.
Tlooth.

ARNO SCHMIDT, *Collected Novellas.*
Collected Stories.
Nobodaddy's Children.
Two Novels.
ASAF SCHURR, *Motti.*
GAIL SCOTT, *My Paris.*
DAMION SEARLS, *What We Were Doing*
and Where We Were Going.
JUNE AKERS SEESE,
Is This What Other Women Feel Too?
What Waiting Really Means.
BERNARD SHARE, *Inish.*
Transit.
VIKTOR SHKLOVSKY, *Bowstring.*
Knight's Move.
A Sentimental Journey:
Memoirs 1917–1922.
Energy of Delusion: A Book on Plot.
Literature and Cinematography.
Theory of Prose.
Third Factory.
Zoo, or Letters Not about Love.
PIERRE SINIAC, *The Collaborators.*
KJERSTI A. SKOMSVOLD, *The Faster I Walk,*
the Smaller I Am.
JOSEF ŠKVORECKÝ, *The Engineer of*
Human Souls.
GILBERT SORRENTINO,
Aberration of Starlight.
Blue Pastoral.
Crystal Vision.
Imaginative Qualities of Actual
Things.
Mulligan Stew.
Pack of Lies.
Red the Fiend.
The Sky Changes.
Something Said.
Splendide-Hôtel.
Steelwork.
Under the Shadow.
W. M. SPACKMAN, *The Complete Fiction.*
ANDRZEJ STASIUK, *Dukla.*
Fado.
GERTRUDE STEIN, *The Making of Americans.*
A Novel of Thank You.
LARS SVENDSEN, *A Philosophy of Evil.*
PIOTR SZEWC, *Annihilation.*
GONÇALO M. TAVARES, *Jerusalem.*
Joseph Walser's Machine.
Learning to Pray in the Age of
Technique.
LUCIAN DAN TEODOROVICI,
Our Circus Presents . . .
NIKANOR TERATOLOGEN, *Assisted Living.*
STEFAN THEMERSON, *Hobson's Island.*
The Mystery of the Sardine.
Tom Harris.
TAEKO TOMIOKA, *Building Waves.*

JOHN TOOMEY, *Sleepwalker.*
JEAN-PHILIPPE TOUSSAINT, *The Bathroom.*
Camera.
Monsieur.
Reticence.
Running Away.
Self-Portrait Abroad.
Television.
The Truth about Marie.
DUMITRU TSEPENEAG, *Hotel Europa.*
The Necessary Marriage.
Pigeon Post.
Vain Art of the Fugue.
ESTHER TUSQUETS, *Stranded.*
DUBRAVKA UGRESIC, *Lend Me Your*
Character.
Thank You for Not Reading.
TOR ULVEN, *Replacement.*
MATI UNT, *Brecht at Night.*
Diary of a Blood Donor.
Things in the Night.
ÁLVARO URIBE AND OLIVIA SEARS, EDS.,
Best of Contemporary Mexican Fiction.
ELOY URROZ, *Friction.*
The Obstacles.
LUISA VALENZUELA, *Dark Desires and*
the Others.
He Who Searches.
PAUL VERHAEGHEN, *Omega Minor.*
AGLAJA VETERANYI, *Why the Child Is*
Cooking in the Polenta.
BORIS VIAN, *Heartsnatcher.*
LLORENÇ VILLALONGA, *The Dolls' Room.*
TOOMAS VINT, *An Unending Landscape.*
ORNELA VORPSI, *The Country Where No*
One Ever Dies.
AUSTRYN WAINHOUSE, *Hedyphagetica.*
CURTIS WHITE, *America's Magic Mountain.*
The Idea of Home.
Memories of My Father Watching TV.
Requiem.
DIANE WILLIAMS, *Excitability:*
Selected Stories.
Romancer Erector.
DOUGLAS WOOLF, *Wall to Wall.*
Ya! & John-Juan.
JAY WRIGHT, *Polynomials and Pollen.*
The Presentable Art of Reading
Absence.
PHILIP WYLIE, *Generation of Vipers.*
MARGUERITE YOUNG, *Angel in the Forest.*
Miss MacIntosh, My Darling.
REYOUNG, *Unbabbling.*
VLADO ŽABOT, *The Succubus.*
ZORAN ŽIVKOVIĆ, *Hidden Camera.*
LOUIS ZUKOFSKY, *Collected Fiction.*
VITOMIL ZUPAN, *Minuet for Guitar.*
SCOTT ZWIREN, *God Head.*